W9-CVY-352

RUE DU BAC

Also by Tony Foster

Fiction
ZIG ZAG TO ARMAGEDDON
THE MONEY BURN

Non-Fiction
BY-PASS
HEART OF OAK
SEA WINGS
MEETING OF GENERALS

RUE DU BAC

TONY FOSTER

◫ METHUEN

Toronto   New York   London   Sydney   Auckland

Copyright © 1987 by Thapex Resources Limited

All rights reserved. No part of this publication may be reproduced, stored in a retrieval system or transmitted in any form, or by any means, electronic, mechanical, photo-copying, recording or otherwise, without the prior written permission of Methuen Publications, 2330 Midland Avenue, Agincourt, Ontario, Canada, M1S 1P7.

This story is based on actual events that took place in France during World War I.

Canadian Cataloguing in Publication Data
Foster, Tony, 1932–
  Rue du Bac

ISBN 0-458-99860-5

I. Title.

PS8561.087R83 1986 C813'.54 C85-099399-7
PR9199.3.F68R83 1986

Design: Brant Cowie/Artplus

Printed and bound in the United States

1 2 3 4 87 91 90 89 88

For Brian and Jill, who reasoned how it all must have happened.

"...Damocles thought himself a lucky man. In the midst of all this display Dionysius had a gleaming sword, attached to a horsehair, let down from the ceiling in such a way that it hung over the neck of this happy man. And so he had no eye either for those beautiful attendants, or the richly-wrought plate, nor did he reach out his hand to the table; presently the garlands slipped from their place of their own accord; at length he besought the tyrant to let him go, as by now he was sure he had no wish to be happy. Dionysius seems (does he not?) to have avowed plainly that there was no happiness for the man who was perpetually menaced by some alarm. Moreover it was not even open to him to retrace his steps to the path of justice, to restore to his fellow citizens their freedom and their rights; for with the inconsiderateness of youth he had entangled himself in such errors and been guilty of such acts as made it impossible for him to be safe...."

From Disputations V. XXI, of
Marcus Tullius Cicero, 61 B.C.

Tuesday, July 10

"Stop!"

Georges stopped the white Citroën at the curb. He checked his rear-view mirror for further orders, but Madame deBrisay had opened the door and was already stepping out on the sidewalk. She was in one hell of a hurry. Nicole met his eyes and shrugged.

"Perhaps she spied a bargain."

"On the Rue du Bac? Quite impossible, chérie."

He got out of the car quickly, smoothed his gray uniform, placed his chauffeur's cap at the proper angle, and went around to wait by the open door. As Nicole leaned out, he was treated to an inspiring and unobstructed view down the front of her blouse. She was braless.

"Don't you ever call me chérie again," she hissed. "My name is Nicole, and don't you forget it!"

He liked a spirited woman. In time he knew she'd come around. He looked away at number 42, a small shop displaying scale models of every known automobile past and present at prices few could afford. Farther down the street, Madame deBrisay stood transfixed in front of another shop window.

The brightly painted storefronts nestled snugly along both sides of the street, renovated antiquity at street level, holding aloft three and four levels of much older and pitted masonry that housed storage rooms, flats, and private offices. The district specialized in expensive objets d'art for the serious collector, the connoisseur, and the frivolous impulse buyer. An ancient Renault edged past on the narrow street. Its driver, glaring in disgust at illegally parked

1

affluence guarded by uniformed subservience, raised two fingers in a universal gesture of universal contempt. Georges replied in kind.

At this hour of the morning Rue du Bac was nearly deserted. On the opposite side of the street a close quartet of Japanese tourists weighted down with leather camera bags chattered amiably. Two very tall blond Scandinavians wearing shorts and carrying enormous red backpacks stood absorbing the July sun and the display of tiny porcelain animals in the window of Lefebvre & Fils at number 24. Madame deBrisay remained transfixed.

The street had begun life as a swath through rich farmland on the Left Bank to the Seine where a small *bac* — ferry — provided the river crossing. After 1564 it had been rutted deeply when stones were carried down to the ferry for construction of the Palais des Tuileries over on the Right Bank. In time the ruts were repaired. Later, the street was paved. But the Palais disappeared into the pages of history.

Georges prided himself on his knowledge of the city's origins. Until Madame deBrisay lifted him out of Montparnasse's squalor into the opulence of Passy to serve as her chauffeur and lover, he'd used the history of Paris as an agreeable basis for conversation with his middle-aged female tourists, once their sexual passions were spent.

A police car turned off Boulevard Saint-Germain onto Rue du Bac. It stopped behind the Citroën. Georges's stomach did a flip. Police made him nervous. The plainclothes man riding on the passenger side climbed out, nodded at Georges, and went into the model shop. His partner stared absently at the Scandinavians from the car window.

"I am ready to leave!"

"Yes, Madame."

He'd missed her approach, so intent had he been on the other car and its occupants. Her appearance startled him. She seemed to have shrunk. Her lips were compressed grimly. Even the makeup from her morning ministrations did not cover the pallor of her elegant features.

He closed the door and looked back at the shop where she had been standing. Nothing. A curiosity window filled with trashy bric-a-brac and a few portrait paintings. The name of Dimitrios Kouridis, Prop., had been gilded on a board sign above the entrance.

He got into the car and started the motor. Nicole too had seen the change. She held her grandmother's hands, attempting to steady the older woman's emotional distress. Georges watched them in his mirror, awaiting orders. It was very puzzling.

Madame deBrisay removed her sunglasses and sat squeezing the bridge of her nose, eyes tightly closed, as though trying to drive away the unpleasant realities crowding in. When her eyes opened he saw fear in them. No, it was more than fear; it was terror.

"Grandmama, what is it? You look like you've seen a ghost!"

"It is nothing, child. A headache, from this suffocating weather. It will pass." She patted Nicole's arm and replaced her sunglasses. "Really, we should move to Charleville before the August holidays. It's so much cooler in the Ardennes. Why torture ourselves in the city suffering this heat? Georges! What on earth are you waiting for? We'll be late. Drive on."

"Yes, Madame."

WEDNESDAY, JULY 11

Paris, 10:35 A.M.

"Death came near midnight. A few minutes before or a few minutes after," the police doctor said, getting to his feet with the painful grunt of a man lacking the physical attributes necessary for prolonged kneeling on a plank floor.

Two effeminate-looking police photographers fluttered around taking different angle shots of the corpse and blinding everyone with their incessant flashes. Bernard Boule growled his impatience. They fluttered faster.

"Is that all his blood?" Boule demanded.

The doctor blinked in surprise and regarded the wide dried stain with renewed interest. It stretched across the uneven floor for three meters, disappearing under a shelf at the back wall.

"The human body holds roughly five liters of blood, Commissaire. Every drop from the deceased drained away from the moment he fell. The blade cut through his carotid artery and jugular vein, and severed the larynx. He'd have been unconscious in ten seconds. Half his blood gone two minutes later. Then suffocation. His heart stopped. A slow draining away of whatever remained. He's ready for embalming fluid now. Ask the undertaker for a discount. I'll send my report over tomorrow. Good day to you, Boule."

The doctor picked up his case and departed. Boule lit a fresh cigarette and hung it on his lip. Smoking was such an idiotic habit. A sign of an undisciplined mind and lack of will power, as his wife reminded him repeatedly. He'd stopped inhaling two years before, limiting his habit to sniffing the acrid smoke from the endless embers

5

consumed in the course of a day. Gabrielle carped continually about this waste of money for cigarettes that were never legitimately smoked.

André Villeneuve, his new assistant — they seemed to change every month — chalked the corpse's outline on the bare floor. Crossing the main channel of dried blood his chalk snapped. André swore. One of the photographers snickered appreciatively.

Boule went to the front of the shop to rest his eyes. He had a headache. A pair of plainclothes detectives were sifting methodically through the wreckage. One of them sat on a leather ottoman making notes. He looked up.

"Well, Fauré?" Boule prompted.

"By the pattern of destruction I'd say it was done to make it appear as though there had been a struggle — which of course there wasn't." He put down his pen and notebook and picked up two large fragments of pottery. "This, for example, came off that shelf behind you. A dust ring fits the base. It was big and bulky. Our intruder picked it up, took it to the center of the room and dropped it onto the floor from about this position."

He got to his feet and stepped across to the spot.

"If he stood roughly here when it smashed then the pieces would break away from the center of contact more or less in an equal distribution."

He let the pottery shards fall. They splintered into a rough circle at his feet.

"Now, this chair was used to smash that wall cabinet. And that old flintlock firing piece became the instrument to bash in the glass countertops. If you look closely you can still see bits of glass in the shoulder stock."

Boule pushed the antique rifle aside.

"Fingerprints?"

"Hundreds, but I'd be willing to bet not one belongs to our vandal."

"Murderer."

"Only when you catch him and prove it, Commissaire," Fauré said.

Two very tall beefy men guarded the front entrance, holding back the growing crowd of curious that was attempting to push its way inside. Out on the street, four more tried to keep pedestrians and traffic moving so that the ambulance, when it arrived, could get through.

Instructions had been given to stop all traffic entering from the Quai and Rue de l'Université until after the police cars and ambulance had left. Somehow a half dozen reporters and cameramen managed to slip past the barricades. They stood at the back of the crowd shouting for recognition. Boule recognized an aggressive, suet-faced reporter from *Le Canard*.

"Only the stretcher-bearers are to enter. Clear?"

"Very clear, Commissaire."

"Tell the gentlemen of the press I shall have a statement for them later in the morning." He had an afterthought. "But should Gilles Fournier from *Le Monde* appear, you may let him pass. Do you know him?"

The guard shook his head.

"He is an impeccably dressed gentleman; he always wears a tie and a waistcoat."

The photographers had stopped their infernal flashing and were lounging on a loveseat watching the handsome young assistant when Boule returned. Everything from the dead man's pockets and person lay on the writing table. André sorted through the pile. There was little of particular interest. Loose change and bills amounted to thirty-four hundred and eleven francs, ten centimes.

"Robbery was not the motive, Commissaire."

"You're certain about that, are you?"

"There's his money!" André grinned while the photographers nodded their approval. "Gold signet ring, gold chain, gold ankh medal, gold Omega watch, and the keys to his car."

"You have a motive then?"

"Crime of passion?"

"It certainly was." Boule growled. The duo on the loveseat giggled. He growled again. "If you two canaries are finished, pick up your gear and get out. Now!"

They grabbed their equipment and fled. Boule sat down at the desk, a heavy pedestal rolltop design with a dozen or more tiny drawers each pimpled with a white porcelain knob. He stubbed his cigarette on the floor with a sigh, and started pulling out the top drawers. When he'd finished he was still no wiser. But when he reached the deeper pedestal drawers his luck changed.

The dead man kept a business diary. At least it looked like a business diary. Boule couldn't read Greek. Yesterday's entries ended at 3:30 P.M. Two words in the short sentence were not written in Greek. A man's name — Roger Marais.

"You are not a classical scholar, André?"

"No, Sir."

"I thought not."

"I speak a little English and German, read a little too."

"But not Greek."

"No, not Greek."

Boule wiped his wide face with a large handkerchief. He carried several. A heavy cylindrical man with light thinning hair and pale eyes, he perspired continuously, even in midwinter. This cruel biological error was responsible for his lack of promotion to the senior levels of the Prefecture. After all, it was reasoned, who would want to share bureaucratic confidences with a perpetually sweating colleague?

Thus denied vertical ascent to power, he devoted his talents to honing his horizontal expertise and in time became the best homicide detective in Paris. While others grabbed headlines solving sensational slayings with a backdrop of politics and sexual perversion, he was left with commonplace homicides. He preferred working on unspectacular murders, the ones with no apparent motives or suspects. There was never any pressure from his judicial superiors for immediate solutions. Which was just as well, because the inspector was a slow, patient, methodical man who disliked being rushed by deadlines or Prefecture ultimatums.

To Boule, murder was an art form. It began with shattered emotions waiting to be painstakingly assembled into a cohesive whole. This was the exciting part: finding the tiny pieces to begin putting the reality together. Never did he doubt his ability to assemble the finished work. Summer was always a good time for murder. Short-fused passions exploded more readily in the heat. Last night emotions had exploded in this shop on the Rue du Bac. The morning had given him another murder to solve.

The Prefecture's awesome power stood behind him. Whatever he needed would be provided. It might take him a week or months, but ultimately he would decide who had killed this Dimitrios Kouridis. Not even a Frenchman, in the name of God! A Greek émigré. A shopkeeper of the seventh arrondissement. Why should anyone want to kill him?

"Commissaire! We've found something," Fauré called.

Boule followed him around the debris to a stack of paintings tilted against the wall. The detective tipped through the first half dozen framed canvases. They were stylized portraits of young and very beautiful girls, each with a startling décolletage. Swelling young breasts, creamy slender throats, unblemished features, eyes laughing naughtily. Each face was completely different, and yet in some indefinable way they were all the same.

The painter was a professional. That much he recognized. An artist who obviously had got himself in a rut churning out slightly naughty portraits of his clients' daughters, then for some reason was unable to collect or deliver the finished work. The Greek must have thought he could bargain them away.

"So?"

"Patience, Commissaire."

"Get to the point!"

The point was that the last four paintings in the row had had their faces sliced out of the canvas. And under the stack next to the wall they found what appeared to be the murder weapon, a wicked-looking broad curved knife with a razor-sharp edge. Very delicately, the detective picked it up by the tip and laid it on Boule's clean handkerchief. His partner came closer to examine the offering.

"An Arab weapon, isn't it? The sort of thing they stuff in their cummerbunds when guarding the harem."

André found the scabbard, a short curved wooden holster covered in black leather and banded by crude hand-beaten metal collars. It held two smaller knives, replicas of the one Boule held in his handkerchief.

Dark smudges stained the shiny wide blade. On closer study he could make out particles of paint and fabric clinging near the point. A brass stamping on the hilt depicted a tiny pair of crossed knives flanking the number "7." He replaced the scabbard and knife on a Louis Quinze end table that had managed to escape destruction.

"See Forensic gets that lot when we're finished here, André."

"Yes, Sir!"

Boule hung another cigarette on his lip and stood staring at the portraits. He took two over by the front window and examined them in the natural light. Neither canvas bore a signature or mark, not even the usual minutely scrawled initials or notations about the artist or his subjects.

"Look for those missing pieces!" he ordered the detectives.

He didn't expect them to find anything, but the effort had to be made or they'd think him derelict. Start with what was missing and try finding it. That was the correct police procedure for every murder investigation. Whose, he wondered, were the missing faces? They must have names, birthdates, identity papers, fingerprints. On the other hand, who owned the remaining faces, the ones that regarded him with such innocent eyes?

A commotion out front distracted him from pursuing the thought further. The young policeman he'd sent over to check on residents in the buildings across the street popped through the uniformed officers guarding the entrance. Behind him, an enormous fat woman in caftan and bedroom slippers prodded her way onto the premises amid much angry abuse from the crowd. Faces pressed against the window mouthing insults. The woman shook herself like a hippo debouching from its morning ablutions.

"Commissaire, this is Madame Clary. Third-floor apartment across the street. She has information."

Boule pocketed the cigarette and inclined his head. "Madame, my pleasure. And of course my apologies for bringing you from the sanctuary of your home. You saw something last night?"

"Yes."

She had petulant rubbery lips that folded out from her teeth. Several chins receded into the buttoned neck of the caftan. For a moment her clever bright eyes scanned the premises.

"Dead, is he?"

"You knew him?" Boule inquired politely.

"So-so. Enough to say hello, nice day, good evening, nothing more than that, you understand. I'm not a mixer. I'm a respectable widow." She spoke with a deep gravel voice pummeled by years of too much alcohol, tobacco, and screeching.

"Of course you are, Madame. I could see it immediately. And I fear you are right. Monsieur Kouridis is dead."

"Murdered, was he?"

"That, Madame, is what we are here to investigate. Now," he continued brusquely, moving quickly to head her off from touring the rear of the shop, "suppose you tell me what you saw or heard last night."

"An hour before midnight, he and another man — a younger man, well dressed, I notice such things — they stood out there in front of the window, talking, then went to the door. The Greek unlocked it and they entered, the other man first, then the Greek. They went into the back of the shop — back there."

"How did you happen to see them? Do you watch the street?"

She stiffened. "Of course not, Commissaire. A chair is by the window, from where I watch television, you understand. In this heat I had the window open. Every sound at night rises from the street. Every conversation can be heard."

He decided her life must revolve around these short summer months of open windows and secrets floating on the limpid night air.

"You heard what they said?"

"But of course. A business matter. I heard them distinctly. The stranger told the Greek he was a thief because he asked too high a price. But the Greek said that there were many expenses and he would open his accounts, proving exactly how much he had paid for any item the man wanted. After this they entered the shop."

"So, they were arguing?"

Thwarted from her first line of reconnaissance, Madame Clary veered off to examine whatever merchandise in the front room could be fondled without stooping. Boule followed as she picked up and discarded a variety of objects, settling finally on a large and particularly beautiful onyx ashtray. She held it covetously, checking the color banding. Boule waited.

He saw André staring at the woman in fascination. Realizing that he was being observed, André had the grace to blush before following with a wink of undisguised amusement. That was the main trouble with the new young ones. Lots of brains and enthusiasm but so little respect for their superiors and the old traditions. He lifted the ashtray from Madame Clary's clutches and set it on the table next to the knife and scabbard.

"You said they were arguing, Madame?"

"Did I? Well, perhaps they were. It wasn't a shouting match, you understand. More. . . ." she flailed the air with fat hands, fighting to grasp an elusive adjective.

"Strong words?" Boule suggested.

"Exactly — strong words. An exchange of strong words."

"Can you describe the other man, Madame?"

"Younger, of course. In his thirties, middle thirties. Well dressed, as I have said. Elegant. Medium height, dark hair."

Her description fit at least five million Frenchmen.

"He spoke with an accent."

"Ah! An accent."

Boule replaced his cigarette, offering Madame Clary a selection from the crumpled package. He lit them both and watched her suck greedily on the frail end, cheeks working like bellows.

A foreigner made things so much easier. Passport pictures, hotel registrations, railways and airports, all could be checked. The Sûreté's mighty arm had long fingers that reached into every corner of every village in the Republic.

"If you saw this man again, Madame, would you be able to identify him?"

"But of course! He looked like..." her eye wandered over the throng congregated beyond the glass window to a solitary man at the back. "That man outside, Commissaire," she squinted past her cigarette smoke. Her eyes widened. "That's the man! The same man! There's your murderer!"

Boule pointed him out to one of the giants at the door.

"Ask him to step inside. No rough stuff. But he's not to get away. Understand?"

The officer charged through the crowd. A brief conversation followed while those in the shop watched. Then without touching the man or arousing his suspicion a pathway was opened, allowing them unimpeded entry to the store.

"Monsieur Fournier, Commissaire," the policeman announced.

Of course it wasn't Gilles Fournier, though the man wore a beautifully tailored suit with waistcoat and striped tie. He glanced around the shop at the policemen.

"I'm afraid there has been some mistake. My name is not Fournier, it is Marais. Roger Marais."

Madame Clary backed away to where the two detectives were working. André closed in beside the commissaire while the young policeman who had delivered Madame Clary stood fiddling with his notebook and ballpoint.

Boule crossed the room and seized the man's hand. "Monsieur

Marais, I am Commissaire Bernard Boule. Bad news! I'm afraid your friend, Monsieur Kouridis, has met with an accident." He dropped cigarette ash on his jacket and tie as he spoke, the lighted tube bouncing dangerously with each lip movement.

Taking the man's hand, he guided him away from the entrance and out of earshot of the nearest spectator. Madame Clary had been quite correct. Marais was of medium height, impeccably attired with a shock of carelessly tossed hair partially covering his ears. His face was boyish but the lines that seamed his eyes and mouth betrayed his true age. Boule guessed him to be thirty-five or thirty-six. His clothes were American but his accent wasn't.

"Last night someone cut his throat. He bled to death."

Marais's eyes widened for an instant, then, like Madame Clary, he headed for the back of the shop. Boule followed, trailed by André and the fat woman. Marais appeared unimpressed.

"You knew him well?" Boule ventured.

"No, not well. He was one of my suppliers here on the continent. I met him last year."

They returned to the front, leaving André to watch the woman and the body. Marais took a chair and sat down.

The man was either a born actor or genuinely unmoved by the sight of death. How long had he been standing out on the street watching the shop? Could he accuse him of being a killer returning to the scene of his crime? But with what justification? A simple Raskolnikov complex? Could Boule ease the burden of Marais's conscience?

"You are a visitor to our city, Monsieur Marais?"

"Yes."

"From?"

"Montréal — Canada."

"I know where it is. The purpose of your trip is business or pleasure?"

He answered warily: "Business, Commissaire. I had an appointment with Dimitrios for breakfast to discuss my list of purchases. Les Antiquaires, you know the restaurant?"

Boule nodded and looked at his wristwatch. "Eleven o'clock in the morning is a little late for breakfast, isn't it, Monsieur Marais?"

"I'm not a big fan of French breakfasts. Too slim."

"You walked from your hotel?"

"Yes, I'm just around the corner at the Pont Royal."

Boule knew the place, a cosy three-star with cheerful lobby, bright rooms, and good service. It had a reasonable restaurant and bar. He bounced a Gauloise Bleu stub against his top lip, shedding ash, while he considered the visitor from Montréal.

Would it not have been more sensible for the Greek to make the five-minute walk around the corner to the hotel and take breakfast with his client rather than make Marais come to him? As the seller, Kouridis would have bent over backwards to accommodate a rich client. Boule offered him a cigarette, but Marais waved it aside with a frown and began examining the surroundings, as though aware of the chaos for the first time. His gaze flickered around the room, over the smashed furniture, finally coming to rest on the Louis Quinze end table.

"That the murder weapon?" He came to his feet.

"Possibly."

Marais smiled. Boule noticed that he had very white, very even teeth. His own were stained and in need of repair.

"That's quite a weapon, Commissaire. May I touch it?"

"I'd prefer you didn't. There may be fingerprints. Do you recognize that knife?"

"Specifically? No. But I recognize the type. It's called a kukri. I've sold a few to collectors and weapons freaks back home. They're hard to come by unless you happen to visit Nepal." He bent over the table to peer at the hilt. "This one came from the 7th Gurkha Regiment."

He straightened and returned to his chair. Boule waited in case there was more.

Sensing an audience, Marais continued: "There's a legend that when a Gurkha soldier dies in battle, one of his comrades must take out his kukri and slice the topknot of hair from his head so his soul may rise to heaven. A comforting tradition, I think. Hindu mythology is always so much more practical than our own dreary religous fables, wouldn't you agree?"

"When did you arrive in Paris, Monsieur Marais?" Boule asked, with a polite cough.

"Yesterday morning. Direct flight. Red-eye special. Up all night watching movies, drinking double scotches, and stargazing."

He gave a man-of-the-world smile. Boule found the smile exasperating. It came and went like a nervous tic with no warmth or meaning. Boule had never been out of France and had no wish to travel abroad. Two weeks every summer fighting traffic to the Côte d'Azur, then trying to find a beach that wasn't completely covered with well-oiled brown bodies was the most he could tolerate, and that only because of his wife.

"Monsieur Kouridis met you at the airport?"

"Dimitrios? God, no! I was too tired to talk business with anyone. As soon as I cleared customs and immigration I hopped a terminal bus into the city and took a taxi over to my hotel. I went straight to bed and slept like a log."

"When did you contact Monsieur Kouridis?"

"I didn't. He phoned me around three-thirty yesterday to say he was on the way over."

"How did he know where to call?"

"He'd made my hotel reservations. I called last week from Montréal when my flight times were confirmed and asked him to use his influence for a room at the Pont Royal. It's difficult because they're booked ahead for months. Last year I got a room by a fluke. A London buyer canceled at the last minute so they fitted me in because I was an antique dealer."

André returned with Madame Clary. She stopped next to the counter and glared at Marais.

"Swine! He was a good man, the Greek. Why did you kill him?"

"Compose yourself, Madame. This is not the time or the place for accusations. I am endeavoring to uncover the facts. I am very grateful for your help, and if there are further questions I will call upon you. My assistant will escort you home."

He turned his attention to Marais.

"Now, Monsieur Marais, you were saying that Monsieur Kouridis called your hotel to inform you that he was on his way over. Did he in fact arrive yesterday afternoon?"

Boule hoped that by smoothing over the interruption he could pick up their conversational threads. Marais might treat the incident as an annoyance rather than an accusation. It was much too early in the game for accusations.

"Yes."

"And . . . ?" Boule prodded.

"And what?"

Boule managed a persuasive shrug: "What happened? Did you leave the hotel together? Where did you go and what did you talk about? Anything you can remember will be of help."

"Yes. We left the hotel together for a bite. We talked business. I went over his list of recommended purchases."

Marais straightened his tie absently, then adjusted his shirt cuffs. His words came slowly.

"Tell me, Commissaire, am I a suspect in this matter?"

Boule sighed. He would have preferred getting a bit more information but that couldn't be helped now. Damn the Clary woman. Great stupid behemoth.

"Anyone who spoke to or knew the deceased is of course a suspect at this stage of proceedings. You can understand that, can't you, Monsieur Marais? I am gathering the threads of events to weave a pattern of the crime. A loose end here, another there, different colors, different textures. But in time — and of course with luck — I'll discover the person responsible for murdering your friend."

"Business acquaintance."

Boule waved a square hand, brushing the error aside: "As you prefer. Friend, confidant, business associate, whatever you wish to call him." He gave a phlegmatic sigh born of infinite patience. "The point is you knew the deceased well and a sizeable portion of his last hours on earth were spent in your company." He left an opening for a reply. There was none. "So naturally that makes you a suspect. Regrettable but understandable, wouldn't you agree, Monsieur Marais?"

The detectives paused in their detritus sifting to examine the first suspect. Sooner or later the visitor would have to be detained for questioning, long, tedious and repetitive hours of intense examination to discover the truth. They looked at Boule for instructions. Would he decide the man should be taken into custody at once, or left to swim a while longer? The Commissaire waved them back to work.

"Did the hotel concierge return your passport this morning, Monsieur Marais?"

"He did."

"May I see it, please?"

For an instant Marais hesitated, appearing on the verge of argument. Reluctantly he withdrew the blue-covered booklet from an inside pocket and placed it on the policeman's outstretched hand. Boule murmured a polite "Thank you."

Roger Jean Marais had been born in Montréal on May 18, 1950. Brown eyes. Brown hair, Medium complexion. Weight 75 kg. Height 175 cm. Several pages of visas for a variety of Latin American and Far Eastern countries had been issued during the past two years, together with dozens of arrival and exit stamps. Boule recognized the most recent, an inked imprint from Charles de Gaulle airport. Marais had indeed arrived the previous day. His profession was listed as "businessman" — certainly a nebulous enough description which could embrace any number of legal or illegal activities.

"You fight with knives, Monsieur Marais?"

"If someone with a knife attacks me."

"Did Monsieur Kouridis attack you?" Boule asked.

But Marais wouldn't rise to that bait. Instead, his face hardened. Two white spots the size of centimes appeared on his cheeks.

Although Boule rarely made the quantum leap to conclusions without benefit of solid facts, instinct told him that in this case he could make an exception. Clearly, Marais was his prime and only suspect for the moment, and quite possibly could be the killer. Boule pocketed the passport.

"I'll keep this for the time being, Monsieur Marais." He gave a bland smile. "It's my insurance that you'll remain in the city until investigations into this matter are complete. I apologize for the inconvenience, but the interests of justice must be served. I'm sure you understand."

Marais cursed under his breath.

11:15 A.M.

Nicole saw the yellow police barricades the moment she turned off the Boulevard Saint-Germain. She assumed there had been a traffic accident. There was a car park just off Rue du Bac on the Rue de Gribeauval, next to the Church of St. Thomas Aquinas. She maneuvered her little Fiat close to the exit and locked the doors.

The attendant, a fat man with protruding eyes and a canvas change apron, stood out on the corner staring at the barricades.

He appeared tempted to desert his post to satisfy his curiosity.

"They say there's been a killing. Are you going that way?"

She nodded. He handed her a ticket.

"Find out what happened for me, will you?"

It was only a short walk past the police and barricades to where a small crowd had collected in front of one of the shops. She took up a position on the opposite side of the street and waited. From what little she could observe through the crush of bodies, it seemed most of the shop's window display had been cleared out. For a moment she thought she had the wrong place, but a gold-lettered signboard above the entrance reconfirmed Georges's description from the previous day: "Dimitrios Kouridis, Prop."

The police must have moved the display. She bit her lip, irritated that she hadn't arrived sooner or visited the shop yesterday after her grandmama took to her bed.

A white ambulance clanged up to the barricades. The police waved it through. Some burly officers guarding the shop entrance elbowed people aside to provide a right-of-way. The ambulance drew up and stopped. Its rear door opened. Two men in spotless white jumpsuits leapt out carrying a folded stretcher. They squeezed deftly through the lines of police and people. Nicole crossed the road for a closer look.

A few minutes passed. The ambulance men came out with their cargo, a white sheet bandaging the lifeless human form. A collective sigh rose from the crowd.

"What happened?" Nicole asked an agile woman who emerged from the crush of spectators.

"Someone cut Kouridis's throat from ear to ear," she said with evident relish.

"Oh?"

"Nasty business, if you ask me. Gives the street a bad name. Scares customers away at the height of the season."

Nicole thanked her and backed away, giving the ambulance room to pass. The crowd began to break up. A few news reporters remained to badger the uniformed policemen for official statements or tried — unsuccessfully — to edge their way past the front door and into the shop. For a while she stood making up her mind what to do: stay and talk to one of the plainclothesmen inside or go back to the car and drive home. She doubted if she would get any information from the police; they were turning the reporters away angrily. As she stood hesitating, a grim-faced man came out of the shop and turned up the street walking quickly, his head high, arms swinging the way men's do when they're heading toward an urgent meeting for which they are already late. On an impulse, she decided to follow him.

He didn't look like a policeman or an official, or even a soldier. His hair was too long, his clothes much too expensive. Thankful that she had worn her flat walking shoes, she trotted along, catching up with him finally as he turned the corner onto Rue Montalembert.

"Excuse me!" she called.

His stride slowed. Then he stopped and looked around.

"Well?" he demanded angrily.

"I saw you at that shop — where the man was killed. Do you know what happened?"

His expression startled her. She knew it was a lame approach to a perfect stranger. He appeared ready to lash out at anyone standing in his way. She took an involuntary step backwards.

"Ask your police. They're the experts. I'm just a visitor."

He spun on his heel and rounded the corner. She hurried after him. When she caught up she tried again.

"I'm sorry. I didn't mean to offend. It was only a simple question. I thought since you were inside with the police you might know what happened. I have a personal reason for wanting to know."

"You knew Dimitrios?"

"The dead man? No, I didn't. I wanted to speak to him this morning. It looks as if I should have come yesterday, doesn't it?"

"What's your interest?"

"I told you. It's personal."

He had a colonial accent. He looked American, dressed like a businessman. Certainly not a tourist. They stopped in front of the entrance to a small hotel — the Pont Royal. She'd never heard of it. But the doorman recognized him and saluted. Her interest in him heightened. He'd been on a first-name basis with the murdered shopkeeper, his hotel was just around the corner, and he was definitely not a Frenchman. She decided to give a little.

"Yesterday morning there were some items in the window. Now they're gone. I want to find out what was there."

"Why?"

She detected a flicker of interest. At least he wasn't trying to escape into his hotel.

"Because my grandmama became so upset by what she saw in that window yesterday she went straight to bed after lunch and stayed there for the rest of the day. That's not like her."

"Did you ask her to explain?"

"Yes. She refused to discuss it and became very angry with me."

"Was it something good or bad?"

"It was something that terrified her. That's why I decided to come back and investigate. But the police got there before me."

"Me too," he said, with the ghost of a smile.

She knew she had him. No longer an irritant, she'd turned into a human form. His face softened, displaying a combination of quiet amusement and curiosity. He glanced quickly at his wristwatch.

"Have you had lunch?"

Nicole shook her head.

"Join me, then."

11:45 A.M.

There is an old and venerable ritual at the Ministry of the Interior that takes place whenever a new man is appointed to this powerful post. The outgoing Minister, before stepping into retirement or political oblivion, places the new Minister's police dossier on his desk. It is a singular honor, a gesture of complete trust. Only a very few citizens of the Republic are permitted to examine their own police files.

It can be a frightening experience. Every success and failure is recorded; each indiscretion, misdemeanor, or sexual aberration is described in vivid detail. There are pages of truths, half-truths, lies, and all shades and varieties of opinion and innuendo. All the good and all the bad are packed neatly between two red file folders and tied together with a black ribbon.

The new Minister is free to make corrections, insert any number of clarifications, remove pages, or take revenge on those civil servants who have, over the years, compiled its contents so faithfully and precisely. Or the Minister may simply put the whole file through his office shredder and begin with a clean slate. The choice is his.

So when François Daumier became Minister of the Interior, he had spent the entire morning of his first day in the comfortable seclusion of his magnificent new office examining his dossier. He was not by nature a vindictive man. But he was a realist, a cautious political animal. In the steady climb to power he'd had to crush many lesser men. And there were certain events and embarrassments in his past that he'd just as soon forget. Nonetheless, some of them were there in his file.

What was not in his file was any in-depth examination of his family background. It simply said that he had been born on May 23, 1919, at Amiens in the region of Picardy and that his father, François, had worked in a sawmill. His mother's name, the report stated, had been Jeanne Catroux until she married and became Jeanne Daumier. No mention of brothers or sisters. Nor was there anything very illuminating about his wife, Monique, other than the observation that they were married in 1947 in Lille, and that she came from the town of Montcornet in the department of Ardennes.

With a sigh of relief he sent his dossier back intact to the Central Registry of Records. Later the same week, he was able to examine his wife's file on a pretext of checking into another matter. Her dossier turned out to be a model of police propriety. Her most notable accomplishment, according to the notes, had been to marry François Daumier and produce two fine children. It ended with a reference to his file for cross-checking. Daumier was content. According to the police, Monique's and his own pasts were without blemish.

For the next three years he had gone about the business of being a Minister of the Republic, the secrets of the past all but forgotten. Then suddenly, today, his wife had phoned him at the office, something he had never done before. When she told him that Gabrielle had called her, he knew that the unthinkable had happened.

After the call he got out of his comfortable leather chair, went to one of the tall polished windows and stared out across the rooftops. Her portrait had been seen in a shop on the Rue du Bac. Now the shop owner was dead. Murdered. No news of what happened to the painting. It was the tip of the iceberg.

He needed a plan, something to blunt the cutting edge of these present circumstances and turn whatever investigations there would be away from him and Monique. It shouldn't be that difficult, he reasoned. After all, his word was the absolute authority for every police activity within the nation. He nodded to himself as an idea began forming in his mind. He returned to his desk and rang for Mirabeau, his appointments secretary.

"Is the Sûreté's Director General in his office today?"

"I believe so, Minister."

"Splendid. Give him my compliments and ask him to come around and see me, will you please?"

"Yes, Minister. At what time do you wish to see him?"

"Now, Mirabeau. I want to see him right now."

"Yes, Minister. I'll ask him to come over at once."

Daumier sat back in his chair. He remembered something the President had told him many years before when they were both starting on the road to political power. "François," he had said, "in this life you will learn there is no such thing as a secret if two people know that it exists."

12:05 P.M.

"Nicole Daladier." She introduced herself to Marais in the hotel lobby. "Same name as one of our former premiers," she explained, as though expecting him to know about such things.

He admitted his ignorance of French politics and steered her into the dining room. At this hour of the morning the only other occupants were a quartet of sleepy-eyed members of a British rock group staying at the hotel. They wore skintight denim and black leather, heavy eye makeup, and tousled shoulder-length hair, and sat drinking tea and smoking cigarettes in one corner of the room. In the opposite corner, an elderly couple studied *Le Matin* and drank coffee.

Marais chose a table near the entrance and ordered salade niçoise with a cold bottle of Chablis.

"This is very kind of you, Monsieur Marais," she said.

"My pleasure, Mademoiselle," he told her gallantly. "Now, what is it you want to know, exactly?"

"What happened at that shop?"

He shook out his napkin and settled it carefully on his lap before answering. It gave him a moment to study the young woman at close quarters. He liked what he saw. She appeared to be about twenty and wore no rings on either hand.

"When I walked over this morning a cop took me inside to meet the investigating officer. A guy named Boule. I think he believes I'm the killer."

"You?" Her eyes widened in disbelief, which he decided was an encouraging sign. Obviously he didn't look like a murderer to her.

"I was with Kouridis last night, so I'm a suspect. Probably the only suspect. Still, it's early in the day. There may be others later this afternoon," he said dryly.

"Then why didn't they arrest you?"

"Good question."

He needed time to think, to sift through the permutations of his predicament. Without his passport he was trapped inside the country. Worse, without notifying the sweaty-faced commissaire, he couldn't leave Paris. Back home he wouldn't have given the matter a second thought. There were legal safeguards. Police suspicions without concrete evidence were worthless. Here he knew things were very different. A man was guilty until he could prove himself innocent. But just how did the game of justice operate in France? He'd better find out swiftly, because he had an uneasy feeling it might be like Mexico or Thailand where a man could sit in jail and rot forever on a whim of police suspicion.

"They lifted my passport, if that's any indication of what they have in mind. I don't know your police procedures. I'm a Canadian."

"I'm very sorry, Monsieur Marais. That sounds unfair."

She seemed genuinely sympathetic. Their waiter poured the wine and left.

"But this Dimitrios was alive when you left?"

"Of course. He has — had — an apartment upstairs. We went up together for a nightcap. I stayed about an hour and let myself out after midnight."

"Did anyone see you?"

"A woman across the street saw us arrive. The night man here will probably remember what time I got back to the hotel — that's assuming I need an alibi."

She held out her glass. He touched his own to it with a tiny musical ping.

"Confusion to your enemies, Monsieur Marais."

He chuckled and drank.

"Let's make it Roger."

"And I'm Nicole," she nodded, setting her glass on the white tablecloth. She leaned forward confidentially.

"When you visited the shop last night did you happen to notice what was in the front window?"

He thought back, remembering Dimitrios searching for his keys. Marais had stood swaying in an alcoholic haze looking in through the glass. What had he seen?

"Nothing but the usual sort of window display."

She leaned further as though fearful of missing some of his words. He toyed absently with his salad, watching her, and at the same time trying to recall what he'd seen. All he remembered were the paintings. The rest of the stuff had been junk. Her gray eyes pinned him. With a start he realized how pretty she looked. A delicate oval face framed by honey-colored hair that kept sliding across her eyes and needing constant attention. Sensual lips. Bare arms, tanned and dusted with freckles in a haze of wispy blond hairs. A miniature gold cross dangled in the vee of her breasts where the buttons of her blouse had been undone to one short of indecency.

"Grandmama's chauffeur told me this morning he remembered a collection of old pistols, a few ceramics, a statue, and two or three portraits. He saw them only from a distance after he stopped the car and got out to wait. I questioned him carefully and he does have a good memory."

Marais agreed: "Yes, I remember the paintings. There were two or three but I didn't notice anything else. It was only a moment before going into the shop. Not much help, I'm afraid."

She leaned back in her chair disappointedly. The kissable lips gave a thoughtful purse.

"I have two theories on what happened yesterday," Nicole said. "First, she must have seen some object in that window she associated with a painful past memory. Or, she recognized a face in one of the portraits."

"Perhaps it was a painting of her," he suggested.

"Perhaps. It would have to be something clearly visible from the back seat of a moving car. That eliminates everything else in the window but the paintings, doesn't it?"

"I suppose so."

He listened politely while she described the events of the previous morning in considerable detail, though he was fast losing interest in her grandmother and the paintings. So what if the old woman saw a painting of herself as a girl? At least it wasn't in the nude. Maybe she'd had a torrid affair with the artist who threw her over for the next girl in his series.

"What I can't understand, Roger, is why she refuses to discuss it with me. It's not like her. We've always been so close. In some ways much closer than my mother and I."

"Do you live in Paris?"

She shook her head: "Grandmama lives in Passy. I live in Lyon. Do you know it?"

He remembered driving through the place on a trip the previous year. He had the impression of a bowl-shaped depression of industrial grime surrounded by urban sprawl. The sky had worn an overcast of yellow smog that stung his eyes like Los Angeles. It had a lovely river — the Rhône, he thought — winding past the city's drab landscape into a deep lush valley.

"I've been through it," he admitted.

"Paris is much more beautiful, I think. Don't you?"

An idea struck him suddenly. She might be of use in solving his passport dilemma. She'd help him escape from France. Why not?

"You know, there were more portraits besides those in the window."

"There were? Where?"

"Inside the shop. Another dozen at least. All of young girls with low necklines. They were part of a collection Dimitrios picked up from a widow in Alsace. It strikes me that if you're interested in following through with that theory about your grandmother's portrait, the widow probably has a record of each model's name and address in her husband's files. It's worth a try. Do you have a car?"

"Yes. But how sure are you of this information? Alsace is a long drive from Paris."

"Dimitrios told me. He stumbled across the old girl on a buying trip last month. Some rustic town near the German border — I've forgotten its name. Her husband died last winter and she'd decided to unload his artwork." The town was Haguenau and the painter's name Karl Dorfmundt, and Marais hadn't forgotten at all. First rule in the antique business: never divulge your sources.

She tilted her head, regarding him thoughtfully. A curtain of hair slid over her eye. She pushed at it absently.

"Did he mention the woman's name?"

"Dortman — Doorman — something like that. Artistically, he wasn't much of a painter. Not the type any of my clients would buy. No signature on the canvases, no dates, and no records of the models — at least on the back of the pictures. Dimitrios picked them up for a song. She practically gave them away."

"What a strange thing to do," Nicole said.

"Maybe her husband had been a dirty old man and she wanted the competition out of the house. I had an aunt like that. First thing she did after my uncle died was throw out his collection of *Playboy* magazines."

"Did she feel any better afterwards?" Nicole inquired.

"I don't think so. She died from a stroke the following summer."

He could tell she didn't know whether or not he was teasing. A smile tugged at the corners of her lips. He decided that he'd planted enough seed on the idea of driving to Alsace. He'd let her think about it. He took a sip of wine, listening as she told him more about herself.

They had a house on the outskirts of Lyon, Nicole and her mother. She said "mother," not "mama," which he thought strange. An older brother had left home already and married. He had children, making her an aunt. The idea of being an aunt at her age was funny, she said. Her father had been an industrial sales representative until a car crash on the autobahn near Cologne killed him. She'd been fifteen when it happened. Her mother received a comfortable pension from the insurance settlement. Nicole was in her third year now at the local university taking a course in computer science. A scholarship covered her tuition.

"But if I hadn't won the scholarship, grandmama would have given me the money. She's quite rich. Just the same, I'm glad I'm doing it on my own."

She had an odd emphatic way of nodding her head several times when making a point.

She and her grandmama, she explained, were very close. Since earliest childhood Nicole had spent the summers with her; Paris in July at her Passy house with its walled formal gardens and servants, then on to the forest country of the Ardennes near Charleville, where she had a modest farm and country home. There were chickens, geese, a cow, and two saddle horses. An old peasant woman managed the place. Nicole loved it.

"It sounds like fun. I'd like to see it for myself sometime."

If memory served him correctly, the Ardennes district butted against the Belgian border. German border, Belgian border, he didn't care just so long as he could get himself out of France.

Through the open doorway he spied the young detective from the shop — Boule's assistant — talking to the desk clerk in the lobby. Had the police decided to arrest him after all?

The clerk, an officious little wimp with plucked eyebrows and fat ears, appeared fascinated by what the policeman had to say. He stabbed a finger at the dining room, looking directly at Marais, then quickly averted his eyes when he saw him seated at the table by the entrance. But the detective only threw him a casual wave before returning his attention to the wimp. A thick leather-bound hotel register was produced. The cop took out a thin notebook and began copying entries while the clerk fawned and continued throwing furtive glances at the dining room.

Marais grew angry. The wimp would tell the concierge, the concierge would tell the management, and by this evening Roger Marais would be asked to vacate his room and find accommodation elsewhere in the city because he'd become a cause célèbre whom the hotel could do without.

Furiously, he reviewed the possibilities for getting himself out of this mess before the vise tightened and he became immobilized. Outwardly he appeared calm and still attentive to Nicole's story, nodding in the right places, smiling in others, filing every word she said away in his mind to be drawn out later and examined at leisure — and probably discarded. While he sat listening politely, several plans began forming in his brain simultaneously.

It had been his grade seven teacher, Madame Duparquet, who had first revealed to him the secrets of his subconscious. She taught language to the students of Abbé Leclerc Grammar School in east-end Montréal. A brittle little woman with a stainless-steel spine, she believed that memory work developed the mind as well as the soul. At the end of every class ten lines of poetry or prose were assigned for memorization. By the time Marais graduated, his brain was stuffed with classical prose and poetry, all of little practical use except to give him an unusual facility for remembering places, names, facts, and faces, and the ability to compartmentalize his mind to solve one problem while working on another. It was a neat trick.

One of the compartments thought about Bobby Pinot.

He assumed Pinot was still in Paris, and free to operate.

Supposing Nicole needed time to make up her mind about that car ride to Alsace? A day. Three days. Marais didn't have the luxury of time. He'd switch to Pinot. Pinot owed him.

In prepubescent youth they had been pals. Later, good friends. Then Pinot went political and started blowing up mailboxes for the FLQ, a brand of terrorism designed to hasten the separation of the province of Quebec from the rest of Canada. To Marais it was a form of insanity provoked by political opportunists.

After a spate of kidnappings and murder the army was called out and the activists fled into Cuban exile. Pinot was wanted by the federal government, but before a warrant could be issued, he escaped to Paris.

Marais knew what Pinot did for a living, but the subject had been skirted carefully during his last visit. It wasn't polite to pry. He seemed to be doing well.

Nicole continued talking. He glanced at the desk. The cop had gone. Even the wimp had disappeared. Sound the all-clear?

"Monsieur Marais?"

He'd popped around the doorway like a jack-in-the-box. Two hefty uniformed policemen stood a few paces behind. They had come to collect him. He resisted an urge to jump up and run like hell.

"Yes."

"I'm André Villeneuve, Commissaire Boule's assistant."

"Yes, I remember."

"I'm sorry to bother you, but additional information has just come to our attention requiring some further explanation."

Villeneuve looked so casual and self-possessed he could have been asking permission to join them for dessert and coffee. All Marais could manage was a slightly strangled "Oh?"

"I'm sure we can clear matters up quickly with your help."

"What's the problem?" Marais asked.

"The problem is that you didn't tell the Commissaire you have a criminal record."

Across the room the British rock group were wide awake and probably wishing they had learned to speak French. No matter, the wimp would fill them in later. He could see the little man peeking around the backs of the policemen, his features working with excitement like someone on the edge of an orgasm. Maybe he was.

"That was a hell of a long time ago," Marais said evenly.

The expression in Nicole's eyes was urging him to fight back. She still believed his side of the story — whatever it turned out to be. He folded his serviette, finished off his wine, and signed the check.

"You want me to come with you, is that it?"

Villeneuve shrugged. "If you wouldn't mind, Monsieur Marais."

1:23 P.M.

Visitors from Great Britain and North America have difficulty understanding how French democracy can survive and flourish in what is so obviously a police state. But the word "police" means different things to different people. In France the suppression of crime and the apprehension of criminals are merely two of many other policing functions.

There are the CRS — "Compagnies Republicaines de Securité" — a type of riot police who are the most vulnerable to public criticism because of their crowd control methods. The "Gendarmes Mobiles," comparable to the American highway patrol or British county police, are a kind of rural police recruited by the army but deployed by the Ministry of the Interior. The Gendarmerie work closely with the "Gendarmes Mobiles." In cities and larger towns there is "L'Agent de Police," who is both traffic cop and patrolman, dressed in distinctive kepi hat with shoulder lanyard and white belt. The DST — "Directorat Surveillance du Territoire" — is the counter-espionage service. Its internal arrangements are an official secret. The DST maintains watch at all airports, docks, and border crossings, checking for undesirables trying to enter the country. Then there are railway police, sanitation police, canal police, secret police, even police for enforcing the purity of the French language. Finally, there is the "Police Judiciare" — or PJ — headquartered in the huge row of somber buildings along the Quai des Orfèvres.

Five separate Directorates and an advisory cabinet report to the Director General of the Sûreté National. Imagined by many to be the force responsible for all criminal investigations, the Sûreté is in reality only a collection of drafty administrative offices around the corner from the Interior Ministry at Number 11 Rue des Saussaies. Its Director General reports directly to the Minister of the Interior, the capstone of this policing pyramid.

Thus, through a chain of command stretching out to the tiniest Breton fishing village, the Minister holds the links of police power through the Sûreté, making him in some respects the most powerful and feared man in the nation.

Daggar Paoli came from Corsica. Although he'd spent most of his life on the French mainland, his heart still belonged to the turbulent island that had given him birth. However, his loyalties were another matter entirely. At the moment they belonged to Director General Beaubien of the Sûreté.

Paoli, a swarthy energetic man with cold dark eyes, considered himself a policeman. Beaubien considered him little more than a wild animal who, at any moment, might revert to his natural state. Paoli made him uncomfortable. Paoli made everybody he met uncomfortable. Paoli was a killer.

Upon concluding his astonishing discussions that morning with the Minister of the Interior, Beaubien phoned Paoli to arrange a meeting. Paoli suggested the Parc Monceau: "By the Colonnade at the end of the lake."

Officially, Daggar Paoli was another unemployed member of the defunct "Service d'Action Civique" force which had been disbanded by the new government. Unofficially, he was still commandant of the SAC's Paris District with a staff of over two hundred men in the field. "Operatives," he called them. Clever, ruthless men, like himself, who were prepared to kill on a phone call.

"There was a murder this morning on the Rue du Bac," Beaubien said when he joined Paoli in the Parc Monceau.

Both wore conservative lightweight summer business suits and looked every inch pillars of community respectability. Uniformed nannies pushed expensive, well-oiled baby carriages along the pathway behind them.

Paoli waited. He leaned with his elbows on the guardrail, hands clasped, watching the various waterfowl paddling after water spiders in the tiny lake. The spiders, he noticed with considerable satisfaction, held the advantage, even at close quarters.

"A Greek shop owner had his throat cut. It wasn't politically inspired. He lived alone on the premises. There were some portraits on display in his front window which we believe may have precipitated his death."

"Portraits?" Paoli interrupted without turning his head.

"Oil paintings of young female models," Beaubien explained. "Not nudes. Respectable pictures of the kind you might see in any family's reception room. However, no mention of these paintings will appear in any news media. Not now, not later when the investigation is finished."

He stopped to give the Corsican a chance to ask the obvious, but Paoli said nothing. There was a large circular bald spot on the top of Paoli's pate with a neatly stitched and faded knife wound. He'd combed some of the surrounding hair over it to mask the defect.

Beaubien stood a full head taller than Paoli. But Paoli was much wider and stronger. The Elegant standing alongside the Egalitarian, Beaubien thought comfortably, touching his neat moustache with the tip of his tongue while he considered the wording of his orders to the Corsican. Nothing in writing ever passed between the Director General and his SAC commandants. That would have been political suicide.

"Our investigating officer is Commissaire Bernard Boule. He's a good man, I'm told. He has been given a free hand to find the murderer and bring him to justice. Nothing more, nothing less. And your job will be to see that he obeys these orders, Daggar. For reasons of his own Boule may decide to exceed his mandate in the search for the killer. We cannot allow that to happen."

Paoli straightened and turned around suddenly. A pair of elderly tourists had stopped within earshot to check the colonnade against their guide book. They spoke German in the loud voices of the slightly deaf. Paoli took Beaubien's arm and steered him along the pathway that skirted the lake.

"A speedy conclusion to this business is needed, Daggar. If Boule has trouble finding the killer we expect you to provide suitable evidence and a corpse for him. On the other hand, if he does arrest a credible suspect, we're relying on you to make certain that that individual does not live long enough to come to trial."

"What are my operating restrictions?" Paoli had a deep gravelly voice marred further by his Corsican accent.

"None. You have carte blanche. I'll expect daily reports from you as usual. The Gare du Nord letter drop under the name of Robert Rampal," Beaubien said. "In an emergency, phone my private number. Take this for expenses to start."

From an inside pocket he produced a thick envelope stuffed with banknotes. Paoli packed it away without comment. They walked awhile in silence, Beaubien waiting for the Corsican to question him further on the assignment. When nothing was forthcoming from the SAC commandant, Beaubien decided the meeting was over. He stopped in the middle of the path.

"I can't give you the reasons for this operation. But I can tell you what I was told. The circumstances relating to the Greek's death and those portraits hold a story within a story within a story — all of which are better left untold."

1:40 P.M.

Rue du Bac ends at the Seine where the Pont Royal crosses over the river to the Right Bank. From the bridge, it is only a three-minute drive along the Quai to the Louvre. Boule's office lay in the same general direction. But before returning to the Brigade Criminelle Headquarters and his detailed interrogation of the Canadian, Marais, he decided to visit the Louvre for an expert opinion from Charles Villier on a few of the portraits.

He needed an art expert to appraise and advise. Who better than Villier? There wasn't a court in the land that would presume to contradict Dr. Villier's opinion on nineteenth- or twentieth-century paintings.

"Bring the ladies," Boule ordered his driver.

He'd chosen six portraits at random from the pile that Detective Fauré was taking over to the Forensic Sciences lab for examination. In the few hours since starting his investigation he'd had an amazing amount of luck: an eyewitness with an unshakable conviction, a prime suspect, and sufficient evidence to keep everyone sifting for weeks while he produced an ironclad motive for the crime.

Repair and restoration were Dr. Villier's specialties. He had an incredible eye for duplicating the color mixes and brush strokes used by the old masters. Yet the preservation of art from the ravages of time, grime, and industrial pollutants was a poorly paid and unending bureaucratic job. Once he'd become a recognized expert in his profession, meritorious advancement was no longer possible, resignation quite unthinkable, and transfer impractical. Villier was trapped. Had he decided to forge Rubenses and Rembrandts instead of devoting his time to the cleaning and repair of the genuine article, his fortune would have been assured. But he was an honest man.

Villier operated from a glass-enclosed office in the corner of a large, airy restoration room on the main floor near the Mollien gallery. There was a view of the river, a photograph of his wife and two children on the desk, and a panoramic display of his workers and apprentices as they labored at making the past more presentable for future generations of museum visitors.

He seized Boule's hand and pumped it enthusiastically. The police driver stood by uncomfortably, a silent robot awkwardly holding the paintings. Villier eyed the one on top, a striking raven-haired beauty with sad eyes and full petulant lips. Her bosom strained against the laced doublet in which the artist had dressed her.

"Is this an official visit, Commissaire, or are you looking for an opinion on artistic merit?"

He slipped the painting of the raven-haired girl from the driver's arms and held it away from him at eye level.

"Official police business," Boule said. "I'm investigating a murder."

"In that case we should retire to my office."

He issued swift orders to his workers then ushered both policemen into his fishbowl. A sweet sickly smell pervaded the premises. Rabbitskin glue, Boule remembered from his last visit.

Villier wore his red beard close-cropped to match his hairstyle. The overall effect was that of a man in an orange balaclava examining the world with a pair of intensely curious blue eyes.

"What can you tell me about that painting, Dr. Villier?"

"What do you want to know?"

Villier's fast darting movements resembled a series of small but continuous explosions. His lips pursed thoughtfully from beneath the red fur.

"Do you recognize the artist?"

Villier shook his head. He took the painting to the window, tilting it to catch the afternoon light. After a moment he shrugged.

"Professionally trained. Classical touch. An old school conventionalist, I'd guess. Stuck to tradition. Not much on imagination. He painted exactly what he saw."

"He?" Boule interjected. "Why not she?"

"Unlikely. When this was painted there were only three professions open to women: motherhood, prostitution, or the Church." He made them sound synonymous.

"Nationality?"

"Any country in Europe — except England. Take your pick."

"But not English?"

"Definitely not English," Villier said. "Too much emotion for an Englishman."

Boule couldn't see any emotion. But then this was the difference between layman and expert, he supposed.

"Can you tell when it was painted?"

Villier peered closer at the paint and canvas. Boule lipped a cigarette from his crumpled package. There were only two left, both bent and leaking tobacco. He'd have to ration himself.

"This one was done before the early 1920s. Say 1913, or thereabouts."

Boule straightened in his chair with a startled expression. Something wasn't right. He'd assumed they were all recent creations, the models still alive — perhaps even the artist.

"You're absolutely positive about that date?"

Villier ran his fingertip over the white lace edging the girl's shoulders. He gave a clucking sound followed by a pair of quick nods.

"Between 1913 and 1920, plus or minus three years to be absolutely certain."

He set the painting on his desk, smiling at Boule's skepticism. His teeth, vaguely visible through the furry fire, were stained and broken. Boule took out a handkerchief and sponged his face.

"You see that white?" Villier pointed. "That came from a lead oxide base, not titanium. White lead oxide produces much softer tones, and tends to yellow slightly with age. Titanium white, on the other hand, is much sharper. But before 1920 there was no titanium white. It hadn't been discovered. During the '20s artists switched to titanium when they found its color qualities easier to control than lead oxide. Which is why I say this portrait was done before 1920."

He appeared pleased by Boule's reluctant conversion.

"Next, your lady is wearing a fashion popular here in the city during 1910. So, by adding a few years to make it acceptable for the lady's parents to allow her to pose in such a garment, I suggest 1913 as the earliest date for her portrait. She's quite a lovely thing, isn't she? Did you know her?"

Boule shook his head. If she was still alive the girl would be well into her eighties, or even her nineties, her youth long fled, her skin turned to wrinkled parchment. Those sad eyes would be dull and dimmed, her mind a morass of wandering memories. Could such a woman be a murderess? He took a second painting from the pile. This one of a blonde girl with cherubic apple cheeks and laughing smile had been caught at the moment of a shared joke. Her gray eyes teased, or taunted, depending on the viewer's mood. Villier studied it with the same care as the first, then set it on top of the other.

"The breasts are different, of course, but the style is the same. Done by the same artist around the same time. Apparently he had a thing about the female breast."

Boule gave him another, scattering cigarette ash over his desk.

Villier gave a vigorous nod. "As I said before, this painter had no imagination. He painted what he saw."

He picked up the next painting and studied it thoughtfully. "Odd, I grant you. Yet it's not uncommon for an artist to develop a fixation for one particular portion of the human anatomy. Titian became infatuated with hands and fingers, Ingres was fascinated by the female rump, Rubens by ample tummies. They painted them over and over again."

Boule shook his head impertinently. "But your old masters painted other things as well. As far as we know at present this man painted only portraits. How can you compare a tit fetish with a Rubens rump?"

"Ingres did rumps. Rubens did bellies," Villier corrected. His brow clouded. He had an angry vein carved diagonally across his forehead that pulsated when aroused. He was not accustomed to being contradicted, considering his opinions expert enough to stand on their own merits.

"And how do you know he painted only portraits, Commissaire? He might have had a preference for landscapes or flowers and fell into the trap of painting portraits on demand for economic reasons. I can tell you with certainty that he did not value this particular work."

"Why?"

"Because he never even bothered to varnish it, for heaven's sake!" Villier exclaimed.

Boule wondered aloud: "Is that an important point?"

"But of course. Every oil painting needs varnish to protect it. Without their protective coatings the world's masterpieces would have disintegrated long ago. It is one of the things I do here. Every fifty to one hundred years the varnish is removed and restored. But . . . " and he shook his finger in Boule's face as though the Commissaire had been one of his students from the Polytechnical Institute, " . . . the varnishing is never done at the time the painting is finished. That would be quite impossible. Time is needed for the oils to dry and cure properly. Eighteen months at least. Usually, if a painting is sold or stored before it's varnished, the artist pencils a note on the back of the canvas when it is to be completed. This one has no date and no varnish so we can assume the work was never sold and that the painter thought it unworthy of further effort. I might add that I'm inclined to agree with the artist in this case," he added smugly.

"But those other two were varnished?" Boule asked.

"Both of them, yes."

The Commissaire dabbed his face and removed his cigarette, using its glowing butt to kindle another. One left in the pack.

"Can you put a date on this one?"

Villier shrugged: "Completed after 1920. How do I know?

Because the whites are titanium. Unmistakable. I can do an energy dispersive x-ray and detail the surface pigments for you if you leave it with me, but I'd be willing to wager most of the iron oxide colors used were synthetics produced around 1939."

Boule missed the rationale but the date came as a surprise. If Villier was right, the artist would have been in his twenties when he painted the first portraits in 1910; by 1939 he'd have been well into middle age, still doing the same sort of pictures. Maybe young girls with swelling bosoms *were* all he ever painted.

Antwerp, 2:00 P.M.

Max Kramer operated a diamond courier service out of Antwerp. A discreet melancholy man with pale gray eyes and nondescript features, he had an ability to blend into the background of any group of people. He was of medium height, medium build, and medium complexion and had thinning mouse-colored hair. In fact it was often said that the most memorable thing about Max Kramer seemed to be that, after meeting him face to face, very few people were able afterwards to describe him either in satisfactory or identifiable terms. He was a physical enigma. His origins were obscure. He preferred keeping them that way. Max worked for the KGB's European Bureau under direct control of Moscow Center. His code name was Traveler.

Arriving in Belgium in early June 1966 on an Austrian passport with a chamois pouch full of high-quality gemstones for which he had elaborate documentation, he claimed to be a diamond broker. Within a week he'd rented a modest three-storey office building along a narrow corridor of ancient monoliths at the edge of Antwerp's diamond district and opened for business. Thus in a few weeks Moscow Center was able to penetrate the tightly controlled world diamond market and begin unloading some of the vast storehouse of uncut diamonds held by the Russian government. Belgium had the best diamond cutters in the world and the marketing infrastructure necessary to produce a steady flow of hard currency back to Moscow. And Belgium had the newly established headquarters for NATO, which was the other reason Max Kramer had been sent there. Slowly and with infinite patience he built a remarkable courier system for his masters. It allowed for the free movement of highly sensitive information and Russian agents around the globe.

In addition to his courier service and diamond brokering, Max Kramer developed an elaborate penetration of NATO Headquarters in Brussels. So successful were his NATO efforts that Moscow Center and the Warsaw Pact nations usually knew the complete minutes of most inner council meetings of the Defense Planning Committee within forty-eight hours of their adjournments.

His method was simple: NATO's weakness in Brussels lay with its method of continually changing intermediate and senior staff from each of the fifteen member countries. Two years' service in Brussels was the average posting. With every change came new faces, new household employees, new opportunities to penetrate and exploit the weaknesses of the new arrivals. Kramer's inside contacts compiled brief histories on every new posting: name, rank, nationality, wife's name, children's names, aides, servants, habits, observed routines. Everything went to the KGB's European Bureau for assessment.

Within a few weeks a courier would arrive with dossiers on the new arrivals, information compiled from Moscow Center's records or drawn from local agents in the new arrivals' country of origin. The decision whether or not to use this information was left to Max Kramer. And Max was very selective. Everyone had an Achilles' heel, he knew. With the Turks it was liquor. For the Americans it was sex. For the British, a loss of prestige. For the Italians, religion, and for the French an idiotic fear of losing their honor.

Brigadier General Rolland Mercure and his wife, Adelaine, were posted to Brussels in the fall of 1979. It was a cushy five-year posting for a politically-minded army officer nearing retirement age.

Unlike other NATO countries, France is not a member of the military organization within NATO. In its early years, NATO Headquarters resided at the Palais de Chaillot in Paris. But in March 1966, General de Gaulle proclaimed France's intention to withdraw from its North Atlantic Alliance military ties. Belgium became headquarters for the Allied Defense Planning Committee (DPC), Supreme Headquarters Allied Powers Europe (SHAPE), and the North Atlantic Treaty Organization (NATO). However, a French Military Mission to Brussels was quickly created. Heading the Mis-

sion required a skilled military officer and diplomat with a technical background and an ingratiating sense of protocol. The man
chosen needed to obtain and pass on every NATO secret which
might be of interest to the French government.

A few weeks after Rolland Mercure's arrival, Max Kramer sent
his usual report on the new staff and family members to the European Bureau of the KGB in Moscow. The Bureau went to work
sifting through the known backgrounds of every person listed in
Kramer's report. Only one turned up with a past that required con-
cealment: the Brigadier's wife, Adelaine Mercure. The details were
passed by courier back to Antwerp.

Kramer read the report carefully and recognized at once that
the woman's vulnerability, when combined with a characteristic
French passion for maintaining personal honor, made her an ideal
candidate for blackmail. He arranged a chance meeting at one of
the NATO receptions and gave her his proposition: his silence about
her past in exchange for a steady flow of NATO military information
plus anything else of value picked up from her husband or at the
rounds of social and diplomatic functions they were required to
attend. Clearly terrified by this threat of exposing her past, a week
later the ashen-faced woman agreed to cooperate.

Unfortunately, she turned out to be a waste of time. An incredibly beautiful but very stupid woman, she was a great disappoint-
ment, and over the ensuing three years most of what she passed
to him turned out to be third-rate bureaucratic garbage of little
value. Only once did she produce what he considered an information gem. So, for the most part, he treated her reports with low
priority, using them mainly for cross-checking material coming in
from other agents in the NATO network.

Twice monthly they met in a café on the Avenue de la Toison
d'Or in Brussels where, without speaking, they exchanged identical
boxes of handmade chocolates. There were much simpler ways of
collecting her reports, but he'd learned that when dealing with nov-
ices an atmosphere of surreptitious activity produced a conscious
reminder about the necessity for secrecy. If things were made too
easy for the amateurs they grew careless. And that would never
do.

Kramer had just returned from a late lunch of cold meat and an
excellent fruit compote to settle into an afternoon of paperwork
when his office manager slipped in to say that Madame Adelaine

Mercure had called asking for an appointment to discuss a flawed two-carat stone. Kramer stiffened. It was her danger signal. Something had gone wrong.

"A flawed two-carat stone. You're certain that's what she told you?"

Piet Arnen nodded: "Without doubt. She repeated it twice to be sure I understood. It's not one of our stones, is it, Sir?"

"I doubt it. Thank you, Piet. That will be all."

He checked Adelaine's telephone number and dialed Brussels. It was risky, he knew, but normal appearances had to be maintained at all costs. At least until he learned more details of the danger.

She answered halfway through the first ring with a voice edging on hysteria. He listened while she repeated with careful diction her litany of the flawed stone. A meeting was imperative. Could they discuss her problem? She suggested the town of Mechelen, exactly halfway between Brussels and Antwerp. Kramer countered with the village of Willebroek, 20 km from Antwerp and 30 km from Brussels, where he was known. She agreed.

"Take the A12. You should be there in a half hour," he said. "There's a small café next to the canal. I'll be at one of the tables."

"I'm leaving now."

She hadn't cracked. That was good. She'd remembered the instructions he'd drilled into her. Quickly, he phoned Herne, the café owner in Willebroek, and ordered some backup in case the meeting turned out to be a trap. Two men from the village, four from Antwerp.

Then he went to his office safe and removed his escape kit, pistol, and silencer and stuck them in a briefcase. Whatever the woman had to tell him, Kramer intended to be prepared. Even if it meant killing her and driving on to the Brussels Luchthaven for the first flight out to an East Bloc country.

Paris, 2:15 P.M.

Marais stretched out on the uncomfortable steel bed, careful not to tear his clothing on one of the rusting spring hooks holding the frame together. The bed gave a weary creak. He looked at his wrist where his watch should have been. After fingerprinting him, they had taken away his shoes, belt, and valuables so he had no way of knowing the time. Two hours, maybe two and a half, seemed to have passed since the polite young detective with the inquisitive eyes had locked him in the room, promising to return shortly.

He had only the vaguest idea where he'd been taken. An island in the Seine, he thought, close to Notre Dame Cathedral. He hadn't paid enough attention during the drive over to be certain. Every ounce of concentration had been given to holding his temper in check. Outrage or anger would be interpreted by the police as a clear indication of guilt. Innocents brought in for further questioning were supposed to go along like lambs, eager to please and anxious to cooperate.

The room, a square box of cracking gray plaster and an uneven wooden floor, had a single barred window near the ceiling, too high to look out and too filthy to provide much illumination. There was no mattress. Instead, a stained striped cotton slipcover provided separation between the occupant and the corroding flat web springs. At the foot of the bed, near the door, someone had thoughtfully placed a galvanized chamber pot with a lid.

One thing that puzzled Marais was how they had managed to learn about his Canadian record in such a short time. It hadn't been more than an hour after he'd left Dimitrios's shop before the keen young cop was at the hotel. If the Paris police were this efficient then they had to know his entire story; what had sent him to prison.

2:37 P.M.

Boule lit another cigarette — his last — and twisted the empty package into his pocket as a reminder to buy more. While his driver sat fidgeting, Boule leaned back in the seat and closed his eyes to think.

The car radio came alive. A Priority One call for him to report immediately to the Police Judiciaire Headquarters. He was told to check at Réception with the duty officer. All very mysterious, no reason given. It smacked of the type of exercise junior police officers were put through after running afoul of one of the pompous senior bureaucrats at the Palais de Justice or the Prefecture. Occupants in every radio car in the city would be speculating now on who Boule had crossed. He took out a fresh handkerchief and smeared his face.

He would have liked to drop in at Forensic on the way and see if the paintings with their faces removed wore a coat of varnish. But all that would have to wait. Any summons from the PJ coupled with an "immédiat" was not the sort of order to be obeyed at personal convenience.

PJ Headquarters is a short drive from the Louvre along the Quai to the Pont Neuf and over that bridge to the Île de la Cité. The island, sitting in the middle of the Seine, was the core upon which the city of Paris had been founded. Only after its conquest by Julius Caesar in 52 B.C. did the original Celtic settlement expand onto the mainland and start growing.

Yet in spite of two thousand years' growth and urban sprawl the island remains the city's judicial and spiritual heart, shared by the Palais de Justice at one end, Notre Dame Cathedral at the other, and the Prefecture of Police in between.

The Brigade Criminelle Headquarters of the Police Judiciaire is located at number 36, Quai des Orfèvres, but even though Boule's office was on the third floor of the building he did not rate a parking space in the courtyard.

"Shall I wait?" the driver asked.

Boule shook his head. He had no idea how long he'd be kept. Better to send the man to Forensic to collect the remaining portraits for Villier to examine. He climbed out, cautioning the driver to make certain Villier signed a receipt listing each painting with its full description. The public prosecutor would need such evidence by the time the matter reached the courts.

At the reception desk inside the building the duty officer, an old sergeant with chest problems and a game leg, handed him a sealed envelope from one of the dark cubbyholes behind his counter.

"He's waiting for you, Commissaire. Worried too, by the looks of him. Someone leaning on him from above, I shouldn't wonder." He jerked a nicotined thumb toward the ornate ceiling.

Boule tore open the letter. Three terse lines informed him that the Sûreté's Director General Beaubien had phoned Chief Henri Dubé at the Brigade Criminelle office at 12:30 requesting details about the Rue du Bac homicide. Commissaire Boule was to present himself at Dubé's office upon arrival. The purple-inked signature swirled majestically across the bottom of the page.

He pocketed the letter. Since when did Director General Beaubien involve himself in a simple murder investigation, Boule wondered. Most unusual, and unsettling. He went along at once through busy corridors that were filled with dawdling clerks and antiseptic odors until he reached Dubé's territory.

Yes, he was expected, the receptionist told him. The Chief and the others were waiting. What others, he wondered? A scrawny secretary with hair piled into a fat plait on top of her head funneled him straight through the outer chambers into the conference room. A thick soundproof door covered with green baize padding whooshed shut behind him, sealing him into the surroundings. Dubé looked up.

"Sit down, Boule, sit down. We've been waiting. Where have you been?" he demanded testily.

Besides Dubé in the chairman's slot at the end of the polished oak table, there were three others seated around the table, each man a section head. Bergeron from Fraud, Jodry from Robbery, and Boule's immediate superior, Martin Robinette from Homicide. Dubé's three Wise Men. He knew them all. They were all younger than Boule, all except the Chief. Boule gave everyone a polite smile.

"My apologies, gentlemen. I was visiting the Louvre," Boule said, and took the chair next to Robinette. Dubé hesitated, on the verge of asking him to elaborate, then thought better of it.

It was not a big room. Few of the PJ rooms were designed to accommodate more than a couple of desks, chairs, and filing cabinets. But because of his rank Dubé had his own conference room with two big windows and a spectacular view of shoreline diners at the outdoor restaurants just across the river. So close were they that had either window been open sounds of glassware and cutlery would have been clearly audible. But with the windows shut there was only silence and an uncomfortable warmth. Boule brought out a handkerchief.

"Can you think of any logical reason why the Director General is interested in this case of yours, Bernard?"

Boule answered carefully: "Not the slightest idea, Sir."

Dubé might have tolerated an amicable "mon ami" or "mon cher chef" within their present closeted circumstances, but never a bold "Henri." That would be too familiar. He was a spare saturnine man with a sharp narrow nose and features that wore the perpetual expression of someone who found the bulk of his daily activities thoroughly distasteful. It was a pose. He was a toady who could always be expected to say the right thing to the right person at the right time.

Boule and Dubé were contemporaries. Same age, same year of graduation from the Police Academy, Boule near the top, Dubé in the middle of the class of one hundred and thirty-one. Both had legitimate claim to having been message runners for the Resistance as teenagers, but there the similarity ended. Affecting an aristocratic manner to cover his colossal ego and ignorance, Dubé managed to arrange a wealthy marriage for himself. No mean accomplishment for the middle son of a Dijon butcher. Boule, on the other hand, had married for love.

Upon reflection Boule decided that this was the basic difference between them. He loved his wife. He loved his job. Dubé loved only himself. Somewhere there was a moral in that. Dubé began:

"Our Director General is very — no, very is not the precise word in this instance. I would say he is extremely interested in this Rue du Bac murder. He insisted on knowing every detail. I said that Boule was handling the investigation and would, in due course, deliver a detailed report. But apparently that wasn't good enough for the Director General. He wanted an immediate assessment of the entire affair."

He leaned forward, shoulders hunched, his beautifully manicured hands pyramided in a benediction above the table.

"Accordingly, I called this meeting so we can discuss the situation between ourselves and try for a consensus as to what it's all about."

Boule said: "Ah!" The others remained silent. It was common knowledge that Dubé was after the Director General's job. Any hint of internal police impropriety would send him scuttling to the Minister of the Interior with a full report on Beaubien's incompetence. One of the three section heads would be suggested as Dubé's replacement.

"Might it be political, Chief?" Jodry asked.

Dubé stopped to consider the possibility. He looked at Boule, who had developed a sudden craving for a cigarette.

"Tell us, Bernard. Is there anything unusual about this particular murder?" Dubé asked.

Boule shrugged. Everything about murder was unusual. Was it a trick question? He hesitated. How the devil had the Director General learned about the affair? Unless the deceased deserved news headlines because of a political background, as Jodry proposed, or because of the unusual method by which he departed life, the Sûreté's office would receive only the barest details until the PJ completed its investigations. Sometimes this could take months. A brief initial report through channels was expected within the first week. That was the way the system worked. Why the sudden rush?

He gave his face another sponging and launched into the story.

"There are a group of portraits, Sir. Seventeen in all, four with the faces removed."

"Removed?" Dubé interrupted. "You mean painted out?"

"Cut out with the murder weapon. Or what I believe to be the murder weapon."

"Then say so."

"Yes, Sir." Boule felt weary.

"He means excised, the faces were excised from the painting. Isn't that what you meant, Boule?" Bergeron smiled.

"Yes, that's what I meant."

Bergeron tipped his head respectfully to Dubé.

"Thank you, Pierre," Dubé said dryly, "Now perhaps we can get on with his story."

As Boule related the events at the shop — the sudden appearance of an eyewitness followed by a prime suspect — Dubé's eyebrows moved higher and higher toward his graying widow's peak. By the time Boule reached the part about phoning the Canadian Embassy and verifying the suspect's passport as genuine only to discover that their computer showed the man had a criminal record, Dubé's pyramid of fingers had collapsed on the table top.

It wasn't proper procedure. Contact with foreign embassies was strictly DST branch business and had nothing to do with the Brigade Criminelle. When Beaubien read this in Boule's report he'd be furious. The Director General believed in total separation of police department responsibilities.

Jodry jumped in, demanding, "Details, Boule. What were the details of his crimes?"

Jodry had a thick protruding lower lip that made him look like a pouting child confined to his bedroom without a favorite toy. His mind, however, worked with a disciplined precision. He was Dubé's anointed heir, or so they all believed.

"I don't know yet. A copy of his Canadian police file will arrive sometime tomorrow morning, I'm told. I'll assess the situation then."

"I'm breathless with anticipation, Boule. Where is this monster now?" Bergeron inquired.

"I've detained him at the Palais de Justice."

"Without charge?"

Boule nodded, watching Bergeron light a cigarette, wishing that he'd pass the package around. But he didn't. It went back into his pocket. Boule licked his lips.

"Tell me, Commissaire, do you think your suspect is guilty?" Robinette asked politely.

The Homicide section head admired Boule. A quiet soft-spoken man with the air of an astute academic, Robinette never raised his voice, his hands, or his blood pressure unless it was absolutely necessary. He was a gentleman.

"I haven't decided. It is possible. He knew the dead man. They were seen together last night entering the shop by an eyewitness."

"How much more do you need to make a case for the public prosecutor, Commissaire?"

Boule shrugged: "A motive, Sir. I need a motive, and so far I haven't found one that makes any sense. But I'll keep looking."

"What about robbery?" Jodry offered.

"So far as we've determined nothing was taken from the place — except four faces out of the portraits."

"Could there be a fraud or blackmail involved? They weren't nudes, were they?" Bergeron took a deep drag on his filter tip, causing Boule to wince with envy.

"No, they were clothed, and there's no indication of either fraud or blackmail, at least for the present."

He screwed his damp handkerchief into a tight ball below the table.

They were all silent for a few moments before Robinette suggested primly that it might have been a crime of passion. He dropped the idea quickly when he saw skepticism on Boule's face. Finally, and pointedly, Bergeron looked at his wristwatch, then picked up his pencil and began drawing pigs on his notepad. He was no longer willing to play Dubé's game. If the Chief needed a pin to stick on Beaubien's ass he'd have to find it for himself. After all, Bergeron reasoned, he wasn't the one who fancied himself to be the Sûreté's next Director General. Dubé could go to hell.

"Anyone have another idea?" Dubé asked. "There must be a reason that our illustrious DG has expressed an interest in this case." He looked at each of them in turn. Jodry shook his head. Boule's stomach rumbled menacingly. He hadn't eaten since breakfast. Worse, he was melting slowly into his dark blue suit.

Dubé fiddled with a file folder, trying to gauge his position. Boule studied him poker-faced, waiting for the shoe to fall. Dubé could take him off the case, replacing him with one of the younger detectives in Robinette's section, a keen university graduate like André Villeneuve, for example, hungry for recognition and press coverage. That was the trouble in France. There were never enough murders to go around.

How had the Director General ordered his Brigade Chief to proceed? That was the key to Boule's remaining on the case. If Beaubien's interest was genuine and either politically or privately inspired, then discretion would take precedence over flamboyance. Of that much Boule was certain. He knew himself to be the very model of discretionary investigation. Dubé knew it as well. There wasn't anyone better in the department. Yet at that moment Dubé seemed to have some difficulty digesting this fact. In the end it came reluctantly, prefaced by a sigh.

"Very well, Bernard. I'll pass your information along to the DG. There will be questions, of course. I expect to be kept informed of developments on a daily basis. Clear?" he added, unnecessarily, Boule thought.

"Perfectly."

Boule got up, pocketing the handkerchief. Outside on the river a white cruise boat slipped silently past the restaurant diners, working its way downriver, its flat-topped superstructure packed with passengers.

"Need any extra men?"

"I can manage, Sir."

"I'm sure you can," Dubé told him confidently.

It wasn't exactly a victory but at least he was still in charge. A feeling of immense relief flooded into every damp pore. He bowed politely to them all and escaped through the baize door to the cooler interior of the building.

Chief Dubé dismissed the others a few minutes later after one last attempt at eliciting support for a theory about Beaubien's involvement. Even the faithful Jodry could think of nothing.

When they'd left, Dubé went to the window and stared down at the garbage-strewn water. His orders had been to tell Boule to drop any reference or investigation concerning the paintings. How the devil had Beaubien known about the paintings in the first place? None of the section heads knew until Boule turned up with that information a few minutes ago. Boule could be trusted to say nothing to the press until the investigation was complete. No worry there. He could let his prize bird dog snuffle through the tall grass, flushing every feather of evidence into Dubé's lap until at last the Director General would betray his position and take flight. When that happened Dubé would be ready to shoot him down with a full report to the Minister of the Interior. After that, it would be Director General Henri Dubé of the Sûreté. The words had a nice ring to them when he said them aloud.

Robinette would step into his shoes here at the Brigade Criminelle and he'd see that Boule took over from Robinette as Homicide's section head. Why not? It was the least he could do for his old sweaty comrade-in-arms. When he became Director General everything would be possible.

Willebroek, 3:04 P.M.

If Max Kramer had been born with a sense of humor he would have laughed. First with relief, later at the absurdity of Adelaine Mercure's concern over her portrait. He'd all but forgotten that the portrait was the reason she had agreed to work as one of his rabbits in the first place.

Three years had passed since his threat of exposing her secret. He'd grown accustomed to their regular covert meetings at the

Brussels café. The reason for her willing cooperation had faded in importance. Every threat of blackmail was swiftly superseded by the more alarming threat of being exposed as a traitor to the authorities. In consequence, the original threat and the reason for it paled to insignificance.

Adelaine had made the transfer from reality to subterfuge without any remorse or aftershock about betraying her country. With some rabbits this became a problem a few months after working in their new environment. Conscience took over and sent them running to the nearest police or government confessional hoping to expiate their traitorous sins. They were ideal candidates then to become double agents. Kramer had caught three of his rabbits turned by the opposition during the past year. Two of them he'd managed to bring back into his warren as triple agents. The other he had eliminated as unsalvageable.

"More coffee, Sir?" Herne, the café owner, inquired.

Kramer nodded: "Thank you, Willi."

Across the room his two backup men, tough-looking local boys with blunt chiseled faces and watchful eyes, waited patiently.

"Tell them they can leave," Kramer ordered.

Herne crossed the room. The men nodded, tugged on their caps, and left. Kramer stirred cream into his coffee. Adelaine Mercure had come and gone and there had been no ambush, but still he was concerned. She had been furious. A snippet of information used to bring her into his warren had misfired. How or why he didn't know. He'd find the specifics in her file back at the office. She spoke as if he knew all the background details to her problem. He didn't. And he wasn't all that interested except as it affected his operations.

He'd implied that his knowledge of her situation was complete, and she had accepted his words as fact when she began working for him. Vaguely, he recalled the reference to a portrait of her as a young woman which the KGB's European Bureau stated would bring her under his control. Now the portrait had been seen in a shop in Paris. Why had Kramer allowed this to happen, she wanted to know? Had she not done everything he asked? Then why had he betrayed her secret?

What secret?

He'd been afraid to ask, realizing he was supposed to know. At first he'd considered countering her volley of abuse with the threat of exposing her to the NATO authorities. However, he realized such a ploy would have been pointless in her present mental state. Public exposure and arrest as a spy appeared to be the least of her concerns compared to the portrait in Paris. So he dropped that idea and sat listening in polite silence. Herne had kept other customers out, so she was free to yell at the top of her lungs. For the sake of discipline, he had been thinking as he listened, she would have to be eliminated. Perhaps a street accident, something neat and simple. The Belgians were such atrocious drivers. But first there would have to be his promise of an immediate investigation to find out which of his associates had disobeyed orders and released her painting. In the meantime, she would promise to remain silent and he would have time to arrange her demise without threat of betrayal. He was on the point of interrupting her tirade to express his shock and offer an apology for the error, together with his hastily improvised proposal, when she said something that guaranteed her survival.

"And what about the other women, Herr Kramer? Will you use their portraits to betray them in the same way you have betrayed me?"

What others? What on earth was she talking about?

Suddenly the entire matter had become a problem for Moscow Center to examine, evaluate, and explain.

THURSDAY, JULY 12

Paris, 9:40 A.M.

During the summer months of daylight saving time there is a five-hour time difference between Paris and Ottawa. The request for details about Roger Marais's criminal record had come from the Canadian Embassy in Paris on Wednesday afternoon, but it was still mid-morning when it reached RCMP Headquarters in Ottawa. The duty sergeant sent the request over to the computer room for search and retrieval. It was lunchtime before the printout was back on the sergeant's desk. He forwarded it to his senior security officer to have it checked for "sensitive material." Another two hours passed. Finally, the file was cleared for transmission to Paris and sent upstairs to the Communications Section. By the time the information reached Paris it was after 9:00 P.M. on the Continent. Inside the imposing stone building at 35 Avenue Montaigne the regular night shift was on duty. The transmission came in plain language, addressed to the RCMP liaison officer, Inspector Barton Géant. Marc Hibbert, the young man holding down the communications desk, simply tore the message off the telex and stuck it neatly into an envelope to be placed in Géant's Embassy letterbox for the morning delivery.

Had the transmission been coded instead of in the clear, the computer operator would not have read its contents, nor made a photocopy for Bobby Pinot, his exiled FLQ friend, whose name had appeared in the original. After all, what were friends for? Besides, he believed stoutly in Quebec's right to independence too.

Inspector Géant had had a fight with his wife and daughter that morning over family finances. Consequently, he was late getting into the city from the Gentilly suburb where the Embassy provided him with a modest but comfortably furnished house near Orly airport. An uncompromising flint-eyed career policeman who had joined the Force as a teenager, his global experiences were limited to a brief stint in Hong Kong on a narcotics investigation during the early seventies, and his Paris Embassy posting, this latter a prelude to retirement.

More social than functional, it was an easy posting, liaison work requiring little effort other than a pair of suspicious ears and eyes to pick up any information of criminal intent directed toward Canada from the French Republic. Additionally, Géant was expected to keep tabs on all known Canadian criminals residing in France and, in a quid pro quo arrangement, provide the various Sûreté directorates with whatever background knowledge might be of interest on a specific individual should they inquire. Roger Marais fitted into that category.

At least in Barton Géant's opinion.

Once a criminal always a criminal, he was fond of repeating. So, when the inquiry on Marais's passport had come in to him the previous day, he had felt duty-bound to provide the gratuitous information to the Brigade Criminelle that even though the passport was genuine, its bearer had a criminal record. A predictable response from the French police resulted: what were the particulars of Roger Marais's crimes in Canada?

Géant turned cautious. What had Marais done to warrant such interest? After all, the man had been paroled from prison for seven years. Maybe Géant had been too hasty in his cooperation with the polite young detective from the Brigade Criminelle.

"It is in connection with a murder investigation, Inspector Géant. You can understand that any clue to this man's background would be of immense help to Commissaire Boule," the polite voice told him.

Géant promised to have the information by the following day.

This morning over breakfast he'd read the murder details in *Le Matin*. Marais had been referred to as a "tourist." No names yet. No accusations. Investigations were continuing. The police were being very cautious. Obviously whatever evidence they had against Marais was thin. Something concrete was needed to justify making a formal charge or arrest. He wished that he'd asked for more details from the man on the phone. Possibly he could have helped Commissaire Boule.

He signed the Embassy's staffing book at 9:36 A.M. and went up to his office on the second floor. A single brown manila envelope lay on his in tray. Géant removed his coat and sat down at his desk.

There were four sheets of printout paper inside the envelope. The perforation edges had been removed and the pages cut to a standard size and stapled together.

The first page was a facsimile of the restricted C-480E form giving details of Marais's conviction and a summary of police information. It showed mail distribution to the FBI in Washington, police headquarters in Montréal, and the prisons in which he'd served his sentence. Copies were on file with the Penitentiary Service in Ottawa and the National Parole Board. Everything was up to date, with the last entry showing the Paris Embassy.

But it was the charge column that held Géant's attention. Marais had been charged with first-degree murder. The man was a killer.

Under the disposition column it showed that the charge had been reduced to second-degree murder. A twelve-year sentence had been imposed. In all, Roger Marais had spent over eight years behind bars and was under lifetime parole supervision. Grim-faced, Géant turned the page and began reading the narrative. Only then did he realize to his disgust that Marais was a cop killer. In his opinion, that was the lowest form of criminal scum.

Yet, despite the overwhelming evidence, it had taken two trials to convict him, and then only of second-degree murder. This was an outrageous miscarriage of justice in Géant's view.

Once a criminal, always a criminal. Was the jury completely mad? As a final absurdity the parole board had released him in April 1977. After an eight-month stint at a halfway house in St. Laurent, he was given permission to travel abroad and develop an art and antique business he'd started in a fashionable area of old Montréal. No restrictions. No exemptions. Roger Marais had, according to the parole board, earned his right to re-enter society and dwell within it as a useful and productive citizen.

"Hah!"

Géant's hand was shaking with indignation as he reached for his phone to call the Brigade Criminelle and tell them that the background information needed to arrest Roger Marais for the Rue du Bac murder had arrived from Canada.

12:10 P.M.

Madame Marie deBrisay's body was discovered in her bathtub shortly before noon. Her housekeeper had become alarmed when repeated knocking on Madame's bedroom door failed to produce a reply. Using a passkey, she entered the en suite apartment and found Madame's body. She phoned the police immediately. Commissaire Jean Blais was now on the scene.

"But I want you to take over this investigation, Bernard," Dubé told Boule. "Get out to Passy as soon as you can. You'll have your hands full with all those damn reporters. An aging but still beautiful divorced wife of a millionaire industrialist is always entertaining news. Especially after she's been stabbed to death in her bath. But try to keep it under control."

Boule shifted the telephone receiver from his right to his left ear, freeing his writing hand to jot down Dubé's information.

He'd spent most of the morning at Forensic going through their laboratory analysis of the paintings. Only one of the portraits with the faces sliced out had been varnished. It had been painted before 1920. The other three were circa 1939 creations. Those models, therefore, could still be very much alive, probably in their late fifties. He felt satisfied with his progress in the case. The last thing he needed was to be saddled with a second murder investigation. Why did Dubé want him on it, he wondered uneasily? It was out of his district entirely.

"Can you handle both jobs?" Dubé demanded in his ear.

Boule hesitated. "I suppose so."

"There is a tie-in," Dubé insisted.

Boule said, "Ah."

"Nicole Daladier. Ever heard the name?"

Boule admitted he hadn't and wrote it down.

"She's been phoning here all morning trying to find out what we're doing with Roger Marais. The street address and telephone number she left are the same as the deBrisay residence in Passy — Rue Raynouard."

"Interesting," Boule said.

"Yes, isn't it? By the way, what are you doing with Marais?"

"We're keeping him."

He'd sent André over to the Canadian Embassy to pick up the information they had received. Boule told Dubé something of Marais's history.

"Food for thought, Boule. Food for thought."

"Yes, Sir," Boule smiled.

He scanned his notes. The Rue Raynouard address was the sort of place he would have liked for his wife. He could imagine the house: vast airy rooms, tastefully furnished and decorated by one of the recognized fashion experts on the Rue Faubourg Saint-Honoré. She deserved the best. Instead, she had him. Ah, the sadness of life. Without wealth and power he had to be content with its reflected glory. Commendations, official congratulations, scrolls of accomplishments, and the countless envious glances from his peers were all he had managed in thirty years of public service, never any power or enough money.

Detectives Fauré and Monceau were still sifting for evidence in the Rue du Bac murder. There were three storeys and an attic to go through, and so far they hadn't got to the second floor. He phoned them at the shop, ordering them to lock the place, put a uniformed guard on the door, and get themselves over to the deBrisay mansion.

André was somewhere between the Canadian Embassy and the PJ. Boule left word with Dispatch for him to go along to Passy the minute he checked in. Then he thanked the patient Forensic man for the use of his office and went down to his car. The day had turned into another scorcher without a shade of cloud to punctuate the yellow glare over the city. By the time he reached the car he was soaked with sweat and decided to find an air-conditioned café where he could cool off over a glass of wine and a cold lunch. So it was mid-afternoon before he made it across the city to the deBrisay residence.

In the enormous central reception hall Jean Blais greeted him with all the confidence of a Marshal of France on the point of coming to grips with an enemy. He shook Boule's hand effusively in an anxious display of professional compatibility.

"Good to see you, Boule. Glad they sent you over and not one of those young know-it-alls," he said, not quite convincingly enough to arouse Boule's cooperative instincts.

The sixteenth arrondissement belonged to Blais. Although the Brigade Criminelle provided the expertise and technical help needed to investigate and solve any homicide within the nation, local precinct commissaires tended to regard any form of assistance from the PJ as meddling. Over the years Boule had learned that tact was his best modus operandi.

Blais, a tall, slim, handsome man with a bright enthusiastic face, had been picked for his administrative abilities and political acumen rather than for any criminal investigative brilliance. Always impeccably attired and coiffured, he reminded Boule of a model in a Rémy-Martin ad. The appointments committee couldn't have found a better image for the sixteenth arrondissement than Jean Blais if they had scoured the entire Republic. Blais had flair.

The sixteenth is a quiet and distinguished part of the city with boundaries that embrace the river Seine, the Arc de Triomphe, and the Bois de Boulogne. The Passy district nestles comfortably between the Bois and the river. Once the home of humble woodcutters, the district flowered in the eighteenth century when rich iron springs were discovered in the area and wealthy Parisians began building summer residences so they could take the waters.

The big ornamental homes and gardens have given way gradually to blocks of flats and high-rise condominiums. But many of the old houses still remain. The deBrisay mansion, set back behind tall trees and an ornamental black iron fence, exemplified the luster of those last Royalist years before the guillotine sliced most of it away forever.

"I have everything under control," Blais announced confidentially, guiding Boule to a wall, away from the streams of people plying the broad carpeted staircase.

"So I see," Boule said, aghast at the numbers tramping past his field of vision.

Fifteen years Boule's junior, Blais was everything the older man was not — an Academy Sword of Honor winner, a First in athletics, a champion debater, and a bachelor and ladies' man. Quickly he filled Boule in, speaking in fast staccato sentences. Throughout the briefing Blais gazed over the top of Boule's head at the front entrance.

"No sign of forced entry. An inside job for my money. One of the household. Wait until you meet them! The granddaughter had a godawful row with her this morning and came storming out of the old lady's bedroom. Both the housekeeper and the cook were on the fiddle and about to be charged with fraud. The gigolo chauffeur had finally run out of gas and got his walking papers last night. Any one of them could have done it. My vote goes to the granddaughter. She phoned, by the way."

"Who?"

"The granddaughter, Nicole Daladier. Two outgoing calls to the PJ. I've put a patch into our office so we can keep track of who is calling whom."

Boule sponged his forehead and searched for Fauré and Monceau among the faces on the stairs. There were at least a dozen reporters mixing with an equal number of uniformed police, a few plainclothesmen from the local precinct, a television crew lugging cameras and lighting equipment and trailing long black umbilicals, and a variety of other people on whose function or involvement he could only speculate.

"And where is the granddaughter?" he inquired.

"Upstairs in her bedroom, wailing and weeping dramatically. I put a man on the door in case she takes it into her mind to hoof it out to the cathedral for a novena."

Boule held his tongue in spite of Blais's smirk. There would be nothing gained by picking a fight.

"The doctor put the time of death at between 7:00 and 9:00 A.M.," Blais continued. "Couldn't pin it tighter than that with the body left in a hot bath. Corpse and water cooled at the same relative rate. Death came from a single stab wound through the heart. Perfect aim. Dead center — forgive the pun. Ha! Ha! Killer used a stiletto or paperknife. No sign of a murder weapon yet. The photographers are finished but the fingerprint boys are still dusting the bedroom."

Suddenly, Blais's eyes widened. He'd seen his target. "A moment, if you don't mind, Boule. Don't go away."

He slipped off to speak with a shaggy-haired man wearing owl glasses and sporting a Radio-France ID tag pinned to his shirt pocket. Boule waited and watched. Several reporters peeled out of the traffic flow and circled Blais and the Radio-France man. Some produced notepads, two waved portable microphones attached to Sony Packs. Blais pushed them aside.

Boule lit a cigarette. The hallway smelled of furniture oil and tobacco smoke. He caught sight of Fauré looking at him across the carved bannister and beckoned him down. Blais and the Radio-France man passed the detective on their way up.

"What the hell is going on here?" Boule demanded.

Fauré smiled. "I think Commissaire Blais has caught the scent of greasepaint, Sir. Nothing like the glare of publicity for quick promotion to public office, is there?"

Boule decided to let that one slide.

Fauré looked around and shook his head. "It was like this when Monceau and I arrived. When I suggested tactfully that reporters be excluded until the detail work was finished the Commissaire told me to mind my own business. I've just been up with the girl."

"How's she taking it?"

"Better now. She's stopped crying. I guess she and the old lady were pretty close."

"Where's Monceau?"

"In the sunroom taking statements from the staff with a couple of Blais's men," Fauré said.

"Has André arrived yet?"

"Haven't seen him, but that doesn't mean anything. It's a hell of a big house and there's quite a mob in here."

"Yes, that's the first thing we have to correct. You'll find my driver outside. He's big and he's in uniform. Stick him at the front door with orders to let no one in without my permission. Check the ground level and see that all doors and windows are locked and bolted, then see what you can do about getting some of these people back on the street where they belong. Only the investigators and household staff to remain. Understood?"

"Understood. What about Commissaire Blais?"

"Leave Blais to me. Now then, how do I find the girl's bedroom?"

It was on the second floor at the end of a wide hall littered with enormous Persian rugs. The rugs, each probably worth a small fortune, dampened every creak and footfall. Paintings of animals and ancestors frolicked or frowned at intervals along the walls. The guard recognized Boule and saluted.

"Another one for you to solve, eh, Commissaire?"

Boule chuckled. The rank and file were behind him, anyway.

The policeman knocked. Boule waited until a muffled voice said "Come in," then opened the door.

It was a large room, decorated in peach and cream colors that suited the girl sitting on the side of the four-poster bed. Her face and eyes were very red from crying and her hair looked damp and untidy. Boule introduced himself. She nodded listlessly.

"May I sit down?" he asked.

Another nod. He pulled a small comfortable armchair away from the wall and drew it closer to the bed. Its castered wheels needed oiling. She had drawn the heavy curtains across the windows, creating a sensation of twilight and intimacy within the room. Boule reached for a porcelain ashtray on the bedside table and held it strategically against his chest below the cigarette.

"Do you mind if I smoke?"

She shrugged and shook her head.

"I dislike intruding, Mademoiselle Daladier, but you understand I must ask a few questions. Something that might provide a clue to the person responsible could be deep in your subconscious waiting for the right question to draw it out. Do you understand?"

He had learned in dealing with the wealthy to adopt a courteous, cautious approach lest someone of importance become offended. It happened frequently with the new boys who tried flexing their bureaucratic muscles at the wrong people. Dealing with the wealthy was like working with politicians. One never knew exactly how far a particular ripple of influence might spread.

"I have answered so many questions already, Commissaire. Couldn't it wait until tomorrow?"

She spoke in a quiet tone of emotional resignation. Boule sympathized, but these were the most important hours spent with witnesses in any investigation. Later, when she had had time to examine her position in relation to events, the girl would become cautious and less cooperative. At the moment her defenses were down and whatever he could persuade her to tell him would be fact.

"My questions are different, Mademoiselle."

"I suppose you've spoken to Bettina. Is that why you're here?"

"Bettina?"

"Grandmama's companion, social secretary."

Boule said "Ah" and waited for more.

The air within the room felt comfortably cool. For the moment he'd stopped sweating.

"Bettina runs the house," the girl explained. "She fights with Georges — the chauffeur — and the cook and anyone else she thinks might be trying to undermine her position. She's really just a glorified maid. I can't stand her. The feeling is mutual. She probably told you I did it," she added bitterly.

Boule shook his head: "I haven't spoken to any member of your household yet — except you."

He stubbed his cigarette and replaced the ashtray near the small color television next to the bed.

"May I ask what your interest is in Roger Marais?"

Her eyes brightened with curiosity. Hesitantly at first, she explained how they had met and why she had visited Rue du Bac, then described their discussions over lunch at his hotel until the police took him away.

"Did your grandmother say anything when you confronted her with your suspicion that it had been the portraits that upset her the previous day?" Boule probed deeper.

"Nothing. She became very angry. Last night and this morning when I tried to discuss it with her she ordered me out of the room. It was horrible. Her face went all red and blotchy. She screamed at me. I've never seen her in such a state."

She shook her head in wonder at the memory. Her eyes filled with tears. "I was really the only one she had, you see," she managed to get out finally. "If only her last hours with me hadn't been spent in argument. I didn't mean to upset her. I was trying to help. That's all. Just trying to help."

Her shoulders heaved as a sob bubbled to the surface. Boule changed the subject immediately. "Why did you phone the PJ inquiring after Roger Marais?" It took a few moments for her emotions to shift onto this new tack.

"I suppose I was curious. He doesn't seem much like a murderer to me."

"They seldom do," Boule observed dryly. "You agreed to meet again?"

She flipped some damp hair away from her eyes and shook her head. "Not really. If the police hadn't come he might have asked me out for dinner tonight."

"Would you have gone?"

"Yes, I liked him."

"Did you know he'd been in prison before — in Canada?"

"No, I didn't."

"Would you still go out with him if he asked?" Boule persisted.

She had to think about that for a minute. "Depends on what he did that sent him to jail."

"Killing a policeman," Boule said softly. "You can appreciate why he is under suspicion, Mademoiselle."

The information rocked her, Boule noted with satisfaction. Perhaps she imagined herself fortunate to have escaped the monster's clutches or having her own throat opened from ear to ear. In any event he'd accomplished his purpose, sensing that now she trusted him for having been responsible in a perverse way for saving her life. He decided to bring her back to his original line of questioning.

"Tell me about your grandmother, Mademoiselle."

"What do you want to know?"

"Anything you care to tell me. What about her friends and acquaintances? Did she have any enemies? Can you think of anyone who might want her dead?"

"No one," she stated positively. Then after a moment's reflection added a caveat: "But of course I never knew many of her friends and certainly none of her enemies. I only come to Paris for the holidays — here and in the Ardennes. Usually we go there during August."

"To stay with friends?"

She shook her head. "No. A farmhouse outside Charleville that Grandmama owns. Old Margot is there."

"Margot?"

"She looked after my mother when she was a little girl and Grandmama was away working in Paris."

"An old retainer?"

"Yes, something like that. She is very old. A man from the village takes care of things around the farm now."

"What year would this be, when she left your mother with Old Margot?" He was trying to understand the sequence of events.

"After the war with Germany."

Her generation gave labels to France's conflicts, he realized. To her they were all history: Algeria, Indochina, Egypt, Korea, Germany.

"Was this before or after she married Comte deBrisay?" he asked.

"Before. She had an affair with an American soldier. They were supposed to be married but he was shipped home."

"Ah," Boule said. It was all so long ago and probably totally irrelevant. "The Comte accepted your mother as his stepdaughter?"

"Never! Nor has he ever spoken to me."

"They were not on friendly terms, your grandmother and the Comte?"

"I don't think they spoke to one another after their divorce. At least Grandmama never mentioned it to me."

"But would she have any reason to mention it, Mademoiselle, even if they had?"

"No, I suppose not."

He had heard enough. Either the girl was the genuine article or a consummate actress. Time would tell.

"Would you do me a great favor?" he asked.

"If I can."

"Make me up a list of everyone you can remember who knew your grandmother here or in the Ardennes."

"Including tradespeople?"

"Everyone."

"I can try. It may take a little time. Is it important?"

Boule shrugged. "Who knows? It might be. Policemen need such lists to solve crimes. Names of people who knew the victim. The more the better. It is a long painstaking task. But always, sooner or later, a tiny clue turns up from something someone says and everything suddenly falls into place." He gave her what he hoped was an encouraging smile.

"I'll do my best," she promised.

He dragged the squeaking chair back to the wall. "Thank you for your cooperation, Mademoiselle. You've been very patient. I hope I won't have to trouble you again. My condolences over your loss."

She left the bed and walked him to the door.

"Does this mean I'm free to leave, Commissaire?"

"But of course. I apologize for the guard at your door." He shrugged companionably and fumbled for a cigarette. "At times our junior officers tend to overreact."

"I understand," she said.

He stopped, his hand on the doorknob. An afterthought: "Your mother is still alive?"

As she stood next to him he saw for the first time how lovely she appeared in the brighter light. Slim, with soft, full lips, she reminded Boule of the way his wife had looked at the same age.

"She lives in Lyon. The other policeman took down our address and phone number. He promised to call her with the news. I was too upset." She nodded earnestly, spilling damp hair over one side of her face.

"A final question: did your mother and grandmother get along well together?"

She hesitated. For the first time her reply was slow and guarded: "No, Commissaire, not very well."

Which probably meant that they hated each other's guts.

Boule wondered why.

Then there was the odd coincidence of Marie deBrisay coming from the Ardennes — from Charleville-Mézières. He wondered about that, too. Could his wife have known the dead woman? They were about the same age, came to Paris at about the same time.

A strange unsettling thought whisked through his mind. Instead of meeting Gabrielle Révier outside the Gare du Nord on a winter afternoon he could just as easily have met Marie deBrisay. Or any one of the thousands of country girls with stars in their eyes who came flocking to Paris each month seeking fame and fortune. Some turned to prostitution, others became clerks or shopgirls, a few wound up on the stage or in a theater company; most settled for good husbands.

They met in the rain, romantically, like movie stars did on the screen in the Saturday afternoon matinées. Heavy drops muzzled with ice splattered across the rim of his new fedora. She was bareheaded, long blonde hair plastered tightly to her ears and forehead. A bulging fiberboard suitcase, already soggy, tied with two turns of rope, rested near her feet. Under normal circumstances he would have passed her by without a second glance. During that winter of 1945 the city had an epidemic of teenage girls wandering the streets with battered suitcases. It was the defiance in her face that made him pause.

"Are you expecting someone?" He wanted time to examine her at close quarters without appearing intrusive. It was wildly out of character. He was usually shy with women.

"No." Her eyes were like tiny coals with pinpoints of light, her facial bones high and imperious, lending a slight oriental cast to her appearance. With her hair dried and brushed, a change of clothes and a touch of lipstick she would be quite lovely, he decided. His pulse quickened.

"How long have you been standing here?"

"Why?"

"Because if you remain much longer you'll be soaked through and catch a cold. Then who is going to take care of you?"

"I'll manage."

"Where did you come from?"

"The Ardennes." She said it like someone expecting an argument.

He felt sorry for her. A beautiful, stupid farm girl. "Do you know anyone in Paris?"

"No."

He made up his mind. "You'd better come along with me then. I'll see if I can talk Madame Doiron into putting you up for a few days until you find yourself a job. No funny business, though! She runs a respectable house."

He started walking, listening for her footsteps, knowing she would follow.

Moscow, 4:46 P.M.

The Ilyushin bounced twice onto the runway at Moscow's Sheremetievo airport and slowed, its engines rumbling against the thrust reversers. Boris Titov gave a long grateful sigh and unfastened his seatbelt. He hated flying. Yet Titov was not a coward. Unlike most of the middle-ranking KGB officers who posed as experienced combat veterans when they were posted abroad, Titov actually had faced foreign troops under fire, first in the Ogaden flatlands of Ethiopia, later in the mountains of Afghanistan.

When the aircraft stopped he remained in his seat, waiting until the crush of apparatchiks deplaned with their bundles of western goods from the airport duty-free stores. Most of the returning Party members were drunk, stumbling foolishly through the aisle. In the end, Titov knew, this would be Mother Russia's downfall — a combination of vodka, greed, and simple gluttony enjoyed by a privileged few. The rancor went deep. Someday it would all explode and bury everybody, East and West alike.

He followed the passenger line into the terminal, veering off to join the group heading for Special Clearance Procedures. In Russia, everything started at the end of a queue. He remembered his mother queuing for hours in midwinter to buy the family groceries. Wives of Party members or local civic officials went to the head of the line. Standing in the cold with his mother and older sister, Boris had thought it unfair. Now he went to the head of the line.

A cherub-faced lieutenant eyed the expensive diplomat's attaché case handcuffed to his wrist, admired the cut of his beautifully tailored suit, then glanced briefly at his travel warrant.

"Welcome home, Colonel." He gave Titov a smart salute and handed back the document.

Beyond the central reception area but before the terminal's main concourse a guarded doorway led to the underground garage where the military, militia, and KGB kept a pool of staff cars and limousines available for the run into Moscow. He showed the militiaman his ID. Another salute.

"Any luggage to follow, Sir?"

Titov shook his head. He passed into a well-lit tunnel walkway that led to the enormous private garage.

A militia major in the dispatch office examined his papers. He'd forgotten how often it was necessary to produce his ID and traveling authority. Living in the West with its unusual freedoms and easy anonymity had quickly become habit.

"Where to, Comrade Colonel?"

The man was Titov's age. But despite the gold-braided gray uniform with its colorful service decorations he looked shabby; his whole presence gave an impression of bored indifference and decay. The uniform and ribbons were spotted with food stains and cigarette ash. Even the gilt buttons were tarnished. Titov recognized the signs: too long on the job, too valuable to replace. At a gunmetal desk behind the major a noncom sat typing forms on an ancient portable.

"Dzerzhinsky Square," Titov said. The noncom looked up and smiled politely.

The major wrote the destination on a clipboard and handed over a small green card. "Car number twenty-six. Give this to the driver. You know the drill. Where are you in from?"

"Brussels."

"Lucky devil," the major said. "Any bags?"

"Just this." Titov held up his shackled wrist and the major nodded as if he'd already known about the attaché case. Titov went out to look for his car.

The decision to go to KGB Headquarters on Dzerzhinsky Square was a last-minute one. On the plane he had planned to go straight to the Foreign Directorate building on Moscow's Ring Road and make his inquiries to the chief of the European Bureau directly. But when he landed something changed his mind. Maybe being back in Mother Russia with all its intrigues and fears made him cautious. Or perhaps it was the knowledge that his career was at stake, that if he made the wrong move initially there wouldn't be a second chance. He'd go first to KGB Headquarters and talk to a friend. Marko Sultal had been his roommate when they attended the Institute of International Relations, before the KGB recruited them. Sultal would advise him on how to proceed.

Titov's official position at the Brussels embassy was that of shipping liaison officer for the Port of Antwerp. In reality he was Max Kramer's control officer. He'd been in his Belgian posting for exactly eight months. Prior to Titov, Traveler's control had been Peter Gretchko. Titov had met him briefly when he took over in January. A Lieutenant Colonel like himself, Gretchko was unhappy with his new posting to Madrid.

"What's happening in Madrid?" he demanded.

"I don't know, Comrade," Titov admitted.

Gretchko polished off his vodka. "Exactly! And what's more, who in hell cares?" Then he slammed his replacement on the back and roared with laughter.

"Have another?"

One was Titov's limit during working hours. He shook his head. Gretchko downed his fifth since inviting Titov into his embassy office. He smacked his lips.

"The real stuff, Comrade. None of that Norwegian shit in a bottle." He poured another. "Know who my understudy is in Madrid? Carlo Maria Bilbao. Now I ask you — what sort of a fucking name is that for an 'illegal'? Sounds like a fairy from the Bolshoi."

Titov had winced. A tightly enforced KGB regulation stated that no controller was permitted to divulge the names of any field agents except during reassignment, and then only to his new replacement. Even the Madrid embassy staff wouldn't know their resident illegal's true identity. Titov let it pass, realizing it was not Gretchko but the vodka talking.

Traveler received high praise from the outgoing controller. No problems, no waves, and no messes to clean up afterwards, Gretchko told him. Running Traveler was light duty. Titov could concentrate on Belgian women during this tour.

Gretchko had been right. Traveler had been Titov's easiest career posting to date. His function became little more than that of intermediary liaison between Kramer and the Center. Quite superfluous, really; Traveler ran his own show. Why not? He'd been at it for years. So Titov kept out of the way and found his own amusements. He'd been away at the coast sunning himself with a dark-haired spitfire from the Portuguese Embassy when Traveler called yesterday. A problem had come up.

He'd expected something serious, but when they met late in the day it turned out to be only a request for more details on an information source provided by the European Bureau in 1981 during Gretchko's tenure. Traveler had brought his copy of the original transmission. It had been initialled by Gretchko and the embassy's decoding officer. For Traveler to have it still in his possession was a serious breach of KGB security and it was this fact that upset Titov more than the message's content. Any decoded documents taken outside the embassy were supposed to be destroyed by the recipient once the contents had been read. He gave Traveler a verbal chastising and a severe lecture on security. When he'd finished, Traveler glanced out at the parking lot of the truck stop on the Ostend highway where they usually met.

"Let me tell you something, Comrade Colonel," he said softly, directing his attention to a tandem lorry with British license plates that was just pulling into the parking area. "The Tsviguns and the Andropovs and the Fedorchuks may come and go at Moscow Center according to the winds of political fortune. But I intend to remain secure in Antwerp. How? By making certain that the Center can't afford the cost or embarrassment of losing either me or my network of couriers through the whim of some Party hack who takes it into his head that I am expendable. I told your predecessor and I'm telling you: if anything happens to me or my network every document, every code, every illegal in Europe that has passed through my hands since 1966 will become public knowledge in the West." The icy eyes swung back on Titov. "Now you be a good Comrade Colonel and find out what the whole story is on this rabbit of mine that's getting ready to bolt."

He walked back to his own car and drove off. Titov, furious at the man's threat, returned to Brussels. Within the hour he had encoded a message for the European Bureau requesting full particulars on the Adelaine Mercure information source, giving the date and number of their original transmission file. Then he went out and got drunk.

Gretchko should have told him about Traveler. But Gretchko couldn't, any more than he could tell his successor about this potential for disaster. If the story ever got back to the Center, or Traveler went over to the West, or died in a car accident — he shuddered at this scenario — then every controller at the Brussels embassy since 1966 would be facing a firing squad in the courtyard at Lubyanka prison for gross incompetence.

Early this morning Moscow's decoded reply had been on Titov's desk when he came in to work at the Brussels Embassy. He had read it and blinked. Then read it again with disbelief and shook his aching head.

The KGB's European Bureau showed nothing in its records on Adelaine Mercure. Nor did its archives hold any record of the transmission made to the Brussels Embassy on the date Titov had referred to in his inquiry.

That was impossible. There had to be something.

He laid the original coded message he'd taken from the Brussels Embassy vault files next to the matching photostat given to him by Traveler. They were identical. They came from Moscow. There had to be a record. Either that or someone had something to hide. He stared at the identical messages:

22/7/81. FILE BRX/EUR 115361006. ATTN: PETER GRETCHKO. REFERENCE YOUR 12/7/81 TRAVELER INQUIRY. INFORMATION AVAILABLE FOR USE ON ONE MEMBER OF FRENCH ARRIVALS. ADELAINE MERCURE. BORN NOUZON-VILLE, FRANCE, MARCH 27, 1928. CONVERSION INFOR-MATION: PORTRAIT OF SUBJECT PAINTED AUGUST 1943.

TRAVELER MUST CLAIM OWNERSHIP OF PORTRAIT PLUS
KNOWLEDGE OF CIRCUMSTANCES UNDER WHICH IT WAS
PAINTED. NO FURTHER DETAILS NECESSARY. SIGNED:
BRANSKY.

What had happened to Bransky? His name had appeared on
every transmission out of the Center until two months ago. The
new KGB administrator signed himself "Galinovsky." Both were
names of real people, not codes. But why had they been changed,
and what had happened between Traveler and Adelaine Mercure
to require more background details? He decided to drive up to
Antwerp immediately and find out.

At the town of Boom he turned off the A12 and found a call
box. No other cars followed him from the main highway. He waited
a full five minutes watching the rearview mirror before getting out
to use the phone.

"Make it the Royal Museum. Nine o'clock," Traveler said and
hung up.

He was already there when Titov arrived. They trailed the
clutches of tourists drifting from room to room admiring the collection of Rubens paintings.

"Center claims to have no record of your rabbit or the original
message," Titov began.

Traveler's face remained impassive. They paused to let the rest
of a tour group press along into the next gallery.

Titov asked, "How important is this information you want?"

Traveler leaned forward to examine the detail of brush strokes
on an enormous dark canvas depicting two coarse-looking buxom
women arguing over a measure of cloth. Titov moved closer.

"I don't know how important it might be, Comrade Colonel."
He then told Titov what had transpired the day before during his
meeting with Adelaine Mercure. He spoke very softly but with an
urgency that the controller found unsettling.

"Before silencing my rabbit, I must know how deep our problem goes. There is a chance the entire NATO network could blow
up in our faces unless we move quickly. Who are these other
women? Where are these paintings? What exactly do they repre-
sent? I tell you, Comrade Colonel, my little rabbit was more frightened of her painting than she was of me."

Titov's stomach tightened with apprehension. "What do you suggest, Comrade?"

"Obvious, isn't it? The problem originated with Moscow Center. That's where you'll find the solution." He stepped back from the painting and sighed. "Always assuming there is a solution left to be found, Comrade Colonel."

Which was why Boris Titov caught the first flight into Moscow.

Paris, 3:11 P.M.

Marais thought his bullet-headed escort was taking him to an interrogation room. That would be normal procedure. Sooner or later he would have to be examined. A Mutt and Jeff routine perhaps, trying to scare him into a confession. Or rapid-fire questioning by some shadowed form behind a pair of 300-watt spotlights while he sat helplessly strapped to an uncomfortable steel chair. His mind conjured up a half dozen possibilities while preceding Bullet Head along the stairs and hallways of the fortress-like building. Where exactly were they holding him? He'd never managed to raise a reply to his questions from any of the guards who brought his meals and changed the latrine pot.

It dawned on him suddenly when they arrived at the property desk on the main floor that he was going to be released. His escort signed him over to another uniformed guard and departed as silently as he'd come.

"You're Roger Marais?"

"I am."

The guard eyed him with stone-faced indifference, handing out a plastic bag from a small aluminum bin. Marais opened it and started pocketing his valuables.

"Everything's there — money, rings — check it out."

He assured the guard nothing was missing. The man grunted and thrust a ballpoint pen and checklist at him with instructions to sign his name beside the X. Marais signed. The guard slid the empty bin back on the rack behind his counter and pressed a buzzer.

A door opened in one of the alcoves that encircled the room, and two tough-looking men in worn leather jackets stepped through it. One said "Hi." The other signed the guard's forms. Both men had an easy casual authority, Marais observed uncomfortably. Cops. What else?

"They been treating you properly in here?" the friendly one inquired. He had a regional accent of some sort.

Marais rubbed his face thoughtfully. "Food's lousy and I could do with a shower and shave. Where are we going?"

The man grinned. He wore a badly broken nose over a pair of scar-sliced lips. "This, like the universe, will unfold."

Marais decided to leave that one alone.

The buzzer opened another alcove. He followed the two men down a narrow corridor to a steel-faced firedoor. They paused. The friendly one introduced himself and his partner.

"I'm Albert, he's Bondi. We work together."

Marais shook hands, trying to decide whose team they were on. He pegged them for undercover cops with hair-trigger reflexes that had been trained to cope with the drug scene. If he was correct then they were out of their territory. His problem was a murder. Or was it? Maybe things had changed during the twenty-four hours he'd been stretched out on that banjo bed.

"Where's Detective Villeneuve?"

"Busy," Albert explained. "Another murder over in Passy. Some rich old lady stabbed in her tub. Can't hang that one on you, can they?" he laughed. "You were on ice."

Bondi pushed open the firedoor and led the way down a flight of steps to a black Opel parked in the courtyard. For the fifth time since putting on his wristwatch, Marais checked the time. It was 3:27 on an afternoon as hot and humid as yesterday's.

They put him in the front seat beside Bondi. Albert slid in back. Once they were across the bridge and hemmed in by traffic, Albert leaned over the front seat.

"It's going to take a couple of days to get your passport — red tape, you know. Meantime we're moving you to another hotel where you won't be bothered."

He didn't reveal what sort of bother could be expected if he remained at the Pont Royal, or the name of the new place.

"Where are we headed now?" Marais asked.

"Back to your hotel so you can check out."

However, they parked a block short of the place, around the corner on Rue du Bac, asking Marais if he wouldn't mind walking the rest of the way. Albert got out of the car and came along to explain.

"We'd prefer you check out of the place on your own. It raises fewer questions for everyone."

Fewer questions for whom, and what sort of questions, Marais wondered? What were these two smoothies trying to promote? Aloud, he asked: "Suppose they want a police clearance from someone before releasing my stuff?"

Albert grinned. "Already taken care of over the phone. They're expecting you. It's official. The PJ have given you a clean bill of health."

"Who or what is the PJ?" It was the first time he'd heard this designation.

"For the moment, we are. Bondi and I." Evidently he thought this funny because he clapped him on the shoulder and laughed.

Marais frowned. "Tell me, Albert — are you and Bondi cops?"

"Sort of." When they got in sight of the hotel Albert turned back to the car, both hands plunged into his jacket pockets. Marais kept going.

Two cabs sat parked outside the hotel waiting for fares. The driver in the first lowered his newspaper and regarded him speculatively. When Marais shook his head, the man returned to his reading.

What was to prevent him from checking out and taking a cab to the airport? Would they sell him a ticket without his passport? He could stop off at the Canadian Embassy and pick up a new one, tell them his had been stolen or lost.

Then he realized he was kidding himself. It had been the embassy that had given the police the information on his record. The embassy already knew who had his passport. Arrive on their doorstep and they'd probably phone young Villeneuve and throw him back to the wolves. For the moment he was boxed. He'd have to play the part of the good guy willing to cooperate, if that's what the pair in the Opel wanted. Wait for the right moment to split.

The hotel doorman stared at him. Marais tossed him a wave and strolled into the lobby as though his unshaven face and rumpled clothes were badges of honor. When he asked for his bill the wimp did a double take and scurried to the office. A heated discussion drifted through the closed door. Finally, the wimp and the manager came out all teeth and apologies.

His account had been closed with yesterday's date, the last luncheon tab omitted, courtesy of the management. Both his bags were packed and parked with the hall porter. They trusted he wouldn't mind, but they needed his room.

"Such a busy time of year, you understand, Monsieur."

He understood perfectly. The wimp slotted his gold American Express card into the machine. A balding man in tan slacks and thick-soled black shoes seated in a club chair on one side of the lobby folded his newspaper and went over to the porter's desk to use one of the house phones. He kept his eyes averted carefully from the desk. The shoes spelled cop.

He figured Baldy would be the lookout posted by Albert and his pal in case he bolted. They weren't being very subtle.

"You had several calls, Monsieur Marais. A woman."

He turned back to the desk. "A woman?"

The manager handed over five pink message slips. They were all from Nicole Daladier, four from yesterday, the last shortly before eight this morning. The first had an address on Rue Raynouard and a phone number, the others just her name and number. Did the cops know about these calls? He checked the house phones. Baldy hung on the desktop deep in conversation. He made a swift mental note of the girl's address and number, then balled the messages with a dropshot into the wastebasket behind the counter. He gave the manager a conspiratorial wink.

"A family friend I'm taking pains to avoid."

He signed his bill, stuffed the receipt and credit card in his pocket and wished them adieu.

Albert stood leaning against the Opel talking to Bondi when Marais turned the corner.

"Thought we'd lost you," Albert said, hoisting the bags into the trunk. He seemed relieved, as if he'd expected him to vanish. "Any problems checking out?"

He shook his head.

Down the street in front of the doorway to Dimitrios's shop a few sightseers snapped pictures and talked with the two police officers guarding the premises. The visitors were oohing and aahing, their voices tingling with excitement. He had an urge to flail into the crowd and tell them to go home and mind their own goddamn business. Poor old Dimitrios. Who would want to kill him? He had been saving his money for an apartment building in Athens where he could retire in comfort. He wasn't interested in women, men, or little boys, as far as Marais could tell. What would anyone gain by killing him?

They drove back across the river and along the Champs Élysées to where it funneled into the phalanx of noisy traffic that perpetually circled the Arc de Triomphe. Albert talked continuously, leaning chummily over the front seat. He spoke of the unusual summer weather this year, the terrible Parisian drivers, the price of food, how the Japs were taking over the world's electronics, why the bankers were being persecuted. Marais realized he was being given some sort of treatment to keep his attention from wandering. While Albert kept spoonfeeding him with bits of trivia, Marais looked at Bondi. So far the sour-faced driver hadn't spoken a word beyond the grunt when he'd shaken his hand back at the ancient detention center. Bondi looked like a professional street fighter. His eyebrows had been carved and stitched a dozen times. The knuckles of the hand on the steering wheel were covered with pink scar tissue. His nose had been flattened.

The car swung off the Arc de Triomphe merry-go-round and headed up Avenue MacMahon. Albert kept up his back-seat chatter. Tourists were his theme now, how they provided such a bonanza for France during the summer. Between breaths Marais interrupted.

"Are you married, Bondi?"

It threw both of them. Albert stopped halfway through a word and Bondi took his eyes off the road to glance at Marais to see if it was a trick question. He shook his head, two sharp shakes before Albert jumped in to make sure Bondi didn't break his vow of silence.

"No, he's not married. But he has a girlfriend, don't you, Bondi? Big German girl with cornsilk hair. I've met her. Oo la la!" He veered off to tell him of a German girl he'd met a couple of months back on the Munich train. But Marais had stopped listening. Something was wrong about Albert and Bondi.

They were driving a rental car. He'd seen inside the trunk when Albert stashed the bags. No radio equipment sitting on black rubber doughnuts next to the spare tire as there should have been. Instead, the trunk had been spotlessly clean with a notice from the rental agency attached to the underside of the lid listing all the things the customer should do in the event of a roadside emergency. And there were no little police extras anywhere to be seen.

There wasn't even a flashlight clipped under the padded dash or a notepad on top.

He wondered if they knew about the stakeout inside the hotel. Were there two different teams involved in his case, one for surveillance and the other for contact? Or were they different teams on different sides of the fence? How many sides and fences were there? And why? There had to be a logical explanation for the inconsistencies.

Bondi eased out of traffic and turned down a side street flanked with older stain-faced buildings spidered with cracking mortar, paint-flecked woodwork, and brightly colored flowerboxes. Shouting children cluttered the pavement at regular intervals, forcing the car to creep past whatever game was in progress.

"Where do they get their energy in this heat?" Albert asked affably of no one in particular. Marais remained silent, refusing to be drawn into the mindless one-sided conversation coming from the back seat.

The car turned again and stopped in front of a hotel. It went by the name Le Palais. But it was hardly that grand any more, just an old six-storey monstrosity with fractured plaster repairs clearly visible under each of the narrow iron balconies which tiered up from the second floor. A green awning with stenciled gold crowns along its borders covered the distance between the curb and hotel entrance. It looked new, and managed, a little deceitfully, to give the place some hint of its undoubted former elegance.

Albert and Marais got out before the elderly doorman made it to the curb. Albert said the rooms were very clean and very reasonable, as if these two points alone justified moving in. A double room with bath had been reserved for Marais on the sixth floor.

The doorman hauled out the two suitcases. He was dressed in an oversized frayed uniform with gold braid on the cap, sleeves, and epaulets. A hundred dry-cleanings had faded the thick cloth until it was almost pink.

"I won't bother coming in," Albert announced. "Bondi and I'll drop by Brigade Criminelle and see if we can get someone there to speed up your passport release. Can you be in your room around eight tonight?" His tone implied that Marais had better be there.

Marais shrugged.

Albert gave his shoulder a pat and said soothingly: "Patience,

Roger. It'll only take a couple of days at the most. You'll see. I'll phone tonight at eight with an update. Be there."

He watched them drive off, then followed the shabby doorman into the lobby. A pervasive odor of disinfectant assailed his nostrils, reminding him of stale mops, squeegee buckets, and prison corridors. An honor guard of tall potted plants on a threadbare runner led up to the front desk. Peeking from behind the languidly drooping plants were a scattering of very old leather sofas and matching chairs in which a few pensioners and prostitutes sat waiting for something to happen. Every eye followed him to Réception.

The doorman deposited his bags with the concierge then hovered expectantly while Marais signed in. A wall-eyed desk clerk handed him a key to a room on the sixth floor. Room 610. The clerk said he hoped Marais would be comfortable and banged the bell for a porter. Nobody asked to see his passport or credit cards. It was strictly a cash on the counter operation.

Marais changed a few bills at the cashier's wicket and handed the doorman a crisp new twenty, holding out a second twenty as a primer. He coaxed him out of earshot from the desk clerk and porter to the privacy of a magazine rack.

"Did you, by any chance, happen to notice that man in the leather jacket I was talking with outside?" he inquired, speaking softly because everyone in the lobby was straining to hear.

The doorman nodded, a movement that caused his too large peaked hat to slip down to his eyebrows. His rheumy gaze held fast on the twenty.

"Have you ever seen him before?"

"Yessir." Carefully, he reset his hat.

"Where?"

"This morning. Here in the hotel. He and his friend are on the sixth floor. You can check with the concierge."

"Did they bring luggage?"

"Yessir, they carried it themselves. Your friend said that it was expensive glassware and if it broke he wanted to be the one who broke it." He reached for the money. Marais withdrew his hand.

"Where's the glassware now?"

The old man appeared perplexed and reset his hat thoughtfully. "I suppose it's still up in their room on the sixth floor. Is something wrong, Sir?"

"No, nothing's wrong. I wanted to make certain the luggage hadn't been moved by the hotel staff. A very important buyer from the Middle East is due in today or tomorrow and those samples must be ready for viewing. You know how difficult things can get when you're dealing with Arabs."

The man said he knew all about Arabs. Whatever he knew wasn't very complimentary, judging by his expression.

"Tell me, how do you know their room is on the sixth floor?" Marais asked as he handed over the money.

The doorman folded his two twenties into a thick wad of bills which he stuffed back in his trouser pocket.

"Our garage driver parked their car," he explained. "We have no street parking except for pickup and delivery. When I turned in the keys at the desk, Edmund — the morning man — placed them in 608's message box. Mr. Leblanc is the name, I believe. I don't know about the other gentleman. He never spoke.

An elevator shuddered him to the sixth floor. He tipped the porter ten francs for carrying his bags and, after assuring him that he didn't want any female companionship for the rest of the afternoon, locked the door.

The room was large and very well appointed with a variety of old veneer furnishings from the Twenties. The black and white television was old and formidable. A few lithographed Impressionist paintings hung from the sky-blue wallpaper. He crossed the room. Rain-stained cream-colored drapes suspended from worn wooden rings and track covered the two windows. Pushing aside the curtains, he unlocked the sill catches on each and opened them both to let out the stale air. Then he took off his jacket and vest and began checking the room.

Systematically, he started with the light fixtures and pictures. Drawers, writing desk, clothes wardrobe, cabinet, curtains, bed and mattress — all were examined minutely. After fifteen minutes he found what he was looking for, stuck to the bottom of his bedside table. For a minute he lay flat on his back, head under the table, trying to decide what he was looking at. It resembled plasticine, the sort of stuff he'd used as a kid for modeling monsters.

The gray mass had been taped securely to the recessed underside so that it was invisible to anyone standing in the room or even lying on the bed. From its center, two filament wires were connected to the telephone cord. And where the cord entered a covered connector on the baseboard above the carpet the wires separated, each going into a tiny hole that had been drilled on either side of the connector directly into room 608.

A telephone tap? He'd seen more sophisticated electronics in toy stores during Christmas. Gingerly, he poked his thumb into the gray putty. It yielded a little. To the touch it resembled bathroom tile caulking when it has dried beyond the point of malleability. Using his nail, he scraped and picked at it, keeping his head sideways to avoid the shavings falling into his eyes. He worked his way around the wires until he'd uncovered what looked like a circular metal button the thickness of a ballpoint pen. A gentle tug and it came away with a shower of gray flakings. For a long time he lay looking at it.

As a teenager one summer he had worked with a highway crew blasting its way through a granite overburden to build a new autoroute extension north of Montréal. The quarrymen had used similar looking metal buttons to touch off the dynamite bundles they'd lowered into their drill holes. This button was a type of sophisticated priming cap. The filaments were contact wires running through the wall to some electrical source next door. Instead of dynamite, an explosive putty had been taped to the table. He'd never seen the stuff before but if it had anywhere near the same explosive properties as dynamite then there was enough of it under his bedside table to blast both him and the room into minute pieces over the city's rooftops. Albert and Bondi had planned to kill him by remote control at eight o'clock.

For Christ's sake, why?

It made no sense. He'd done nothing, seen nothing, and knew nothing. His only desire was to haul ass out of France while he still had an ass to haul.

Someone had fingered him. What worried him was that he hadn't the slightest idea why it had happened or who was the enemy.

He twisted the wires until they broke free from the button, then tore the other leads out from the wall. With the threat of sudden extinction eliminated for the moment he felt a little better, although his hands had started shaking.

He squirmed from under the table and sat on the bed, waiting for his nerves to steady. Could there be other explosives in the room? Perhaps they knew he'd locate and neutralize this one, and cunningly concealed a second elsewhere in a place he would never think of looking. That thought brought him to his feet, and he continued his sweep, finishing up in the bathroom. He peered under the tub. It was an unusual old highbacked model with splayed lion's feet at its four corners. Over the years its dripping tap had left a yellow stain on the white porcelain around the drain hole. Everything appeared normal. If a second booby trap existed, he couldn't find it. He decided to take a bath and shave, give himself time to think about what to do next.

He had to assume the room next door was vacant. There would be a timing device set for eight o'clock, or shortly before when he was supposed to be sitting on the bed waiting patiently for Albert to call. If he could get into 608 and remove whatever had been left inside the room it would increase his bargaining position enormously. He'd have the evidence to prove his case for an assassination attempt. Without all the equipment in his hands, it would be his word against theirs. And with a record like his he wouldn't stand a chance of being believed.

By the time he had bathed, shaved, and changed into clean clothes his brain had started to function the way it should. He had a plan which, with luck, would get him out of the country by tomorrow afternoon with enough hard evidence to bring the accusations of his being a murderer to a grinding halt.

Quickly, he set to work on the bedside table. Using his pocketknife, he removed the gray putty, placing every bit of the innocuous-looking material into three small plastic bags he'd removed from the freshly laundered shirts in his suitcase. By the time he finished, cleaned the carpet and set the table back in position, every bit of evidence had been packed away in his bags.

Next, he unlocked the door and stepped into the hallway. It appeared deserted. A fast check of the floor revealed nothing unusual — no wandering housemaids with jingling keys, no open doors, no television sounds from the other rooms. Maybe everybody had gone shopping or maybe 610 and 608 were the only rooms rented on this floor today. He paused by the elevators to listen. Neither of them was in operation.

He raced back to room 608 and hurled himself shoulder first against the door. Once, twice — with a splintered crack like a pistol shot the door swung open and he fell into the room. The brass striker-plate holding the latching mechanism had torn loose, spraying screws and woodchips across the carpet. But the hinges and handle were intact.

He scrambled to his feet and peered into the hall. No response anywhere to the noise. He closed the door quietly and propped a chair against it. His chest heaved from his exertions and his shoulder ached. He rubbed it gently as he looked around the room.

The décor was pink, not blue. Other than that, its layout was identical to his own except for the luggage stand. It should have been at the end of the bed. Instead, it was against one wall at roughly the same place where his bedside table was situated on the other side of the pale pink wallpaper. A black rectangular sample case rested on the stand. Its pebbled surface had been designed for rough wear. He bent to examine it.

Two white metal clasps held the lid. There was always the chance the case had been booby-trapped to explode when the clasps were opened or the lid raised, but he thought that unlikely, reasoning that it would have been too dangerous to leave unattended. A nosy housemaid could blow herself to kingdom come. All the same, when he snapped open the clasps, both eyes were screwed tightly shut until he heard a comforting snick and realized he was still in the land of the living. With a sigh of relief he sat down on the floor until his heart stopped pounding. Then, inch by inch, very gradually he raised the lid.

Inside the case and secured by a mounting collar lay a square gray metallic box resembling the electronics pack used with a radio-controlled model airplane. Except on this pack where the two control sticks should have been a pair of timing dials had been installed, one for hours, the other for minutes. They had been twisted around to 20 and 00. A small red indicator needle under a plastic cover indicated the mechanism had been switched to "battery." Filament wires attached to the box threaded out through the back of the carrying case and dropped to the baseboard where they disappeared into a pair of small drill holes.

He switched off the battery, drew the broken contact wires out of the baseboard, then coiled them back into the case. He cleared the screws and wood splinters from the carpet and reset the striker-plate in the door frame. Then, after wedging the door shut behind him, he carried his new electronic suitcase back to his room.

The problem now would be to get out of the hotel carrying three bags without being seen by any of the staff. There had to be a fire exit somewhere. He went exploring around the floor. Nowhere did he see an "exit" or "sortie" sign. What did guests do in case of fire, jump out of windows? He found the answer at the end of the hall. A narrow window set at knee level opened onto an outside fire escape attached to the side of the building. He opened it and stepped outside onto the iron grating.

The structure spidered down to a narrow lane where a garbage truck was being loaded with refuse. He started down, checking for broken steps or loose anchor bolts. When he reached the second-floor window he climbed back inside and took the elevator up to his floor. Quickly, he changed clothes, then carried the suitcases out to the fire escape and left them on the second-floor landing above the garbage cans. He climbed back inside and took the elevator to the lobby.

Shaved, scrubbed, and dressed in neatly pressed flannels and sports jacket he looked much less like one of the lobby-watchers than when he had arrived. This time when he turned up at her wicket the cashier gave him a polite smile. He asked for *jetons*.

She frowned as though payphone coinage was forbidden to registered guests.

"Your room phone is not working, Sir?"

"Perfectly, Madame. However, this is not a call I wish to make from my room," he smiled.

She counted out ten of the metallic slugs and took his money. He couldn't leave it this way. If she decided his action deserved discussion there was always the chance she'd take it up with the manager or concierge. For all he knew they might be pals of Albert and Bondi. He managed what he hoped was a sly wink.

"The call is to a lady. It could be a long conversation and I don't want to tie up my room phone or have the operator break in with another call. That way the young lady might know where I'm staying in Paris and that would never do, now would it?"

She reached through the wicket and gave his hand a maternal pat. But of course, she understood perfectly.

He put on his sunglasses and strolled out under the front awning.

The old doorman asked if he needed a taxi. Marais thanked him and said he preferred to walk.

Outside a café on the next block he found a call box with an undamaged telephone. He stepped inside, fed in a *jeton*, and dialed Nicole Daladier's number in Passy.

Moscow, 6:00 P.M.

Marko Sultal's office looked out from a fourth-floor window of KGB Headquarters to the back of the pitted metal cloak covering Feliks Edmundovich Dzerzhinsky, first head of the Soviet Secret Police. The statue, Titov noted, was splattered with bird droppings about its head and shoulders. A current Moscow joke claimed that the KGB refused to clean the statue of their famous Polish expatriate because history had proved no Pole could ever be completely happy unless Moscow was shitting on him.

Beyond the statue an assortment of foreign tourists wandered about on Dzerzhinsky Square snapping pictures and ogling the security guards manning the front entrance. The late afternoon sun had slanted, giving softer tones to the KGB's massive ochre-tinted building. Times had changed. Once, any attempt to photograph Headquarters would have brought plainclothes security agents rushing out to seize the film and camera and strongarm the hapless photographer.

Had officialdom become less paranoid, Titov wondered, or had their paranoia merely turned in other directions? He stepped back from the window, folding himself into a chair. Marko glanced up, then continued reading the file Titov had brought from Brussels. The office had a single carpet, several wooden chairs, and three metal filing cabinets. Heavy green curtains framed the double windows. A roller blind covered the top third of the glass. On the white wall behind Sultal's head hung the standard-issue Lenin portrait with its gaze of zealot-eyed intensity. Titov stifled a yawn. Personally he preferred Lenin's bearded face to those dreadful crucifixes adorning the walls of so many government offices in the West.

Finally, Marko looked up. "So?" He put his elbows on the desk.

"So, what do you suggest I do?" Titov demanded.

"Do?" Sultal scratched his head as though such a question was beyond comprehension and should never have been asked in the first place. He had a round clever face surmounted by high cheekbones and perceptibly oriental eyes.

"You do nothing, Boris. That's what you do," Sultal said. "The Directorate has denied all knowledge of the woman and your transmission." He held up the offending papers. "So obviously they are forgeries."

Titov frowned. He'd expected better than this. "I removed them from the embassy files this morning myself."

Sultal's eyes blinked with stubborn disregard for the facts. "Pah!" he sneered. "What does that prove? Gretchko could have planted them before he went to Madrid. Maybe it's something he and Traveler cooked up as an added persuasion to tighten down this NATO contact." He looked at his watch. "You'll come home and have supper with Anna and me? Don't say no. I have a surprise. No, I refuse to speak of it until we get there." He smiled and slipped on his uniform jacket.

Titov took back his Brussels file. He couldn't blame his friend. The official line was all that mattered to Marko.

"How popular is your office, Marko?" Titov asked after his friend had buttoned his tunic and begun straightening the desk preparatory to leaving.

At the suggestion that his office might be wired, Sultal's eyes narrowed suspiciously. Except for designated meeting rooms, KGB Headquarters offices were possibly the most private in the Soviet Union.

"Why?" he demanded truculently.

Titov smiled, a thin tightening of the lips. "Because old friend, I have something to tell you, and I'd just as soon it remains here in this room."

Sultal dropped back in his chair and took a package of Byelomor cigarettes from his desk drawer. He offered one to Titov.

Titov shook his head. "I gave it up."

"Purist," Sultal joked, and twisted the rice paper to hold the tobacco in place. He set the end alight. For a second it flared. Motes of black ash drifted over the desk top. "Speak freely. My office is private." He inhaled deeply, waiting.

Titov tapped the Brussels folder. "These are not forgeries. You know it and I know it. And it is not my transmission that is being denied, but theirs. Now why would the Directorate want to deny its existence?" He waved Sultal's reply aside. "Let me finish. I've come a long way to ask your advice. Wait until you hear all the facts before providing me with any answers."

Sultal leaned back in his chair, prepared to listen. He owed Titov at least that much.

"Either our information on the woman was misfiled when the European Bureau went from paper records to computer storage, or the information was deliberately removed and erased. The question is why? And on whose authority? I have about seventy-two hours to find out. If I don't, our NATO penetration through Traveler may blow up in our faces because of one neurotic woman and her portrait."

Paris, 4:02 P.M.

When Boule came downstairs from Nicole's bedroom he noted with satisfaction that the crowd on the main floor had thinned. Fauré, standing by the front door with Boule's burly driver arguing with two reporters, broke away to greet him at the bottom step with a sardonic smile.

"Are you interested in hearing a lecture on the importance of freedom of the press, Commissaire?"

Boule grimaced. "Where's Blais?"

Fauré shrugged. "Hasn't returned from upstairs. Probably giving them his life story — off the record."

"André?"

Fauré shook his head. "No sign of him either. What about the girl? Any prospects there?"

Boule rubbed his chin, feeling the stubble beginning to poke through. Perhaps. I've taken the guard off her door. She's free to leave. Blais may howl, but let him. We'll see where she leads us. Now, where are these other suspects?

"Still in the sunroom. Straight down the hall then left to the end. You'll see a pair of glass doors. I'll send André along when he shows."

"Thank you."

The sunroom turned out to be an enormous room stuffed with massive peekaboo vegetation and wicker furniture. Tall leaded glass windows surrounded the room on three sides. Bamboo slatted blinds helped deflect the sun. In spite of the blinds the place was at least ten degrees warmer than the rest of the house. Boule took out his handkerchief and introduced himself.

Besides Detective Monceau and the household staff, three of Blais's men were present — a uniformed officer and two plainclothes detectives. The latter pair had the courtesy to come to their feet and introduce themselves properly. Boule settled into a wicker chair beside Monceau and proceeded to decipher the body language confronting him while the detectives continued their examination of the housekeeper. Monceau scribbled notes.

The staff all looked guilty — arms folded defensively across their chests, eyes watchful, toes and heels shifting nervously. Could one or more of them have committed murder? Boule leaned over and borrowed Monceau's notes, then put on his reading glasses.

Georges Vadim, the chauffeur, had been employed for fifteen months. He'd been selected over twenty-three applicants. Monceau had written "Why?" beside this last item. Vadim's living quarters were over the garage. A house phone connected him to Madame deBrisay's bedroom. A keyed shutoff installed on her phone prevented eavesdropping by the rest of the staff. Georges could be summoned through a private door and narrow inside stairwell connecting her second-floor bedroom with the ground level at the back of the house near the rose garden.

"Who had the key?" Boule whispered loudly to Monceau.

"I beg your pardon, Commissaire?" one of Blais's detectives said. Giroux or Galbert, Boule had forgotten which was which.

"That key to her private entrance from the rose garden. . ." Boule asked inquisitively, "did Monsieur Vadim let himself in when his employer called, or did she have to come down and open the door?"

"I had my own key, Commissaire," Georges said quietly.

"Ah! Thank you, Monsieur Vadim," Boule smiled. "Did anyone else have a key?" He took out a cigarette and lit it slowly, watching the trio on the high-backed wicker sofa.

After a few moments of uncomfortable silence the housekeeper and cook shook their heads emphatically. They knew all about the private door, but it had nothing to do with them. If Madame wished to summon her chauffeur at odd hours, that was her privilege, was it not? Boule shut his eyes to think. The detective waited a discreet moment then continued questioning the housekeeper.

The alliances were obvious. Cook and housekeeper against the chauffeur, and probably the girl as well. How kindly would she take to this young buck spending his nights with her grandmother? A midnight call on the house phone. A secret entrance from the rose garden. It sounded like a sordid melodrama straight out of the nineteenth century.

Bettina Denoir, the housekeeper, had been employed for four and a half years. She handled all Madame's affairs, business and social. She'd made the arrangements for hiring Georges and, she added archly: "His engagement was not due to my recommendation, I can tell you!"

"You handled her financial affairs as well, wrote checks, paid the accounts, paid the tradesmen?" the detective asked.

"I wrote the checks but Madame signed them."

Boule opened his eyes. "Tell me, Monsieur Vadim," he interrupted, "from which rooms in the house would it be possible to observe someone entering or leaving that private door beside the rose garden?"

The chauffeur blinked. "I can see it clearly from my apartment above the garage."

Boule shook his head. "I mean from the rear of this house." He pursed his lips, tilting his cigarette dangerously close to his nose. "Let's suppose somebody came down the driveway from the street early this morning. Keeping close to the side of the house he reaches the back and flattens himself — or herself — against the wall. Got the picture?" They all nodded and leaned forward so as not to miss anything. Boule continued: "He eases around the corner, along the rose garden to the door, then up to the bedroom. Minutes later, he slips back through the garden and disappears onto the street. Now then, from which rooms might he — or she — have been observed?"

They considered his proposition in silence. It was a slim chance the killer had been seen by any of them.

"Madame's private door is visible only from a side window in the dining room, I believe, Commissaire," the housekeeper offered.

"But, by taking the route you suggest, the murderer would have been seen passing the library and dining room windows. Both have glass doors at ground level." She gave a self-conscious shrug. "Assuming anyone was in either of those rooms this morning and happened to be looking out the window, of course."

"Of course," Boule agreed. "And naturally none of you was in the library or dining room between seven and nine this morning?"

They shook their heads.

"Unless . . ." the cook began, only to be silenced by a withering glance from the housekeeper. The cook had fat red hands and a florid complexion. Her bright plum cheeks appeared to be on the verge of exploding. Boule gave her an encouraging smile. The room was uncomfortably warm; he sympathized with the poor woman. Why Blais's men had to pick this hothouse for their interrogation over all the other empty rooms in the place. . . . He swabbed his face.

"Unless what, Madame?"

She shrugged and remained silent. Under the thumb of the Denoir woman, no doubt. He tried a different tack.

"Besides you three, Madame deBrisay and her granddaughter, who else was in the house this morning?"

"Colette," the housekeeper said. "She works half days until noon, you see."

"Ah! And when Colette works what does she do?"

"Cleans, dusts, polishes the furniture and silverware. That sort of thing."

"At what time does she report for work?"

"Eight o'clock Monday to Friday. She comes in by the side door. Cook and I were in the kitchen when she arrived today." The cook nodded vigorously in agreement.

Boule handed Monceau the notebook so he could enter these facts. The other two detectives were writing their notes already, both apparently content now to let Boule take over the questioning.

"Now — I assume Colette arrived at her usual time? Yes? Good. What work did you assign for her, Madame Denoir?"

"Downstairs dusting and cleaning."

"Including the dining room and library?"

"But of course, Commissaire. They are both downstairs, no?"

Her sarcasm was enough to pique but not sufficient to reprimand. He let it pass. Monceau shifted uncomfortably in his chair. The wicker creaked. The detective was ready to pounce on the woman. Boule laid a hand on his arm, holding him back.

"So it is possible Colette might have seen the killer?"

The interplay between Monceau and himself had not gone unnoticed. Her reply was both polite and accommodating.

"It is possible, but unlikely, Commissaire. If she had seen a prowler she would have reported to me at once."

"Or if not at once, certainly after the body had been found," Boule added. "Colette seemed untroubled when she left at noon?" he continued.

"I don't know, Commissaire. I didn't see her leave."

"Did anyone see her after the body was discovered?"

Vadim and the cook shook their heads in unison and looked for guidance toward the housekeeper. Apparently she held some power over the chauffeur as well as the cook. Was Georges in on their financial fiddle? Blais hadn't mentioned it. He needed to talk to them separately to squeeze out the truth. Meanwhile, he extracted the cleaning girl's address. She had no telephone. She shared an apartment with a friend. Boule changed the subject.

"At what time did you awake this morning, Madame?"

"I beg your pardon?"

The question was simple enough but for some reason it flustered her. He took back Monceau's notes and flipped the pages over to the beginning of her interview.

"You stated the fight between your employer and her granddaughter began while you were in your bedroom across the hall. Somewhere close to six-thirty, you said."

Bettina nodded. "I was getting up — no, I was in bed, then got up."

"The noise awakened you, was that it?"

"Yes."

"So you went to your door to listen?"

"Yes."

"You were curious. They fought often, did they?"

"Never."

"You opened your door to hear. Isn't that right?"

"I was concerned."

"Naturally. And what did you hear?"

She turned to the others for support but they were staring at Monceau's pad that Boule held resting on his knee. Judging by their expressions it had just dawned on them that everything they had said had been taken down in evidence. The chauffeur looked particularly uncomfortable.

"I heard only a few snatches of their conversation, you understand," Bettina said, folding her hands primly on her lap. "It had to do with information Madame refused to tell Nicole. Madame told her to mind her own business. That what she had seen was a private matter."

"Seen?" Boule interjected.

"Yes, that's what she said."

"Go on."

"They argued further, their voices getting louder. Finally, Madame ordered Nicole out of the room. On her way out she slammed the door. That was all. I dressed and went downstairs to the kitchen."

"Did it sound as if they were arguing in the bedroom or bathroom?"

"It sounded as though Madame was still in bed."

"What time was this again?" Boule inquired.

She hesitated, perhaps remembering that Monceau's notes stated "close to six-thirty." Was she that certain, he wondered? In his experience it was a rare witness who could recall the exact timing of an event, and then only in relation to some other event that was happening simultaneously.

"Six-thirty, perhaps a quarter to seven," she said.

"Maybe even seven?" Boule prodded.

"It is possible."

"Maybe even seven-fifteen?"

"Possibly."

Boule sighed. In other words she didn't know.

"How long after this argument did Madame deBrisay's granddaughter leave the house?"

"I don't know, Commissaire. I didn't hear her leave. Georges brought the car around and took me shopping for the weekend's supplies. When we returned Nicole's car was gone from the garage."

Boule switched his attention to the cook. "How about you, Madame, do you have anything to add to that?"

He received a tiny shrug of uncertainty.

"Is that a yes or a no, Madame?"

She shook her head, quivering her chins. A no. Another exasperating female, he decided. Vadim remained silent when he looked in his direction. Nothing further could be discovered while they were seated together and posturing among themselves.

He butted the cigarette and got to his feet, deciding to steal the chauffeur away for a private chat. Georges's face looked familiar. He'd seen it before, but where? No matter, it would come to him.

"Monsieur Vadim, please be good enough to accompany me to your living quarters."

Boule gave his face and neck a final sponging then stowed the handkerchief away. Blais's detectives came angrily to their feet; they did not appreciate one of their witnesses being spirited off under their noses. However, they had enough sense to hold their tongues as Boule ushered the chauffeur out a side door onto the stone balcony that overlooked the back gardens.

Outside the sunroom the air was delightfully cool. Boule took a deep breath and lit another cigarette. Birds chirped in unison among the trees. A fountain splashed shimmering diamond drops over a lily pond in which fat goldfish stared up in bulbous-eyed curiosity. Below the balustrade platoons of precisely planted flowers were marshaled in orderly multi-colored rows. He rested his palms on the warm stone railing.

"Who does the gardening, Monsieur Vadim?"

"I do."

"Really? Then you are a man of remarkable talent. A most tasteful display."

"Thanks."

Such a garden was another of the elusive things he wished for his wife. Whenever she spoke fondly of her garden and the flowers she had grown as a child, each so carefully planted and nurtured, it nearly broke his heart. She deserved a garden.

For an instant he visualized her kneeling on the grass that edged the flowerbed. She would be wearing cloth gloves to protect her beautiful hands, a wide-brimmed sunhat with pink ribbons to guard against freckles. She worried about freckles. He pictured her digging in that dark rich loam, humming happily, looking up at him finally and smiling with pleasure.

"You said you had a key to that private door — past tense?"

"Past tense," Vadim agreed. "She took it back last night."

"Any reason?"

"I don't know, Commissaire. It came as quite a shock, I can tell you."

But he didn't elaborate. Boule waited, staring down at the flowers. He took Vadim's arm and guided him down the steps to the garden.

"Come, come, Monsieur Vadim. We are both men of the world. It is not unusual for a wealthy older woman at the peak of her sexuality to desire a handsome young man to provide her with companionship and satisfaction. Especially when she has no husband. I am not a moralist. I'm a simple policeman, shocked by nothing. Trust my instincts. By asking questions I am eliminating suspects. There are no witnesses out here. No notebooks. Just you and I trying to solve a mystery. Help me, Monsieur Vadim, and I'll help you. Now then, you were her lover, weren't you?"

"Yes."

"For how long?"

"From the beginning — the first day she hired me. Marie — Madame deBrisay — had enormous sexual appetites, Commissaire." He smiled with pleasure at the memory. "I've known a lot of women who enjoyed a roll but never one with sex on her mind all day every day. She could never get enough. At first I thought it was me, because of my considerable experience. But my God, I was no more than a donkey for her! It hurt my pride, I can tell you. Love should be a slow and gentle building of passion. A kiss, a touch, a fondling, gradual arousal, no? Not with her. Twice a day she'd call on the house phone. Georges, she would say, I'm feeling very moist. Can you come over, please? It wasn't easy for me, I can tell you!"

They paused at the lily pond and watched the goldfish scatter to the far end. An enormous pale green frog sat hunched on one of the flat leaves. A butterfly swooped low. The frog missed it.

"You spent the nights with her, Monsieur Vadim?"

"That's what you would think she'd want, wouldn't you? To fall asleep in a man's arms once her desires had been properly attended to. But not Marie — Madame deBrisay. Oh no, when she'd had enough, that was it. Goodnight, Georges, she'd say, and I'd creep away down those damn stairs like some moonstruck teenager and go back to my garage."

He stopped suddenly and faced Boule.

"I'll let you in on a secret, Commissaire."

"Please do."

"She hated men. All men."

"Really?"

"Absolutely, but you see she still needed us to satisfy herself. She told me masturbation and dildoes weren't enough. It had to be a man. A man's fingers, lips, tongue, and erection. Whenever we made love she started muttering how men were all disgusting animals and how she hated us. Later she'd start cursing. Then, when her orgasm began, she'd scream that I was a brute, that she despised me. She'd bite and scratch. But after the first time I was ready for her. It lasted only a few moments, then she'd relax and act as if nothing had happened."

They crossed the thick green lawn to the garage. A white Citroën sat parked outside an open bay. The other overhead doors were all closed. Vadim led him up an exposed staircase attached to the side of the building. Instead of facing the main house, his second-floor windows looked out on a back fence that enclosed the property. The quarters had been converted from a rustic horsebarn hayloft into accommodations as good as any first-class hotel. Thick rough-hewn beams stretched overhead from front to back holding the structure together. Boule butted his cigarette and sank into an overstuffed armchair.

"Coffee, Commissaire?"

"Yes, thank you."

Vadim produced a coffee tin from a cupboard. He measured out four spoonfuls and switched on the percolator. Boule watched, envying his youth and looks. Sex with his wife once a week was about all he could manage these days. Self-consciously, he compared his own libido, even as a young man, with Vadim's. There was no comparison. He resisted an urge to inquire at what age the chauffeur had begun his promiscuous career. It had been Gabrielle who had introduced Boule to the wondrous world of sex on the sofa-bed in his one room flat at Madame Doiron's *pension*.

Madame had been in bed and sedated, recovering from a visit to the dentist, when Gabrielle came tapping at his door. She'd been in Paris less than a month, and already she had found respectable employment with the telephone company. On the surface their relationship had developed into nothing more than regular friendly exchanges on the stairwell or while waiting in line with other household members to use the bathroom. One thing he never discussed was her appearance. Her beauty was beyond belief — at least to him. He wondered if she affected the other male roomers the same way. But it would have been gauche to discuss the matter with any of them. Consequently, he found their conversational exchanges emotionally painful, leaving him drained and feeling like a tongue-tied teen-age idiot.

"May I come in?"

Surprised — because she knew the house rules as well as he did — he stepped aside, then quickly closed the door. He offered her the wicker chair. She declined, explaining that there were too many split canes waiting to rip her dress.

"You could always take it off," he suggested, trying to be funny, never for a moment dreaming that she would.

"You are a good man, Bernard. Did you know that?"

He muttered something with appropriate modesty.

"I was paid today. So I have come to pay my debt to you." She held out a few new tissue-paper francs.

He shook his head. "You owe me nothing. I was happy to help. I can't take your money."

"Why not?" She seemed surprised.

"Because it might spoil things between us." He knew the words sounded awkward and trite, but he meant them. "You'll need that to buy a heavy coat and new shoes." He had heard her complain to Madame Doiron about the amount of time it would take to save enough money to buy these items from a second-hand store.

"What can I do for you, then?" she inquired, solemnly pocketing the bills.

"Just be my friend."

"That's all?"

"It's enough for me," he lied, then watched in silence as she began slowly undoing the buttons down the front of her dress. After folding the garment carefully over the bureau, she sat on the sofa and smiled. "Here, Bernard!" She patted the cushion. "Beside me."

Later, still mystified by what it was she saw in him, he summoned enough courage to ask her to be his wife. Without a moment's hesitation she accepted. It was ridiculous. He knew nothing about her — or she him. The word love hadn't even been mentioned. For his part there was no need. He was infatuated by her beauty, her strength, and the fact that she had found something immensely appealing in him. When stacked against the ecstasy and turmoil of his emotions any statement of love would have sounded weak.

Why *had* she agreed to marry him, he wondered a few weeks later?

"You're having second thoughts?" she accused.

She had an unnerving way of staring into his eyes as though reading his mind.

"Not at all," he replied with little conviction. "I am merely curious."

As he had every right to be. Gabrielle could have had her pick of the handsomest young men in Paris, rich men from good families who had money to spend in expensive restaurants and owned cars, who could look forward to secure careers with the government or in family businesses. Why had she chosen the plain-looking and impoverished student, Bernard Boule? Was there something in her past unable to bear detailed scrutiny? A family history of insanity? Some slowly debilitating and incurable disease of the body? Maybe he was already carrying the infection? Her answer surprised him.

"Dear, sweet Bernard. You are the only man I've known who has never asked me for anything or attached conditions to our relationship. You are strong. You are good. You are honest. And you love me. Fifty years from now I believe you'll still love me." She shrugged. "Tell me, what more can any woman ask?"

He recalled their honeymoon, two glorious weeks spent mostly in bed with his beautiful new wife. Days and nights of mutual and spontaneous passion until they were exhausted and — as he remembered — a little sore. He'd been much younger than Vadim. But near the end of that holiday they'd had enough. There had been other things to consider besides sex.

The war years were past, the accusations stilled, the medals awarded, pride rekindled. He had been accepted for the Police Academy. This was to be the first rung on his ladder to fortune and fame, maybe even a Prefecture before retirement. His ambition was for his wife more than for himself. But instead of reaching

the summit where they belonged he'd turned into a smelly dia-
phoretic cripple hobbled by handkerchiefs and shunned by his col-
leagues. Poor woman; he had failed her.

My God, it was so unfair! He contemplated the contrast between
his life and that of this successful young gigolo living in the lap of
luxury.

Suddenly the penny dropped. He remembered where he'd seen
Vadim's face. It was a police photograph, one from a collection of
known gigolos who were working the summer tourists. There had
been a nasty killing three — no, four years ago that had never been
solved. A wealthy Baltimore woman had been found with her throat
cut. Self-inflicted, it was decided, although her jewels had obviously been stolen. Vadim had been one of her escorts. Only his
name hadn't been Georges Vadim then but Marcel . . . Marcel . . .
Marcel what? One of Chief Henri Dubé's many personally unsolved
cases. Boule had watched in amusement from the sidelines while
he made one mistake after another. In the end the Director relieved
him by promoting Dubé to Chief and assigning someone else to
the case. But by then the spoor was cold so the new man wound
up saddled with the blame for Dubé's earlier incompetence.

"She decided to end your relationship last night, did she, Monsieur Vadim?"

He shrugged and tilted his head to one side, giving Boule a
querulous stare. "That's right. Straight out of the blue. Hit me
like a thunderbolt, I can tell you."

He came around from behind the kitchen counter and perched
on one of the padded bar stools, hooking his heels comfortably
against its steel foot ring.

"It all started the day before yesterday when she ordered me to
stop the car in the Rue du Bac," Vadim began.

4:52 P.M.

Marais paid off his taxi near the métro station, adding a circumspect tip for the driver. Too circumspect, as it turned out, because
the man cursed him roundly and flung the coins disdainfully into
the street. Great. Just what he needed — an idiot taxi driver roaring "Thief!" on the Montparnasse in the middle of the afternoon.

He crossed quickly to Rue Vavin and hurried down the sidewalk to Pinot's apartment. The street had pleasant shops and a couple of well-patronized bistros that provided a comfortable middle-class environment for those who could afford to rent flats from among the shark-toothed windows that overlooked the street. Pinot's flat peered down at a sidewalk café from the third floor.

As he climbed the worn stairs to the second landing the concierge appeared magically from a toilet closet. Sounds of water flooding through pipes gurgled from behind the door. He gave her a polite nod and continued along the landing.

There was nothing on Pinot's door to indicate an occupant, a flat number, or what lay beyond the sturdy oak. For an instant he thought he'd come to the wrong building. The premises looked the same but the concierge was different. Last year there had been a man. Maybe the woman was his wife. He knocked softly. Then more loudly.

"He's out!" the concierge called.

Marais went to the head of the stairs and looked down.

"I'm a friend," he said lamely.

"Well, he's not in!"

The concierge held both hands on her ample hips, her feet spaced astride the landing.

"Do you know when he'll be back?"

"No."

He tried a little historical background: "I'm from his home town in Canada. I have an important message to deliver."

"What town in Canada?"

"Montréal."

The answer satisfied her. She came slowly up the stairs, her entire demeanor much less aggressive now. Marais produced an encouraging smile as she reached the landing. She took a moment to catch her breath.

"He left at noon to go to the races at Longchamps. If he stops for dinner then it will be late before he returns. Otherwise I'd expect him around seven.

"Was he alone?" Marais asked.

"Alone? Monsieur Pinot is seldom alone." She nodded approvingly at his living arrangements.

He thanked her, promising to call back. The concierge suggested that if he wanted to wait there was a quiet bistro across the street that served reasonable coffee. Marais knew the spot from last year's visit. It was where, after some hesitation, Nicole Daladier had agreed to meet him at six o'clock.

He picked a vacant table on the sidewalk just under the awning and ordered croissants and coffee. Kitchen food smells set his stomach rumbling with anticipation. He'd eaten nothing since his meager morning feeding at the detention center. When the waiter returned he ordered an omelet.

The coffee, a dark bitter Turkish blend, scalded his tongue. He studied the entrance to Pinot's building, wondering how long he would have to wait. After polishing off the food and coffee he felt much better, more alert. He paid his bill and sauntered down the street to a kiosk for some newspapers.

There were no glaring headlines about Dimitrios's murder. The front pages were all on the latest Middle East conference. A Jewish group was demanding an end to American hypocrisy over arms shipments. Good luck! And Claude Faubert of the Ministry of Finance had been caught with his hand in the till and resigned. Traffic snarled along the Rue d'Assas behind him while he read. The murder was on page two. He folded the paper carefully.

"Hey, are you memorizing or buying?" the vendor demanded.

Marais apologized, counting out change for three of the dailies. A bottle green delivery van pulled in at the curb. Brightly illustrated signboards affixed to its side proclaimed "Murder in Millionaire's Mansion." The bold crimson letters blended into a line drawing of a dripping dagger. Intrigued, Marais decided to wait for a paper.

Two men in gray smocks leapt from the van and unloaded a half dozen bundles of the latest editions, stacking them beside the kiosk. Once the vendor had counted them and signed a receipt, the van roared away. He split the plastic strappings and lugged an armload of the papers into his sanctuary. Marais was his first customer for the new edition. He shoved it under his arm with the others and walked back to his table at the bistro and ordered another coffee.

He began with the morning edition of *Le Matin*, then went quickly through the two noonday papers, saving the millionaire's mansion murder for last. In the first three, Dimitrios's death had dropped to the inside pages. All he could find was a recap of what the papers termed yesterday's facts covering the Rue du Bac murder; there was a veiled suggestion that today's facts, should they become known, would be quite different.

Commissaire Bernard Boule — one paper had changed his name to Voule — chief investigating officer, stated that a suspect was still in custody and charges were pending. When asked to name his suspect the Commissaire would say only that the man was a tourist, male, thirty-five years of age. Not even a Frenchman, the paper pointed out indignantly. Thoughtfully, Marais sipped his coffee. Something was missing from the stories. They were drab, as if upon overnight reflection the editors had made up their collective minds that the story wasn't newsworthy in the first place and were now trying to kill it as swiftly as possible. He wished he could have read a copy of the evening papers from yesterday. Had the story been headlined like the "Mansion Murder"?

He opened his last paper and started reading. It was pure sensationalism.

"Twice within the past twenty-four hours," he read, "a knife-wielding killer has struck at a citizen of Paris. According to Commissaire Jean Blais, investigating officer at the scene, some time during the early hours of today Madame Marie deBrisay, 55, divorced wife of millionaire industrialist and war hero Comte Maurice deBrisay, 60, was stabbed to death in her bath. Present in the family's palatial Rue Raynouard residence at the time of her death were the chauffeur, Georges Vadim, 26, her granddaughter, Nicole Daladier, 20 . . . "

Thunderstruck, Marais stopped reading. He reread the story to make sure his eyes weren't deceiving him. No mistake, it was Nicole. Someone had done in her grandmother. Did they suspect her? If she was a suspect then how could she get away from the house without being followed? The idea made him nervous. Paris made him nervous.

Yesterday it was Dimitrios, this morning Nicole's grandmother, and tonight at eight he, Marais, was supposed to explode into little pieces. Near the end of the news article it stated that the police were satisfied for the moment that no connection existed between the deBrisay killing and the shop owner in the Rue du Bac. It concluded by saying that a tourist was in custody and awaiting formal charges. Obviously their information was dated. He set the paper aside with a frown.

But there was a connection between the two deaths: Nicole. According to his Michelin Guide the population of the city and its suburbs came to ten million plus. So what were the odds of one girl being involved in the only two murders in town — three, if he hadn't uncovered the explosive in his hotel room? About the same as being hit by lightning twice on consecutive days.

He checked his watch. Nicole was due any minute. Wouldn't it be safer to be a spectator to her arrival rather than a participant? For all he knew she might have a dozen surveillance cops trailing her. After just sliding out from one tight situation he didn't need to sit in the sun like a fool waiting to be guzzled up by another. He finished his coffee, paid the bill, and left a few coins on the table beside the discarded newspapers.

He sauntered along the sidewalk for a half block before crossing over to take up a position in front of an angled shop window. The vantage point was ideal. Without moving his head he had the glass reflection of the bistro and was still able to watch the oncoming traffic from the opposite direction up the one-way street. The late afternoon sun had dropped behind the rooftops, leaving the building fronts in softening shadows. Rush-hour traffic had peaked in a cacophony of engine noises, tires, and loudly farting exhausts without so much as a breeze to waft away the fumes.

He checked the flow of vehicles coming from Rue d'Assas: taxis, trucks, several vans, single drivers, men and women sharing the front seats. None of them slowed or stopped.

In the glass Marais saw Nicole hesitate on the sidewalk in front of the café. She was two minutes late. Not bad considering she'd come on foot. He'd expected a car. She peered inside, scanning the tables, then stepped back to reread the sign above the sidewalk awning. He waited until she'd taken a table — the one he had vacated — before moving from his window. Keeping to the opposite side of the street he walked slowly back toward the bistro, all the time studying the pedestrian traffic for something unusual. But there was nothing out of the ordinary — no loitering newspaper readers, no casual male strollers in high-collared trenchcoats. Not even one surreptitious café customer entered the place after Nicole sat down. So what in hell had he been expecting to happen? Sirens and gunfire? A swat team? He'd have to hold his imagination in check. But that explosive under the night table wasn't imaginary.

For a moment he stood directly opposite the café watching her fiddle absently with the menu. At last she caught his eye and folded her hands onto her lap. She wore a white summer dress with a narrow red belt and low-heeled walking shoes. She carried no handbag, only a small red leather wallet with a gold clasp that she'd left on top of the table. He crossed the street and sat down.

She wasn't smiling. Behind the large sunglasses her eyes were red and puffy from weeping.

"Sorry about your grandmother," he began.

"You knew?" He'd startled her.

"From the newspapers. Front-page coverage. Your name was mentioned." The waiter came and hovered with an order pad. Marais glanced back at the street. Still nothing suspicious. "Do you mind if we walk?"

She gave a tiny shrug and stood up, reclaiming her wallet. The waiter looked annoyed. Marais took her arm. She flinched at his touch. He sensed her uneasiness.

"I'm not going to bite you," he said.

"I'm sorry. I'm upset."

"I can imagine. If I'd known the news earlier I would have called to cancel our meeting, but I just found out. How did you manage to get away? Didn't the police want you to stick around?"

She shook her head, spilling hair across the sunglasses. "The Commissaire said I was free to leave after he finished questioning me. Boule — the same one you met at Rue du Bac."

"He's on this case too?" Marais said in wonder.

"There were others, but he was the last one I spoke with." She pushed the hair away from her glasses. "You phoned shortly after that. So I got dressed and came out." She looked at him accusingly. "Where are we going?" She stopped abruptly in the middle of the sidewalk as though he might be trying to spirit her away.

He tried a smile, but it didn't work. She was frightened of him. Had she reassessed his image since yesterday and decided he'd killed Dimitrios after all? He was afraid to ask in case she panicked and started screaming for help. Anything was possible in her present emotional state. He mustn't push too hard.

"I thought a quiet walk in the Luxembourg Gardens if you're up to it. I've never seen them."

But she held her ground. "What was wrong with that bistro?"

"Nothing," he rubbed his nose, deciding how to justify his caution, "only you may have been followed."

Her brows knit. "I don't understand." She looked past him, searching pedestrians and traffic for pursuers. "Who'd want to follow me?"

He took a deep breath. "The police." His hands lifted, their fingers spread defensively. "I know, you'll think I'm paranoid. But I'm positive your police are trying to kill me."

She stared at him in disbelief, trying to decide if he was serious. "You're joking!" She gave a short nervous laugh.

"No, Nicole, I'm not." He took her arm, steering her toward the Gardens. This time she didn't resist. "Something very strange is going on. I don't understand what or why it's all happening, but believe me, it is happening. I've got a suitcase filled with explosives checked in at the Gare du Nord with the rest of my luggage to prove it."

He told her his story, beginning with his uncomfortable room at the old detention center on an island in the Seine.

"The Palais de Justice," she interjected; "it's on the Île de la Cité."

He told her about Albert and Bondi, the trip across town to another hotel and how in both instances they wouldn't go inside with him; how he was supposed to be by his phone at eight; what he'd found in the room next door; and how, after phoning Nicole, he'd returned to the hotel to lug his suitcases down the fire escape into a taxi. He dug the railway baggage checks out of his pocket and showed them to her.

"If you're still in doubt we can take a cab to the Gare du Nord and I'll show you their equipment — timer, wires, detonator, it's all there."

"Is it safe to leave it at the station?"

"It won't blow up. Everything has been disconnected."

They crossed with the lights at Rue d'Assas while the brooding traffic waited, and went into the Gardens. It was a magical place with tall forest trees at one end and formally arranged flowerbeds at the other. Hundreds of young people and students sat or read or cuddled on the grass, oblivious to the world. There was a small lake, dozens of statues, and the Medici Fountain that sprayed scattered rainbows when the sun touched it at the right angle. Carefully tended pathways meandered among the trees, and there was a miraculous feeling of solitude beneath their canopy of whispering leaves and chattering birds.

"I'm going to try to arrange a passport through a friend. He has the connections. When I had it in my pocket I was planning on asking you to drive me to the nearest border crossing. But that was before I read about your grandmother," he hastened to add, not wanting to sound churlish.

"Is that why you phoned?"

"Yes and no. You left messages at the Pont Royal for me to call when I came in. Four yesterday, one this morning."

"I'd forgotten."

"I'm not surprised. You've had other things on your mind." He gave a shrug and clasped her hand. "Anyway, I apologize for dragging you away like this. Maybe my friend can make transport arrangements for me at the same time as getting the passport."

Her hand was soft, a gentle hand with long fingers that curled comfortably around his own. He took a sidelong glance at her face behind the sunglasses. She was incredibly beautiful in profile.

"Just the same, I'm glad to see you again. Someday when all this is a memory I'll take you out to dinner and we can talk about the time we held hands in the Luxembourg Gardens."

She didn't smile or even acknowledge that she had heard what he'd said.

"Did it occur to you there might be a connection?" she asked suddenly, stopping in the middle of the path. He released her hand. "I mean between grandmama and that man yesterday on the Rue du Bac." She whipped off her sunglasses and stared at him thoughtfully.

Marais nodded. "That occurred to me when I read the news about your grandmother. You're right. In both instances there's a common denominator and the odds are too great for it to be coincidence."

Her grasp of the fact that she had been on the scene before and after both murders surprised him. What surprised him even more was how she took his original premise a step further.

"It's those portraits, Roger. I feel they're the key to everything that's been happening. If we can find out what they're about I'll bet anything we'll find the killer." Her lips tightened with determination.

It wasn't what he'd expected to hear, but it was an idea he'd overlooked.

5:10 P.M.

Boule heard footsteps climbing to the second-floor landing. Vadim went to the door. It was André.

"My apologies for the interruption, Sir. But if it's not too inconvenient, Commissaire Blais would like to speak with you."

Boule gulped the rest of his coffee and thanked Vadim for the courtesy and conversation, promising to finish their talk a little later. "You'll be looking for a new employer, Monsieur Vadim?"

The chauffeur bit his lip. "I suppose so."

"You will let me know when you move?" He gave him one of his Brigade Criminelle cards listing his office extension. Vadim promised to call.

Down on the white concrete driveway Boule stopped to light a cigarette. "How would you describe the Commissaire's mood?"

André smiled. "Apoplectic, I should say. Fauré and your driver refuse to budge from the front door."

"Well then, there's no rush, is there?" Boule said with relish. "We should give the poor man time to either succumb or settle down." He started across the lawn at a leisurely pace, hands clasped behind his back, cigarette bouncing on his lip. André fell into step.

"Is that the embassy information?" Boule inquired.

"Yes, Sir." André opened the large brown manila envelope. "Care to read it?"

Boule shook his head. "Later. A précis of the facts will do for now."

André rewound the flap string around the red eyelets and stuck the envelope back in his case. "Marais is under lifetime parole in Canada for killing a policeman during an attempted bank robbery. His sentence was twelve years."

"They should have given him the chair."

"That's only in America. I believe Canada used the rope until banning the death penalty, Sir."

"So they could parole their murderers and let them visit Paris. An unhealthy situation for both countries, wouldn't you say?"

"Yes, Sir. The Canadians have promised full cooperation."

"I should think so. After all, they turned him loose on us," Boule said.

"I'll make out the formal charges and arrest him in the morning, then notify the Director of Public Prosecutions," André volunteered.

Boule stopped in his tracks. "You'll do no such thing! What is our case against him? Tell me that, eh?"

"His record, Sir. Isn't that enough to start?"

"Not for me it isn't. Where's the motive? Unless Marais is a psychotic, he had to have a motive for killing the Greek. Does his police record say anything about mental instability?"

"No, Commissaire."

"Exactly! So he had to have a motive. What was it?"

"Helping the granddaughter?" André suggested. "He kills the Greek while she kills her grandmother?"

"A death pact sealed over lunch at the Pont Royal Hotel? Don't be an ass! He'd just met the girl — her story, not his. Where's their motive, lad? You'll have to do better than that or the Public Prosecutor will laugh you out of his office."

André lowered his head, examining the polished tips of his shoes with idle interest. Quickly, Boule recovered his composure, regretting his outburst. He was tired. That was it. Too many late nights and early mornings. Middle-aged decrepitude, he supposed.

"On the other hand, young André," Boule softened his voice engagingly, "if you can find a solid piece of evidence that points to a conspiracy between Marais and the granddaughter for either murder I'll trumpet your achievement from the bell tower of Notre Dame Cathedral — either that or buy you a first-class lunch in the police caféteria."

They started walking. Boule sighed. "We're going to be under considerable pressure to solve this mess in the days ahead. The PJ will want an arrest quickly. Not so much for the Greek's murder as the one here. Where politics and money are concerned you will find, no doubt to your utter amazement, that the district of Passy will always take precedence over the Faubourg Saint-Germain." He shook his head. "One of life's unfortunate realities. But we have something in our favor. The two killings are related. Solve one and we solve both. Marais and the granddaughter are the common link. So we must continue working from that base and assumption. Something will break our way. I know. It always does."

André put the Marais dossier back in the envelope. "What do you want me to do next, Commissaire?"

"Look for a clue. There is one waiting for us somewhere — here, at the shop on the Rue du Bac, among Marais's luggage — somewhere."

"Right. Where do you want me to start?"

"Start by using your imagination. After that the rest should be easy. You do have an imagination?"

"Yes, Sir."

"Good."

They came around the side of the enormous house. Two *flics* guarded the driveway keeping reporters from sprinting around back for Peeping Tom photographs. On the front portico a knot of angry people jostled for position. André cleared a path through the squirming bodies while Boule, following closely behind, elbowed them aside. When they reached the door Boule was sweating torrents and inwardly cursing himself for not returning through one of the rear doors.

André made a clever little speech introducing Boule, who waved everyone into silence and announced in a clear menacing voice that until he'd finished his investigations no one would be allowed in the house except family members and staff.

"Where's the granddaughter?" someone yelled.

From another, "Isn't Commissaire Blais in charge here?"

He zeroed in on the second speaker: "Only if the Chief of the Brigade Criminelle changed his mind after ordering me over here this afternoon."

Another indignant voice insisted that Blais had told him personally he was in command. Did he have any comments on that?

"Ah, that is a matter between yourself and Commissaire Blais," Boule replied owlishly, "or between Commissaire Blais and his conscience. In neither case am I involved."

This produced a few laughs and the tension eased.

"Now, if you will excuse us . . . "

A polished black seven-passenger Mercedes nosed into the drive from the street and drew up in front of the steps. Before its uniformed chauffeur could manage to get around to open the door, a tall slender man with iron-gray hair climbed out and stood glaring at the crowded entrance. A newsman recognized him.

"Comte deBrisay! By heaven, it's the Comte himself!"

Within seconds the man was engulfed by electronic flashes and an avalanche of questions. Boule forced his way into the mêlée, quickly introduced himself and took hold of deBrisay's arm, escorting him up the steps. André roared at everyone to stand aside. The door opened a few inches and Fauré peered out to see the cause of the sudden disturbance. Finding Boule surrounded by shouting faces, he opened wider. The Comte, Boule, and André popped through the opening and into the vestibule.

Indoors, the crowd — nearly as large as the one outside — was more subdued. Every gaze fastened on the new arrivals. Blais pushed through to the front of his group while Boule stepped past Fauré, his driver, André, and the Comte. No one spoke. One of the uniformed policemen gave a nervous cough. Blais's handsome features reddened. A television cameraman swung his unit onto a hunched shoulder and adjusted the focus. Behind the front row of menacing faces a soundman lowered a drop mike on the end of a long boom and waited to see who would be the first to speak. Real-life drama, Boule decided cynically, giving Blais an affable smile.

"Comte deBrisay, permit me to introduce Commissaire Blais of the sixteenth arrondissement, who is assisting me in this difficult investigation."

As the Comte stepped forward Blais switched instantly to form, delivering a magnificent bow followed by a pumping of the Comte's unwilling hand with all the enthusiasm of a true supporter of the restoration of the monarchy.

Officialdom then retired to the main floor library and closed the doors on the common herd. "My sincere condolences on your bereavement," Blais began unctuously.

The Comte smiled. A nasty smile, Boule thought, devoid of any humor or pity. "What are all these people doing here?" he demanded of Boule.

"They are in the process of being removed. There was some delay in my reaching the house. The newspaper, radio, and television people were here first. As you know, they're difficult to dislodge once established on the scent of what they believe to be a promising scandal."

Blais looked horrified but kept his mouth shut. André stood near the door with Fauré, ready to grapple with any trespasser who might try crashing past the guard posted on the other side.

"Scandal, is it?" deBrisay muttered. He had pale patrician features of the sort associated with men who spend most of their time indoors on the telephone or attending board meetings, even when on holiday. His movements around the room were proprietary, a picture tilted, a volume reset on its shelf, an ivory figurine lovingly held, then replaced on the fireplace mantle. The policemen watched in silence. When he extracted a humidor from his breast pocket and removed a slim cigar, Blais instantly produced a gold lighter. The Comte seated himself in one of the big brown leather chairs near the empty fireplace and looked morosely at Boule.

"I heard about it an hour ago and came immediately. Why wasn't I notified earlier? Or do you make it a habit to call the media first?"

Blais flinched, and Boule launched into an explanation of how reporters were posted at the desk of every police precinct and hospital in the city waiting for just such an event. To prevent interception was next to impossible except in matters of national security. It was Boule's standard patter for such occasions. He could have saved his breath.

"I'm well aware of how the system works, Sir," deBrisay glared. "I own a chain of newspapers. Is she still upstairs in my bathtub?"

Boule shook his head. "The body has been taken to the police morgue for the customary examination."

"Good! Cleaned the mess up afterwards, did you? Hope so. I hate messes. The radio said she'd been murdered. That so?"

"Without question," Boule affirmed.

"Not surprising when you consider the way she carried on her love life. The only surprise is that it's taken this long before someone took it into his head to kill her. If you ask me, the damn woman had it coming!" Everyone in the room was taken aback.

His voice held a deep authoritative resonance. He'd be a magnificent witness in open court. Boule judged the Comte to be about his age; this would be a decided advantage for interrogation purposes.

Looking at deBrisay in his elegant light gray summer suit, sitting there in the rich leather chair surrounded by books he'd never read, in a magnificent house that he had inherited, Boule thought that the handsome Comte epitomized the decadence of that portion of French nobility who managed in 1793 to slip through the net of Citizen Robespierre's Committee of Public Safety. He swung a matching chair away from the fireplace so it was opposite deBrisay and sat down. All five pocket handkerchiefs were soaked. He gave his face an uncomfortable swipe with the driest while the Comte regarded him with interest from behind a tendril of cigar smoke.

"When did you last see your wife, Comte deBrisay?"

"This morning over breakfast."

"You were here this morning?" Boule asked incredulously.

"No, Sir. I haven't crossed the doorstep to this place since divorcing Marie Carnot."

Had the Comte decided purposely to be clever? Boule took a moment to sort it out. Ah well, what was in a name? He pressed on. "The deceased woman's maiden name was Carnot, I take it?"

"Maiden, did you say?" deBrisay exploded. "Marie a maiden? You're joking, Sir! I'll warrant she was born without a hymen. Probably started copulating in her crib."

From the center of the room Jean Blais gave a sly smile, its implication as clear as if he'd spoken the words: Your case, Boule? Are you sure you know what you're doing?

Boule tried again for a common ground of understanding with the Comte.

"You've had no contact with the deceased since what date?"

"October 1962, our divorce. Messy business. I suppose you saw it in the papers?"

"No, I didn't." Sensational divorces held little interest for Boule except when they involved murder.

DeBrisay sighed. "Dreadful experience. Went on for weeks. In the end I settled her with an income and occupancy of this place until she remarried. A farmhouse and land near Charleville I gave her outright. Why not? Who in their right mind would want to live in the Ardennes?"

"My wife is from the Ardennes," Boule said.

"Is she now? Well then, there you are. Sensible woman, she married a Parisian. Still together, are you?"

"Yes."

DeBrisay studied his cigar tip with a faraway look that stretched beyond the thick gray-blue smoke, past the room off into his memories. A wistful smile tugged at the corners of his mouth.

"May I inquire why you divorced Marie Carnot?" Boule interrupted his reverie.

"You may not! It was a private matter, except what appeared in the newspapers at the time. I suggest you read them. Beyond that it's none of your business."

Boule attempted a different approach. "You were married how long?"

The Comte reflected a moment. "Fourteen years."

"Then incompatibility was not a factor in your separation, I assume."

"Assume whatever you like."

He was not an easy man to interview. Boule took a deep breath and tried again. "How did you meet?"

"Does it matter?"

"It might."

"Thirty-six years ago? You must be joking, Commissaire." He thought about the question over a mouthful of cigar smoke, decided there was nothing damaging in it and replied: "In one of the big couturier houses in the Faubourg Saint-Honoré. My mother had dragged me along to see the latest spring fashions."

"And you were married how soon after that?"

"Six weeks, more or less."

"A whirlwind courtship?"

"Yes, if you like."

"You must have loved her very much."

DeBrisay frowned. "Yes, I did. Very much. She wasn't always a bitch."

"Did your family approve of the match?"

"I think so. They wanted me to settle down and raise heirs for the deBrisay name. My brothers were killed in the Dunkirk perimeter at the beginning of the war. I was the only one left to continue the line. Under normal circumstances my father would have forbidden such a union. Marie was a nobody from the Ardennes without name, dowry, or property." He made it sound as if she had been a carrier of some social disease.

"Then you took the trouble to check her background?" Boule interjected.

"I didn't, but my father did. He used our company's attorneys."

"And . . . ?"

"And what?"

"What did they find?" Boule asked reasonably.

DeBrisay waved his cigar in annoyance. "Really, Commissaire, I don't see what this has to do with her death. Shouldn't you be looking for a suspect instead of rehashing my marital errors?"

Boule sorted out one of his damp handkerchiefs. "Please answer the question, Comte deBrisay." Out of the corner of his eye he saw Blais frown. The hell with Blais and his precious nobility, he thought. Fourteen years of marriage ends in divorce. Why? He'd send André out to comb the newspaper stories covering the period.

DeBrisay was not accustomed to confrontations with his class inferiors. He cleared his throat uncertainly. "They found nothing damaging, if that's what you're after."

"Let me be the judge of that."

Reluctantly, the Comte outlined what he remembered. Marie Carnot had grown up in a village close to the Belgian border where the river Meuse winds back upon itself briefly before setting sail across the frontier for Namur and Liège. Her father, a minor official in the Ministry responsible for canals and river traffic, had two sons and two daughters. The sons died in 1940 when France's defenses crumbled near Sedan and the mighty *Wehrmacht* juggernaut poured across the Meuse. As word arrived first that his younger, then the elder boy had been slaughtered, her father gave up his will to live. Twice in his lifetime he'd watched as nearly everything he loved and valued was swept away by the Boche.

Two days before Christmas he died. Cardiac arrest, the doctor said. But since he'd just turned 45, the more likely cause was a broken heart. Marie was 13 years old at the time. Her mother took Marie and her sister to Charleville, a few kilometers south of their village. The girls were sent to the convent school. Somehow, Madame Carnot managed to arrange employment for herself across the river in Mézières at the office of the Prefecture for the Department of the Ardennes.

"Her mother was accused of collaboration after the war. But our attorneys could find no substance to that accusation. The Boche controlled the Prefecture with their own appointees, so naturally anybody working in the place was suspect," deBrisay concluded.

"What about her sister?"

"Disappeared near the end of the war. She was never seen or heard from again."

"Can you recall her sister's name?"

"No. I have forgotten."

"But in due course Marie came to Paris where you married her?"

"Not in Paris. We were married in the chapel of my family's estate at Cléry. It was my mother's wish. But we lived in Paris, in this house."

"For fourteen years," Boule added.

The Comte's features tightened perceptibly. "Yes."

Boule shifted position in his chair. Its leather hide cover had begun sticking to the back of his suitcoat. He wanted to get up and move around a little, giving himself a chance to dry off. But that might break the spell he was trying to create with deBrisay. The man was finally beginning to open up a little.

"Marie had a child?" he asked softly.

"Yes." The Comte's jaw thrust forward. "Not mine though, by God! It belonged to some American soldier who'd put her up the stump and left for home." He sounded outraged. Justifiably, Boule decided.

"This was before you married her?"

"Yes."

"Something the company lawyers overlooked."

"They were looking at her background in the Ardennes, not Paris."

"An understandable oversight," Boule agreed sympathetically. "How did you find out?"

"From my doctor. She was unable to conceive. I wanted to know if it was my fault or hers. Once I had been pronounced fertile I arranged for Marie to see him. He discovered that she was barren and had already had a child."

"You were angry over her deception?"

"Furious."

"You confronted her and demanded an explanation?"

"I demanded more than an explanation. I demanded a divorce."

"And she refused?"

"Yes."

"So it became a matter for your company lawyers to settle with as little scandal as possible to the deBrisay name."

"Yes, a settlement was arranged. I gave her a virtual carte blanche to live and do as she pleased. The only limit placed on her spending was that property acquisitions were all to be registered in my name for taxation purposes. The Charleville farm was the only exception. I think I treated her fairly."

Boule didn't. But he let it slide. Had he given Marie time to tell her side of the story? What had been her side of the story back then and would it be any different if she was able to tell it now, he wondered?

"You remarried after the divorce settlement?"

"Yes. I have three children."

"Did you see Marie again?"

DeBrisay shrugged. "From time to time. Mostly by accident at the opera, the races, once at Orly when she was flying out to South America on the arm of a handsome young escort. Turned out to be her chauffeur, if you can believe it!" He muttered and tamped his dead cigar into a flaking mess in the ashtray at his elbow. "My curiosity got the better of me. I hired a private detective to investigate. She'd spent an unusually large sum that month. Until then, her expenditures overall had been relatively modest, other than the Charleville farm purchased a few years earlier on some whim. Not that she was frugal, Sir. She lived well, dressed well, and maintained this house and herself in luxury. I accepted that. Blood money, conscience money, or whatever you want to call it. But when the monthly draw-down from my bank suddenly shot up to one hundred thousand new francs in a single month I became alarmed. Maybe one of her gigolo drivers had decided to set himself up a retirement income. You see my problem?"

Boule nodded absently, his mind still on poor barren Marie. Boule understood. His own wife had been unable to conceive after being butchered by an abortionist. Yet never once during those first sorrowful years did he contemplate a mistress and mother for his unborn children. What Comte deBrisay had done to Marie Carnot was as despicable a thing as any man could do to his wife, in Boule's eyes. How could he claim to have loved her in the first place?

There was a quiet knock at the door. Fauré stepped out to talk with Monceau.

"It turned out she'd spent the money on a portrait of herself as a girl painted by some fellow in Haguenau. Dorfmundt was his name, I believe. Somewhat overpriced, I thought. At any rate she wasn't being blackmailed by one of her gigolos. That's all I cared about."

Boule sucked in his lower lip. "Perhaps she was being black-mailed by the painter?"

The Comte didn't answer, and Boule was left wondering whose portrait Marie *had* seen in that window on the Rue du Bac. Fauré returned to the room with a perplexed expression, stopping to mutter a few words to André, who shook his head with wonder.

"Well, what is it?" Boule demanded.

"A message from the PJ, Commissaire," Fauré told him, glancing pointedly at Blais and the Comte.

Boule excused himself and stepped out into the hall.

"Do you know officers Targout and Clévis, Commissaire?" Fauré inquired.

Boule shook his head. Monceau looked uncomfortable and said, "They had an authorization signed by you to take Roger Marais to the magistrate's court in Versailles this afternoon. Chief Dubé wants to know what happened since no one turned up at Versailles. All three men have vanished."

"Which is just as well," Fauré added laconically, "since that magistrate's court isn't open until next Monday."

8:03 P.M.

Bondi had parked the car two blocks from the hotel, close enough to watch the sixth-floor explosion but not close enough to be collared as an eyewitness. Albert looked at his wristwatch, cross-checking it with the electric clock on the dash.

"It's after eight," he said.

Bondi grunted.

"Give it another five minutes."

Another grunt.

"Those timers can be off a little. Remember that one we used in Narbonne?"

Bondi remembered.

"Quality control, that's what's lacking. Nothing's made the way it used to be. Slapdash — no pride of workmanship. Nobody gives a shit any more about quality. Not like the old days. You remember the old days?"

Bondi remembered them.

"A man knew where he stood," Albert mused, his attention held by the hotel's sixth-floor windows. "Everything straight up and in black and white. Remember what it was like? Everybody followed the rules. You know why, Bondi. . . . "

"Albert," Bondi interrupted wearily, "do me a favor."

"Sure, Bondi, name it."

"For Christ's sake shut up, you're driving me crazy."

At twenty-five minutes past eight they knew they were in serious trouble. Albert got out of the car and went to find a telephone. First he called Le Palais and asked for Room 610. At seven rings the hotel operator came on the line again asking him to leave a message for the occupant. Albert hung up. Then he took a deep breath and dialed Commandant Daggar Paoli for instructions.

8:17 P.M.

Marais had been expecting a taxi or a man and woman on foot coming from the métro station. Instead, a gorgeous new yellow four-door Renault stopped across the street in a no-parking zone and a single man got out. It took him several seconds to realize it was Pinot. The curly hair had been clipped neatly, a smart summer suit had replaced the old leather jacket and blue denims, but there was no mistaking the ferret face.

He told Nicole to wait and sprinted across the road, entering the building at the same moment as Pinot.

"Hello, Bobby. How's Paris been treating you?" he called.

Pinot stopped. "Rog!" His face split in a grin. He'd had his teeth capped. "When did you hit town?"

"Day before yesterday."

"Still working the old antique and art dodge?"

"Still the same. Look, Bobby, I need some help."

"Name it."

"A passport."

Pinot's eyes narrowed. "You got heat?"

"I think so."

"Hey, man, never mind the head games. Either you got heat or you haven't. Which is it?"

"I got heat."

"How much heat?"

"The police think I sliced that guy's throat on Rue du Bac yesterday and a couple of beauts tried blowing me up about a half hour ago on the other side of town. Now that they know it didn't work they're going to come looking."

Pinot stuffed the mail in his pocket and went to the door. Through the glass he checked the street in both directions then took Marais's arm and drew him into the foyer's dimmer light away from prying eyes. His voice sank almost to a whisper.

"Where you staying?"

"At the moment, nowhere. I spent last night in some cop shop. They sprung me this afternoon."

"Who?"

"The pair that are trying to kill me."

Pinot's brow furrowed. "Are you putting me on?"

Marais shook his head. It sounded far-fetched even to him. Small wonder Pinot had trouble digesting it.

"Here isn't the place to talk about it. Can't we go somewhere — unless you want me to get lost?"

Pinot's lips tightened. It was a hell of a favor Marais was asking. "Passports cost big. You got the bread to pay for one? Fouquet, the guy I know, doesn't take checks or American Express."

"I can phone home for a bank transfer in the morning, but I'll need you to pick it up. I'll be out of your hair by tomorrow night. What do you say?"

Pinot filled his cheeks, held them inflated for an instant, then blew away his doubts in a long sigh.

"What the hell! Okay, Rog, let's go."

They went out to the car. There was a girl in the front seat. Marais hesitated.

"Don't worry about Danielle," Pinot said. "She doesn't like cops any better than I do."

"I'm not worried about your girl. It's the one with me."

"Where does she fit?"

"Somebody stuck a knife in her grandmother this morning while she was taking a bath. We met yesterday on the Rue du Bac. She's waiting across the street."

"Sweet Jesus!" Pinot said numbly. "Is there anything else?"

Marais hurried to get Nicole, realizing that if he lingered Pinot might reconsider his position. The car was rolling from the second they climbed in, and no one spoke until they had turned onto the cluttered safety of Boulevard Raspail.

He introduced Nicole. Pinot nodded through the mirror. Danielle turned and smiled. She was very pretty, with full lips and jet-black hair.

"Okay, Rog, give me a story," Pinot said when he was sure they weren't being followed.

Marais's tale began with his arrival at Charles de Gaulle airport two days before. Pinot listened without comment, driving aimlessly along the wide, well-lit boulevards that connect the city's heart and soul. When he finally finished, Pinot asked, "Why are you involving Nicole?"

"He's not," Nicole interrupted. "I'm involving myself."

She and Roger had discussed their respective positions over coffee while waiting for Pinot to appear. They had agreed that Marais stood a better chance of getting out of the country now if Nicole traveled with him, since whoever was after him would be searching for a lone man. In exchange for her company, he had agreed to go with her to Alsace to interview the widow of the painter from whom Dimitrios had bought the portraits.

Pinot turned off on a hilly side street in the village of Montmartre and parked. The lights of Pigalle and the city streamed out below. He turned in the seat so they could see at least one half of the concern on his face.

"Let me tell you how the system works over here, Rog, old buddy," he began dryly. "Because it takes a while for it to sink in, and when it does it's scary. Purely and simply, this is a police state. Don't get me wrong. I'm not talking about a banana republic police dictatorship. That's not in the French character. This is more subtle, more impersonal. Cops here are just another branch of the huge faceless bureaucracy that runs this country. They're the armed branch. Get the picture? They're all in bed together: cops, magistrates, judges, water-meter inspectors. It's the old-boy network gone wild."

He squinted earnestly at Marais in the dim yellow street light that filled the car's interior.

"If this guy Boule thinks he's got a case against you, you're gone. Au revoir. They'll lug you in front of a magistrate who will examine the case based on what Boule tells him are the facts. You got nothing to say about it. There's no bail bondsman because there's no bail. You'll sit in the slammer two or three years while a judge, magistrates, and the fuzz investigate the crime. There's no rush. If their report to the Public Prosecutor says you should go to trial, it means they're all in agreement you're guilty beyond the shadow of a doubt.

"Guilt, you see, is decided at the investigative level, not at your trial. But — and it's a big but — if you can come up with a reasonable explanation for your actions the jury might cut you loose. That's so unusual that if it happens they put it on the front page."

Marais cleared his throat, which suddenly felt very tight. He didn't need a lecture on French jurisprudence. All he wanted was a passport and an idea — if Bobby had one — on why someone wanted him dead. For the first time, he noticed that Nicole had reached over to hold his hand.

"You've made me feel better already, Bobby," he said. Nicole gave his fingers an encouraging squeeze. Pinot's hand went nervously over the top of his head.

"I wasn't trying to scare you. It's just that I know French cops don't pick up tourists at first-class hotels over lunch, toss them into the slammer overnight and release them the next day without some explanation unless they're working an angle of their own. Whatever you're involved with, Rog, is way out of my league. The faster you can get out of this country the better for all of us."

He started the car and took them to a cheap hotel near the Montmartre village square where squalid rooms rented by the hour for twenty-five francs. There were no registration cards required, no identification needed, and no questions asked, and guests were expected to arrive in pairs.

"Do you have any money with you?" Pinot inquired.

Marais nodded.

"Try and act like a stud in heat. Nicole will be expected to slip the deskman a twenty on the way out. I'll go and try to find my passport connection. It may take a couple of hours." He squinted at his gold wristwatch. "I'll meet you back here on the street at eleven."

Marais patted him on the arm. "We'll be waiting. By the way, Bobby, how's business?"

Pinot smiled. "Don't ask. You're in enough trouble already."

The small hotel exuded an atmosphere of despair. Odors of urine and stale cigarettes clung to its peeling walls. Marais gave his best shot at a lascivious smile when Nicole wiggled over to the desk and ordered a room from a pale thin clerk with boils who sat reading *Le Canard*. Room prices had gone up. Marais paid him thirty-five francs plus another twenty-two for towels and linen.

"Toilet's at the end of the corridor. Remember to give the chain a good sharp pull after you use it or the damn thing will overflow!"

Marais promised. He followed Nicole up the dark stairwell to the third floor. They passed a girl with enormous breasts squeezed into a skintight silver lamé jumpsuit unzipped to the navel. Her trick trailed along self-consciously, wishing Marais an incongruous "Good evening, Sir" on his way down the worn stairs. An ecstatic howl filled the third-floor landing from one of the rooms down the hall. From the opposite direction a man's voice yelled, "Well done! Long live the Republic!"

Their room had been furnished with one objective in mind: to get rid of its occupants as speedily as possible once the purpose for their visit had been concluded. Marais sat down on a shriek of bedsprings.

"From the Pont Royal to the slammer to Le Palais to this tomb. How much lower can I get?"

"At least the place isn't going to blow up."

"Not at the moment," he agreed, as he lay back on a glissandi of squeals, easing his feet up on the mattress. Nicole took the chair and sat gingerly on its curved plywood lip. He sensed her unease. They were alone. No one at the next table she could call for help to ward off his advances. She refused to meet his eyes. He propped himself on one elbow and examined her.

"I still don't really understand why you're here," he said.

The comment startled her and she paused to consider it before replying, shaking a swatch of hair across her face in the process. "You think I should be in Passy making funeral arrangements, is that it?"

"Something like that. Don't get me wrong; I'm glad you came. It's just that this scene of mine doesn't suit you."

"What's that supposed to mean?" she challenged.

He shrugged his free shoulder. "You may get yourself into a lot of trouble. You live here. I don't. Once I'm across the border I'm home free. You're already home. It makes a difference."

She flipped her hair aside. "I don't think I could face going back to the house at the moment, and there's no point driving to Lyons because Mama will be on her way to Paris." She slid a little further back on her chair, adopting a less defensive posture. "I'd prefer to leave it to Mama to make the funeral arrangements. It's the least she can do now for poor Grandmama."

"I take it they didn't get along very well?" he inquired politely. "It happens in families," he continued. "A mother and daughter are too much alike to get along with each other. They become competitors instead of friends."

"Oh, no, they weren't at all alike," Nicole said. "Right from the day Old Margot told Mama that Grandmama was her mother she refused to believe it because they were so different."

And then she told Marais her mother's story as it had been told by the three women closest to her: her mother, her grandmother, and Old Margot.

For as far back as Irène could remember there had been Old Margot. Irène was twelve when the old woman explained that Marie deBrisay was her natural mother. Until that time all her affections had been directed at Mama Margot, the only parent she knew. Vaguely, she'd been aware that Mama Margot was too old to be her real mother. But that didn't matter, because whenever love and comfort were needed, whenever there were tears to be dried and kissed into smiles or laughter, Mama Margot had been there. The pretty dark-haired woman from Paris had not. She was a stranger.

She came twice a year, at Easter and Irène's birthday, bringing armloads of gifts. For a time after each visit Mama Margot would be sad, sometimes crying in her sleep, deep agonizing sobs that wrenched Irène's heart. Yet, when she tiptoed into the old woman's bedroom and touched her gently awake to ask what was wrong, Mama Margot would put her arms around Irène's shoulders and hug her tightly, saying that every woman had a cross to bear. For a little while they would weep together before Irène went back to her own bed.

They lived on a small farm in the blissfully peaceful country-side along the road to Charleville. Twice weekly a hired man came from Arreux to help with the chores. A dull morose individual, he spoke rarely and then only in grunts, so that Irène's first impression of the male of the species came from this personification of ignorance. When she started her schooling at the local parish she found other children like herself whose fathers had left for parts unknown. Hauteville, Hamburg, heaven, or hell; to the children they were just names. So it came as a shock to learn that this strange woman from Paris, and not Mama Margot, was her mother.

"She couldn't believe it," Nicole explained. "They didn't even look alike. Grandmama's eyes were brown, her hair black, while Mama was blonde, like me, with blue eyes. She told Mama that she'd inherited her father's good looks. When Mama asked who her father was and where he'd gone, all she would say was that he was a handsome American soldier who had loved her very much but that now she was married to a Comte and her name had been changed to deBrisay. At the same time, she discovered Paris had been her birthplace and not the farm as she'd always believed; that the farm, the house, and Mama Margot had all been arranged, bought and paid for by Grandmama."

"It must have come as an awful shock," Marais said sympathetically.

"Oh, it did! She never forgave Grandmama for the deception. In a way she blamed Mama Margot too for hiding the truth from her all those years. It seems silly to you or me who have always known who their mother and father were. But look at it from Mama's point of view. Suddenly the only parent she'd ever known had turned into a fraud while a total stranger suddenly became her mother. Grandmama would tell her nothing, only those same vague stories she told me about that village where she'd grown up. She once took me through the Charleville school she attended, but she wouldn't take me to her village. You see, she was hiding something — from Mama and from me."

Restlessly, Nicole came to her feet, crossing the fractured lino-leum to the window. Outside it had started raining. Thin wet tracings skittered down the panes carving channels through the grime and turning the view into a dapple of impressionistic shapes and forms. She stared at the street below as she continued her story.

Irène's entrance to university had coincided with the Comte's divorcing her mother. Forensic medicine at the State University at Lille had been her choice of study, but Marie would not hear of it. Irène was summoned to Paris and chauffeured daily to and from her classes at the Sorbonne. Living in Passy with Marie deBrisay was pure hell. Irène lasted a year before meeting Charles Daladier, a third-year engineering student, and marrying him to escape the tyranny of Passy.

"It was to get away from Grandmama. At least in the beginning, though I know she loved my father. He was just the sort of man Mama needed, a kind, generous soul with a sympathetic smile or word for everyone." She mused, "That's not much of a description, is it? Because he was lots of other things too. But that's how I remember him best. I'm sure it's how Mama remembers him. Whenever she got into one of her black moods — on top of the thunderclouds is what my brother used to call it — my father could always find a way of making her laugh. I haven't seen Mama laugh since he died. Smile, yes, but she has never laughed. I think that's sad, don't you?"

He nodded to her reflection in the window.

She turned, resting both hands behind her on the paint-flecked sill, half sitting, half standing against it. "Anyway, that's why Mama and Grandmama never saw eye to eye." For a moment she studied him in the quizzical manner of someone searching for a long word for a crossword puzzle.

"Tell me something, Roger Marais, Canadian citizen from Montréal."

"If I can." He swung his legs off the bed to a motet of squeaks and sat on its edge. The damn thing was uncomfortable in any position.

"Commissaire Boule told me that you were convicted for the murder of a policeman. At the time I didn't believe him. Too many other things on my mind, I suppose. Is it true or false?"

His gaze never shifted. "It's true and false."

"I don't understand."

"It's true that I was convicted for the crime. False that I committed it."

She looked doubtful. "How is that possible?"

He could sense her shrinking from him. "Our system isn't that different from yours. When the *flics* decide you're guilty then that's it. Game over. Justice, truth, compassion or logic don't enter into it."

He could see that she didn't believe him. "Let me tell you what happened, then you decide."

It had started with a rack of pool at Cormier's Billiard Parlor in downtown Rue St. Denis on a Friday afternoon in June. He'd cleaned a pair in six straight games. They were visiting from Longeuil just across the river. Young guys with shoulder-length hair and nails chewed to the quick. They asked him for a lift home. Why not? He was up six hundred and fifty dollars. The least he could do was drive them across the Jacques Cartier Bridge. They all squeezed into the front seat of his fire-engine red Mustang.

As they were cruising along Rue Montcalm the older of the two asked him to stop in front of a branch of the Imperial Bank of Commerce. They had a government check to cash. Marais obliged, waiting outside in a no parking zone, windows open, radio turned up, motor running.

Two or three minutes passed, long enough for Bob Dylan to finish his song and Stevie Wonder to get a few bars into his. A police cruiser pulled in behind the Mustang. Its driver got out. Marais, who had been thumping time to the music on his padded dash, didn't notice the cop until he asked to see Marais's ownership and driver's license. Disgusted, he turned down the radio and reached into a hip pocket for his wallet and ID. At the same moment gunfire erupted inside the bank, muffled cracks like beer bottles smashing against rocks.

The policeman dropped his notebook and went into a crouch until only the top of his cap was visible outside the door. He ordered Marais to keep his hands on the steering wheel where he could see them.

Seconds later the two men backed out of the bank. Both held white canvas money satchels and black pistols. Not until they turned for the car did they see the cruiser. The other policeman was already out on the pavement, kneeling behind the front fender. He and the older punk traded bullets. The cop was the better shot. The younger one made it to the car, tossed his bag onto the front seat and ran back to his partner who was already dying on a slab of sidewalk. He jerked the other satchel from his hand and raced to the car screaming: "Go! Go! Go!" as he leapt inside.

A .38 caliber police special on the end of a uniformed sleeve passed in front of Marais's nose. Everything seemed suddenly to slip into slow motion, like the sound of an old 78 r.p.m. record when the switch is on 33⅓.

The cop started to say something but the punk shot him in the face. Marais stiffened. For a split second he thought the flash and bullet had been aimed at him and had dealt a mortal blow. The breath froze in his lungs. He expected a fading light but it never came.

Then the blue sleeve jerked back across his nose and the gun exploded before his eyes in red flame and acrid smoke. It dropped into his lap while the hand that had held it slipped slowly out the window and disappeared from view. Marais's ears rang with the pealing of a hundred church bells, his eyes saw a myriad of brilliant pinpoint lights, and still he held fast to the steering wheel.

Then silence came. A terrible silence where the tiniest sound filtered in from the other side of the universe with a soft and deadly whisper:

"One teeny little move and I blow your fucking brains out. So, very, very slowly now: pass those guns out to me," the dead cop's partner ordered. He held the hot tip of his gun barrel pressed against Marais's ear.

And Roger Marais did exactly as he was told.

"I had no witnesses. When you're sitting alone in your car waiting for two men to come out of a bank they've just robbed, how do you go about proving that you don't know them? You see the problem?" To his relief she nodded. "But I was lucky. The judge gave me only twelve years for being an accessory. He could have given me life. Another triumph for the little people." He watched her reaction closely, satisfied that he had made his point.

"How can such things happen?"

He shrugged. "Luck of the draw. If I had waited a week before coming to Paris, poor old Dimitrios would already have been dead and your police would be out looking for the real killer."

"It's not fair!"

He sighed. "Tell me about it."

Moscow, 10:20 P.M.

Feodor Ivanovich Bransky lived alone on the eighth floor of a massive apartment complex on the Mozhaiskoye Highway. Bransky was the logical starting point, in Sultal's opinion. Titov agreed. Bransky had signed the original communication to Brussels in 1981. After a phone call to the KGB Director of Personnel produced their man's home address, an elated Titov insisted they go to him at once. Reluctantly, Sultal changed out of uniform and they drove across the city to find Bransky.

Number 17 was the last door at the end of the hall. A corner apartment, which meant that Bransky had windows on two sides. He'd used his rank to get the best view of the river.

Sultal hammered the door. After a moment he hammered it again, this time longer and louder. There was a snick of sliding bolts as Bransky opened up.

"Yes, what is it?" he demanded.

"Comrade Feodor Ivanovich?" Sultal stated in his flat official voice.

"Yes." Bransky hesitated, a fleck of uncertainty crossing his eyes. He had the pale face of a man who shuns sunlight.

Titov produced an ID folder, holding it close enough for him to read his rank. The effect was instantaneous.

"Comrade Colonel, come in, please."

Bransky stood uncertainly in the center of the room trying to decide which of the two visitors was in charge. Since Sultal had produced no identification and sat down uninvited while Titov remained standing, he assumed Sultal to be a high-ranking Party official and Titov his assistant.

"Something to drink, Comrades?" Bransky suggested.

Titov waved his hand. Sultal roused himself a little. "What have you got that's good?"

Bransky winked respectfully. "The best, Comrade Minister. A bottle of Kohjakbi. And it's unopened!" He beamed.

Sultal scratched his dimpled chin. "Well, what are you waiting for, man, go get it!"

Bransky brought three dirty tumblers down from a cupboard above the sink.

"Not for me, Comrade," Titov said brusquely. "I have something I'd like you to read."

"Is it official or unofficial, Comrades?"

"Just do as you're told, Captain," Sultal told him evenly.

Which made it official to Bransky. He filled the tumblers, bringing one to Sultal.

"Na zdarovye!" he toasted respectfully.

Sultal grunted, tossed the brandy down with a gulp, and passed the glass back for a refill.

Titov handed Bransky the copy of his Brussels transmission. "Do you happen to remember sending this?"

Bransky gave a brisk nod. "You must understand, Comrades, I only follow orders."

"That," Sultal observed coldly, "is exactly what Lavrentia Pavlovich Beria said before he was executed at Lubyanka in 1953. You see, Comrade, everything depends on whose orders you were following as to whether or not you are guilty of a crime."

"Read this," Titov ordered, producing the most recent message from Moscow Center signed by Galinovsky in which all knowledge of Bransky's 1981 communication was denied. After reading it slowly he passed it back to Titov. His hand shook.

"Any comment, Captain?" Titov stuffed the papers into his file. "Somebody is telling lies to the Brussels Embassy, aren't they? Either it's got to be you in 1981 or our Comrade Galinovsky yesterday. We're here to find out who and why." He sat back waiting.

Bransky poured himself another brandy. "You must understand me, Comrades, when I tell you that I'm a loyal officer and Party man. I do what I'm told — like you."

Titov waved the words aside with annoyance. "Can we dispense with the rhetoric? We're not here to arrest you. We're seeking information. Let's start at the beginning. And sit down before you spill that drink."

Bransky took a straight-backed chair, positioning himself in the center of the room between his inquisitors. When at last he spoke his voice was nearly calm.

"The information contained in that original transmission to Brussels came from the European Records Branch of the GRU. It wasn't a KGB source. We collected it into our Alien Agent computer bank when the GRU replied to one of our standard inquiries for background details on suspected foreign sympathizers; those in a position to provide technical assistance and information to the local KGB Resident. But the GRU's response was considered too vague to be of value until Colonel Radomsky — that's Colonel Vladimir Alexeyevich — spoke with a senior GRU records officer. "Send it as is," he told me. So I put it out to Brussels in its original form and entered a computer transcript with the Alien Agent storage bank. That's the proper procedure, you must understand."

"Who was this senior GRU officer? Titov inquired.

"General Nikolai Vereshchagin," Bransky said, readjusting his bathrobe, which had opened at the knees. Titov saw that he had nothing on under the robe. "I didn't know it had been the general himself that Vladimir Alexeyevich had been talking to over the phone. How could I? I was a green lieutenant, and colonels don't confide in lieutenants, do they?" He paused a moment as if actually expecting a reply to the question.

Titov knew Vereshchagin. One of the GRU's old untouchables. In theory, a warm comradeship supposedly existed between the military intelligence and state security agencies but in reality each was fiercely jealous of the other's role. Wherever a GRU officer was posted abroad for purposes of military intelligence gathering, a KGB officer worked alongside him to ensure the same information reached Moscow Center. By law all GRU information files were available to the KGB upon request. But generally it was a one-way street for information, because the KGB was not required to open its files to anybody except its Kremlin masters. The men inside the Kremlin were realists. They knew that the only organized force capable of toppling the government was the Soviet Army. The KGB's function was to make sure that never happened.

"Go on, Captain," Titov prompted.

Bransky shrugged. "That was the end of it. I never thought about the matter again until last winter." He massaged his forehead, bringing back the memories. "Mid-November, it was. I got a call to report to Personnel Classification for reassignment. Temporary duty with the GRU. Not a bad posting, more of an overseeing job than any actual work. And I got my captaincy to boot. They gave me eighteen men and an old commissar to work with the GRU crowd." He sucked reflectively on his bottom lip. "The GRU had this warehouse full of files at Solntsevo. Some of the stuff went as far back as 1923, if you can believe it. Most of it was dated junk — which was why GRU wanted to dump it. Every item had to be checked before it was burned in case something popped up that should be routed into KGB information storage. That was my job — checking it out. Crazy, if you ask me. To do it properly would have taken three lifetimes.

"By month's end we were up to 1925, and trashing just about everything. My commissar, Lebedev, had lost interest and spent most of his time either drunk or sleeping it off in my office. Don't misunderstand me, Comrades, I did my job. But when ten boxes of paper covering the Baltic arsenals of 1924 turned up along with crates of old uniform designs and Weimar Republic naval secrets, you wouldn't expect me to waste time sifting it, would you?" He shook his head. "Of course not, so I signed the trashing orders and sent everything out to the furnace. You'd have done the same."

"Early in February General Vereshchagin roared into the compound with a big ZIL and a pansy NCO. The snow was up to our knees. An inspection visit to see how we were getting along with the job — at least that was his story. It didn't fit."

"Why?" Titov was curious.

"Heroes of the Soviet Union don't arrive unannounced in the middle of winter to visit drunken commissars and junior captains in old unheated barns, at least in my limited experience. They wait until spring, don't they? Or send a colonel — no offense."

He had a point, although Titov refrained from comment.

"Lebedev had served under Koniev in a Guards Regiment during the Battle of Berlin. Forever telling me what a great goddamn hero he was and how he'd known Zhukov, Petrov, and Rokossovsky personally. To hear him tell it you'd think the generals spent half their time conferring with Lebedev on tactics instead of fighting the war. But I'll be damned if the old son of a bitch didn't know Vereshchagin. 'Hey, Nikolai Timofeevich!' he yells as the general comes through the door with his pansy. 'Hah! I thought they'd have put you out to pasture by now!' And they embraced; kisses on both cheeks. Why, Lebedev even started to cry a little. Turned out they had fought together in the front line all the way from Warsaw, across the river Oder and on to Berlin.

"Lebedev showed him around the place as if he'd been doing all the work and I'd been the one asleep. He poked boxes, barked at our noncoms, cracked jokes. But I could see the general wasn't interested. When we got back to the office he sent his pansy out to sit with the driver so we could talk privately. 'Comrades,' he said confidentially, 'I need your help to protect the memory and reputation of an old friend and hero of the Soviet Union. Will you help?' Before agreeing I waited until old Lebedev had nodded, figuring that if a GRU general and a senior commissar decided to do something then it must be legitimate, and if I valued my career I'd be a fool not to go along."

The logic was irrefutable.

"Marshal Yuli Kurminov," he nodded, "that's who the general wanted to protect. 'Protect his sacred memory' — those were his exact words, Colonel." He crossed his legs, decorously resetting the bathrobe. He had very hairy legs. "The Comrade general told us that back in 1946 when the army was being purged of wartime revisionists, the Marshal gave some inaccurate information to military intelligence during his interrogation. His statement was placed in GRU files where it lay dormant until July 1981. That's when I processed the Brussels inquiry. Of course I didn't know what he was talking about. Why would I? I mean, do you have any idea of the number of alien background requests that come through the European Bureau in a week? Then he brought out copies of our internal communications with the GRU together with their reply on the Frenchwoman, Adelaine Mercure. When I'd read it through I remembered the case because it was one of the few times Comrade Radomsky had queried a GRU source for more details." Bransky shrugged. "You know what happened after that."

"GRU said to send the material as it stood." Titov said.

"Exactly."

"Even though it was false," Sultal rebuked him.

Bransky turned his head. "Not false, Comrade Minister, just inaccurate."

"Weren't you suspicious, Captain?" Titov asked.

"It wasn't my place to be suspicious, Colonel. But now that you ask, yes, I was. I felt Comrade Radomsky should have used KGB authority and requested GRU to produce the complete dossiers on the woman; sources, backup, everything they had on file. If the Brussels Resident had come back with a request for additional information maybe that's what would have happened."

Titov gave a wintry smile. "But Brussels didn't, did they?"

Bransky shook his head. "Nothing until a week later when we got notification that the woman had been turned and was to be entered into our Alien Agent files. I keyed the computer entry myself, cross-indexing it with our GRU source."

Sultal came off the wall, balancing on the balls of his feet like a boxer looking for an opening. "You haven't told us what the general wanted you to do."

Bransky hesitated, lowering his gaze to the pitted linoleum floor covering. In places it had worn through to the cement. The only sounds in the room were a dripping tap and an annoying squeak in one of Sultal's shoes as he rocked back and forth. At last Bransky looked up.

"He wanted all GRU source references on the woman that were in the KGB files erased."

"What about her GRU records?" Titov demanded.

"He said he'd already taken care of that himself. All he wanted from me was to clear the KGB computer of any reference to a GRU source on Adelaine Mercure because it was inaccurate."

Sultal stopped squeaking. The faucet paused its drip. Silence hung on a thread of anticipation, then broke.

"And did you do what General Vereshchagin asked?" Titov inquired, not unkindly.

"Yes, Comrade Colonel, I did."

Paris, 11:37 P.M.

A great weariness had settled over Boule as he stretched out on the camp cot in his office. His brain was tired. A tired brain makes little mistakes. Little mistakes add up to big mistakes. Two days ago it had been a simple, straightforward murder investigation. He'd found a reasonable suspect and at least one presentable witness and had the situation firmly in hand. Now everything appeared to be slipping out of his control. Face it, he told himself. No one had control of events.

He squirmed on the uncomfortable cot, fighting to shut his mind against a succession of intruding thoughts. A solitary desk lamp in the middle of the small office held the surrounding darkness at bay. Next to the lamp a black telephone sat poised and waiting to ring. Boule stared at it with torpid disinterest.

"Call me the moment you hear anything. I don't care what time of the day or night," were Dubé's parting instructions. He spoke figuratively, of course, the way he always did when there was a crisis. Boule could imagine the reaction if he actually dialed his chief at four in the morning with an update. But maybe this time Dubé meant it. "We need to get to the bottom of this business." With the corollary, "I'm not ruling out a conspiracy within the department. Think on that, Boule!" As if Boule was one of the arch-conspirators in the plot. Surely someone trying to usurp Dubé's position would select a less oblique approach than removing a prisoner from detention.

But someone had done it. Someone intimately familiar with procedures at the PJ. Who? Boule's hands were tied. No help was forthcoming from other departments until he found those responsible for the kidnapping. Kidnapping? Did he think the abductors would make ransom demands for their captive? Sourly, he realized that Dubé hadn't thought the matter through sufficiently to come up with a sensible plan. He was reacting instead of acting. The full resources of the country's policing departments were placed out of bounds, and Boule would have to content himself with three detectives and his own experience to find the fugitive. "Try it for a couple of days," Dubé told him. "If nothing turns up then I'll reconsider the advisability of bringing in other branches."

By which time the bird would have flown and he'd be looking for another suspect to take Marais's place. Dubé was an idiot.

First Boule had phoned his wife to say he'd be spending the night at the PJ.

"You've been given both murders to solve? When does Dubé expect you to sleep?" She sounded annoyed. He could almost see her eyes flashing with indignation.

"He doesn't. I'm too valuable to waste on the horizontal."

That brought a laugh. She asked him about Marie deBrisay. Radio and television bulletins had been pouring out the story all afternoon.

"What was she like?"

"From the Ardennes."

"Really?"

"Charleville-Mézières, to be exact. About your age. Family name Carnot."

"What a coincidence!"

She always enjoyed discussing his investigations. He had spent that morning talking about the Rue du Bac affair with her across the breakfast table. She agreed that for the moment Marais was his most likely suspect, though at other times some of her suggestions were inspirational.

"You didn't by any chance know her, did you, Gabrielle?"

"Carnot ... Carnot. ..." She hesitated. "No, the name is not familiar. Have you any clues?"

He sighed. "Nothing concrete, I'm afraid. Colette, the part-time housemaid, might have seen the killer. Other than that it's a process of elimination." He told her about Vadim's sexual athletics, Bettina and the cook's conspiracy and Nicole's disappearance with Marais, and the fact that he was very tired.

"Now you mustn't overdo it, Bernard!" she reminded him sharply. "You're not as young as you used to be — none of us are. Promise me you'll get a good night's rest."

"I promise."

"Goodnight, Bernard."

As always, Gabrielle understood. Next he had sent Fauré and Monceau home to get some sleep, extracting promises from each that they would be in his office by eight the next morning. Finally, he had asked André to stop off on his way across town and interview the property reclamation officer to see if the man remembered any specific details about those two mysterious police officers who had collected Marais.

As he settled one more time into the cot he thought that if that fool operator working the Passy telephone patch had reported the incoming call from Marais to the granddaughter instead of waiting until he went off shift they might have caught their man on the Rue Vavin. Too late now. But why Rue Vavin? Vaguely he remembered there was a reason for Marais choosing that street, but before the thought could coalesce he was fast asleep.

11:54 P.M.

Near midnight the vehicles passing through the Porte Maillot in and out of the Bois de Boulogne change from private cars to slow cruising cabs, most carrying a prostitute in the front seat next to the driver. Daggar Paoli had parked his car under the trees and turned on the flashers. He lit a cigarette and waited, watching the taxis drift past, their wipers sloshing at the rain. A red Audi pulled in front of him and stopped. Its driver turned on his flashing lights and ran back to Paoli's car. When his wet face appeared at the passenger window Daggar unlocked the door.

"Lousy night, Commandant," the man said. He had broad Slavic features with close-set eyes. Ginger hair lay plastered across his scalp. He shut the door with a grunt, wedging himself against Paoli.

Within the minute a black vw Rabbit pulled in front of the Slavic man's car. Its occupants ran back to join Paoli. The last man apologized for being late. Paoli stubbed his cigarette.

"The target's name is Roger Marais," he told them without preamble. "A French Canadian. He was supposed to die tonight at eight. Someone erred. I've called you in to correct the matter."

The Slavic man shifted his position so he could open his window a crack. The air within the car was very close. Paoli's gaze held fast on the rain-smeared windshield as if turning his head might cause him to lose the thread of his monologue.

"My information is that Marais will contact an expatriate named Robert Pinot for help. Pinot has a flat on the Rue Vavin. He lives alone." A police car crept past the window then sped away. "They are old friends," Paoli continued, "so Pinot will help. There is a possibility Marais will be accompanied by a young woman. An unfortunate liaison, but one which in no way should affect your instructions. Understood?"

All three nodded.

"Questions?"

There were no questions. Paoli gave them Pinot's apartment number, then reached across the Slavic man's lap and opened the door. "Call me when the job is finished," he said.

FRIDAY, JULY 13

Paris, 12:07 A.M.

Fouquet, to Marais's surprise, turned out to be an ugly dwarf with a face as long as a Lenten Sunday. He suppressed a desire to lift him onto one of the café stools. Fouquet managed unaided and with a practiced agility. When they were all more or less at eye level with each other, Pinot introduced him. The dwarf took Marais's hand in an iron grip and murmured pleasantly, the sound rumbling from his small body in basso profundo. Pinot came straight to the point.

"My friend requires a passport, Marcel."

Fouquet scrutinized Marais carefully, moving from the Bally footwear to his expensive sports jacket.

"What's he done?"

Pinot gave a disarming smile. "Nothing that getting him out of the country won't solve."

The dwarf swung around to the counter and studied the evening's menu chalked on a big blackboard tilted against the wall behind a row of wine bottles. He ordered onion soup and a glass of Bordeau.

"You have photographs?"

They had taken a color strip of three in a coin-operated booth on the way over. Marais had parted his hair down the middle like a teenager and with a contrived studious expression looked no different than dozens of other young men he'd seen sprawled on the grass with textbooks in the Luxembourg Gardens. With horn-rimmed glasses he could have been a card-carrying communist from the Sorbonne. He passed the pictures along the counter. Fouquet pocketed them without a glance.

"What nationality?"

"Anything but French. He has an accent — like me," Pinot explained unnecessarily.

"No one has an accent like you," the dwarf observed, and Pinot laughed. To Marais he confided in his deep voice, "My fee is thirty thousand francs. Do you have such a sum?"

"He has it," Pinot volunteered.

"Your height and weight?" Fouquet's voice was so soft it was difficult to hear it over the clatter of voices and cutlery.

Marais told him. The waiter brought the soup and wine. Pinot paid. Fouquet stirred the crusty soup.

"Everything I sell is stolen," he said confidentially in case Marais had mistaken his source of supply as the Ministry of Foreign Affairs. "I have friends working the hotels and tour buses. Mine is a brokerage service, so my stock is considerable. No doubt there will be something fitting your general description. I simply switch the pictures. My work is first class. But there's no guarantee you won't be arrested the first time you present the passport at a border crossing."

"When can I have it?" Marais pressed.

Fouquet slurped his soup and took a swallow of the Bordeaux. "Say at eleven o'clock tomorrow morning in front of the Omnia Theater. And don't forget to bring the money — in cash. Understand?"

Marais understood.

Outside at the curb they waited for the Renault. They had told Danielle and Nicole to circle the block. Pinot lit a cigarette, an exotic oval filter tip. He stared glumly at the approaching traffic, considering his options.

"Where to next?" Marais asked.

"A safe place where you can hole up for the night. Is the lady staying or going home?"

"Staying. What about another one of those first-class hotels in Montmartre?"

Pinot shook his head. "Too risky. Anyone holding a room over two hours gets a knock on the door from management. Those guys operate a high-turnover business."

"What about your place?"

"No way, Rog. I don't need your heat."

"Your concierge has already seen my face, for Christ's sake."

"But she hasn't seen us together, and that makes all the difference. I want to keep it that way."

He was being obstinate.

"Sure, Bobby, whatever you say."

"You think I'm being unreasonable?" Pinot asked.

Marais shrugged. He could have reminded his friend about the time back in Montréal when he had provided the airtight alibi that Pinot needed to stay out of jail. Pinot took a deep drag on the oval, expelling twin smoke streams through his nostrils.

"Remember what the Monk used to say: never shit in your own nest. It's the reason gorillas are nearly extinct. Besides leaving a bad smell the Monk said it was a sure sign of moral decay. Paris is my nest. I don't want to shit in it. This is my country now. And you're out of bounds."

"I'm also in trouble," Marais told him. "But I won't rock the boat, Bobby."

Pinot grimaced. "It's too late, Rog. You already have."

His Renault arrived curbside. He spun the lighted cigarette into the gutter where it died with a hiss. Danielle slid over as Pinot got in on the driver's side; Marais climbed into the back beside Nicole.

"Tomorrow morning at eleven," Marais told Nicole.

She gave a quizzical look to the back of Pinot's head as they rejoined the traffic. There was an uncomfortable silence. "What's wrong with him?" she whispered. Marais shrugged.

The car swung about the floodlit circle at the Arc de Triomphe and arrowed down Avenue Victor Hugo.

"Where are we headed?" Marais inquired finally.

"Danielle's flat near the Bois. You two can spend the night there. There's only one bedroom but the sofa's comfortable. I'll take Danielle home with me. That way everything looks normal and if anyone asks I can claim we never made contact." He didn't sound happy about the arrangement.

Nicole touched his shoulder hesitantly. "We're causing you a lot of trouble, aren't we?"

"Yes, you are," Pinot agreed. "I'm insane. Let's not talk about it."

The flat, in a new high-rise apartment building, had an underground garage and a spectacular sixteenth-floor view of the Bois de Boulogne from a small curved balcony. Gold damask drapes tracking the full width of the picture windows muzzled the traffic sounds. The furnishings were small-scale and functionally comfortable, graced by a woman's touch in the choice of colors and wall hangings.

Pinot sat in the only upholstered armchair while Danielle opened a clever little liquor cabinet that folded out from a bookcase. She poured everyone a Courvoisier. Pinot held up his glass.

"What the hell! Here's to a clean getaway — and no hair left behind when it's all over."

Marais drank to that. Pinot seemed to have accepted his involvement, and the atmosphere eased considerably. They small-talked their way to the bottom of the snifters until Danielle smothered a yawn, apologized, and yawned again. She worked at the Air France ticket office and had to be at work by seven, Pinot explained. She went into the bedroom to collect her uniform and overnight case.

"If the phone rings don't answer," Pinot warned on their way out. "I'll be back around nine-thirty for breakfast."

When they'd gone Marais went out on the balcony and breathed in the night air. By tomorrow night he'd be over the border. Frankfurt the next morning and a direct flight to Montréal. Home, where he knew how the game was played and the names of the players.

"He really didn't want to help you, did he?" Nicole joined him. Her hands rested on the railing. She gave an involuntary shiver.

"He's been down the route before with other visiting Québécois who called for help. Bobby's a sucker for a sad story."

"And what happened?"

"He played Sister of Mercy. After a few years they all flew home for token jail terms and instant paroles. Bobby stayed behind. He's a little bitter about it all."

She huddled her arms around her chest protectively, clasping her shoulders to ward off the chilly night air. She looked very beautiful standing in the half-light, and very vulnerable.

"You should put on a sweater or jacket. There's probably something hanging in the closet," he offered without making a move to assist in the search.

"I'm okay. If I get cold I'll go inside," she told him logically. "For a minute I want to enjoy the peace and quiet out here. It feels and smells like the country."

He could have put out an arm and drawn her into his warmth. The excuse, if not the direct invitation, had been provided. But he held back. Eight years in prison had done that to him — made him into someone who regarded women not as companions but as objects to be used. He didn't want to do that to Nicole.

Nevertheless, he felt the need. For Nicole or her femaleness? He studied her profile. Her eyes were shut. She stood sniffing the pungent rain-washed night. A bedroom tussle might be good for both of them. But he wondered whether she was still unsure of him. Back at the hotel when he'd tried explaining the circumstances that sent him to prison, the truth had sounded implausible even to his ears. He could sense her disbelief when he'd finished.

"I think I'll take a shower and go to bed." Nicole said.

She stepped through the doorway like a slender song, breaking that momentary spell of magic he had felt standing beside her. He followed her inside and drew the drapes.

When she'd gone into the bedroom, he tried the television, switching over the three available channels. Too late for a news update. He heard the bathroom door close. Unconsciously, he listened for the snick of the lock. Instead the shower exploded into muffled thunder. He turned off the television and poured another brandy. His mental timeclock was still set to Montréal. Food was what he needed, not booze. He found a package of sliced cold cuts and a jar of pickles in the fridge and fixed himself a thick sandwich. The shower continued. What was her usual time for a shower, he wondered? He imagined her long-legged and naked like a woodland water nymph. The hand holding the sandwich began to tremble.

He took a bite from the sandwich and chewed thoughtfully. Surely she had been in there too long? Maybe something had happened. He pictured her lying unconscious at the bottom of the tub, blood swirling down the drain in pale pink bathwater.

Quickly he set his sandwich on the counter and went to the bathroom door. He knocked lightly, his hand on the knob. No reply. She had left it unlocked. He stepped inside. Her outline moved behind the glass partition. She was alive and unhurt. Wet fingers slid the panel open.

"I was ready to give up on you," she smiled. "Do hurry! I'm beginning to feel like a lobster."

He undressed quickly and joined her. As she soaped him and he groaned with the pleasure of it he prayed to whatever deity governed such events that this time he wouldn't feel shabby in the morning.

1:38 A.M.

Earlier that evening when François Daumier was making love to Monique, it occurred to him that he was probably the only minister of the government in bed with his own wife at that moment. His confrères enjoyed no such sexual constancy and were either involved with mistresses, divorced, separated, or recovering from the effects of a prostatectomy — a dreadful thought. Two were practicing homosexuals and one a widower of such advanced years that any sexual plumbing left to him had long since ceased to function. Daumier in fact suspected that he had become Minister of the Interior because of his wife's unique sexual qualities. Had he chosen anyone but Monique, by now he'd no doubt be making a fool of himself with some younger woman, spending extravagantly, and wasting valuable time in pursuit of an elusive sexual nirvana. Would the President have given him the Interior Ministry if Daumier had lacked marital constancy? Probably not, for the job required a man whose moral integrity was without blemish and above reproach. With the Defense or Finance portfolios a system of internal checks and balances tended to prevent excesses by the responsible Ministers. As Minister of the Interior he was a law unto himself. Monique had made it all possible. There was no question in his mind about that.

However, a price had been exacted for his successful marriage: a slowly swinging sword of Damocles hung suspended above his head threatening at any minute to drop, slicing the honor of the government of France to pieces. That price was the past. His past, and hers, and the secret they shared. Even thinking about it now in their warm bedroom sanctuary, with Monique asleep in his arms, caused him palpitations.

Atrial fibrillation. A twitching of the heart muscle, giving him a feeling of bird's wings fluttering within his chest. "Stress and old age, Daumier, stress and old age," Dr. Évard told him. It was true his job was stressful. But old age at sixty-five? Ridiculous. His small compact body was still in superb physical condition even if most of his dark curly hair had long since grayed and gone. But that was hereditary, nothing to do with the heart. His father and grandfather had both been bald in middle age.

He felt the fluttering. Gently, he disengaged himself from Monique. Shifting his body position helped still the wings. She stirred; her breathing tempo altered for a moment then resumed the slow steady rhythm of deep sleep. Poor darling. After their lovemaking she had cried herself to sleep in great soul-shattering sobs. Almost forty years had passed since that autumn afternoon when they had brought her before him, ragged and dirty, her face a misery with one eye swollen nearly shut from fighting off her tormentors. Why didn't every memory slip away unnoticed when the physical pain was gone?

He lay remembering the smell of sweat and plaster in the small interrogation room at Mézières. She hung between two Maquis, young men like himself, wearing FFI armbands and side-arms. They had raped her a few minutes earlier. One had a dribbled semen stain on his trousers that was still wet.

The memory set off the fluttering again. Very slowly he eased himself off the bed and into his slippers and dressing gown. The gown, a dark blue Shantung silk with delicately embroidered lions, had been her present to him on his last birthday. He was a Leo, she a Pisces. He'd reciprocated with a gold brooch in the shape of a fish with oversized ruby eyes. According to her astrology charts — she subscribed to the *Astrologer's Monthly* — they were not supposed to be compatible. He'd have done better with a Virgo or a Sagittarius, she claimed half in amusement. It was difficult to know whether she believed in such rubbish or used it simply to tease.

He stood a moment in the near darkness looking down at her. She was still lovely as an angel. Her dark hair spilled gracefully across the satin pillowcase as though arranged by a professional photographer. Her small breasts had sunk. But no matter, at least they didn't sag, and their neat pink nipples still coned and hardened seductively whenever she was aroused. He adjusted the bedsheet, covering her shoulders, then turned out the night lamp and tiptoed softly from the room.

Near the bottom of the stairs a man suddenly materialized from the shadows like a giant hologram. Every cabinet minister was provided with around-the-clock police protection. Try as he might he could never get used to bodyguards skulking about the house and grounds at all hours, scaring the wits out of everyone, himself included, when they popped out of thin air.

He waved his hand in annoyance. "I'll be in my study." Such a bizarre way to live, imprisoned in his own house as protection against the citizens he was supposed to serve. Soon he could turn the job over to his successor, and good riddance. They'd go back to the Ardennes and buy a small country estate where Monique could plant vegetables and flowers while he wrote erudite editorials in the regional papers and presented prizes at local fairs. Together they would savor their old age.

He turned on the fluorescent desk lamp in his study and sat down with a sigh. Physically he was tired, yet his brain refused to shut down. For two days he had been on edge with no word from Beaubien. He'd left everything to the Sûreté's Director. Had that been wise? Who else could he turn to for help without getting personally involved?

He reached for a cigarette from the humidor on the corner of his desk. It was empty. The digital clock's numbers flicked. 1:43 A.M. In one of the desk drawers he found a very old package of stale cigarettes. He lit one, filling his lungs with smoke, then gave a contented cough.

He reflected once more on Beaubien. There was always the chance the coverup would fail. Then there'd be no erudite editorials or prize presentations. He'd be forced to resign in disgrace. That mustn't happen. He realized that he should have been more forthcoming with his Sûreté Director, given him the complete story instead of forcing him to work in the dark. He'd call Beaubien in the morning and meet him for lunch. They could discuss details.

His motives weren't entirely selfish. There were after all others besides his own wife and children and their families whose lives would be ruined if the facts became public knowledge. Franco-German relations would suffer. The Russians would have a propaganda field day.

He blew an imperfect smoke ring. Yes, he would call Beaubien and together they would work out a swift solution to the problem. Beaubien understood the need for discretion. As a closet homosexual he was the epitome of intelligent sensibility in the conduct of his private life. He blew another smoke ring. A perfect halo floated toward the ceiling. Daumier felt better already.

1:45 A.M.

When Pinot slid his apartment key into the lock and opened the door his mind still dwelled on the problem of his friend Marais. So when he was confronted by a heavyset man with a Slavic face who asked, "Roger Marais?" Pinot very foolishly replied "Yes?"

It was only after he'd spoken and felt Danielle's hand tighten on his arm that he realized they were in danger. There were two others with the Slavic man. They stood well back on either side of the room holding Ingram M-10 nine-millimeter submachine guns equipped with silencers. Danielle began to scream, Pinot to explain — too late. She took sixteen bullets in the face and neck from a two-second cyclic burst; he eleven more through his head and heart. The only sounds were their falling bodies. The three men folded away their weapons and departed as silently as they had come.

Moscow, 5:00 A.M.

In Moscow the summer dawns come very early. There is a chill and stillness in the vast empty streets and sidewalks where paired uniformed militiamen stamp their feet and lounge in doorways or on corners waiting for their shift to end. From Sultal's front window Titov watched a pair on the corner across the street from the apartment. He couldn't sleep. He'd slept for three solid hours when they got home last night after dissecting Comrade Bransky. But then he'd awakened with a start, mind alert and scrambling frantically after the fragments of a complicated dream. For a few moments he had fought the soft cushions seeking sleep before giving up, pulling on his trousers and going over to the window to await the dawn.

Sultal's third-floor apartment overlooked Leningradsky Prospekt and provided an angular view of the Sovietskaya Hotel. Idly, he wondered if the living room window had been used for occasional stakeouts on hotel guests. He wondered too about Traveler. Had his straying rabbit gone to the Belgian authorities with her fantastic tale of Russian spies and NATO betrayals? He'd given himself three days to find the answers. Tomorrow was Saturday. All NATO and government offices would be closed for the weekend. World War III could never begin after four P.M. on Thursdays when everyone vanished to their dachas. He was safe until Monday. Could he have the answers by Monday? He'd better.

Titov sighed. Once the problem of Traveler's rabbit had been solved there was still the matter of Traveler himself. He was the arch-villain in the piece, too dangerous to eliminate and far too clever to cross. Something would have to be done about Traveler.

All things considered, Titov decided he wasn't doing too badly. He'd found Bransky. The young captain had fingered a GRU general as the man behind the plot, claiming the KGB erasures were done to protect the reputation of an old comrade. The story was so bizarre it had to be true.

On their way home Sultal was all for issuing a warrant to bring General Vereshchagin into Lubyanka prison for grilling. Titov talked him out of it. Dealing with generals, especially a GRU general, on an investigative basis could be very sticky when the investigating officer wasn't absolutely certain of his facts.

"Where does arresting Vereshchagin get us?" Titov demanded.

"To the bottom of the barrel."

"Or in it," Titov countered. Sultal's incautious suggestion had come from too much vodka and not enough thought. By the time they reached the apartment Sultal had sobered up enough to postpone any decision until morning.

Sometime after five Titov heard the toilet flush and turned to see Anna, bulbous and drooping under a silk kimono, go into the tiny kitchen to begin preparing breakfast. She looked wrecked. Titov murmured a good morning and was rewarded with a halfhearted smile.

"I hope you had a comfortable night, Boris," she said without enthusiasm as she turned on a tap to fill the coffee pot.

"Perfectly satisfactory. Is Marko up?"

She nodded. "Awake, but not up. He has a hangover."

"I'm not surprised."

"He drinks too much," she said gloomily.

"We all do from time to time."

"Not from time to time. All the time. Daytime, nighttime, anytime. Sometimes he frightens me when he gets so drunk. I hate to think what sort of an example he'll be for the baby."

They traded small talk in the cramped kitchen while the coffee perked and the apartment filled with pleasant breakfast smells that set his stomach rumbling in anticipation.

Anna arranged a breakfast tray and shuffled back to the bedroom. Titov gulped his coffee, ate two lovely fat sausages straight out of the frying pan with his fingers, then carted his shaving gear into the bathroom to ready himself for the day.

By 7:30 A.M. they were turning off the Ring Road onto the highway to Dmitrov and the sprawling Uchinskoye Lakes where Sultal's GRU information source said Vereshchagin had his dacha. A motorcycle militiaman at the turnoff ramp glanced at the car's official Moscow license plate and waved them through into the countryside. He was poised to salute until he saw that both occupants wore civilian clothes.

Beyond the Ring Road the land changed to undulating fields of ripening grain. Comfortable copses lay scattered among the distant slopes. Morning air blasted crisp and clean through the side vents, chilling Titov's knees. But he said nothing. He was enjoying the rich feeling of fresh air and freedom under the cloudless skies and the varieties of earthy smells that filled his nostrils.

After a bit they turned off the main highway onto a narrower secondary road. Near the top of a rise past a small village they came upon a private road that disappeared among the trees. A barricade manned by a half dozen soldiers barred the way. Sultal pulled up to the gate and stopped.

A tall slim lieutenant with a lantern jaw and ramrod back came over and asked politely for identification. The fact that they were both KGB colonels neither impressed nor cowed him. He examined their photographs carefully, bending like a gymnast at the waist so he could look in the window and check their features in the flesh. With a smart salute the identity folders were returned.

"You've been here before, Comrade Colonel?"

Although Sultal had visited the area a number of times, he admitted to needing directions for the general's dacha.

"He is expecting you?"

"Possibly."

It sounded sufficiently innocuous. The lieutenant didn't press for details. He took a small notepad from his tunic and sketched a tidy little route map complete with landmark symbols and terrain contours. Sultal thanked him. The barrier was raised.

Now that they were on the verge of confronting Vereshchagin, Titov began to worry. Russian generals on active service wielded enormous power and privilege, especially war veterans who wore the star proclaiming them to be Heroes of the Soviet Union.

The general's dacha lay at the end of a gravel road that had recently been oiled. A black ZIL limousine and two Chaikas painted an olive drab were parked under the trees next to a crudely constructed woodshed. Sultal pulled in next to the ZIL.

Whoever had built the main lodge had spared no expense. It was a huge one-storey rectangular affair built entirely with peeled white pine logs. The place glowed with warmth and comfort in the silky morning sunshine. Sultal knocked on the front door. Sounds of music drifted from an open window, something by Glazunov. The door opened.

"KGB colonels to see the General, right?"

Except for his tight cut-off jean shorts the handsome young man was naked. "I'm Georgi. One of Comrade Nikolai Timofeevich's aides," he told them as he closed the door.

Georgi led them through the front hall and into a broad reception room where giant picture windows looked out across a narrow lawn to the lake. There was a good sandy beach, a well-constructed dock with overhead lighting, and three pleasure boats tethered on slack lines to bright fluorescent buoys in the glassy water.

"Care for anything to eat, drink — coffee, vodka?"

Titov ordered coffee, Sultal a vodka. Georgi left them. Sultal lit a cigarette and eased himself into one of the padded armchairs. Titov settled into a chair and stared at the lake. Georgi reappeared with a tray. The vodka was Stolichnaya; the coffee Turkish, thick, and very hot.

Vereshchagin came striding in behind him with outstretched arms as if the visitors had arrived by invitation. "Ah, Comrade Colonels, welcome, welcome! I see Georgi has looked after you."

Titov came to his feet. After putting out his cigarette, Sultal followed suit. The general wore tan slacks, a dark orange polo shirt, and open-toed sandals. He looked more like a retired American golf pro than a Soviet Army intelligence general. There didn't appear to be an ounce of fat on his spare frame. He had a lean leathery face filled with cracks and crevasses that accordioned his cheeks when he spoke. He fairly bubbled with enthusiasm.

"It's not often I have the pleasure of entertaining our KGB comrades-in-arms," he said without a trace of sarcasm, followed by a thin-lipped smile. "Sit, sit! I hate standing when there's no reason for it. Help yourself to the bottle, Colonel. No need to observe any formality, eh?"

He folded himself into a straight-backed chair and examined them expectantly. Although the smile was casual and friendly, his gray eyes were hard and calculating.

"We have been investigating the erasure of a KGB reference file, Comrade General. Since the originating source came from GRU records, we thought you could help clarify the matter," Titov opened smoothly. "Our information comes from a KGB coding officer. His story is that the erasures were made under your authority this past February when you visited an old GRU storage warehouse at Solntsevo. You told this officer that our file information was inaccurate. That you had already removed the GRU source from your own records and wanted the KGB records to be amended accordingly. The reason you gave for your action was a desire to protect the memory of Marshal Yuli Kurminov."

He paused, waiting for some response. The general, sipping at his coffee, appeared wrapped in a reflective veil.

"On whose authority are you here, Colonel?" He addressed Titov. Sultal took the opportunity to pour himself another drink. His features had lost some of their earlier pallor.

Titov tilted his head thoughtfully. "On my authority," he told him.

"You suspect I'm guilty of some political conspiracy, is that it? Some far-reaching implications for the State?"

Titov shrugged coolly. "A record has been erased by an officer claiming to have been acting on your orders. The circumstances, you must admit, are unusual."

"I admit nothing," he said pleasantly.

"Then you deny knowing Feodor Ivanovich Bransky?" Sultal demanded with the tiniest suggestion of sarcasm. The second drink had loosened his tongue. Titov winced.

"I deny nothing, admit nothing," Vereshchagin assured him blandly. "But if you suspect a crime has been committed, your duty is to report it at once to your commanding officer together with all relevant facts. Why come bothering me? Unless of course you plan on making an arrest." The idea seemed to amuse him.

"Of course not, Sir," Titov said hastily, before Sultal got them thrown out on their ear, or worse. "We've come seeking information. It's as simple as that. But there is an urgency which makes it imperative we omit the luxury of normal chain-of-command procedures. Besides, we're not interested in causing anyone embarrassment."

"Really, Colonel? Your being here at all is an embarrassment to me."

Titov realized they were on very shaky ground. He decided to try an appeal to the general's patriotism.

"The European Bureau has been running a Resident from our Brussels Embassy. Code name Traveler. He's a man with fifteen years' field experience, our senior officer for northwest Europe. The day before yesterday he came to me with a problem." Titov shifted forward, leading with his chin. "One of his agents, a Frenchwoman by the name of Adelaine Mercure, threatened to turn herself in to NATO authorities, thereby exposing Traveler in the process. Under normal circumstances she would have been dealt with swiftly. But in this instance there were complications which made that impossible — at least until certain questions could be answered satisfactorily. It was a very delicate matter. This woman, you see, had been persuaded into working for us through fear of Traveler exposing the complete facts about a portrait of her he claimed to hold. That information originated with your office, was passed to the European Bureau in July 1981, and forwarded to Brussels. I have a copy of the original transmission, if you'd care to see it?" He reached for his attaché case. Vereshchagin waved an indolent hand and shook his head.

"That won't be necessary, Colonel. I'll take your word that it exists. Get to the point." He appeared bored by the whole business.

"The point is that Traveler hadn't the slightest idea what it all meant. But he used the information as instructed and, as predicted, Adelaine Mercure became his agent. She turned out to be of little value, although her husband was France's military representative at NATO. It might have been more productive had Traveler gone after the husband in the first place," Titov said with the perspicacity of hindsight. But he'd finally caught the general's interest. He continued: "Their relationship might have gone on until her husband's tour of duty ended and they returned to France. Then suddenly out of the blue on Wednesday she phoned for an emergency meeting and accused Traveler of treachery. Her portrait had been seen in a Paris shop window together with several others. Did he intend to betray those other women as well?" Titov sat back, giving his nose an absent-minded scratch before taking a sip of coffee.

"You see the difficulty, Comrade General? Not only didn't he know what the woman was talking about when she spoke of her own painting, but now there were other portraits, other women. Who were they? Where were they? How much had Adelaine Mercure told them about her work with Traveler? He couldn't eliminate her without knowing what risks he might be running of exposure by the others. So he came to me with his problem. Now I come to you with mine." He held the coffee cup with both hands, absorbing its warmth. "Will you give me the benefit of your advice, Comrade?"

"KGB records have nothing on Adelaine Mercure?" The general asked.

"Nothing."

He seemed pleased by this answer. "Nor GRU records, Colonel. Nothing there, I assure you."

"I accept that, Sir."

"So all you have left is that copy of the original transmission and the word of Comrade Bransky. A KGB captain, Class Two Coding clerk. My word against his. Doesn't give you much to go on, does it, Colonel?"

"But Commissar Lebedev was present when you gave your orders," Sultal reminded him through a cloud of cigarette smoke.

"True," Vereshchagin pursed his lips thoughtfully. "Alas, Comrade Lebedev is no longer with us. His excesses finally caught up with him."

"You mean he's dead?"

"Since early June. Liver and heart. Nasty combination. But a true Hero of the Soviet Union." He came to his feet, signifying the discussion had ended. "You want my advice, Colonel? Tell your Traveler to use his best judgment in dealing with the woman. I doubt if he has anything to fear from the others."

"I wish it were that simple, Sir." Titov spoke regretfully. "But if I am put in the position of being unable to answer any of Traveler's questions, then he will surrender himself to NATO authorities."

"You mean defect?" To a patriot the idea was inconceivable.

"Exactly."

"He told you this?"

"He did. We have until Monday morning to come up with the answers. I assure you, Comrade General, my only interest in this affair — and the Directorate's only interest — is to avert a disaster to our Western Europe network through a simple misunderstanding. It is in the interests of Mother Russia that you tell us everything you know. Nothing you say will ever be used against you now or in the future. You have our word."

Vereshchagin looked at Sultal for confirmation and was treated to a verifying nod.

"On the other hand," Titov continued wistfully, "if our man defects, the truth about the woman, the portraits, and your part in the affair will certainly come to light during the subsequent investigations. Somewhere the blame will have to be attached, punishment meted out.... " He left the implications dangling.

The general went over to the window and stood staring at his bay, hands clasped behind him, shoulders erect like a drill sergeant's. Without turning he asked absently: "How old are you, Colonel?" He had a clear, precise way of articulating, as though measuring the quality of each word.

"Thirty-four, General," Titov told him.

"I was twenty-two when the war ended. You weren't even born then." Spoken with wonder.

"No, Sir."

"Tell me, have you ever been in a battle with bullets flying?"

"Yes, Sir."

"I mean a real battle. A war, fighting fanatical well-trained troops that are brave as lions. A war where a soldier walks on sore feet for a million kilometers, guts churning every step of the way. And, if he's very lucky, with a friend to cover his back. Get the picture?"

Titov got it. Fighting black rabble in the Ogaden desert wouldn't qualify. "Then no, General. I've never been in that kind of war."

"I was. My generation. Over thirty million dead. Oh, I know the records say twenty. But it was really thirty-two million. When losses are that high, what difference are a few million more or less, eh?" He turned, facing them. "And the friend that covered my back was Yuli Kurminov." His sad smile was almost apologetic. "I loved him, you see. Do you think it unnatural for one man to love another?"

"I've never given it much thought one way or the other." This was a lie. Titov despised everything that smacked of homosexuality. Vereshchagin read it in his face.

"Of course you have, Colonel. Bah! The problem with men your age is your fear of letting your emotions surface. You're to be pitied."

With an audible sigh Vereshchagin sat down, legs extended, ankles crossed, the picture of informality. A shadow of resignation relaxed the crevices and creases in his face. His eyes closed as he collected his thoughts.

"It begins in Berlin, April 1945. The German beast was dying and Hitler knew it. Yet that raving lunatic still kept issuing orders to his mythical armies from the bunker under the Chancellery. Fight to the last man! No retreat! Their situation was hopeless, yet they kept fighting. It was insane.

"I was a sergeant in the 6th Guards Rifle Division of Koniev's 1st Ukrainian Army Front. A wild Cossack general named Ivanov commanded the division. Any type of a rotten job that had to be done, he'd volunteer the 6th Guards as spearhead. From the Vistula to the river Oder our poor division went first, and Ivanov covered himself with medals and glory. By the time we reached Berlin there wasn't much of my company left. They promoted Yuli Kurminov to company commander after Captain Serov stepped on a land mine. I became his sergeant-major. We'd been together since the beginning, two frightened soldiers collecting each promotion over the body of a fallen comrade. In two and a half years Yuli went from rifleman to company commander, I all the way up to senior sergeant. Our only qualifications were luck and an ability to stay alive. We took care of each other, you see. So finally, here we were in Berlin with the war almost over. It began to look as though we might make it through after all.

"On the morning of April 23 we smashed through the city's outer defense ring and fought our way up the ruined streets and avenues, through parklands blasted by shellfire, toward the Chancellery. It was spring, but most of the trees were dead. By evening German resistance had started stiffening again. Our company ran into a pocket of Volkssturm and Hitler Youth, old men and boys who should have been home in bed.

"Yuli decided on a reconnaissance to learn what we were up against. He picked a corporal and five men to go with him. I begged him not to go. The commissar agreed with me. By this time Lebedev had grown fond of us. We were all that was left of the original company. But Yuli insisted. Ten minutes after they left I heard grenades and small arms fire coming from the end of the street. When they hadn't returned by midnight I asked permission to take a patrol and go looking. Lebedev said no. With Yuli gone I was the only experienced noncom left in the company. We stayed up all night waiting.

"Shortly before dawn Yuli limped in through our barricades leaning on a soldier. They'd been ambushed by a bunch of those fourteen-year-old fanatics. He'd been wounded. Not seriously, but he'd lost a lot of blood. "The girl saved my life," he told us. "What girl?" Lebedev asked. Yuli pointed at the soldier who'd helped him back. Lebedev and I burst out laughing. Our brave strong invincible company commander saved by a German girl. Yuli didn't laugh. She had saved his hide. In exchange he'd guaranteed her safety and her life. He'd given his word she wouldn't be raped or molested. So she joined our company as a soldier.

"It wasn't difficult to hide the girl in a Russian uniform. There were a number of female units in the Soviet Army, and Russian forces were converging on Berlin from all over the Soviet Union in a variety of uniforms and speaking a dozen different dialects. One female soldier unable to respond to an officer's orders or questions wasn't that unusual.

"She stuck to him like a lap dog. Couldn't speak a word of Russian, of course. Hand signals kept her in food and whatever she needed. When Yuli went off to Regimental briefings he turned her over to me to look after, knowing my interests didn't run to girls. She looked like a thin young boy. Half starved, with big inquisitive eyes. I taught her a few words: water, food, sleep, toilet — that sort of thing.

"A few weeks later the war was over. Marshal Zhukov collected the glory and wound up Supreme Commander. His troops were given garrison duty as a reward while Marshal Koniev's units were put to work dismantling German factories and rolling stock for shipment home. Poor old Koniev nearly had a mutiny on his hands when word came down from Zhukov's HQ that we weren't going home.

The regiment disbanded. We all said goodbye, swearing brotherly love and promising to keep in touch. I was shipped off to East Prussia with a newly formed engineering battalion. Yuli took the girl with him to Leipzig. Lebedev returned to Moscow, and Marshal Ivan Stephanovich Koniev, the hero and liberator of Kharkov, Kirovograd, and Berlin, was given the sop of Soviet representative on the Allied Control Commission in Vienna. Zhukov wasn't going to share his glory with anyone, you see," he said bitterly. He closed his eyes as he continued his recollections.

"Of course none of us kept in touch. But from time to time I'd see Yuli's name in the papers — first in the *Red Star*, then later, after he'd been promoted to general and appointed a candidate member of the Central Committee of the Party, he appeared periodically in *Izvestia* and *Pravda*. I knew it was only a question of time before he made Marshal. Our paths never crossed. We were in different branches of the service.

"I transferred into military intelligence. It was the best place for someone with my predilections to make a career for himself. I graduated top of my class. Best of all I was safe. You see, back in Comrade Stalin's day they put homosexuals in front of a firing squad. The Intelligence Service never bothered with a man's personal life as long as he did his job and minded his own business. The years went by and eventually I became a general."

His eyes blinked open as if the extent of his success had only just dawned on him. Hands gripping the armrests, he leaned forward in his chair, his voice deepening dramatically.

"Then, about four years ago, I ran into Yuli at a Beriozka shop. There he was, large as life. Larger, in fact. He'd put on a little weight around the tummy. Too many Embassy receptions. 'You remember my wife, Soulange, of course?' he asked after we'd finished the bear hugs and kisses. I mumbled something suitable and shook hands, trying to place her. 'Don't you remember me, Nikolai

Timofeevich?' she demanded. I felt a fool because no one should forget a woman like that. Slim, fine features, a few elegant wrinkles around the eyes, close-cropped dark hair: she reminded me of a male dancer from the Bolshoi I used to know. 'Water, food, sleep, toilet,' she laughed, imitating the broken Russian words I'd taught her. Our skinny German girl from Berlin, that's who she was — the one who had saved Yuli's life. Only now she spoke perfect Russian and she wasn't German. She was French."

"French?" Titov repeated. The information took him by surprise. His brain raced ahead to the obvious conclusions. He held his excitement in check, waiting.

The general nodded. "From a town up near the Belgian border. Yuli married her in Leipzig, a German civil ceremony. All quite legal, at least in Germany. When his duty tour ended he smuggled her home as his personal orderly. By then he'd been promoted to captain so it wasn't difficult to arrange. Who knows how long they might have gotten away with it if she hadn't got pregnant. More coffee? It's still warm," he suggested affably.

Titov waved the offer aside. Sultal poured himself another drink.

"Quite right, Colonel, help yourself." He spoke wryly, pausing long enough for Sultal to toss it back before continuing with his story. "I heard the complete details later in Sochi when they invited me down for a weekend at their summer place. He had cancer, you see. Lymphatic cancer, the slow kind. They'd given him two, maybe three years at most. We took a walk along the beach, just the two of us. He hadn't told his wife the news. 'Old friend,' he said, 'I want you to do something for us.' 'Name it,' I said. 'Not now, but when I'm gone. And it's not for me. It's to protect Soulange and our sons and their families.' 'If I can help I will. You know that,' I told him. Well, as it turned out, he had a very big problem for me to solve." He frowned at the memory.

"The authorities learned about his marriage in 1949. Yuli and the girl were arrested. Our Berlin Blockade had failed and Comrade Beria saw Western spies under every lamppost. If the MVD had got wind of the business it would have meant a firing squad for both of them. Fortunately, the army decided wisely to keep it to themselves as strictly an internal affair. Weeks of interrogation followed. Were they working for the West? Was she a French or German spy? Had Yuli defected? Their defense stories were models of artlessness. He'd saved her life because she had saved his. Later, he had fallen hopelessly in love. Not very original, you must admit. Soulange, on the other hand, claimed to have been abducted by a German officer and brought to Berlin as his mistress, which, if true, made her little more than a French whore and possible enemy collaborator in the interrogators' eyes. But why admit such damaging information voluntarily except to hide something much worse, they wondered? Yet search as they might for that dark secret they came up with nothing to prove their thesis.

"She claimed that she owed her life and freedom to Russia now, that she loved Yuli and wanted their child born as a Soviet citizen. Even under sodium pentothal her story remained unchanged. She promised to fight the forces of fascism and imperialism in any way she could. And she meant it. Oh yes, she meant every word."

The general gave an emphatic nod as if he'd been present throughout her grilling.

"She told a very curious tale about having been invited to have her portrait painted by a local artist. A dozen or more girls like herself from respectable families likewise had their portraits done at about the same time. She provided names and in a few cases family backgrounds on each. Her story was checked through our people living in the area. Soviet underground contacts in those days were first-rate. A report came back that everything she'd told us was true. So the next question was how could her information be used for long-term military advantage?

"Intelligence opened a file for the girls with provision for regular five-year updates; see what happened to each of them, who they married, where they worked, that sort of thing. In theory at least, one of them might reach a position of power or influence where she could be compromised by our knowledge about her past. In due course Yuli and Soulange were released with suitable apologies. Of course your people were never notified of the proceedings. Not then, nor later when MVD reorganized into the KGB, of which we are all so extremely proud," he added unnecessarily. To his credit, Sultal managed to hold his tongue.

"When Yuli learned he was dying he wanted the file removed from the records. It had to be done by somebody with direct access and sufficient authority to prevent questions being asked. As senior records officer I was his natural choice, you see. It was a small enough favor to ask in view of the circumstances. For all intents and purposes the matter had become a dead issue. Over the years none of the girls had amounted to much, so their importance to GRU was marginal at best. As I recall, several had died already, two or three never married and were living alone on modest family inheritances, and the rest had turned into normal dull-witted wives and mothers, marrying a shop clerk, a baker, a policeman, a petty bureaucrat, and such like. Only one had showed any initial promise. She married an army officer. But he had a disappointing career. Never managed to make it beyond lieutenant colonel. His name escapes me."

"Brigadier General Rolland Mercure," Titov volunteered.

Vereshchagin didn't bat an eye. "Really? Then he must have been promoted after our last update on his wife's file."

"But before you erased everything."

The general shrugged. "My instructions were to wait until Yuli's death before acting. How could anyone have anticipated a KGB background inquiry out of Brussels before he died? Our first inquiry in thirty years on a practically dormant file! Can you imagine the odds on such a coincidence, Comrade?"

There followed an uncomfortable silence. Vereshchagin stared morosely at his sandals. "I ordered an information hold on those files so that any incoming query would have to cross my desk. When the KGB request arrived I limited our reply strictly to the portrait information. A few months later Yuli was dead. I cleaned out the GRU records, and then contacted old Lebedev to help me figure out some way of wiping the duplicate correspondence from the KGB's central data bank. Using your man Bransky for temporary duty at that warehouse was his idea," he concluded with a long sigh, half relief, half resignation. He regarded Titov warily. "End of story."

Which Titov knew wasn't true. The general had told an interesting story that led nowhere. What was so terrible about a group of girls getting their pictures painted? He needed names, leads, some substance. But Vereshchagin shook his head with annoyance when pressed for more details.

"Names you want? It's been two years since I read the file. As to what happened to the others . . ." He shrugged. "Your guess is as good as mine. There was nothing more in the files, beyond what I've told you already."

"Except what you've forgotten," Titov said.

The general ran a hand over his close-cropped hair. "There's a chance you might get one or two names from Soulange," he said thoughtfully. "It might be worth a try. She still lives in Moscow. I have her address."

He was really trying, Titov decided with relief. "That would be most helpful, Comrade General."

Paris, 7:10 A.M.

Irène Daladier spent the night dozing in a reclining chair on the night train to Paris. First-class ticket for third-class accommodation. Past Dijon she finally fell into a fretful sleep, awakening with the dawn on the Paris outskirts. Morning mists trailing yellow-washed tendrils coiled through the suburbs and changed into a gray wet overcast as the train slid under the ancient roof of Gare de Lyon and stopped.

Paris. Crush of sleepy people. Odors of damp canvas, unwashed bodies, hot croissants, cigarette smoke, and urine. She hated the place. It represented misery and deceit.

"How much to Passy?"

"Where in Passy?"

"Rue Raynouard."

She stood waiting while the cabbie reflected on her clothes, hand luggage, severely tightened ash-blond hair, and flinty-eyed demeanor.

"Seventy-five francs." He had to start somewhere.

"I'm not looking for a business investment, Monsieur. I'll give you forty-five and not another centime."

The morning traffic hadn't started to build. She sat upright, head erect, looking neither left nor right on the trip across town. The city had never held any interest for her. She tipped the driver five francs for his silence and got out half a block from the house. She needed a short walk to clear the cobwebs, and the suitcases were light. The street and sidewalk were empty, the overcast morning breathless.

At the edge of the driveway she stopped and put down her bags. The house appeared the same. Ageless, like the city itself. And impersonal, waiting for generations of future deBrisays. That had been her mother's single greatest flaw: her inability to compre-hend that even with the deBrisay name, wealth, and family home, she could never be more than Marie Carnot, country girl from the Ardennes who struck it rich in the big city.

Irène had been expected to mold herself in her mother's image. How little Marie understood her daughter! The transition from Mama Margot and the peaceful farm to Mama Marie — she insisted on being called Mama — and Paris was simply too much for her to accept. She was the country girl with the country accent and the stink of dung on her shoes, trying to put on social airs in a society she despised.

As she stood looking at the empty driveway and the silent house with its drawn curtains and professionally tended grass and gar-dens, all the memories of her unhappy past returned. She picked up her suitcases and strode up to the front door. Its heavy brass knocker was ornamentation, she knew. When struck its sound dis-solved into the thick oak, discouraging the uninvited and unan-nounced. A small recessed button lay hidden at the rear of one of the white stone columns supporting the portico. The button rang a jarring bell in the staff room next to the kitchen. She pressed it long and hard. After a time she pressed it again.

Finally, a sleepy young man with tousled hair wearing an open-necked shirt and field gray uniform trousers appeared from around the side of the house. He saw the suitcases and scratched his head.

"You looking for someone?"

"I am." Irène glared. "Who are you?"

He hesitated. Something in her tone and stance made him answer respectfully, "Georges Vadim. I am the chauffeur, Madame."

"Are you the only one here?"

"No, Madame. The housekeeper phoned my apartment to say there was a caller and asked me to investigate. We've had a death in the family."

"Do you have a key to this door, Georges?"

"No, Madame, mine is for the servant's entrance."

"Your housekeeper's name?"

"Madame Bettina Denoir."

"Be good enough to inform the lady that I wish to enter the premises through the front door."

He stood awkwardly, his gaze roaming the curtained windows.

Finally he managed, "And your name, Madame?"

She wondered idly if he had the key to that secret door to her mother's bedroom from the rose garden. He was her mother's type of male animal. Over the years Vadim had probably worn out the lock.

"Tell her Irène Daladier has arrived. I'm here to collect my daughter and my mother's personal belongings, and to make the necessary arrangements for the funeral and requiem mass."

If she'd struck him across the face he couldn't have been more surprised.

"At once, Madame." He spun on his heel.

"And Georges," she called, "before you go into the house. . ."

He pivoted back.

"Do up your fly."

7:15 A.M.

A powdering of pleasurable images dusted through Nicole's consciousness as the telephone brought her awake.

In her ear Marais murmured, "Don't answer."

Her brain focused, then her eyes, and she remembered. He drew her close to his nakedness, holding her in a long languid kiss. She felt his hardness and began responding with slow rhythmic intensity. She didn't remember hearing when the phone stopped because their passion filled the silence. It was 7:15 A.M.

At 8:09 A.M. it rang again.

She'd fallen asleep. This time she was awake instantly. Marais sat up. Six rings. After a few seconds' pause it started again. Seven rings and then silence.

"Air France calling because she's late for work? Thought they misdialed the first time?" she suggested, propping herself up on an elbow.

"Or Bobby phoning with a change of plans," he countered. "I should have worked out a telephone code before they left last night so we could stay in touch. Stupid of me to forget." He swung his legs off the bed and sat frowning at the telephone.

She sensed his unease and reached out with a comforting hand to his thigh.

"Last night we were all tired."

He gave a weary smile. "I still am."

The pink satin sheets were stained and pungent with sex and sweat. Marais went to the bathroom. She heard the shower and lay back with a sigh against the pillows. He was a fantastic lover. She lay considering other lovers she had had. What made the difference? Perhaps his age? He was much older than she. Was that what it was? Not something she could discuss with her mother. Perhaps with her grandmama.

But grandmama was dead.

The mental barricades went tumbling down as reality dawned again. She realized she'd used him as a place to hide. A night of high adventure and sensual passion with a stranger had allowed her to squeeze back the feeling of helplessness that had engulfed her. He had been good for her; tender, gentle, and loving, and for a while she had forgotten reality. Now she had to face it.

"I'm going to phone his flat," he announced.

Startled by his sudden reappearance, she pulled defensively at the sheet to cover herself. He stood toweling himself in the middle of the room. The merest suggestion of fat had begun to form around the middle of his supple, well-muscled body. A ten-inch scar ran diagonally across his torso. She hadn't noticed that before. There were small white-sliced scars on his upper arms as well. The sight of them made her uneasy.

"He said he'd be here for breakfast." With an effort she sat up, holding the sheet demurely. "He may have left already."

"In which case there will be no reply."

He found his address book in the pile of abandoned clothes and dialed Pinot's number. No answer.

"See, I told you he was on his way!"

"Maybe."

Preoccupied, he began dressing, seeing yet not seeing her. She slipped out of bed and, after winding the sheet about herself like a toga, headed for the bathroom. She felt embarrassed and a little shallow for having used him. Would it make any difference if he knew? It was unlikely he'd give their brief relationship a second thought once his own difficulties were solved. So in a sense they had been using each other. She felt better as she turned on the shower.

9:07 A.M.

Judge Jacques Guérin assumed a metaphorical lotus position while his sad brown eyes contemplated Commissaire Boule. A rotund melancholy man with snow-white curling hair embracing a freckle-spattered pate, Guérin placed a thick finger on Boule's report.

"Not good enough. Not good enough at all. My function is to establish responsibilities. Yours is to bring me facts, not wishful thinking, Commissaire. You suspect Marais? Excellent. Bring me proof that it is his crime. To do less is to do us both a disservice. And the suspect an injustice. No?"

A short nettlesome-looking crone entered the judge's office with an armload of files. She walked sideways like a crab and dropped the lot unceremoniously on the desk. Blue files, green files, yellow files. Boule's report lay in an open brown folder. Was that significant, he wondered?

The Procureur de la République will be called in the case of unexplained death. That's how the law reads, but in practice that's not what happens. The Procureur is far too important a man to waste his time listening to homicide reports. So the Procureur's office is staffed with keen young assistants known as substitutes. If the substitute considers that the superficial facts and evidence indicate a crime, the matter is turned over to a judge of instruction under whose authority the police inquiry begins.

Any incident classified as a crime by the Penal Code is studied by a judge of instruction. Homicides are examined more thoroughly. A study of evidence by a judge of instruction is about as close to an impartial and independent inquiry as any Frenchman or woman suspected of a crime is liable to receive. There are eighty-six judges of instruction in Paris and, like Guérin, they are all overworked.

The old woman shuffled out. Guérin removed his bifocals, holding them carefully by the silvered ear wires. A hot puff on either lens and he began polishing the glass with a tissue. Unmasked, his eyes displayed the bafflement of blurred vision.

"You see my position, Commissaire?"

Boule nodded and said: "Certainly."

"It is difficult to tie your suspect in with both misadventures."

He liked Boule, considering him competent and thorough, although a little too phlegmatic in his approach to criminal investigation. He'd worked with him on two other cases, both satisfactorily resolved. Boule's pursuit had been relentless, his periodic progress reports above reproach. On the Rue du Bac affair, he had expected a progress report in a week or two at the earliest. Perhaps after the August holidays. But no. Last night Boule's young assistant had delivered an interim report. Guérin took it home to read.

A suspect had been found and detained, who somehow managed to escape custody the following day, having given himself an unassailable alibi for a second misadventure with which Boule, and Guérin by association, was now saddled. Why, the first corpse hadn't even cooled and here they were with another! And Boule putting his name to wildly inflammatory depositions. Not at all like the Boule he remembered. The moment he reached the sanctuary of his cluttered office in the Palais Royal he summoned the Commissaire. Guérin smelled politics.

"It is so unlike you, Commissaire." He adjusted the silver wires over his ears, bringing Boule back into focus. "To be sure, the girl is a common denominator. But that doesn't imply the guilt of your suspect directly or indirectly with either deceased, now does it?"

Boule was not prepared to contradict himself at this juncture. Guérin used the time gap to close the brown file.

"You're not being pressured?" It had just occurred to him.

"Pressured?"

"From above."

"You mean formally? No. I — we have two homicides to solve. They are connected, Monsieur le Juge. Marais is the most logical suspect for the first." He shifted position in order to retrieve a handkerchief from his trouser pocket. "Admittedly his connection to the second is thin." He mopped his forehead.

"Non-existent, I should say," Guérin observed primly. "Dear me, I can't imagine what possessed you." His stubby fingers fluttered like a pianist's searching a keyboard. Another thought. "This was prepared by your assistant, young — what's his name?"

"André Villeneuve."

"And you signed it without reading it through. Exactly. It happens under pressure. I can understand." Guérin sighed.

"You have spoken with the Director General?"

Boule blinked.

"No?"

Something was in the wind. Beaubien had phoned him late the same morning Boule was investigating events over on the Rue du Bac. Guérin's signature was barely dry on the authorization for a police inquiry, and here was the DG calling him. Who was the investigating officer? Did it look like murder? What evidence had been uncovered to date? He was fishing. For himself or someone else? Reluctantly, Guérin gave him the answers.

Senior government bureaucrats and politicians dislike judges of instruction because they don't mesh with the "system." Which is another way of saying they are independent and have too much power.

"You have had no discussions with anyone outside those directly connected with the investigation, Commissaire?"

"None." Boule remolded the handkerchief and dabbed his cheeks.

"Then you must be on your guard. There are others besides ourselves who are interested in this investigation. Who, you ask? Dear me, I wish I knew." His rounded shoulders shrugged in bafflement.

"First the DG phones. Then Chief Dubé wants a copy of the substitute's report immediately. Commissaire Blais calls like a Minister of State, demanding an explanation as to why you were given this investigation in the sixteenth arrondissement. As if I would know the answer to that!" He plucked at an imaginary thread on his sleeve. "And late yesterday the DG phoned again suggesting that any reference to the portraits and their Haguenau painter be omitted from my final brief. Gracious, I've never seen such interest in a case." He stopped plucking and looked owlish. "Yet you say nobody has called you."

"Nobody," Boule replied evenly.

Their gaze met and held. Staccato sounds started up in the outer office from an electric typewriter. At last Guérin cleared his throat.

"Which brings us back to your — if I may use the term — precipitate report." He took up an ornate paperknife, holding it lightly between his index fingers, raising it above the desk so that Boule could see the inscription etched in its silver blade: "A knife cuts — knowledge heals."

Boule stared impassively.

Guérin handed over the brown file folder. "Less speculation next time, Commissaire, if you wouldn't mind." Followed by a gentle smile. "Not trying to hide anything from me, are you?"

"Certainly not, Monsieur le Juge."

For several minutes after Boule had left, Guérin sat frowning at the piles of papers on his desk. Then he adjusted his spectacles and returned to work.

9:45 A.M.

At nine forty-five Marais decided something had gone wrong. Still no answer from Pinot's flat. A call to Air France's Personnel Department for a tracer on Danielle Coty's whereabouts on behalf of her newly arrived Canadian cousin confirmed that she had not arrived for work that morning at the Aérogare des Invalides, but that she could probably be reached now at her apartment because at that moment her line was engaged.

Marais thanked the man and hung up. Warning bells sounded. Time to go. He gulped the rest of the coffee and cleared away the breakfast dishes. The phone rang. Nicole started for it. He grabbed her arm.

"Air France calling back. They know someone is here because the line was busy. Let it ring."

"But if no one answers they'll know something's wrong, won't they?"

Nothing wrong with her logic. He nodded. "I figure we have about ten minutes to make our exit before someone comes knocking."

They made it in eight, leaving the apartment immaculate: dishes washed and stacked, clean sheets on the bed, fluffed-up pillows, dirty linen in the wicker hamper next to the bathroom.

The elevator was in service, so they walked down two floors and pushed the button. Just in case. But they were the only two on board for the trip to the lobby. An overripe cleaning woman in a yellow smock wielding a bottle of ammonia spray stood polishing the thick glass doors. She grumbled about paw prints when they pushed their way out to the sidewalk.

He took Nicole's hand for an unhurried stroll. Walk a few blocks, then hail a taxi. That would sever their connection with the apartment. He checked the time. The dwarf would be waiting in front of the Omnia Theater with his passport in another hour. No traveler's checks, please. Cash business.

"Do you have any identification?"

She held up the red billfold with her free hand. "Sure, driver's license, identity card, credit cards."

"How about a bank reference?"

"Are you serious?"

"A city bank where you're known, then? A place where you could walk in with a fistful of traveler's checks from a pal and turn the lot into francs."

"Will they do that?"

"They might. I've plenty of backup ID but no passport."

"Wouldn't any bank do? You could tell them the hotel is holding your passport."

He shook his head. "Suppose the bank wants to phone the hotel and check with the concierge? What do I say: I've forgotten the name of the place? Lost my room key in a métro toilet when my pants were down this morning? It wouldn't work. If I were a banker I'd tell me to get the hotel to cash my traveler's checks. You can have all the ID in the world but if you haven't got your passport, it's no go at the banks. Take my word for it."

"How much do you need to cash?"

"Thirty thousand francs for the passport plus another thirty to get me out of the country and home."

She stopped, clutching his arm. "So much?"

Stationary couples clutching and talking in the middle of a sidewalk draw curious stares. Marais led her along.

"Grandmama's bank is near the Trocadéro. I've cashed checks there before. The manager might remember my face from last summer."

He'd be senile if he didn't.

"We'll give it a try."

9:54 A.M.

Fridays and Sundays were Marc Hibbert's days off work from the communication room in the Canadian Embassy during the months of July and August. He could have mailed the photocopy of the RCMP telex to his friend, Bobby Pinot, but that would have taken too long. In any case the telex concerned Roger Marais. Only peripherally had Pinot been mentioned. But by delivering it personally he would make Bobby feel indebted, wouldn't he? Maybe he would fix him up with one of those luscious creatures he had working the racetracks at Auteuil and Longchamps.

He greeted the concierge by name, bidding him a good morning on his way into the building. Monsieur Carbonnet stooped polishing brass facings on the apartment's letter boxes. He straightened, examining the horse-faced visitor.

"Do I know you, young man?"

"Marc Hibbert. I'm a friend of Bobby's — you know, Bobby Pinot — third floor front. We've met."

"To be sure."

But obviously he wasn't. Still, he seemed to think Marc looked harmless enough.

"Is he in?"

The concierge reflected, chewing a pendulous lip. "Hard to say. I haven't seen him this morning. But he doesn't usually go out before noon. And I didn't hear him come in last night."

Capping this lack of knowledge with an indifferent shrug, he returned to his brasswork, polishing in a slow methodical circular motion.

On the third-floor landing Marc paused to catch his breath. He coughed uncomfortably, eyes adjusting to the dim light. He knocked politely on Bobby's door. After all he had arrived unannounced. No answer. He tried again, harder. The wood panel dissolved under his knuckles like rotting timber. A cluster of dull metallic objects sprinkled the floor. Through the opening he saw the two punctured bodies in their disjointed attitude of death. After staring bug-eyed for the briefest moment he threw up.

10:04 A.M.

Marais decided to go into the bank with Nicole. On the ride over she'd become so caught up in the drama of making an authentic presentation that he was afraid she might overdo it and give the game away.

The bank was one of those pretentious bastions of fiscal propriety, solemn and hushed. Obsequious uniformed doorman, polished mahogany, blazing brass, thick pile underfoot, all designed to create an illusion of judicious financial management.

A chief teller was the best they could manage without an appointment. Nicole presented the traveler's checks and launched into her Canadian cousin story. If the teller, a stooped and cadaverous man with a sharp pointed nose, recognized her he had decided to keep the information to himself. Marais's spirits sagged.

"These are all your signatures, Monsieur?" he asked suspiciously.

The checks were made out to Nicole Daladier, the duplicate signatures of Roger Marais at the bottom of each. He assured the man they were his, then produced an accordion of credit cards and ID, shoving the signature on his Québec driver's license under the man's nose.

"Monsieur, shouldn't you have signed these in the presence of the payee?" he chided.

"But I am the payee," Nicole interrupted. "He signed them in front of me. They are now my property and it is I who wish to have them cashed."

The concept troubled him. He tugged at an earlobe while considering his position. Did Marais have an account or line of credit with a local bank? Did Nicole? Why hadn't they gone straight to the American Express office where perhaps Monsieur was known; would not that have been more sensible? Indeed, why bother coming to this bank in the first place, two strangers, not even customers? He sniffed with indignation.

Nicole insisted on seeing the manager. That required an appointment, which could be arranged through Madame Bozec, as he had already explained.

Nicole drew herself up and glared: "Monsieur clerk, I am the only granddaughter of the late Comtesse Marie deBrisay, a client of this establishment, and I wish to see the manager this instant."

Her icy words carried well beyond the counter and polished desks where the scribes and scribblers sat. The chief teller blanched. Curious stares from other customers and frightened faces from those bank employees within earshot brought him to his senses.

"Our manager is away in Zurich at a conference. I will inquire whether his assistant, Monsieur Pomereu, can spare a moment to see you, Mademoiselle. If you will step this way."

They followed him to a break in the countertop where he conducted them through a swing gate and out of sight of the uneasy employees.

"How am I doing?" Nicole murmured.

Marais rolled his eyes. They padded down a paneled corridor that smelled of lemon oil and old wax, stopping before a door on which a brass plate had been affixed: Achille Delaray Pomereu, Assistant Manager. The Chief Teller knocked politely, then ushered them inside.

As they entered, a leggy secretary in a sundress that barely covered her beautiful buns folded a notepad and slipped out the side door into an adjoining office. Pomereu's eyes came alive with recognition before the introduction was complete. He waved his Chief Teller into silence.

"But of course, Mademoiselle Nicole Daladier. Delighted to see you again." Coming to his feet. "But under such distressing circumstances. My condolences on your grandmother's untimely passing. Shocking, shocking. Such a fine woman."

Pomereu was a rotund little man with oil-slick hair and a smarmy smile that fell away into several baby-smooth chins. He wore charcoal gray and a white boutonnière.

Marais introduced himself. Nicole placed the traveler's checks on Pomereu's desk as if the bank had already agreed to take possession.

"I'd like these cashed," she said in a matter-of-fact tone, then sat down in one of the red leather tub chairs on the supplicant's side of the desk. Marais remained on his feet. The suspicious teller launched into his side of the story. Pomereu listened politely, fat hands folded against his belly.

"And what is the sum, Mademoiselle?" he inquired when the teller had finished.

"Ten thousand dollars," Marais interjected.

Pomereu's brows creased ever so slightly. "So much?"

"My cousin has a financial problem," Marais slotted smoothly. "The funds normally at her disposal during the summer months from her grandmother are no longer available. The Comtesse's estate and financial affairs have been frozen pending the outcome of the police investigation. I happened to be in the city on a buying trip. She asked for help. Naturally, as a member of the family, I'm prepared to help in any way I can."

"Naturally," Pomereu agreed.

"To save her worry and avoid the usual delays involved in a cable transfer of funds, I decided to sign over some of my traveler's checks."

"You have an account in Canada, Monsieur Marais?"

"I do. Royal Bank, Place Ville Marie branch in downtown Montréal. Donald MacIntosh is the manager's name. He knows me if you'd care to call . . . "

He left it hanging while Pomereu jotted down the information on his desk pad. The chief teller cleared his throat.

"Your hotel, Monsieur?" Pomereu's gold pencil paused.

"Pont Royal until yesterday afternoon when I heard about the tragedy. Since then I've been with Nicole giving what comfort and assistance I could. My business activities will be suspended until after the funeral."

Pomereu pawed through the checks. With a smile he extended the slim pencil.

"If you wouldn't mind, Monsieur. Three specimen signatures. A formality."

Home free. He could have leaned down and kissed Pomereu's chubby cheek. Quickly, he slashed five signatures on to a sheet of bank letterhead. Pomereu compared them carefully to those on the checks. His smile remained.

"You have seen his identification, Claude?" he asked the teller.

"Yes, sir." Judicious pause. "Everything was quite in order with the exception of Monsieur's passport."

"Oh?" The smile faded. "You do have a passport, Monsieur?"

"But of course. Couldn't very well get into the country without it, could I?"

"Might I see it?" Pomereu inquired.

"It's in my briefcase back at the house. If I'd known Nicole was going to have such difficulty here I'd have taken her across town to my bank's Paris branch." Just the right touch of petulance.

"You are known at the Royal Bank in Paris?"

"No, I'm not. But I know them well enough to be able to cash a few traveler's checks using my driver's license for ID. I've done it before." Which was only partly true because he'd had to produce his passport as well and the bank's officer had written the passport number on the back of each check as an added precaution. He waited, poker-faced. Pomereu, he could see, was weighing his options. He re-examined the checks, sucked his bottom lip, set the stack down in a tidy tier at the edge of his desk. How important had Marie deBrisay's account been, Marais wondered? Did the old Comte deal here as well?

"I think we can look after Mademoiselle Nicole's requirements, Claude. You will be opening an account with the money?"

"But of course, Monsieur," Nicole said blandly.

That clinched it. Pomereu handed Claude the checks. "You'll make the usual inquiry with American Express?" An apologetic smile in Marais's direction. "Normal banking procedure, Monsieur." He clasped his hands in the manner of a novice seeking benediction. "It is nothing personal, I assure you."

Handshakes and toothy smiles all around, murmured apologies for any inconvenience, and they were on their way back through the musk of lemon oil and cordoba wax to wait at the front counter.

"A moment, Mademoiselle. It will take a few minutes to process the account."

The chief teller slipped away. According to an electric clock over the accountant's desk Marais had fifteen minutes left before his appointment with Fouquet. Would the little man wait, he wondered?

As soon as they had gone Achille Pomereu made four phone calls in rapid succession. The first was to Comte Maurice deBrisay, a director of the bank. He was assured immediately that Mademoiselle Daladier had no claim whatsoever on either the financial estate of her grandmother or the contents of the house on Rue Raynouard. Nor did the Comte know of any Canadian relatives on his ex-wife's side of the family.

His second call was to the deBrisay residence. The housekeeper answered the phone. No, she did not know Monsieur Roger Marais from Montréal, Canada. Most assuredly he had not spent the night under the deBrisay roof on Rue Raynouard. And no, Madame had never spoken of having any overseas relations, but she was very glad to hear that young Nicole was safe because her mother had arrived unexpectedly from Lyon and was furious to discover that her daughter had been out all night doing heaven knew what and with whom. Would Monsieur be good enough to ask Nicole to phone home at once. Pomereu promised he would.

He used his office intercom on the next call, instructing the chief teller to try to hold Marais and the girl on the premises for as long as possible without arousing their suspicions.

"Under no circumstances are you to give them any money."

"But I have checked with American Express, Monsieur Pomereu, and there is nothing irregular about the checks," the chief teller said.

"No doubt. However, Claude, there may be something irregular about Monsieur Marais."

Then he dialed police headquarters for the sixteenth arrondissement and asked to speak to his friend Commissaire Jean Blais. "At once, if you please."

Marais realized suddenly that the chief teller had been gone far too long. He'd been leafing through an assortment of the bank's promotional circulars lifted from a little wooden rack on the counter. He dropped them back in the display and glanced around.

Something felt wrong. He sensed impending disaster like that eerie silence preceding a storm. Nicole appeared oblivious to the danger. He leaned over and whispered: "I think we're being set up."

"What?" Too loudly. A clerk looked up from her desk on the other side of the counter.

"We've got trouble. Keep your voice down." He could almost smell it now. His mouth felt dry. He gave her hand a pat. "Wait here, I'll only be a minute."

With a tightly fixed smile he sauntered across to the front entrance. A uniformed bank guard stood next to a giant rubber plant, his eyes covering the doors through a spray of waxy leaves.

"Excuse me, but are you armed?" Marais asked the startled man.

Yes, he carried a lovely little Smith and Wesson .32 caliber pop gun. Why did the gentleman wish to know? His eyes were cautious.

"I'm picking up rather a large sum of money." Conspiratorial wink. "I'd like an escort back to my shop in Vincennes. Achille said you were the most competent man for the job. It's worth five hundred francs to me. What do you say?"

The eyes switched from caution to greed. He sucked in his gut and squared both shoulders. "At your service, Monsieur." Courtly bow straight from the Restoration.

"You accept? Splendid. Let's go tell Achille."

Without the least hesitation the guard dropped into step behind him. They marched across the concourse, past a startled Nicole, then beyond the swing-gate barrier and along the corridor to the manager's office. Marais knocked twice and stood aside.

"Enter!" called a voice from within.

As the guard opened the door Marais lifted the gun from his shiny leather holster and pushed him into the room, kicking the door shut behind.

"If somebody moves, somebody dies!" he yelled dramatically, waving the Smitty around so they all got a good look at it. His hands were steady and his brain clear, but his heart started flipping like a beached eel as the adrenaline flowed. Marais took a deep breath. "Everybody on their feet! Move, move, move!" he shouted. Four frozen faces stared at him with wide-eyed uncertainty: the guard, Pomereu, his secretary, and the chief teller. "Against the wall, hands clasped above your heads. Pomereu, get on the phone and call the police again. Tell them they're too late. Say the girl and I have already left. Last seen heading off down Avenue Georges Mandel in a taxi. Tell them I took the traveler's checks with me. Quickly, quickly!"

It was surprising how fast the sleek little man could move. Marais went around behind him and pressed the muzzle against the base of his skull. "Say it exactly as I said, Achille," he said softly. "And if you happen to dial the wrong precinct and the police arrive before I'm ready to leave then I'm going to kill you. Is that loud and clear?"

Pomereu made the call, spoke exactly as instructed, apologized for the inconvenience, wished the police good luck, and hung up. He sat absolutely still until Marais removed the gun from his head.

"Now get hold of a teller and order the full amount of my traveler's checks delivered to Mademoiselle Daladier. She's waiting at the front counter. Nothing smaller than thousand-franc notes. When she has the money I want to speak to her on this phone. Do it!"

Pomereu did it and replaced the receiver. His face had turned the color of chalk.

"While we're waiting I want everyone to take off their clothes. Pile everything on the carpet in front of you." He gave a demented giggle. The girl hesitated. He waved the gun.

"Everything!"

She got the message. Skirt and pantyhose came off together.

Her pubis had been shaved and looked oddly indecent, like seeing a bald man without his toupee for the first time. The men kept their gaze studiously at eye level.

When they were all standing in bare-assed impotence he ordered the cadaverous chief teller to collect everything and lock it away in the office credenza. Marais pocketed the key. The telephone rang. He signaled Pomereu to answer and pressed the gun to his temple.

Sixty thousand francs had been turned over to Nicole. Did Monsieur Pomereu wish to speak to Mademoiselle Daladier? He certainly did. Marais took the phone, waving the manager back against the wall, well out of jumping distance. Nicole came on the line.

"Act as though you're speaking to the manager. Do you have the money?"

"Yes, Monsieur."

Good girl, he thought. She caught on quickly. "Sixty thousand in thousand-franc notes, old bills?"

"Yes, Monsieur."

"Fine. Any sign of trouble out there?"

"I don't understand."

"Any unusual activity, plainclothes policemen milling around, that sort of thing?"

Pause while she checked.

"Not at all, Monsieur."

"Do you remember that bistro where we met yesterday?"

"I do."

"Leave the bank now and get a taxi. I'll meet you in half an hour out front of the métro station with the same name as the street it's on. Understand?" She did. He hung up.

A five-minute head start should be enough. He ordered his captives to face the wall at the other end of the room. There had to be some type of alarm running from the manager's office to signal the police or those out front in case of emergency. He got down on his hands and knees under the desk and began carefully patting the thick carpet searching for a telltale lump. But there was nothing to be found, no wire filaments from the support legs, no pressure button, not even a simple buzzer. He decided everything was operated from the telephone console on the desk.

"Keep your faces to the wall!" he screamed, and the guard's

head snapped back into position. The row of buttocks tightened. "I'm not through with you yet!"

But he was. The yelling had covered the sound of the console wires being torn out. With luck he had two minutes before all hell broke loose. Quickly, he let himself out the door, pocketing the gun in the process. The corridor was empty. It was a short sprint to the end, followed by a casual stroll across the marble floor and out the front door with his heart jackhammering over the entire distance. Another forty seconds and he'd reached the safe ano- nymity of the Trocadéro métro station. Blessings upon that un- known bureaucrat who had decreed that no point in the city should be more than five hundred meters from a métro station.

He purchased a ticket and inserted it into the machine. Trocadéro station was an interchange point with a choice of two lines: the number 9 to Pont Sèvres or a number 6 to Montparnasse and beyond. He made it onto a number 6 before the doors closed and found himself an empty seat. As the car swayed into the under- ground's lighted darkness he relaxed a little and tried analyzing the events of the past half hour. What had prompted the manager to phone the cops, he wondered? Had his face appeared on a morn- ing news broadcast or newspaper, or was it just a lucky guess on Pomereu's part that something was wrong? It seemed every time he made a move all he did was dig himself into a deeper hole. They'd be trumpeting bank robbery now, although technically the only thing he'd taken without legal justification had been the guard's gun. Try arguing that in a French court of law. After a time he gave up trying to figure reasons and turned to study a route display map. If he changed at Montparnasse to a number 4 it would take him directly to Rue Vavin.

Nicole told the driver to drop her a block short of the station on the Boulevard Raspail. There appeared to be some sort of traffic tie-up down Rue Vavin. She decided to take a quick walk and investigate. As she got closer she saw that the activity was cen- tered around the front of the building across from the bistro. An ambulance, several police cars and a swarm of uniformed officers holding back the crowd of people seemed a replay of events in the Rue du Bac. She took a seat at one of the vacant sidewalk tables. The café was deserted. Everyone had left to join the crowd in the street. The proprietor, a square little man with an apron and thinning hair, stood on his toes at the back of the pack keeping one eye on the action and the other on his cash drawer. When he saw Nicole he hurried over, rubbing his hands with excitement and barely suppressed relish.

"My apologies, Mademoiselle, but there has been a murder." He stood by the table trembling with delight. "Two actually. Man and a woman. Lived right across the street on the third floor."

"Really?" An alarming thought slashed her brain.

"Of course I knew the man," the proprietor told her proudly. "A Canadian from Montréal. He ran a new car. Ate here regularly. They say there were enough bullets in each body to sink them in the Seine. Probably a gang killing."

He continued speaking but Nicole had stopped listening as his words sank in. She felt very hot. There was a strangling sensation in her throat and a bilious churning from her stomach. She got up suddenly, excused herself, and went to the washroom. Gripping the sides of the washbasin with both hands to keep from fainting, she vomited into the sink. The cubicle lurched and swayed alarmingly. She hung on. After a few minutes her heaves flattened into a sour feeling of bewilderment and fear. Every dreadful sensation she had experienced after the death of her grandmama resurfaced. Only this time, instead of being a sorrowing observer to the horror of violent death, she felt herself a responsible participant. Her shoulders sagged from the enormity of her guilt.

She splashed her face with water and rinsed her mouth. A pair of wide and frightened eyes regarded her from the small mirror. Defiantly, she set her jaw, made a minor hair adjustment and, after rinsing the sink, unlocked the door and returned to her table.

The owner had rejoined the street gawkers. The ambulance doors were still open. A policeman stood at the rear talking to one of the attendants. The other sat in the vehicle smoking a cigarette. There appeared to be a delay of some sort.

Then she caught sight of Roger coming down the street. He too had come to investigate. As he examined the scene in front of the apartment his pace slowed until finally he stopped and stared. He caught sight of her, turned on his heel, signaling her to follow, and started off quickly back toward Boulevard Raspail. Nicole grabbed her bulging billfold and hurried after him.

She caught up with him when he paused in front of the Civil

Aviation Building. "Oh, Roger, they're dead! Murdered. A gang-land killing, the café owner told me." He took hold of her arm and began walking along the Montparnasse.

"This is probably going to sound crazy, but I'm almost certain somebody made a mistake."

A mistake! My God, what was he saying? This hadn't been an error in multiplication or addition. It was murder. His face barely registered surprise.

"What sort of mistake?"

Drops of rain tumbled onto the sidewalk, splattering like buck-shot. He hurried her past a trio of well-tanned office girls on an early lunch break from the Ministry.

"Where's the money?" he asked sharply.

She offered the red billfold but he only nodded. "Good work. Any trouble leaving the bank?"

"No." She was perplexed. Had he no feelings? "Roger?"

"Yes?"

"What mistake?"

Montparnasse traffic rumbled past. He hesitated.

"I have a hunch that whoever killed them thought they were killing someone else."

"Who did the killer think they were, then?"

He gave her hand a reassuring squeeze. "You and me."

She stopped abruptly, her mouth open with astonishment. He had to be making it up. She wanted to get away from him, take the first train back to Lyon.

The feeling passed as quickly as it came. She held tightly to his hand. He gave her an encouraging nod. "They seem to be after both of us now."

"Who?"

"Wish I knew. But we've got to get out of Paris. Gare du Nord. I left my bags there. We'll get two tickets on the first train out."

"To where?"

"Anywhere — the nearest border crossing."

He spotted a taxi row in front of the Théâtre de Poche. His pace quickened. She ran to keep up.

"What about your passport?"

"Forget it. I was supposed to meet Fouquet at eleven. He didn't strike me as a man who'd hang around waiting for anybody."

"I don't understand what's happening," she insisted, yanking him to a stop a few paces short of the taxis.

"Neither do I," he admitted. "Somehow it's all tied together: the business on Rue du Bac, the death of your grandmother, those two phony cops trying to blow me away, and now Bobby and the girl. We're the common denominator in everything." He chewed his lip, considering the evidence. "We've stumbled into the middle of something we're not supposed to know." His brow furrowed. He checked the street and sidewalk in both directions.

"I don't mean to sound melodramatic, but I have the distinct feeling that unless we come up with answers fast we're going to be dead."

His sigh of worldly resignation didn't deceive her. He was frightened too. They sauntered past the taxis. He had more to say. The expectant driver at the front of the line returned to his newspaper.

"I don't know about you, my sweet, but I'm definitely too young to die just yet," he said. "That bank manager, by the way, did phone the police. It wasn't my imagination." He told her what had happened and how he'd taken his leave. "They'll be looking for you as my accomplice. 'Blonde Bombshell Bolts with Bundle' is how the evening paper will have it." Pinot, he explained, was a high-class pimp who operated a stable of very expensive girls working the racetrack. He didn't know the details, but Pinot wasn't the sort who made enemies.

"In fact," he added reflectively, "I'd call him a helpful pacifist with a touch of larceny in his soul.

"A pimp might die during an argument with one of his girls. Or from blackmailing a customer. In the first instance death would be from a knife or poison; in the second by a bullet through the head or heart. But when it's a case of heavy lead in an apartment fronting a busy street and no one hears a thing, then it doesn't sound much like a lover's quarrel or the result of an avenging customer with herpes. All those bullets and no one hearing a thing means that a silencer was used. Big league stuff." His eyes were bright with alarm.

"Big league?" she repeated.

"Organized crime. Contract killings a specialty of the house."

More raindrops fell. He took her hand. They ran back to the taxi row. His face was wet as if he'd been crying.

"Gare du Nord," he told the driver.

10:30 A.M.

Bettina Denoir phoned for help. Madame deBrisay's daughter had arrived unexpectedly from Lyon to collect her mother's effects. She'd been told nothing was to be touched without police permission. It made no difference. What was she to do?

Boule promised help.

"You go," he told André, because André happened to be sitting in the cramped office.

Fauré had gone to Versailles for the Comte's signature on last night's statement. His reminiscences had been condensed into four typewritten, double-spaced pages. Whether Fauré's phlegmatic police prose warranted the Comte's signature remained to be seen.

Monceau was churning through the bowels of the Latin Quarter trying to find and interview Colette, who hadn't come to work according to Madame Denoir, and learn why she'd left the Passy house so abruptly yesterday morning.

Although the canvas cot had been folded into a corner, the smell of bedroom lingered. Socks, sweat, and smoke. André's eyes watered. The fumes stifled without the mercy of suffocation. Boule appeared oblivious.

"Be firm but polite," he cautioned. "Explain the reasons for the autopsy. You'd be surprised how touchy next-of-kin are on these matters. The morgue has promised to release the body sometime this afternoon."

He pulled the cigarette from his lip, leaving behind a strip of rice paper. His tongue felt for it. "Find out where she wants it delivered. Our sincere condolences for her loss, naturally."

He spat the sliver of paper onto the floor.

"List everything she wants but tell her nothing can be removed until the Comte gives his permission. We don't want her making off with any family heirlooms." He smiled owlishly. In spite of rumpled clothes and overnighting on a camp cot his pale eyes were alert and bright, his face clean-shaven. The Commissaire, André reasoned, must have the constitution of an ox.

On the drive to Passy, André could hear Dispatch working calls on a double murder in the Montparnasse. A man and woman gunned down. Police Identité had their names. No suspects. No witnesses. Nine-millimeter automatic. A gangland slaying? He resisted an urge to call in and ask the PI for names.

Near Rue Raynouard, Dispatch switched from the shootings to a bomb threat at the Foreign Ministry. Six patrol cars were ordered to converge on the Quai d'Orsay.

Rain squalls pelted the windshield. He turned in the drive, parking as close to the front steps as he dared without actually mounting them. Through his side window the blurred image of the housekeeper motioned him inside. He pocketed the keys and made a run for it.

"You are the police?" she demanded.

He produced his identity folder. "I was here yesterday with Commissaire Boule. André Villeneuve."

She locked the door behind him. Two chains, top and bottom, plus a brass slider covered with fingerprints.

"She's upstairs in Madame's apartment." She jerked her thumb at the second floor. "I've tried reasoning but it's no use. I don't know what the Comte is going to think when he hears of this."

He sensed she could hardly wait to tell him. She trailed him up the staircase, carping over the difficulties in fulfilling her responsibilities to the family. At the landing he paused and told her firmly: "I will deal with Madame Daladier alone. I'll ring if I need you."

He left her smoldering on the stairs. He waited until he heard her descending before he knocked.

"Yes?" The voice was strong and penetrating.

"Police, Madame. May I come in?"

"It's open."

She was seated on the enormous four-poster bed surrounded by bundles of letters, file folders, notebooks, and monogrammed stationery. A red leather jewelry box lay upended, its sparkling contents scattered across the satin bedcover. She held a photo album on her lap.

"Here to arrest me, is that it, young man?" A swift smile followed the question, not exactly patronizing but enough to annoy.

"André Villeneuve, Madame." He bowed and closed the door carefully behind him. "Commissaire Boule's assistant. The Commissaire sends his condolences. He asked me to assure you that the Brigade Criminelle will pursue every avenue to apprehend the person or persons responsible."

She appeared not to have heard. He'd expected tears, even hysterics. If this one felt sorrow she was doing a remarkable job of concealing it. Not quite middle-aged, he decided. A strong determined face that might have been soft and yielding in youth. Square chin to match her shoulders. Her hair was too blonde to be real.

"I've been sorting." She set the album aside and stood, smoothing her skirt. "Clearing the estate. Isn't that what you call it? I'm afraid it's a mess." A statement of fact, not an apology.

Coats, suits, dresses, and furs lay in orderly mounds about the carpet. Slips, blouses, underclothing, and brightly colored scarves had been sorted then folded neatly into open suitcases. Toilet articles, cosmetics, and perfumes were set out in shoe boxes beside the bed along with pairs of fragile leather footwear that looked terribly expensive. She'd certainly been busy.

She caught him staring. Her dark blue eyes skewered him. "Well?"

He had the grace to blush. "My apologies, Madame."

The photo album lay open at a group picture. He couldn't see the details because it was upside down. It looked like a wedding photograph, color-tinted from a black and white enlargement. He picked up the album.

"Is there any word from my daughter?" she demanded.

"No, Madame. I believe the Commissaire spoke with her yesterday."

"Didn't the Commissaire inform her I'd be arriving?"

André didn't answer. He stared at the photograph: a youthfully handsome Comte deBrisay and his bride, flanked by the best man and ten bridesmaids. Christian names were written in white pencil under the picture. It was the bridesmaids that held his attention. Four of their faces he recognized instantly from among those portraits taken from the shop on the Rue du Bac.

11:56 A.M.

Daggar Paoli shouldered his way through the crowded concourse of the Gare du Nord. Only seventy-two hours had elapsed since Director General Beaubien had spoken to him in the Parc Monceau, and already the task with which he'd been entrusted was complete. To be sure, things hadn't worked out exactly as the DG might have expected. Who could have predicted that slow, plodding Boule would have a suspect behind bars on the first day? Such efficiency from the PJ was unheard of! Paoli had been forced to move swiftly.

"If he does arrest a credible suspect we're relying on you to make certain that individual doesn't live long enough to come to trial." He remembered Beaubien's exact words. The DG would be pleased. Once more the SAC had proved its value to the Sûreté in a time of emergency. He hoped Beaubien would be generous with his praise in the right quarters. Perhaps even to the Minister himself? Disbanding the SAC had been a political decision. With proper incentive given to the right people that decision could just as easily be reversed. The SAC could emerge from the shadows.

Although Beaubien had requested daily progress reports, Daggar had prepared only one, the final one. This single typewritten page in the breast pocket of his gray summer suit detailed the events involving his SAC units from the abduction of Boule's suspect from under the noses of the PJ through to the execution of Marais and the Daladier girl in the flat on Rue Vavin. It had been a typical SAC textbook operation. No fuss. No loose ends.

Well, not many. He'd left out that part about the missing suitcase bomb in the hotel room. No need to bother Beaubien with trivia. Results were all that mattered.

He elbowed his way into a group of passengers waiting to collect their luggage at the porter's desk. One glance at his powerful shoulders and dark expressionless features and people stepped aside without a murmur. He enjoyed the effect he could create on others by his physical presence.

"A letter for Robert Rampal," he told the baggage attendant once he'd pushed his way to the front of the line. The man took it. There was a form to fill out. Daggar waited.

In another lineup a man and a young woman were collecting two bags and a leather attaché case. He studied the blonde's face and figure approvingly. Tall and lithe, just the type he enjoyed bedding. Something about her companion struck a familiar chord. It was a face he'd seen recently. As recently as . . . like a thunderclap it hit him. The clamor of people, porter's yells and squeals of baggage carts were drowned by the roaring in his brain.

He reached across the counter and snapped back his letter, mumbling that he'd forgotten an enclosure. The agent gave a derisive sneer as he turned away.

Marais and the girl walked toward an exit. Daggar followed. How could it be? If they were alive then who in hell was dead? My God, what a mess! He needed to get to a phone at once. But how? If he stopped to call they'd be gone again.

Instead of leaving, they turned into the métro station, pausing to buy a newspaper. Daggar sauntered after them, picking up one for himself. Where in hell were they going?

They went through the barrier down to the crowded platform. He moved in as close as he dared. They were talking but he was too far away to hear. A southbound Number 4 swept in and stopped. He pushed himself into the crush, keeping his eyes on his quarry. When the doors closed he was near enough to reach out and touch the girl. They stood facing each other, holding the overhead supports. The flashing tempo of subway lights increased as the train picked up speed. He studied his quarry, searching their faces for emotional reflections.

First stop Gare de l'Est. They eased past with an apology for the suitcases. Their abrupt departure startled him. He nearly missed his footing squeezing past the sliding doors. They chose the stairs to the railway station instead of the street.

They weren't trying to evade pursuit by changing direction. There was an objective to their actions. They intended to leave Paris. A train to the German border?

Of course!

That's exactly what he'd do in their place. The DST would be expecting them to try for one of the busy crossings along the Belgian border, or the Channel ferries to England. Every airport would be alerted. But no one would be looking for them in the east. Clever move.

At the top of the stairs they stopped to find their bearings. Daggar caught up, drifting past in the general direction of the ticket counters, hoping his theory was right. He didn't dare turn around. He paused to scratch his head then examined the ancient overhead clock. Twelve-eighteen. He checked his watch. Same time exactly. He unfolded the newspaper.

Marais and the girl came into view, crossing to the wickets at the administration island in the concourse. Daggar relaxed and fell in behind at a slow walk. They bought first-class tickets, spoke a few words with the clerk who pointed them at the track numbers, then moved off.

He waited until they were halfway across the floor, heading to the barrier gates and lines of passengers waiting to board their trains, then moved quickly to the wicket and showed his face against the metal grate.

"Police! That man and girl who just left. Where were they headed?"

The clerk, a balding middle-aged skeptic with narrow face and tiny eyes, remained unmoved. "Police, eh? Where's your badge, Mister Policeman?"

In an instant the barrel of Daggar's snub-nosed revolver was pointing through the grating at the man's heart.

"Refusing to cooperate with an officer of the Republic in the pursuit of his lawful duty is an indictable offense. You have five seconds to answer or you're under arrest!" he snarled.

The clerk blanched.

"They're on the twelve-thirty to Haguenau. Track 7. If you hurry you can just make it."

Daggar pocketed the gun. "Haguenau," he repeated.

"Yes, Sir. Near the Rhine."

"I know where it is."

He sprinted for the nearest payphone.

12:22 P.M.

When the self-righteous concierge began screaming, Detective Monceau's first inclination was to slap her face. He resisted the urge, deciding to let her get it all out of her system. Besides, if she yelled long and loud enough, perhaps other occupants of the seedy premises would materialize in the hallways, thus saving him the necessity of knocking on every door.

"Oh, my God! Murder!" the concierge howled between screams, in case anyone doubted the fate of the two women occupying the fourth-floor front room.

Within minutes a sizable crowd had collected on the landing: three old men, a skinny youth wearing a long-sleeved shirt to hide the needle marks on his arms, and a clutch of middle-aged women. In the pale light their faces registered shock and varying degrees of curiosity. The women stood with arms folded, craning to see inside the room. Monceau's bulk blocked their view.

At last the concierge subsided into sobs. Someone put an arm around her shoulders. Monceau faced them.

"Anyone hear anything or see anything last night or this morning?"

No one had.

"A stranger on the premises, then?"

He got a few giggles from the women. Rooms on the second and third floors were used by prostitutes, he was told. Every night there was a continuous movement of strangers entering and leaving. Where were the girls? It was explained that they slept until well into the afternoon. He'd check with them later.

The concierge agreed to telephone the Brigade Criminelle and ask to speak to Commissaire Boule. Monceau went into the room and shut the door. He reexamined the chaos.

The first thing that struck him was the size of the place. It was little more than a shabbily furnished rectangle with peeling walls and pocked linoleum. There was a door at one end and a single polished window at the other. A small table with two wood chairs had been placed next to the window so the street could be viewed during mealtimes. Crowded into this kitchen corner were a stained enamel sink with dripping faucet, a wall cupboard painted a garish lemon yellow and a narrow ledge on which an ancient two-burner heating element sat in the last stages of disintegration. Crammed into the remaining space was a plywood clothing wardrobe minus its door, a double bed with coil springs, and a hideous sofa with one corner propped up by a pile of paperbacks to compensate for its missing leg. The place was in shambles. Pictures were broken, clothing — some bloodied — had been torn into shreds, the wardrobe emptied, magazines scattered across the floor. The bodies, both naked, lay beside each other on the bed. Each had been stabbed once through the heart. A deranged necrophiliac, he wondered? Anything was possible in the Latin Quarter. That was what someone wanted him to think.

He leaned over them, checking for bruises, broken fingernails, or scrapings of blood and skin which might have been sustained beating off an attacker. There was nothing: no bruises, no cuts, and not the least sign of sperm around the pubic hairs of either body. Even the bedsheet was clean. Which corpse had been Colette? Not that it made any difference now.

He straightened. This murderer had been very selective in his destruction. Only those things that could be wrecked in silence had been chosen. Broken picture frames with the glass intact. The wardrobe left standing against the wall. Every dish, cup, pot, and piece of crockery left untouched.

Why?

Because it would have made too much noise, that's why. The murderer was someone who was afraid any noise might bring one of the residents to the door. Someone who didn't realize that the building's occupants were accustomed to hearing strange noises from people who came and left at all hours of the night. Which meant the murderer must have been a stranger to the district.

None of it made sense.

12:25 P.M.

Salon Gaston Poincaré et fils, Photographes, occupied the entire first floor of a venerable nineteenth-century gray stone building off the Avenue de la Grand Armée. André found a parking spot around the corner and walked back. There was a pretty young man with buffed nails, eye shadow, and a gold medallion behind the counter. André asked to speak to the manager. The young man inquired whether he had an appointment. André produced his ID folder.

"Gracious! The Brigade Criminelle!" the shop assistant said in a high fluted voice straight from the sixteenth arrondissement. "Monsieur Poincaré is occupied with a client. If you're absolutely sure it's important I'll run and fetch him." He gave André a precious smile. "Perhaps I can help."

"Perhaps you can. How far back do your client records go?"

"Eighteen-eighty-nine, our first year in Paris, when Monsieur Gaston moved here from Amiens."

André brought out his photograph of the deBrisay wedding party and placed it on the counter.

"What can you tell me about this?"

"Ah, a wedding party!" he announced brightly, and turned the picture over very delicately to examine the ink-stamped information on the back. "Taken June 25, 1948, by Léo Laurier. He's no longer with us, I'm afraid. Our file number is B-184, meaning the groom's surname begins with the letter B."

"Maurice deBrisay," André confirmed.

"This is one of thirty-two copies. The color tinting is quite good. Of course we don't do that any more. What else do you want to know?"

"You have the complete file?"

"But of course!"

"Would it include the names and addresses of everyone who got a copy of this picture?"

"If the customer's instructions were that Poincaré et fils was to do the mailing, yes, naturally the names and addresses would be in the file."

"I want it."

He turned petulant. "That will take time, Monsieur. A search through boxes and boxes of records. Perhaps several days."

"Is it on the premises?"

"Yes."

"Good. I'll give you two hours to come up with it, or we lock the front doors and bring in a police team to do the search. They're efficient but messy. It's up to you."

"Monsieur Poincaré will have to be told," he sniffed.

"Tell him. Two hours. I haven't got time to argue."

The young man decided to forgo a scene. Quickly he wrote down the information from the back of the photograph on his notepad.

"Remember! Two hours."

André pocketed the picture and went back to his car. Had

Poincaré et fils mailed a copy to each of the bridesmaids? Why not? Marie and her new husband would have been off on their honeymoon. It would be logical to let the photographer handle the mailings to members of the wedding party. When he knew their maiden names he'd try locating them, find out who they married and how each happened to have her portrait done by the same artist during World War II. Could one of them be a murderer?

Or one of their husbands?

He decided to drive back to the office and discuss the matter with Commissaire Boule.

12:28 P.M.

Wagon Number 477047, First Class Compartment Number Seven. The little room was clean and compact with polished honey-colored wood, seating for two and an adjacent cubicle toilette with full-length mirror. Marais lifted the suitcases onto the overhead rack and returned to the platform, joining the groups of well-wishers that are endemic to departures everywhere. Nicole watched anxiously from the compartment window.

Starting at the front of the train and working his way back, he scanned the faces on the platform slowly looking . . . for what? Something out of place, perhaps. He didn't know. Everyone seemed normal. But what exactly was normal for a noon departure at the Gare de l'Est?

A whistle shrieked. With a tiny jerk the train began to move. He resisted the urge to run and board. It was important to know if he would be the last passenger. In the open doorway of the next coach an attendant stood grasping the handrails. He waved. A few of the children waved back. Marais moved closer to the front.

As a boy he'd spent an occasional summer afternoon jumping slow-moving freights in the Montréal yards with some of his pals. But they had been little yard diesels shunting empty boxcars. A passenger train with an electric engine was altogether different.

The platform clusters stood transfixed as the coaches rumbled past. He ran forward, deciding to try for an open door on the next car. As he pivoted to race in the same direction as the train he caught sight of another man running from the exit gate toward the last car. They swung aboard together and for an instant their eyes met in recognition down the line of coaches.

"We're being followed," he said matter-of-factly when he got back to the compartment. His forehead glistened with a film of rain, sweat, and fear. His chest heaved from exertion. He closed the door and slid the brass bolt.

"Are you certain?"

He sat down. "The same stocky guy with the hard face who joined us in the subway. He swung aboard the last car."

She remembered the man. "Shouldn't we try to get off?" Her voice held a tinge of resignation. Every time they made a move something went wrong. He took her hand and gave it a squeeze.

"No point. If he's police he'll have reinforcements. Probably get the conductor to help him search every compartment until they find me. Remember it's me they're after, not you."

They crossed a bridge over the canal Saint-Denis, moving at the restricted yard speed. If he wanted to get off there was still time. Once the train connected with the main line in the city's outskirts its speed would increase and it would be too risky to jump. He'd have to decide quickly. It would be so simple to go, leave her with the luggage and try making it on his own. He could hire a car, even charter a small aircraft from some satellite field that could fly him straight to Germany. He travels fastest who travels alone.

He'd lose her for sure then. Did she realize the danger she was in? Unlikely. If he decided to split at the last minute he owed her at least enough information to enable her to protect herself.

"I don't think this guy's police. He's from the other side."

She didn't understand. Small wonder. He didn't understand himself. He explained: "If he'd been a cop he could have taken us into custody any time after we left the subway. All he had to do was blow his tin whistle and a half dozen uniforms would have come running to assist. But instead he stood back in the weeds waiting, then jumped the train at the last minute."

"But why is he following us if he's not a policeman?"

"Because he wants to kill me." And probably Nicole as well. But he didn't come out and say it. He had a game plan, something that would force the man to show his hand while leaving them with a small advantage. As he explained the details to her it sounded plausible enough to his own ears. By the time he finished they were already through the town of Thorigny-sur-Marne, paralleling the river and moving at a respectable speed. Certainly too fast to jump from the train without breaking a leg.

A few minutes later there was a knock at the door. Nicole picked up a magazine. Marais slid the bolt.

"Billets?"

There were three men in the corridor: the collector, a polite gray-headed man with a worn leather purse hanging from his shoulder; his young pimply-faced deputy; and the man from the métro staring impassively from behind the two uniformed officials.

Marais concentrated his gaze on the older man as he handed over their tickets.

"Haguenau?"

"That's right."

"A pleasant town this time of year."

Then they were gone.

He figured muscle-face would stick with the other two until they finished their collections, then he'd be back. Two more coaches. Perhaps ten minutes. He gave Nicole a reassuring pat on the cheek. She managed a smile.

"Make it look real," he said.

"I'll try."

The bathroom cubicle was very cramped. He had two choices: either sit on the toilet and watch through the crack in the door from the piece of folded paper towel he'd wedged between the jamb and locking mechanism, or stand with his butt resting against the wash basin. He decided to stand. It wasn't as comfortable as the toilet but he could make it to the center of the room in a single step. Speed was essential.

He checked the .32 Smith and Wesson he had taken from the bank guard. It wasn't much of a weapon but it would have to do. At least it was loaded. He took a few deep breaths to steady his nerves. Blood pounded at his temples.

Through the slice of open door he watched Nicole undress down to her panties. It was a cheap shot, but he needed that extra two seconds of distraction when their visitor arrived.

Nicole folded her clothes neatly onto the seat and sat down. The minutes dragged. On the opposite track an inbound Paris express thundered past and was gone. Nicole jumped with fright. The cubicle grew hot and stuffy. He shifted his legs uncomfortably and waited, listening to the wheels rumbling over switches, through crossings and past junctions. He felt a need to urinate.

Someone knocked.

One loud rap. The same one used by the ticket collector. He eased the safety catch off his gun. Nicole got up, looked in his direction uncertainly and went to answer the door, passing out of his viewing angle. He heard the bolt slide. She sprang back into sight, hands not quite covering her breasts. Then, very slowly and seductively, she raised her arms over her head. He tensed.

A silencer and pistol appeared held by a disembodied hand. He took a deep breath and plunged into the room. That extra two seconds gave Marais time to slam his gun barrel against the intruder's ear hard enough to hurt. The man grunted and turned, pistol swinging. Marais grabbed him around the neck, turning with him, keeping his body clear of the fat silencer. The man was amazingly strong for his size.

"Drop it," he hissed, "or I'll kill you!"

Enraged by pain and the sudden turn of events the man hurled them backwards against the door. For a split second Marais saw stars but managed to hold on, even to tighten his grip on the thick neck by locking his arm against the Adam's apple and squeezing for leverage against the arm holding his own weapon. He was choking him. The man's free hand clawed at his arm trying to break its grip. Then he must have realized it was the other arm, the one holding the gun against his ear, that gave his assailant the edge. In desperation he lunged for the wrist and twisted.

The gun went off.

Instantly the man went limp, dragging Marais down with him. There seemed to be a lot of blood, most of it from the jagged red hole in the top of the skull. Marais sat on the floor, stunned, staring at the wound. Then he remembered Nicole. She was on her knees by the window.

"Are you all right?"

She nodded. "Is he dead?"

He felt for a pulse. The lifeless dark eyes stared in pained surprise. He pressed the lids down and got to his feet, listening for activity in the corridor. Surely people in the next compartments must have heard something. Seconds passed. The wheels rumbled across a bridge. A freight train passed. Nicole began putting on her clothes.

He relaxed a little. There had been only two distinct sounds: their bodies crashing against the door and the gunshot. Not enough to produce an inquisitive knock on the walls or door, it seemed.

The only identification in the dead man's pockets was a plain envelope addressed to Robert Rampal, Gare du Nord. Marais tore it open. Nicole sat staring at the body on the floor. The man's mouth had opened, revealing a collection of gold-encased molars. A gray light filtered around the edges of the window blind, holding the compartment in a middle darkness.

Marais finished the letter, then sat down beside Nicole and read it again. His heart was hammering wildly. What he was reading was their obituary, prepared by the man responsible for murdering Bobby Pinot and his girlfriend. Which was why he'd jumped aboard at the last minute to try killing them again.

The name on the envelope — Robert Rampal. Was he the corpse with the gold molars?

He considered the facts. A sealed envelope in a man's pocket would indicate a sender, not a receiver. Unless of course that someone had grabbed it in a rush from a post box at the railway station as he ran to catch a train. Then he wouldn't have time to open it. But that didn't square. A message as important as this one would have been opened and read at the first opportunity — if not while he was searching the train, then certainly later on his way back to their compartment to kill them. No, he decided, the dead man wasn't Robert Rampal. More likely he'd written it, addressed it, and then while on his way to deliver it to Rampal realized his mistake after the million-to-one chance encounter in the métro.

He passed the letter over to Nicole and reached across to crack the blind for a few more centimeters of light. He studied her reaction as she read. What little color remained drained slowly from her face. Wordlessly she handed it back.

It had been done on a portable typewriter in need of a new ribbon. It bore no salutation and no signature. The contents listed in point form a series of events culminating in "the elimination of the subjects at the residence on Rue Vavin." It read like a police report. He'd seen enough of those to recognize the style and the compulsion to use acronyms and capital letters in place of words for the sake of brevity: CRS, SAC, PJ, IJ. The last sentence was a terse self-congratulatory observation that confirmed his worst fears: "Your instructions concerning the portraits have been observed to the letter. At no time was this matter discussed or mentioned to or by any subordinate engaged in these operations."

Suddenly a new realization hit him. He wasn't a suspect. He'd never been a suspect. He'd been set up as the fall guy. Somewhere along the way they had decided Nicole had to go too. Why, for Christ's sake?

"What do you make of it?" he asked once his emotions were firmly under control. They needed a plan. Haguenau was the right direction to be going to try for answers, but sitting in a train compartment with a fresh corpse on the floor all the way to the Rhine seemed a bit simple-minded. He wanted her opinion.

"The Barbouzes are after us, Roger." She answered his query in a tight strangled voice. "We are already dead."

"Bullshit!" He twisted in the seat. What the hell was she talking about? The letter had said nothing of barbouzes. He took her hand. It was like ice. She slumped in the seat, defeated.

"I don't get it."

"The Bearded Ones," she whispered.

She took away her hand and clasped both arms protectively across her chest.

"Read the letter. It's all there." When she saw that he didn't understand, she tried explaining: "SAC stands for the Service d'Action Civique. Officially, it's not supposed to exist any more. The government said it was disbanded in 1982." She took a deep hesitant breath before going on. "SAC members are called Barbouzes because of their undercover work as a branch of the SDECE. The SDECE is France's secret service. That man must have worked for the SAC. Whenever the SDECE didn't want its hands dirtied these people were used and then protected so no one would ever know what happened or what they did."

It sounded far-fetched. "How do you know all this?"

She made a face. "Every boy and girl in France knows about our Bearded Ones. They've become a cult object."

"Where does the secret service fit in?" he asked.

"It's just another police force working under the Sûreté," she said. "All police departments work under the Sûreté, I think."

"Who commands the Sûreté?"

She shrugged. "Its director — Director General he's called in the newspapers."

"And above him?"

She thought a moment. "The Minister of the Interior, I suppose."

"He's the top of the cop heap?"

"Except for the Premier and President of the Republic."

He came to his feet and stood swaying with the train's motion, looking down at the corpse. The revolver with its bulbous black metallic silencer lay near the suppurating skull wound. He picked it up and unscrewed the silencer, then pocketed the two parts. Their arsenal was growing: a suitcase bomb and two handguns, one with a silencer. He began thinking out loud, trying to make sense of everything, for his own benefit as much as hers.

"Assume our friend here did work for the SAC. He must have held some rank because of his age. He'd be — what, in his forties? Maybe older. Not one of your regular hit men. I'm betting he was the boss. His orders came from the SDECE. Or maybe even one step higher — the Sûreté, right?" But he didn't wait for her nod. "His assignment was to kill us. First me, then later both of us when, as it says in the report, 'it became obvious the girl was a security risk.' He had cooperation from the PJ and IJ, as well as the SDECE.

"You don't know that!" she interrupted.

"We can assume it. How else would he have the connections to get me out of jail within twenty-four hours? I've never seen this man, yet he recognized me in the métro. He must have had a copy of my passport photograph or the one taken by the IJ when they were fingerprinting me. That means he had the authority to get anything he wanted from other police sources. Only someone very high up in the Sûreté could give that sort of authorization. Those two that lifted me out of jail then tried blowing up my hotel room were probably Barbouzes. But the bomb didn't go off. I didn't die. I phoned you. We met. It was then that whoever wanted me dead decided you had to go too. Our friend here."

"Why?"

"Because of what I knew — or what he thought I knew and might have passed on to you."

She appeared unconvinced but said nothing. Beyond the blind another train thundered past in a rush of sound and was gone. They both jumped with fright.

"Don't you see how it happened? He knew your name already. Remember? You phoned the PJ and asked about me. You left messages at the hotel Pont Royal for me to call. And by the time I did, your grandmother was dead and the place was swarming with eager cops. One of them could have listened in on an extension or, even better, had the telephone tapped. It's normal police procedure during a murder investigation to eavesdrop and see what can be picked up."

Now he had her attention. Slowly the arms came down until both hands rested on her lap.

"You were tailed. We were observed together, talking, walking, eating, and driving off in Bobby Pinot's car. How long do you think it takes to put a name and address on a car once they have its license number?"

She started to say something but he cut her off. Ideas came tumbling out: "He couldn't kill us in public, you see. There had to be a set-up. Like the bomb in my hotel room. That way it could be blamed on gangsters or terrorists. When we drove off with Bobby it must have shaken him. But it didn't make any difference in the long run because he had the Renault's license number. From then on it was easy. He'd find a name, street address, and apartment number, and the fact Pinot came from Montréal with a history of helping Canadian lame ducks who were running from the law. Obviously we'd be given shelter. The heavy weapons squad was called in for an early-morning hit. They were expecting three or four. Instead they found two. And thought they were killing you and me. Their boss here writes up his report with a brilliant suggestion for 'our friends at the PJ' — his words. Blame our deaths on Bobby's competitors trying to muscle in on his territory. A case of mistaken identity. Shocking, the news media would say. A formal apology to the Canadian Embassy along with a suitable letter of condolence to your mother. Game over. Everybody can go home clean and the secret of the portraits stays safe with whoever the nut is that dreamt the whole thing up in the first place."

"Robert Rampal?" she suggested.

"If such a person exists. The name may be only a cover."

She pointed at the corpse without looking at it directly. "Why couldn't he be Rampal?"

He shook his head. "This character was the sender. Remember he met us on the métro yet almost missed the train. Why?"

"Because he stopped to pick up the letter," she reasoned.

"No. If he'd picked it up at the station wouldn't he open it sometime before coming in here? My bet is he wrote it at home on his portable." His lips pursed while he thought. "Okay, so what delayed him at the station?"

"He needed help?" she offered. "He had to make a phone call."

Marais gave her an approving nod. "Right! He's delivering his report when he sees us and realizes suddenly that everything is screwed up. He needs manpower fast. Working undercover on a murder assignment he can't bring in regular police patrols or railway cops, so he phones his SAC base for help. It takes time to set up a plan where they can grab us somewhere along the route. Then he runs like hell and jumps aboard, bullshits the ticket collector by flashing his gun and follows him through the cars until we're found. He plays it cute until they've checked the entire train, then doubles back. When he came through that door he didn't intend to kill us unless he had to. His idea probably was to wait until his buddies came aboard and carted us away."

He sat down and reached across to raise the blind higher.

"Any idea where we are?"

"Not the slightest." The scene outside the window held no interest. "Do you know what you're saying? That it's the police who are trying to kill us! My God! Do you know what that means?"

He nodded. "For starters it means we shouldn't report anything to the police."

Which brought a smile. Not a big smile but enough to tell him her crisis had passed. He kissed her suddenly. She clung to him.

"I'm scared, Roger."

"So am I. But the thing is we mustn't let it beat us. We're still ahead of them. Don't give up on me. Please."

"I won't," she murmured.

"I need you," he said, and meant it. "Besides, the odds aren't all that bad. Just you and me against every police force in France."

That elicited an honest laugh. Relieved, he pulled her from the seat. "C'mon, let's move him into the lavatory where he'll be out of sight in case someone comes knocking. Then we'll try cleaning up the mess."

He gave her the feet to hoist so she wouldn't have to look at the man's ugly slack-jawed features.

Moscow, 2:30 P.M.

Madame Soulange Kurminova occupied three large rooms on the third floor in one of the drab gray apartment blocks on Petrovka Street, near the Bolshoi. Part of the week she worked as a translator for *Novosti* in the French department producing propaganda booklets on disarmament. Thursdays and Fridays she worked at home on her articles for *Sovieska Cultura*.

"And since today is Friday, Comrade Colonel, she will be at home. May I give you her telephone number?" asked the *Novosti* editor.

Titov told him no; he preferred to arrive unannounced. He wrote down the street address and flat number and returned to the car. Marshal Yuli Kurminov's widow would be his last call. There was an afternoon flight into Brussels and he intended to be on it. All the information Traveler needed to settle the Adelaine Mercure matter had been collected. The frightened rabbit could be eliminated without fear of repercussion from other quarters.

There was, however, the matter of Traveler himself to be settled. Something would have to be arranged. He was too dangerous to remain alive, and even more dangerous dead.

"She's moved to Murmansk?" Sultal suggested when he got back.

"She has a flat near the Bolshoi."

"I might have guessed. You take the car. Drop me off at the office. I have work to do."

He missed his turn and had to drive around the block. There was no such thing as a left turn in Moscow traffic. Did anyone in authority realize how idiotic the ban on left-hand turns was in a modern city? More to the point, did anyone care?

A severe-looking woman in her late thirties with plaits and horn-rimmed glasses met him at the door. In careful non-threatening tones Titov explained the reason for the visit, but when she saw his ID with the sword and shield she blanched. He was shown into a dark vestibule hung with house plants. The place smelled of strong cigarette smoke and the mustiness of carpets in need of a good beating.

"Who is it, Tatanya?" someone demanded from beyond the Swedish ivy.

"An officer from the KGB."

"Bring him in here!"

He entered a large room paneled on two sides with dark walnut. An enormous bookcase stretched from floor to ceiling. Near one of the windows sat an elfin woman working at an escritoire. She held a long cigarette holder. Lazy gray tendrils of smoke curled toward the ceiling. She had stark white skin and enormous inquisitive eyes. Her lips were full and fixed in an expectant smile. She was magnetic. She belonged in a fashion magazine. Or the theater.

"Soulange Kurminova?" He felt like a flushed teenager at the first sight of a naked female.

"Sit down, General. Tatanya! A chair for the gentleman. Coffee? I have an excellent Arabian blend. Tatanya!" She used the cigarette holder like a conductor's baton.

When he was settled finally before the escritoire Titov admitted his official rank.

"Only a colonel?" she exclaimed. "Then they should promote you. You have the bearing of a general." Her eyes twinkled. "I should know. I've met a lot of generals in my time."

"So I understand," he said ungraciously. Soulange Kurminova smiled impishly and fitted a fresh Byelomor on the end of her filter.

"So, Colonel, you've been talking to Nikolai Timofeevich." It wasn't a question. She used a wooden match, snapping the head expertly with a thumbnail to light the cigarette. Her hand, he noticed, was quite steady. After the first deep drag she became convulsed by a series of deep-seated, dry, racking coughs that must have hurt. Titov winced. Obviously she was seriously ill. She took a handkerchief from the desk drawer and dabbed her eyes. He waited until she caught her breath.

"I'm seeking information."

She laid the filter aside carefully on an oval glass ashtray. "Not unusual for the KGB." The coughing spasm had shaken her.

"Owing to a minor administrative error, details of your interviews with the GRU have been misplaced." He gave a tiny helpless shrug. "Thirty-five years is a long time. Files go missing. You can understand how it might happen."

If she did she wasn't ready to admit it. Her head tilted comfortably against one hand, the elbow resting on the escritoire. She waited to hear the rest.

"I'm in an awkward situation," he said uncomfortably. "That information you gave to the GRU after the war could be of vital importance today in preventing a disaster in our European Foreign Service." He held up his hands. "But the file on one Soulange Kurminova no longer exists. So what must I do? I must come directly to the source." He produced what he hoped was an encouraging smile. "How good is your memory?"

She gave a dry laugh that blended into a brief cough and picked up the filter. For a few moments she studied the drifting smoke. "So the old reprobate kept his word." She said it with wonder, shaking her head. "Such a foolish risk to take for a friend. Poor old Nikolai. All my husband's idea, of course. Marshal Yuli Kurminov, the Great Manipulator. It wasn't done just to protect me, you know." She shook her head again. "There were our children to consider. How would they feel if the information came out one day that their mother had been a German officer's whore and suspected spy from the West?"

She spit the word "whore." For an instant her face clouded angrily. "Even in our modern, enlightened, egalitarian Soviet society there are those who'd use such knowledge to destroy a man's career. My son, Oleg, has a sensitive position in the Ministry of Agricultural Planning. My daughter's husband is Third Secretary at the embassy in Mexico City. A whiff of scandal and their careers would be finished."

She took a cautious mouthful of smoke, releasing it without inhaling.

"In the end I suppose Yuli was right," she sighed. "Without his power and influence there would be no protection for any of us. We'd wind up like Comrade Brezhnev's family. Not that it makes any difference in my case. In less than a year I'll be dead. Six months if the doctors are to be believed. But what do they know?" She grimaced. "Bah! I've decided to stay alive till next summer. Summer is the only proper time to die, Colonel, don't you think? I mean when the ground is warm."

Titov murmured sympathetically.

"I can tell you nothing more, I'm afraid. I stayed with Lieutenant Maier until he was killed by English bombers early in 1945. As for the other girls, I know what happened to two of them. And my husband told me that our intelligence people located some of the others."

She sipped her coffee, letting the cigarette burn into ash at the end of its holder. Titov set his cup back on the escritoire.

"You never attempted to contact your family after the war?"

"To tell them what? There were only my mother and sister left. What could they do for me or I for them, except open up the memories of old wounds? Besides, private correspondence with the West was very difficult at that time — and very dangerous. I had no wish to cast suspicion on myself or my husband."

He could hardly fault her prudence. "By any chance do you remember any of the girls' names?"

She appeared to reflect, but whether on his question or the need of divulging such information at this late date he couldn't determine. There was no reason for her telling him anything, even if she did remember. Soulange Kurminova was past the point of intimidation. The GRU and KGB records were gone, and with them any proof that might damage her family. Within the year she too would be no more.

So it all depended on her sense of loyalty.

She had been given refuge in the Soviet Union, enjoyed a full and privileged life among the ruling elite, watched her children achieve political and financial security. In the final analysis her reply would be based on whatever sense of obligation she felt for the system that had given her a chance to reclaim her self-respect. How much value did she place on that, he wondered?

She cleared her throat. "I remember the names of five — two that came after I left."

Titov took out his notebook and wrote down the names: Marie Carnot, Monique Dessauer, Gabrielle Révier, Adelaine Plaunt, Hélène Gauthier. "You said that you knew what had happened to two of them?" His pencil remained poised.

"Yes. Marie Carnot and Monique Dessauer. Yuli and I were attending the Leipzig Trade Fair in 1961 when I ran into Monique at the Center. Her husband was an official with the French exhibitors. Monique told me about Marie."

"You knew Marie Carnot?"

"Yes, Colonel. She is my sister."

Titov blinked with surprise.

"Fortunately, Marie married sensibly. A rich industrialist, Comte deBrisay, publishing and electronics, I believe. It was Monique's husband who gave me the shock. She had married a politician. When she introduced us I nearly fainted."

"You knew him?"

"He was older, and his hair had thinned, but there was no mistaking the face and voice. He was my eldest brother, the one reported killed by the Germans in 1940. Only his name was no longer Charles Carnot. It was François Daumier."

Paris, 1:30 P.M.

Boule set his office telephone carefully on its cradle and frowned. Another *immédiat* summons, this time from the Director General. A meeting was ordered in Beaubien's office at Number 11 Rue des Saussaies. Department heads — and Boule. Most unusual! Something serious was in the wind. The Rue du Bac or Passy murder, you could bet on that. Or the Marais escape? They could hardly pin that on him, though Dubé might try. The hell with Dubé.

He went over to the window and stared out absently at the traffic rushing soundlessly along the Quai. His window needed cleaning again.

"Pardon?"

He hadn't heard André enter, so intent had he been on his thoughts. It was embarrassing to be caught talking to himself, particularly by a junior. Like being found in a farmer's cornfield with his pants down during a weekend picnic. How his wife had laughed at that one.

"Well?" he said rather more sharply than he'd intended. It wasn't André's fault he was entering his dotage.

"I found something at Passy, Commissaire. I thought you should see it."

"You explained matters to the daughter?"

"But of course. A formidable woman. She understands completely. Not a tear. I think she despised her mother." He unzipped his sparkling new attaché case and brought out the wedding photograph. "This was the best part, though. I think we've discovered the identity of our girls."

André continued talking but Boule no longer heard. Every fiber of his being concentrated on keeping the hand that held the photograph from shaking. Color drained from his face. Ice enveloped his heart. André stopped his monologue and regarded Boule expectantly.

"Good work, young André." He managed to keep his voice neutral and maintained a proper degree of cautious skepticism as he pointed out that it might take time to locate and identify each member of the wedding party. But André was optimistic.

"I'll have names and addresses for us before the weekend is out," he promised.

He wanted to discuss the approach, but Boule begged off, explaining his summons by the DG. An encouraging pat on the shoulder coupled with a clichéd exhortation to leave no stone unturned, and he was gone, leaving André to sort things out for himself.

In the corridor outside his office Boule leaned against the wall. He felt as if he was going to vomit. A stabbing pain knifed through his chest. He had difficulty breathing. He staggered down the hall to the stairway and held the bannister tightly to keep his balance. Near the main entrance he found a bench and sat down. One of the security guards came over.

"Are you all right, Sir?"

"Yes. Yes. I'm fine. Something I ate. It will pass." He lurched outside and began walking toward the Pont Neuf. André had uncovered the answer. That tiny clue he'd told him they needed. André had found it. He had only to use his imagination to find where it led and what it meant. Boule knew already.

One look at the date and faces in the photograph and he had realized the killer's identity. Only the Rue Vavin murders remained as question marks. With such interest from the DG's office he assumed they had probably been done by Beaubien's Barbouzes. It was their style. Slick and silent. But for the Rue du Bac and Passy murders there could be no doubt.

The anguish of this knowledge brought an involuntary groan to his lips. My God, what suffering a man must endure! He found an empty table under an awning at a sidewalk bistro and sat down. Sprinkles of rain ticked the canvas and dampened the street. He ordered a cognac, drank it, then ordered another. Tears and sweat trickled down his face.

What he faced now was nothing less than the total loss of his honor as a policeman. Was he capable of such sacrifice? "We're all corrupt," he muttered sadly. "Or corruptible." An elderly man at the next table regarded him curiously.

How long would it take André to find the answers? A day or two, perhaps. Not much of a head start, but it would have to do. He had to get there first. A point of honor. He finished his drink, paid the bill and hailed a taxi.

Épernay, 1:36 P.M.

They left the train just over an hour out of Paris at Épernay, center of the Champagne wine country. It seemed a sensible choice. If the dead man had phoned for help back in Paris, the nearest major police center he could have reached would be Reims. If reinforcements managed to get themselves organized in time, they'd have two choices for boarding. They could either drive fifteen minutes to Épernay on an uncomfortable road through the Montagne Forest or join the train farther along the line at Châlons-sur-Marne after a high-speed trip down the A4 autoroute. Marais bet on Châlons-sur-Marne. It was a bigger town and the cops would blend more easily with the platform crowd when they came aboard.

Before stepping out at Épernay, Marais checked the platform for signs of any unusual activity. He saw nothing other than two men with an old iron-wheeled baggage cart and a half dozen people waiting to board. He kept Nicole close, waiting until the last minute while the departures came aboard and the arrivals dispersed through the exit. Once the platform was deserted except for the uniformed attendants with the baggage cart, they stepped off the train with their suitcases and made for the exit, looking for all the world like a pair of honeymooners from the city on a champagne tour of the district.

Once outside the station they breathed easier and paused to examine their surroundings. They were in the middle of a small town split by the river Marne and cluttered with cut stone and

white plaster medieval buildings, narrow streets, and lethargic traffic. There was a taxi stand across the road from the station with
two cars, neither indicating whether it was for hire or simply a
private vehicle whose driver had found a convenient parking space
and intended to hold on to it.

"What do we do now?" Nicole asked.

She looked a lot better in the fresh air. Color had come back to
her cheeks and she seemed much more in control. He figured
they had about forty-five minutes before the ticket collector would
take the reinforcements into the compartment and find the body.
Then they'd start backtracking from Châlons-sur-Marne, Épernay,
Château-Thierry, Meaux, Claye-Souilly, trying to decide where
their quarry had left the train. Would they phone the local gendarmerie or bring in more of their own kind? It would be nice to
know exactly from whom he and Nicole were running.

He put the suitcases down and gave her arm an affectionate
squeeze. "We get out of town as fast as our little legs will carry us."
He studied the taxi stand. "Wait here. That may be our transport."

Crossing the street he went to the second car because the driver
in the first was fast asleep.

"Is this a taxi?" The old sun-faded red Peugeot looked like a
museum piece.

The startled driver lowered his newspaper. He had a dull round
face set with a pair of scheming eyes and an enormous belly that
pressed against the steering wheel.

"Taxi? I'll be damned if it isn't! Not much to look at but she runs
like a Piaget watch. My Piaget Peugeot. I call her 'Licka.' Get in!"
he chortled.

Marais wasn't ready to commit himself.

"Where's the nearest airport?"

"Plivot. It's about ten minutes from town." He looked across
the street to Nicole and hoisted a fat yellowed thumb in her direction. "Is she with you?"

Marais nodded.

"Wife?"

"Yes."

"Nice. You're honeymooners, I suppose?" He folded the paper
away on the front seat. "It's two hundred francs to the airport.
Suitcases are ten francs extra each."

Inflation had arrived in Épernay. Marais leaned in the window.

"This airport of yours, does it have aircraft for charter?" He resented the overcharge but didn't have time to argue.

"Certainly! An air taxi. Fly you anywhere in Europe." He winked a dark inky eye. "Provided you've got the money. Ferdinand Gervais runs it. 'Taxi Plivot.' Good name, eh? We're competitors," he added, as though the thought had just occurred to him. He burst into laughter. The entire car shook.

Marais got into the back. "Okay, I'm sold. Let's go!"

There was a delay while the ancient motor was coaxed to life. "Hear that?" the driver yelled over the racket. The muffler had been holed in several places. "The tappets need adjusting. That's where she gets her name . . . lickalickalickalicka!" He laughed loudly again.

They made a U-turn over to Nicole and stopped. The driver heaved himself out to get their suitcases. Marais opened his door.

"Get in. He's taking us to the local airport."

Her eyes widened in alarm. "You said they'd be watching all airports!" She slipped in beside him. The driver was out of earshot.

"Not the small ones. Plivot? Who's ever heard of Plivot? Don't worry, we're safe for a couple of hours. By then I hope we'll be in Haguenau." He put his arm around her, drawing her close.

"Does Haguenau have an airport?" she whispered.

"Why not? It's bigger than this place."

They stopped talking when the fat man got in and started a long story about his own honeymoon at Saint-Tropez during the '50s before the tourists came and ruined it for decent Frenchmen.

The village of Plivot was just big enough to warrant a bypass on the main highway into Châlons-sur-Marne. The airport lay amid farmland a few hundred meters off the highway. A row of single- and twin-motored airplanes were tethered neatly with yellow ropes beside the airport fence. They looked like toys. A single Toyota pickup sat parked behind the hangar. They stopped beside it and got out. The place appeared deserted.

They walked around to the front of the prefab steel building. The folding doors had been left open, exposing a dozen small airplanes squeezed inside under the low roof, their wings interlocking like a child's giant jigsaw puzzle. A workshop area lay crammed against one wall. Its focal point was a long oil-stained wood table scattered with a variety of tools, wire spools, masking tape, a drill press, a vise, and a vast collection of rusting coffee tins filled to overflowing with bits and pieces of metal. The place smelled strongly of acetone-based paint and hydraulic fluid.

Next to the workbench a man and a youth, both dressed in green coveralls, stood adjusting a metal jig set up to repair a damaged wing removed from one of the aircraft. They knew the driver.

"Ferdi's in his office, Gaston," the older man said.

"Couple of customers for him," he said proudly, jerking a thumb over his shoulder. "Honeymooners wanting a charter to paradise!"

On that cue Marais took Nicole's hand, remembering she wasn't wearing a ring. Did people wear wedding rings in France? He'd never noticed.

"Congratulations!" the mechanic said automatically. He had a quiet bemused way of speaking. His helper said nothing but turned red in the face and grinned self-consciously.

Nicole thanked him.

"Where do you want to go?" His eyes were on Nicole.

"Strasbourg," Marais told him. The riverport city lay thirty kilometers south of Haguenau and, for flying purposes, in the same general direction. He didn't want Gaston to know their destination.

"Return trip or one way?" He picked a waste rag from the workbench and began wiping his hands.

"One way. We're going on to Munich tomorrow by car."

"Any luggage?"

"Two bags and an attaché case," the taxi driver offered.

"When do you want to leave?"

"Now." Marais said.

"Okay, go and make your deal with Ferdi and I'll get a machine ready. Any particular preference? We have twins and singles." He tossed the rag back on the bench and started unbuttoning his coveralls.

It dawned on Marais that the mechanic was a pilot. "What's the difference?"

The bemused smile returned, crinkling his eyes. "Price and one engine," he replied succinctly.

In normal circumstances Marais would have laughed. Today his heart wasn't in it. "We'll take whatever's cheapest," he said. "We're trying to economize."

"Right." The pilot understood. "In that case tell Ferdi we'll be taking the old Horizon."

He wondered whether "old" was meant as a term of endearment or aircraft vintage. He was afraid to ask.

They went to look for the owner, with the taxi driver acting like one of the company's founding directors. The offices were in a lean-to attached to the main structure and connected by a firedoor. The inside was as cluttered and confused as the hangar.

The forward section consisted of a small waiting room for transient pilots and passengers. It was littered with torn paperback books and magazines, cigarette butts, empty and partially filled plastic thermal coffee cups, and shredded paper. Beyond this mess, in an adjoining office behind an unmanned reception counter, they found Ferdinand Gervais. He was a frantic little man with a spade beard and nervous fingers that kept dancing about his desk straightening the piles of invoices he'd been checking, most of which carried the word "Overdue" in large red letters.

He jumped to his feet, introduced himself, and quickly sat down, leaving everyone to sort themselves out. Marais remained standing. The driver did a little more bragging. Gervais listened politely, fingering the invoices, his gaze devouring the two prospective customers. Gaston finished his monologue and took a chair.

"Strasbourg?" Gervais repeated. He went to a wall map and measured the distance with a length of weighted string tied to a metal hook that protruded from the village of Plivot.

"Two hundred and seventy-one kilometers," he announced. "One way. An hour and ten minutes flying time."

The Horizon rented for eight hundred and fifty francs per hour with pilot. But since they were honeymooners he'd give them a break. Sixteen hundred francs return trip. Cash deal. No receipts.

He seemed taken aback when Marais agreed and began counting out the money plus a hundred on the side for Gaston. The fat man beamed and scurried after their luggage. Gervais pocketed his money, wishing them a safe trip, many children, and a long and happy life together. They went outside to wait on the tarmac, leaving him with those troublesome invoices.

The pilot and his helper had rolled a small low-wing four-seater over to the gas pump. Painted in a royal blue with silver trim, the little plane looked very smart and new. Marais felt better.

"They'll all remember us here, won't they?" Nicole muttered.

He wished she would stop worrying. "Probably. What does it matter? Concentrate on what's going to happen, not what's passed."

She bit her lip. "I'm scared, Roger."

"So am I," he told her quietly.

A break in the overcast bathed them momentarily in sunlight. He glanced up at the patch of blue. "Cheer up! Even the weather's decided to cooperate."

She gave a resigned smile. "I can't help feeling somehow responsible for getting us into this mess in the first place. If you hadn't phoned after they let you out of jail none of it would have happened. You could be safe at home by now, convinced that everyone in France is crazy."

He grabbed her arm. "Don't feel guilty, my sweet. They wouldn't have let me out of the country anyway, at least not alive. And without you I couldn't have got this far. Besides, I don't want to lose you."

She thought about that a moment. "Why?"

He shrugged. "I'm getting used to your company. We sort of fit together, don't we? Haven't you noticed?"

It wasn't exactly a long-term commitment but it was enough to tell her he was interested.

Gaston huffed their suitcases to the plane. The pilot lifted them into a baggage space behind the rear seats.

"Did you notice that wall map in the office?" Marais asked.

Nicole nodded.

"There's an airport called Weinumshof right on the outskirts of Haguenau."

"Then why don't we land there instead of Strasbourg?"

"Yes, why don't we?" he agreed.

The pilot signalled that they were ready to go.

Paris, 1:43 P.M.

Daumier ordered another coffee. The café's lunchtime regulars had gone back to their offices, leaving the premises to the afternoon shoppers who would begin arriving sometime after three. Daumier felt relaxed and a little sleepy. His talk with Director General Beaubien had been like a tonic. He experienced the same feeling he had had as a young man leaving the confessional after baring his transgressions to the village priest. His sins had never been very serious, though they had seemed so at the time. Then finally, when he did have something to confess, he couldn't bring himself to trust even a simple man like Father Henri, much less an outsider from another parish. But the years had softened his perspective.

Beaubien had been truly horrified by what Daumier had told him. But then how often in French history had a Director General of the Sûreté been informed that his Minister of the Interior was a charlatan, fraud, murderer, and — at least on the surface — a double agent? And if not a Russian agent, then at least a grave security risk. No wonder Beaubien had lost his composure during lunch.

It hadn't been the sexual aberrations in his story that had upset the DG as much as Daumier admitting to shooting his superior officer during wartime. In spite of using Daggar Paoli and his thugs from time to time when necessary, Beaubien was a decent, honorable man. But, as Daumier had reminded Beaubien over dessert, it is politics and circumstance that dictate the degree of decency and honor to be found in any man or woman. Beaubien agreed time was crucial in solving the problem before matters got any further out of hand. He left without finishing his coffee to assemble his forces and set whatever additional wheels were needed into motion. After his departure Daumier grew reflective. Looking back over the years he couldn't see what he might have done differently in the beginning that would have changed his situation in the end. At least not if he had wanted to stay alive.

Sedan, May 14, 1940. One thousand German tanks had driven through the Ardennes during the day. By nightfall the Boche had reached the Meuse from Liège to Sedan. Lieutenant Franchet ordered his men to fight to the last. Lieutenant Franchet was an asshole. He had taken over the company after the Captain had lost both legs in a mortar blast and bled to death. Throughout the night they fought, dropping one by one until by morning there were less than thirty of them left alive. Charles Carnot had had enough.

"Carnot! Where do you think you're going?" Lieutenant Franchet demanded, waving his pistol.

"I'm getting out, Sir. We're surrounded. If I can make it out perhaps I can find somewhere else to fight."

Morning mist draped the fields and woods. It would cover his escape to the river, where he could shed his uniform and hole up for a few days until the main German assault forces moved out of the district.

"Get back to your post, Carnot!"

"Fuck off, Lieutenant. We're finished. Maybe you want to stay here and die. I don't." He turned away and started through the short grass, crouching low so he wouldn't be seen from the enemy observation post in the next field.

"One more step and I shoot!" The Lieutenant's voice was edged with hysteria.

Something snapped in Carnot's brain. The stupidity of the French general who allowed an idiot like Franchet to command men to die for nothing when anyone with a gram of intelligence could see the battle had been lost the day before! He whirled about, bringing up his rifle. At the same time Franchet raised his pistol. Two shots cracked simultaneously. The Lieutenant missed. But Carnot's rifle bullet took Franchet through the heart. He dropped where he stood. From the adjacent fields the Boche opened up with machine guns, cross-hatching the French positions. Carnot ran back to his trench.

"Did you kill him?" one of the men asked.

"Yes."

"Good shot. He deserved it. Now what do we do?"

"I guess we have to fight."

Forty minutes later their positions were overrun. Those that were left alive surrendered. Carnot was not one of them. He had been bending over an ammunition box when Private François Daumier fell across his shoulders. Daumier and Carnot had been the last two alive in the trench. Daumier had a bullet through the neck. He twitched and gurgled briefly, then he died. Blood poured over Carnot's face and uniform. He heard the Boche soldiers talking as they advanced. He lay very still. They paused above the lip of the trench long enough to see that everyone was dead, then moved on.

For a long time he lay under Private Daumier thinking about his chances for escape, first from the Boche, later from a courtmartial when the Army heard how he'd shot his commanding officer on the battlefield. And they would hear about it. Of that he was sure. His captured comrades would talk to their friends, not out of malice but because they'd think Charles Carnot was dead.

The sun rose. Private Daumier stopped bleeding. Big green flies buzzed about the trench feasting on the dried blood. Very gently Carnot eased Private Daumier off his shoulders and peered out over the surrounding grass. Not a soul could he see in any direction. Quickly, he traded his paybook, identity tags, papers, and billfold for Private Daumier's. He made the sign of the cross on Daumier's forehead and crawled out of the trench.

Charleville-Mézières, September 24, 1944. An administrative hiatus had developed. The Americans had swept past in pursuit of von Rundstedt's fleeing Wehrmacht who were regrouping in the Belgian Ardennes. Until the transition to a properly constituted civil government could be arranged by the liberators, local Maquis units were left in charge of maintaining law and order under supervision of a few junior officers from the American Army Provost Corps. The American non-combatants were a joke. They knew nothing about administration and less about structuring a civilian government, and spoke not a word of French beyond a few childish requests for "vins" and "femmes." Once these basics had been supplied, the Maquis was left to handle local affairs in whatever manner they saw fit.

Daumier had spent the war in Lille working with the underground, becoming one of the bravest and luckiest commanders in the district. His forces welcomed the Americans as they sped north toward Belgium. He arranged to have himself appointed as investigator into collaboration activities for the Charleville-Mézières region. His purpose was twofold: he wanted to find out what had happened to his family and whether anyone in the area would recognize him under the beard he now wore.

He had, on several occasions during the war, toyed with the idea of returning home to his village for a visit. But each time he had decided it would be too dangerous. If the Gestapo caught him and discovered his true identity he knew they'd have no compunction in using his family members as bargaining chips for extracting a confession about his underground connections and activities. Better to wait until the Germans had gone.

Now, with the Germans in retreat, he felt it was safe to visit the village where he grew up. To his sorrow, he learned that his father and younger brother had died during the war. His mother had taken his sisters and gone to Charleville to work for the Germans, he was told by one of the local busybodies who should have recognized him but didn't. Back at the Prefecture he found his mother's name among those accused of col-

laboration. Her head had been shaved along with a group of prostitutes who had been rounded up the day after the Germans pulled out. He didn't have the courage to face her. Instead, he ordered all prostitutes and women over the age of 40 to be released at once. But nowhere could he find any information about his sisters. Nuns from the convent told him that both girls had left school suddenly a year apart. They had no idea why.

In Mézières the local Maquis Commandant had taken over the Prefecture. A small interrogation room was arranged on the main floor next to the Magistrate's office. It was a mess. The departing German clerical staff had wrecked the premises in a scramble to destroy all evidence of misdeeds by occupation forces. Daumier located a trestle table and two chairs and opened for business.

He looked deceptively pliant and, because of his size, much younger than his years. Dark curly hair crowning an untroubled brow, rosebud lips, credulous gray-green eyes set in an almost saintly bearded face — these were the first impressions to greet the accused as they came through the doorway. He'd smile politely and listen to every story until each plaintiff felt certain his arguments had carried the day. Then, like a cobra, he would strike, silencing them with a cold fury of words. Some turned indignant, others meek and frightened; most shouted their innocence in strident invective as they were taken away. He began wondering if there was anyone left in Charleville-Mézières and the surrounding district who had not collaborated.

In the beginning anyone his men produced was turned over to the police. Then he became more selective, realizing that many of the "collaborators" were guilty of nothing more sinister than offending a suspicious neighbor. Additionally, the police were running out of adequate facilities to house and feed his horde of detainees.

Then one day out of the blue he found out what had happened to his sisters.

"Name?"

Slowly her head came up. Her bright brown eye met his gaze with unblinking curiosity. It was the first time anyone younger than him had been brought in. They stared at each other in silence until, in embarrassment, he was forced to shift his gaze to the two men who had brought her in.

"Where did you find her?" he asked the one with the semen-stained trousers.

"Hiding in a cellar," he snickered.

"Well?" Daumier demanded of the woman.

She was sizing him up.

"Would you like to sit down?" His tone was bland.

She nodded. He ordered up a chair. She shook free of her captors and seated herself gingerly.

"Cigarette?"

He offered a package. She shook her head. Daumier lit one slowly as he studied her. Despite the swollen eye and bruises, the tangled hair and torn clothing, she was beautiful. He guessed her to be no more than sixteen or seventeen. And her lips were enticingly sensual, formed into a seductive pout. No wonder his men had jumped her first before bringing her into town. He'd deal with that later.

"Are you from around here?"

Nod.

"Where?"

Shrug.

"Family? Father and mother? Brothers?"

No response.

"Answer the Captain's question, slut!" one of her escorts shouted.

Daumier glared at the man. "Wait outside," he ordered curtly. The men hesitated, then left, muttering darkly. Now that the excitement of war was over, they found it difficult to accept the restrictions of peace.

"My name is François Daumier," he tried encouragingly. "What's yours?"

Now that they were alone she shrank from him, expecting another rape.

"I'm not going to harm you. And I am sorry for what happened."

She smoothed her torn dress, carefully pulling the hem to her knees, both of which were scraped and bleeding slightly. He waited for her to recover a little self-respect.

"I have to ask you a few questions."

"Are you going to shave off my hair, Sir?" she murmured in a deep contralto. Her lips trembled. He set her mind at rest. His job was to protect, not molest, teenage girls.

"Where are you from?" he asked her.

"Does it matter?"

"It could."

"You want to tell everyone that I'm a collaborator, is that it?"

"Are you?"

"No!" She spoke defiantly. Her chin came up. "I hated them — all of *them. They were no better than animals — like those two." She jerked her head back toward the door. "If I were stronger I would have killed them!"*

"Who, the Germans or my men?"

"Brave Germans, brave Frenchmen, what's the difference? You're all animals." Her good eye blazed with outrage.

Taken aback, he changed direction. "Let me look at that eye." He came around the desk. She recoiled from his touch. He held her face gently, examining the injury. She had translucent skin that magnified the slightest injury out of all proportion to its gravity. The girl's cheek was bruised and swollen, but from a slap, not a fist. Behind the puffy skin her eye was clear.

"You bruise easily."

He could feel her relaxing beneath his fingers. She would be all right in a week or two with nothing to show for the experience but its memory. He went back to his desk and picked up a pencil.

"Tell me what happened." He waited.

She hesitated. "My name is Monique Dessauer."

Daumier began writing. It took an hour to ease the entire shocking story from her. When she had finished he could only stare at her in dumb amazement. She had known Soulange and Marie, shared with them the same anguish and helplessness. The thought of it ripped his very soul. In frustration he screamed his rage, smashing the table with his fist again and again until it collapsed and the guards rushed in to see what had happened.

He had torn up his notes that day and spirited Monique off to the house of one of his wartime friends in Lille, far enough away to prevent any chance encounter with someone who might recognize her. Yet still close enough for him to visit. And later to fall in love and marry. Their secret remained hidden and secure, cementing their love throughout the years.

He found Marie in Paris; Soulange by accident in Leipzig. Neither had wanted to discuss the past. His own life had been exemplary. Each had followed a separate path. In one form or another they had found happiness, except perhaps poor Marie. Tiny Marie. She had been his favorite. So beautiful, so vulnerable, and so tormented. Who had killed her, he wondered, and why? Not that it made any difference now. What mattered was protecting the repu-

tations of those who were still alive; their families, their children
— and the honor of France.

Daumier paid his bill and walked back to the office.

Moscow, 4:34 P.M.

"You could have pushed her more," Sultal said.

Titov nodded. "Perhaps." He had given his friend the list of names
he'd obtained from Madame Kurminova. But not the facts that her
maiden name had been Carnot and that her brother was France's
Minister of the Interior. That information he wanted to save for
himself. It was valuable enough to make him a general if he handled
things properly with a personal report to the head of the KGB. But
first there was the problem in Brussels to be settled. He didn't
want his past coming back to haunt him, as had happened to
Vereshchagin. When the Daumier story came out in *Pravda*, it
would shake the French government to its very foundations. NATO
would immediately assume that every secret since its formation
had been relayed to Moscow by Daumier through his sister. It
would be better than the Philby–Maclean affair. A delicious
thought. He could take his pick of postings after that.

"She's still hiding something. I can smell it."

"What?" Titov asked.

Sultal squinted his Mongol eyes at the road ahead. They were
nearly at the airport. A Sabena flight left for Brussels at 5:00 P.M.
"I don't know," he admitted finally. Rain splattered the windshield. A
motorcade of black ZIL limousines sped past on the way into Moscow, their windows darkened against the curious. Secrets. Everybody had secrets. Soulange Kurminova still held her secret.

"I shall have to report her," Sultal announced.

"Why?"

"You ask?" He glanced at Titov quickly, then back at the road.

"She gave me the names," Titov argued. "Even that Alsatian
painter's. It's been over thirty-five years! You can't expect her to
remember everything. GRU interrogated her years ago. She's done
nothing wrong. They used sodium pentothal on her. She couldn't
have lied."

"Maybe she didn't have to lie." Sultal said slyly. "Suppose she told the truth, back then and today."

"Meaning?"

"Meaning GRU didn't ask the right questions — and neither did you. Think about it."

Titov thought. Then aloud: "Leave her alone, Marko. She's dying."

Sultal stopped in front of the arrivals section and left the motor running.

"I won't come in," he said.

Titov thanked him for his help. They embraced awkwardly. But when he started to leave Sultal held him back.

"Two things, comrade."

"Yes?"

"Captain Feodor Ivanovich Bransky."

"What about him?"

Sultal frowned. "The man's a traitor. I'm recommending he be shot. Will you co-sign that recommendation?"

If he did, Titov knew the frightened captain would be dead in a week. True, Bransky had been stupid. But if stupidity was treasonous then most of the Soviet Army should end up in front of a firing squad at Lubyanka.

"I'll co-sign an order for reduction in rank with a five-year transfer to Arctic duty."

"You're going soft, Boris, do you know that?" Sultal sighed phlegmatically.

"It's too much Belgian chocolate that does it, Marko. Be glad they keep you at home." He waited. Eventually Sultal gave a reluctant nod. Bransky would live. "You said there were two things?" His hand rested on the door handle.

Sultal turned in his seat. "I will tell you a story that we have on file which may help you to understand the French mentality. In a Paris museum — I've forgotten which — there is a stuffed pigeon with glass eyes. It lived during World War I and was the last carrier pigeon to fly from Fort Souville to Verdun before the place capitulated to the German Army. Gassed and badly wounded, it carried its message through the lines and dropped dead upon arrival. In early June 1916, it was awarded the Legion of Honor." He released Titov's arm and smiled. "What sort of nation would award a medal to a dead bird? It isn't rational. Take care, Boris, if you intend pursuing these women. Remember that they are French."

Paris, 2:43 P.M.

In a small conference room on the third floor of the Sûreté's administrative offices at Number 11 Rue des Saussaies six men had gathered around a beige leather-topped table. They were men of enormous power. And they were worried. The room in which they sat was secure and tightly soundproofed against eavesdroppers. Twice daily it was swept for hidden microphones. No conversational records were ever kept of these meetings. Each man could speak frankly and without fear of exposure.

Director General Beaubien had called the meeting for 2:30 P.M. after his unsettling lunch with François Daumier. The elegant Beaubien would have preferred not to know Daumier's complete life story. But now that he did and realized its full implications he knew it was necessary to move swiftly before matters developed into a national scandal that would in all probability bring down the government. The portraits had to be picked up and destroyed at once, and Marais and the Daladier girl found and silenced.

He summoned his Directors of the Gendarmerie, Police Judiciaire (PJ), Compagnies Républicaines de Sécurité (CRS), Directorat Surveillance du Territoire (DST), and the austere head of the nation's secret police, the SDECE.

Chief Henri Dubé of the Brigade Criminelle and Commissaire Bernard Boule arrived thirteen minutes late, Boule sweating like a basting goose and Dubé effusive with apologies for their tardiness. The DG waved his apologies aside and told them both to sit down. Boule and Dubé took chairs at the end of the table.

With the exception of the PJ's Jean Foulon, Boule knew the other directors only as names and faces. He hadn't the slightest idea why any of them had been summoned. Dubé, pale and silent on their way over, had offered no suggestions, appearing unnerved by this summons to Olympus. Boule searched his pocket for a fresh handkerchief to dry his face. Dubé sat bolt upright, eyes riveted on Beaubien, his lips compressed with anxiety.

"We have an emergency," Beaubien began. "The Rue du Bac

murder, the deBrisay stabbing, the man and woman machine-gunned in the Rue Vavin, and two prostitutes stabbed in the Latin Quarter. You two are here to offer ideas and opinions as we examine the facts."

Dubé's color returned and Boule sensed his Chief's ego beginning to inflate. A tête-à-tête with the DG and his directors would be interpreted as a reinforcement of Dubé's value to the Sûreté. He would become even more insufferable.

Beaubien smoothed his moustache. "Six murders in less than a week and apparently all related."

"We don't know that for certain," Foulon said carefully. He had a Burgundian accent and tended to roll his r's.

"You're suggesting coincidence?" Beaubien asked.

"It's possible."

The DG shook his head while the others at the table picked up their photocopies and reread the pages. Boule and Dubé watched in silence.

"Then I must have missed something in your department's reports," the DG countered. "As I understand the latest facts, one of the dead prostitutes was employed in the deBrisay household, which the granddaughter left after Madame deBrisay's death to meet the only suspect in the Rue du Bac murder. That suspect, Marais, already knew the deceased, Pinot. In fact, the café where the granddaughter met Marais is directly across the street from Pinot's flat. Surely such a linkage of people and events precludes coincidence? Dubé, what do you think?"

But the Chief was too alert to get trapped on that one, Boule noted regretfully. The phlegmatic PJ director with his provincial mannerisms might be badly misplaced in his present post, and no doubt in Dubé's opinion was, but on a day-to-day basis he still held the power to advance or destroy Dubé's career. On the other hand Dubé couldn't afford to have Beaubien think him a complete fool. He hesitated a fraction of a second before replying.

"Agreed, Sir. A tenuous connection does exist between the events and people. But there's no way to connect the suspect Marais with the deBrisay killing. He was in our custody at the time." He glanced at Boule for confirmation, but the Commissaire was busy watching a fat gray pigeon that had alighted on the outside window ledge and was trying for a morsel hidden in the cracked mortar. "He'd have opportunity for five murders only, not six. That's where the linkage theory breaks down."

Boule had to admire the man's aplomb.

"Motive?" demanded the SDECE Director.

"For which killing?" Dubé countered.

"You choose. Tourists don't go around Paris murdering people without a motive." He stabbed his forefinger on the report. "It states only that this Marais 'might' have quarreled with the Greek. Quarreled about what? It doesn't say. Did the witness see or hear them quarrel?"

Dubé was getting in over his head.

"No, Sir."

"Then why report it?" he asked frostily.

"It does seem to me," the CRS Director smiled, "that if this Marais had cut the Greek's throat he'd have had a splash or two of blood on his clothing. Did you find any blood?"

"Did you look for any?" the SDECE Director demanded.

"His clothes were given to our forensic people," Dubé said stoutly.

Which was pure horseshit, Boule knew. They had gone through his things and found nothing. The pigeon gave up and flew off.

"Where is this suspect now?" the Gendarmerie Director asked.

"He was taken from custody by two men posing as police officers. We haven't seen him since." His voice lowered with embarrassment.

"No leads?"

"Nothing worthwhile."

"But you must have something. What about your *mouchards*?"

Every police group had its informers. Ex-convicts, prostitutes, petty criminals with phony papers who were allowed to exist unharassed in exchange for information from the street.

Dubé swallowed quickly before replying. "Sixteenth Arrondissement received a report this morning that Marais and the granddaughter were in a bank near the Trocadéro exchanging traveler's checks. But by the time Commissaire Blais and his men arrived on the scene they were gone, taking a pistol stolen from the bank's security guard."

Foulon turned to Dubé and blinked. "You mean they held up a bank with the bank guard's gun?" This was information he hadn't heard yet.

"Not exactly."

"What do you mean, not exactly? Either they did or they didn't."

Boule was enjoying the PJ's exasperation. Most of the time Dubé affected him exactly the same way.

"The bank refused to discuss details. The assistant manager claimed that it was a private matter." Dubé colored. "Apparently Marais cashed his checks at gunpoint with a weapon taken from the guard. The checks were all valid American Express. There was no theft."

"Incredible!" the DST said.

Beaubien interjected, "In any event they are still at large, armed, and obviously dangerous."

"And surprisingly resourceful," the SDECE commented to no one in particular.

"This man is on a lifetime parole in Canada?" The CRS looked up from his report and glanced around the table, his gaze fixing finally on the DST. "He killed a policeman. And you let him into the country?"

"Like hell I did!" the DST snarled.

"Then see you don't let him out."

"Now, just a minute —"

But before it got out of hand Beaubien stepped in smoothly. "I'm sure we're all agreed errors have been made. What we're after now are ideas, gentlemen. Motives, a theory as to what happened, and a course of action to bring those responsible to justice."

Bravo! Sound words. Boule reached for a cigarette until he remembered there were no ashtrays on the table and no one else present smoked. Instead, he reballed the handkerchief and dabbed his forehead.

Over the past few hours something had happened to worry the DG. Was some sensitive political nerve being pressed, drawing a panic response from someone high in government? Whatever had happened, Beaubien was under pressure to get this mess cleaned up swiftly and all the crumbs swept under the carpet, safe from public scrutiny. He listened while the directors discussed their plans.

After ten minutes of conversational ping-pong it was decided that within the next thirty-six hours pictures of the fugitives could be in the hands of every police officer in the nation. This was in addition to the photographs of Marais already posted at each airport, train station, and border crossing since late Thursday evening.

The CRS and PJ would join forces with the Gendarmerie and comb the city and its suburbs checking hotels, pensions, youth hostels, and car rental agencies. Since the SDECE operated the nation's best undercover network, they would exert pressure on known underground political and suspected terrorist groups to assist in tracking down the quarry. Operations would start in Paris and later, if required, expand into the rest of the country.

Costs for such an operation would be enormous, Boule knew. But if the directors had any misgivings over the amount of effort the DG had decided to put into the case they kept it to themselves. With the exception of the CRS.

"How sure are we that these are the right people? A tourist and a Comte's granddaughter — an unlikely pair of multiple murderers, wouldn't you say?"

Blasphemy from the CRS. The others looked at each other quite prepared to discuss it. Boule stepped into the breach in the nick of time.

"I am very sure," he said emphatically. "But proof will take time. It always does in a murder investigation."

He paused. He had their attention and decided to press his advantage. Even Beaubien nodded in approval. At Boule's elbow Dubé squirmed uncomfortably at having lost the limelight.

"Marais killed the Greek, make no mistake. Probably as a result of a drunken business quarrel. We are able to place him at the scene at the approximate time of death through an eyewitness and the autopsy report. His alibi about the hour he returned to his hotel cannot be verified by the desk clerk or porter. And if all this isn't enough, he has a history of settling personal differences with a knife. He's a tried and convicted killer."

They were all listening closely. Even the CRS stopped tapping his damn pencil. Boule reassembled the handkerchief and dabbed his face.

"Marie deBrisay was murdered by her granddaughter who, by the way, is only the Comte's granddaughter through marriage." He sighed like a patient Job forced reluctantly into revealing a partially conceived analysis of events. "I suspect it was done in a fit of anger or revulsion, perhaps a little jealousy — who knows — after learning about Marie deBrisay's flagrant sexual appetites and her liaison with the household chauffeur. Maybe she wanted the man for herself." He reflected a moment before resuming, as if an idea had just occurred to him. It was good theater.

"She entered her grandmother's apartment through an outside entrance next to the rose garden. But she was seen by the maid, either coming or going. When it dawned on her the damage such a witness might do to her in a police investigation she had to enlist Marais's help. They met on the Rue Vavin. Last night in the Latin Quarter they stabbed the maid and her roommate."

He regarded each of them in turn, waiting for questions. So far so good.

"It's my belief Marais and the Daladier girl knew each other from his visit last year. Both were in Paris at the same time. While there's no evidence they met, logic indicates they did. How else could she have dined with him at his hotel the day after he arrived in Paris? There is no other explanation. They were good friends, possibly lovers. She knew his background, knew he would help." A dramatic pause. "And so he did."

With that thought he left them all hanging. It seemed a long time before anyone spoke, then the DST stirred himself to ask: "And the Rue Vavin murders, Commissaire? Do you have a theory on those as well?"

Boule gave a gracious smile. "I do indeed, Sir. They are a matter of coincidence. Unrelated either to Marais or to the girl. He tried contacting his friend Pinot, that much is certain. But before they met, Pinot and his girlfriend were gunned down by another warring faction."

"Why?" SDECE asked.

"Pinot was a very wealthy pimp."

"Oh, I see."

The meeting adjourned with promises of speedy results to the DG. Not a word had been said about the paintings. Beaubien caught Boule at the door and steered him over to a window. Chief Dubé hung back, thought better of it, and reluctantly left them alone, closing the thick soundproof door on his way out.

"How are you handling the portraits?" The DG stood studying traffic in the street below.

Boule relaxed a little. "All at the Louvre with a friend of mine. They're quite safe."

"They're to be destroyed," he insisted.

"There may be others. I suggest we wait until Marais and the girl have been caught."

"Isn't that risky?"

Boule shrugged. "Only if they talk to someone before we arrest them. Afterwards it doesn't make any difference, does it?"

"How much do they know?"

"That's hard to say. Marais is no fool. For all we know he may have figured the whole thing out for himself already, in which case someone will have a lot of explaining to do if he decides to talk."

"How will you proceed?" Beaubien inquired.

"I will wait. If he knows nothing his only interest will be getting out of France with or without the girl. In which case I'd let him go. Complain to his Embassy, of course. But I shouldn't press the issue in case they offered to return him."

"I'll pass on that recommendation," the DG said.

Boule took a fresh handkerchief from his hip pocket and unfolded it carefully. "On the other hand, if he's realized what you're doing to him then he may decide to stay in France, either to prove his innocence or to satisfy his curiosity."

He wiped his neck, pulling his shirt collar away from the skin, after which he patted his face and forehead until they were dry. Beaubien watched him with barely concealed distaste.

"What happens then?" He spoke testily.

Boule smiled. "Why then, in that case we'll have to find him, won't we?"

Nancy, 3:21 P.M.

The Horizon caught up with the heavy clouds and rain showers near Nancy. "Cold front," the pilot announced laconically as the deluge swept around them and rivers of water poured across the plexiglass to be whipped away into the dark clouds. The machine bucked and yawed, flinging them against their seatbelts.

Marais nodded in an off-hand manner as though he'd spent a good part of his life riding through cold fronts in small planes. Behind him, Nicole scrunched down and clung tightly to her seat, swaying with the violent motion. When they'd been airborne for three-quarters of an hour and the turbulence seemed to be moderating he asked the pilot where they were.

"On course," he said, lifting one earphone higher on his head so he could listen simultaneously to the air traffic controller and Marais.

"Would it be too much trouble landing at Haguenau instead of Strasbourg?" Marais inquired. They were still in cloud. Light lamb's wool now, with an occasional bright spot overhead where the sun was trying to penetrate.

"Haguenau?" the pilot repeated.

"If it isn't too much trouble."

"No trouble. Same distance more or less." He checked his air map. "Strasbourg's closer to the German border."

"Haguenau, if you wouldn't mind," Marais told him evenly.

The pilot nodded, fiddled with his radio dial for a new signal, then picked up his mike and talked to the ground controller for permission to alter course. Marais held his breath in apprehension. If the authorities in Strasbourg had been alerted and were waiting at the airport, this sudden request for a course change would be refused. Instructions impregnated with static crackled from the raised earphone. A brief response from the pilot and they were turning onto the new course and starting their descent. Marais relaxed.

The aircraft slipped from beneath the cloud cover above the Vosges's forest-clad hills. Minutes later they landed at Weinumshof in a light but steady downpour. The pilot carried their bags into the terminal and wished them a happy honeymoon.

"I don't think he believed a word of your story," Nicole said after he'd gone into the airport office. "You should have tipped him."

"For what? Keeping his mouth shut?" He looked at his wristwatch. "Let's see if we can get a lift into town."

It cost a hundred francs for the five-minute ride. Inflation had reached Haguenau as well. A teenage apprentice delivered them to the town center in the airport manager's pickup truck. He had to go into town anyway for the mail, he explained.

The town looked like a period painting from the sixteenth century. Cobblestone streets, tall ancient houses, many half-timbered with overhanging storeys and flower-encrusted balconies, a few with delicate Gothic or Renaissance oriels, all creating a sense of timelessness and peace. Rain was keeping the tourists indoors, so there were few people about. Down a side street they found a small café, the Relais St Francis. They went inside, partly to get out of the rain and plan their next move and partly because they were hungry.

The waiter suggested a sausage produced by a local butcher. It was revolting, but they ate it anyway and rinsed away the taste with a bottle of tongue-rasping Chablis. By four o'clock they were feeling much better.

"No, Monsieur, there is no art gallery in Haguenau, but we have a fine museum," the waiter informed them. "There's an art gallery in Strasbourg you should see while you're in the district."

Marais tried a different tack. "Any local artists? My wife and I are interested primarily in paintings. Portraits in particular."

But it didn't strike a chord. Perhaps he was too young to know about the local talent.

"I could ask Monsieur Wirtz. He might know."

A beefy red-faced man with a trio of chins emerged from the kitchen and introduced himself as owner of the premises. First he wanted to know if they'd enjoyed his sausage, to which Nicole gave an appreciative smile. After a modest bow he launched into a brief history of the town starting in the fourth century. Marais let him get as far as the ninth before interrupting.

"A portrait painter from the town. I believe his name was Dorfmundt?"

"Of course! Old Karl." His face fell. "Died this spring, poor man, after a long illness. He was quite famous in his day, I understand. Appointed Court painter to the Hohenzollern family. That would be back in World War I. I was in the Algerian business myself," and he was off on the Ben Barka disappearance and how it had been necessary to murder the poor man. Marais interrupted, "Did the painter Dorfmundt live here in town?"

"No, not in town. Just outside of town on the highway to Wissembourg before you reach the forest station. Quite a big house with a studio at the rear. You can't miss it. His widow still lives there. Strange woman. Kept to herself, not a mixer. He wasn't much of a mixer himself. Artists are like that, I suppose. Why, the other day I read a story on Picasso . . ." And he was off again.

The rain came in heavy gusts borne on the frontal winds they'd flown through near Nancy. Marais asked if he could call a taxi to take them back to the garage where their car was being repaired. Wirtz sent the waiter off to phone.

When the taxi came they paid the bill, thanked the owner for his courtesy and fled.

"Take the Wissembourg highway out of town," Marais told the driver.

"You got it! Any place in particular?"

"The Dorfmundt house."

"I know the place."

They were there in minutes. It was enclosed on three sides by tall firs and sat a short distance back from the highway. At its rear the manicured trees of the Haguenau Forest paraded away into the mist and rain. A paved driveway ran up to a single-car garage separated from the house by a flagstone walkway.

"Want me to wait? I mean in case there's no one home."

Marais shook his head. "No, thanks. We're expected."

The fare came to forty francs. In gratitude he handed the driver sixty. Their first encounter with Alsatian integrity deserved to be rewarded.

They took their luggage and walked around back of the house in case he decided to wait after all and make sure they got in the front door. After a couple of minutes pressed against the side of the house they heard the car turn around and drive away.

The flagstone walkway ended with three stone steps ascending to a cosy patio. Double sliding glass doors provided access to the house. He set down the suitcases and tried the door. It opened.

"Now what do we do?" Nicole asked.

He shut the door. "We knock."

But no one came. They were getting very wet. He slid it open again. Nicole followed him inside.

"Anyone at home?" he called.

Silence.

"Hello!" Nicole tried.

Silence.

"Maybe she's asleep."

"Or deaf."

"Or dead," he suggested.

"Very funny."

He brought the suitcases in and closed the door. The room they had entered extended from the patio doors across to where two casement windows looked out on the front garden. An enormous open fireplace hung with decorative copper pots and pans provided a baronial touch. All the furnishings had been covered with dust sheets. There were no photographs, paintings, lithographs, or wall hangings to be seen anywhere, not even hooks or nails. Threadbare Persian carpets with fading mosaic designs covered the floor. A grandfather clock had stopped at 10:23.

"What happens when she finds us in her house?" Nicole asked softly.

"We introduce ourselves, I suppose. C'mon, let's explore."

They checked the downstairs first: reading room, library, den, dining room, pantry, and kitchen. Only the kitchen appeared to have been used recently. There was bread in the breadbox and milk in the refrigerator. He checked the milk. It wasn't sour.

On the second-floor landing they stopped and looked at each other. They'd both heard it: a sound somewhere between a creaking floor and a cracking ankle bone. He placed a finger to his lips, waiting.

"It must have been the wind. Old houses have a habit of cracking when the humidity changes," he said softly.

She looked unconvinced. "If she heard us, Roger, won't she think we're burglars trying to steal the silver or something?"

Of course she would.

"Hello! Madame Dorfmundt!" he yelled suddenly. Nicole jumped with fright. "We're not going to harm you. We want to talk to you about your husband's paintings. You know, the ones you sold last April to that art dealer from Paris. The Greek, Dimitrios Kouridis, remember him?"

They went from room to room, Marais continuing his explanations in loud tones as they searched for the terrified old woman. At last, in a front bedroom near the end of the hall, they found her. But she wasn't frightened and hiding.

She was dead.

Stone cold and stiff in rigor mortis she lay face down on a violet shag rug. Two neat bullet holes were visible at the base of her skull where the long gray hair had parted when she fell. Her hand was outstretched and reaching for the telephone on her dressing table.

She would have been in her late sixties or early seventies, he guessed. She was dressed in a skirt and sweater. There were no signs of struggle, no tipped drawers, toppled furniture or broken lamps. He went over and checked the phone. It too was quite dead.

"They got here before we did, Roger."

He nodded. "Probably sometime yesterday afternoon. Someone who knew we'd be heading in this direction looking for answers."

"It's all so senseless! What is it that's so terrible . . ."

When she stopped in mid-sentence he looked up from the corpse and saw her eyes widen as the slim elegant man standing directly behind her began prodding her into the room with the gun he was holding.

In German-accented French, the man said, "If you'd be good enough to raise your hands very high above your head I'd be most grateful."

Paris, 4:08 P.M.

When André returned to the photographic studio, Poincaré himself presented him with the list of names of the deBrisay wedding party. André plucked the sheet from the little man's manicured fingers. There were twelve names and addresses of guests who'd been sent copies of the wedding photograph. The bridesmaids were among them. He thanked Poincaré gravely and promised a letter of commendation — suitable for framing — from the Brigade Criminelle for his splendid cooperation. Poincaré was overwhelmed. Even his assistant, sulking behind the counter, appeared impressed.

He went back to the car and sat studying the names, trying to decide what to do next. It was after four o'clock. Everything would be shutting down for the weekend. Should he report his latest findings to Boule? Seek his advice on how next to proceed? He hesitated. The Commissaire might think that a sign of indecision. The seasoned veteran hadn't turned the Rue du Bac business over to him simply because he liked the color of André Villeneuve's dark brown eyes. No, he was expected to perform. If he got into trouble along the way the Commissaire could be reached by phone over the weekend at his home in Villejuif.

With that decision made, some of his earlier hesitancy lifted. Now, how to find the present whereabouts of his bridesmaids?

Start with the first, Hélène Gauthier. Would she still be living at number 16 Rue Brancion after thirty-five years? Unlikely.

Traffic flowed around the car. He realized suddenly that it was rush hour and he was blocking the curb lane. Passing drivers glared angrily or shook their fists. He started the motor and joined the slow-moving stream. Why did today have to be Friday?

Somewhere someone had records of these women filed away. The police? Not unless they had criminal records. Then what about tax department records, or the voters lists from polling stations closest to each woman's residence? Where did that lead? Nowhere if they had all been unemployed and too young to vote.

He radioed Dispatch and asked for a driver's license address on Hélène Gauthier, age about fifty-five. When they came back with an answer he'd crossed to the Left Bank and was within a short distance of Rue Brancion.

Computer records of driver's licenses didn't extend beyond 1962. There were twenty-eight Hélène Gauthiers in Paris alone, seven of them in their fifties. Records needed a birthdate, color of eyes, a middle name or an occupation before they could narrow the choice. It would be no use asking them to try the next name on his list.

Boule would know where to look. So he tried putting himself in the Commissaire's shoes, reasoning the way he would. It was no use. He hadn't the foggiest idea how to proceed other than by a lengthy and tedious process of elimination which might take weeks.

An elderly concierge at the Rue Brancion address told him that he'd held the post for twenty-two years and he'd never heard of Hélène Gauthier.

"Was she a nurse?"

Most of his residents worked at the Pasteur Institute or its hospital. Why not give them a try? "Thirty-five years ago, you say? That'd be just after the war."

"Three years after," André agreed.

The concierge sucked his lower lip and thought a moment. "Have you checked with the Prefect of Paris records for the fifteenth arrondissement? They'd probably have her on file if you fellows don't."

"Oh, why?"

"Identity papers were issued by the Prefect's office. Without identity papers she couldn't have got a ration book or a job. Things were very strict after the war. Not like now."

"This was in 1948," André reminded him.

"So you said. But restrictions remained in force until long after the war ended." He sniffed condescendingly. "You young fellows don't know how lucky you are today."

André thanked him politely and returned to the car. It was no use. The Prefecture's offices were closed until Monday morning. He might just as well pack it in, take the car back to the motor pool and catch the métro home. The late afternoon sky had cleared, promising a lovely summer weekend. He'd call his girlfriend and they'd take the train to the beach tomorrow. They both enjoyed Deauville.

As he started the motor two fashionably dressed young women sauntered past the car. They were chatting amicably and looked like models from the Rue du Faubourg Saint-Honoré. Then a thought struck him. The deBrisay woman had worked in one of those fashion houses. That was where the Comte first saw her. Maybe Hélène or one of the others — or all of them — had worked at the same establishment. They were all beautiful enough to be models. And at least five had come to Paris from the Ardennes after having their portraits done. Of course, how stupid! Where better to start looking than at the fashion house where they might have been employed? One of the older employees might remember something useful. First a call to the Comte in Versailles, jogging his memory for the name of that couturier house in the Faubourg Saint-Honoré where he had met his future wife. All thoughts of a weekend at the beach vanished as he put the car in gear and headed back across the city.

Vitry-le-François, 4:10 P.M.

Daggar Paoli's corpse was discovered by three hard-faced men outside of Vitry-le-François. They had got on at Châlons-sur-Marne, one at the front of the train, two at the rear. Taking the ticket collector with them to open any unyielding doors, they made a thorough search. The two in the rear found the compartment with the bloodstained carpet first. They dragged the body from the toilet and laid it on the floor. For an instant both men stared at the corpse in disbelief.

"Go and find Vincetti," the one examining Paoli's clothing told the other man. To the ticket collector he said: "You sit down for a minute."

The man obeyed without question. His legs felt weak. In all his years on the railroad such a thing had never happened.

"Is the train to be stopped, Monsieur?" he asked.

"No! We have transport waiting at Vitry-le-François. We'll carry him off the train. You keep to the schedule."

"The police will have to be notified."

"You will say nothing!" the man interrupted sternly. "This is a matter of national security and we *are* the police."

The other two returned, crowding into the tiny compartment.

"The moment we arrive in Vitry, get to the van and bring that body bag, two sheets, and the stretcher. You'll have four minutes to get him off. Go now!"

He spoke rapidly like a man used to giving orders. The train began slowing after its run across the flatlands from Châlons-sur-Marne. Vincetti and the other man left immediately.

"A man and a woman were in this compartment, traveling to Haguenau. Blonde woman in a white dress. Man in a sports jacket. Do you remember them?"

The ticket collector nodded slowly.

"Where did they get off the train?"

"I don't know."

"Did they have luggage?"

"I think so."

"This dead man," he pointed at the body. "Ever see him before?"

The collector shrugged. "But of course, he accompanied me through the train from Paris to Meaux while I checked the first-class compartments. He must have come back here later."

"Did you see him after Meaux?"

"Yes, in the corridor."

"And after that?"

The collector shook his head. "I didn't see him again." He glanced at the corpse. "Until now."

"So they must have got off between Meaux and Châlons." He was thinking aloud, deciding who he would call to check those intermediate stops. Strasbourg should send a team back to Haguenau in case they made it through the net. Paris would have to be notified immediately.

The train slowed into the station and stopped.

"I shall be wanted on the platform," the collector observed, stirring himself. "Regulations require that..."

The man interrupted: "Go, then. And remember, not a word!"

It took a minute and forty seconds before the other two were back. Working swiftly, they hoisted Paoli into the dark green body bag and wrapped him with the sheets. With the package strapped securely on the stretcher they worked their cargo awkwardly out of the compartment, down the corridor and onto the platform with seconds to spare.

There were a few curious stares as they crossed the platform. An elderly priest paused when they passed and made the sign of the cross. The hard-faced men inclined their heads.

The driver of the van, a muscular young man with a wisp of hair on his upper lip, stood waiting anxiously at the vehicle's open rear. Once the others had loaded the stretcher and climbed in he slammed the doors. Moments later the van left the parking lot and was racing back along the highway toward Châlons-sur-Marne and Reims.

Haguenau, 4:11 P.M.

"Where do you fit into all this?" the elegant man with the pistol asked Marais. He had a narrow aesthetic face, high forehead, and determined chin. His hair, snow white and plentiful, was combed straight back from a widow's peak.

"I'm an innocent bystander trying to find out what's going on."

"Why?"

"The police are trying to kill me for a murder I didn't commit." It didn't sound very plausible.

"Interesting," the man said and turned to Nicole, his gun still pointed at Marais. "And what is your part in this affair, young lady?"

"The police are trying to kill me too." Even more implausible.

"Why?"

She dropped her arms a little, then caught herself and raised them higher.

"Because I'm with him. They think we know something about the portraits, but we don't. That's why we came here. We thought Madame Dorfmundt might tell us something."

"Such as what?" He sounded mildly curious.

She shrugged, raising her arms even higher, "How they came to be painted and why. If there were any others. What happened to the models. Can I put my arms down? They're beginning to ache."

"Yes, of course — not you, Monsieur, just the lady," he cautioned politely.

Marais judged him to be in his early sixties. He wore an old-fashioned belted tan raincoat with epaulettes and leather weave buttons. His gray eyes were alert and his hand remarkably steady.

"Your name, Monsieur?"

Marais introduced himself, then Nicole.

"Daladier, did you say?" The gun wavered ever so slightly.

"From Lyon," Marais amplified.

He turned to Nicole. "Your mother's name?"

"Irène," she said.

"Then your grandmother was . . . ?"

"Marie deBrisay."

"Quite right." He pocketed the gun. A fleeting sadness seemed to cross his face. "Please, lower your arms, Monsieur. My apologies for putting you through this, but I had to find out who you were and why you came."

Marais let out a long sigh of relief. "You scared the hell out of us!" He sat down beside Nicole on the bed, blocking her view of the body. The man's gaze remained fixed, studying Nicole as one might examine a medical curiosity. Marais felt his own assertiveness beginning to return.

"Suppose you tell us what you're doing here and who you are?"

"Of course!" He smiled politely and took off the raincoat. "I was on the point of leaving when you arrived. For a moment I thought you were police. That would have been most awkward for me."

Without the coat he looked like a genial yachtsman or English country squire in his gray flannels and navy blue blazer with emblematic brass buttons.

"I am German," he announced, bowing from the waist. "Hans Schefler, at your service. My home is near Baden-Baden, on the edge of the Black Forest. Two days ago my employer received a phone call from Elsa." He paused and pointed to the corpse. "She was very worried. There had been a television news story that afternoon on Marie de Brisay's murder. Two hours later a man arrived from Strasbourg wanting to know if she had any more of Karl's paintings for sale. She asked him to leave and threatened to call the police. He laughed and told her that he was with the police and would be back to see her later when she was in a better temper. As she had sold a number of her husband's canvases to a dealer from Paris last April, my employer told her not to worry. Her visitor could have been joking about being from the police, and in all probability the fact that he'd arrived within two hours of the murder announcement had been coincidence."

"Excuse me, but can we continue this conversation downstairs?" Nicole asked.

"Why, certainly! How stupid of me," Schefler apologized.

Schefler took her hand and led her from the room and along the hall to the staircase, Marais following. They went back to the patio room at the end of the house. Schefler saw the suitcases.

"You came prepared to stay?"

"Not really. Just a quick visit before crossing the border."

"And then?"

"We hadn't planned that far ahead," Marais admitted.

They sat on the dust sheets and watched the rain, Schefler examining Nicole once more in that same curious manner.

"You were saying that your employer told Madame Dorfmundt not to worry," Marais prompted, bringing him around.

"Yes. Then yesterday after thinking about it again he phoned back to see if she was all right. There was no answer. He started to worry. When there was no answer again today I was sent to find out why."

"You came by car?" Marais asked.

"Yes. It's a half hour's drive. I parked off the road near the forestry station and walked back. The rest you know." He reflected a moment. "Except that all the paintings are gone. Portraits, landscapes — everything, including sketches and pencil drawings. I searched the atelier out back and every room in the house." A frown creased his high forehead. "Could it be possible," he mused, "that the French police killed Elsa and took the paintings?"

"Not only possible but probable," Marais said emphatically.

Schefler blinked at the enormity of the accusation. "But why? What was accomplished?"

Marais shrugged. "Silence. Elimination of damning evidence.

Suppression of facts. Who knows?" He turned to Nicole. "Why don't you tell him what's been happening to us."

Schefler listened intently as she spoke. "Mein Gott!" he exclaimed when she'd finished, his composure shaken for the first time since they'd met. "What did you do with the guns and bomb parts?"

"In the black suitcase," Nicole said. "Roger thought we should keep everything for evidence. Who would believe such a story without proof?"

Schefler nodded. "I believe you." He stood up. "We must leave immediately before someone returns. I'll fetch the car. Meet me in the driveway, and don't forget your bags."

He slipped out the patio door and disappeared around the corner of the house. The rain had slackened a little.

"Shouldn't we wipe away our fingerprints or something?" Nicole asked.

Marais smiled. "Why bother? What's one murder more or less? If they can't hang us with this one then perhaps the next."

"The next?"

"Or the one after that," he said. "They're all madmen."

He picked up the suitcases. She followed him outside with the attaché case. The car was a Mercedes four-door sedan, dark gray in color, with such a high polish that the raindrops slithered off without pooling. Schefler deposited their luggage in the trunk.

The car's interior smelled of leather and expensive aftershave. Schefler turned the car around and pointed it onto the highway back to Haguenau.

"I will phone my employer for instructions," he announced. "It is certain he will want to meet you." He didn't explain why. He stopped at a service station in Kaltenhaus, a suburb on the other side of Haguenau within sight of the airport. While an attendant checked the car he went inside to use the telephone. He was gone a long time.

"My employer asks if it would be convenient for you to come to Baden-Baden?" Schefler asked when he got back in the car.

Marais and Nicole looked at each other. Why not, if he could get them over the border with their suitcases. They nodded.

"There may be a problem." He started the car. "If the French police are looking for you it is possible your photographs have been distributed to all border crossings."

"Would they have had time?" Marais asked.

Schefler nodded. "They can be extremely efficient when it suits their purposes. What I propose is to drop you off in Drusenheim while I visit the border guards at the bridge. I know most of them personally. If there is a problem I'll find out."

"And if there is a problem? We have no passports and all my ID is in my own name."

"In that case we will try another way." He gave Marais an avuncular pat on the knee. "I am not without resources in these matters."

Ten minutes later he dropped them at a crowded café on the edge of the village of Drusenheim. After they'd ordered two beers, speaking in English as a precaution, Nicole asked, "Do you trust him?" She had to raise her voice over the noise.

"Who, Schefler? Sure, why not?"

"He keeps looking at me in a very strange way. Have you noticed?"

"I noticed."

"It's not sexual. It's something else."

The waiter brought their beer. Made from locally grown hops, he explained in broken English.

"Cheers!" they said loudly in unison. The waiter smiled approvingly.

"Supposing he's gone?" she said suddenly. "Across the bridge with the bags and all our evidence?"

"Why would he do that?"

"I don't know. After the last couple of days I'm suspicious of everyone and everything."

"Except me?" he asked hopefully.

She laced her fingers into his. "Except you, Roger." She leaned over and kissed him very tenderly. Her lips tasted like the beer, cool and refreshing and — surprisingly — romantic. When they finally separated, those sitting nearest to their table clapped. One man shouted "Bravo!" in a bass voice. Marais felt self-conscious. Nicole blushed. He caught sight of the car through the front window. They excused themselves. "Jolly good show, Englander!" the waiter said when Marais paid the bill. "Come back soon again."

Schefler had visited with his friends in the border crossing office. Marais's picture had been tacked on the bulletin board near the front entrance.

"Not a very good likeness. But close enough for identification, I'm afraid. Especially if they're the least bit suspicious and demand your passport," the German said.

"Not Nicole?"

He shook his head. "Not so far. I can take her across but you'll have to go by boat. I will arrange it."

Less than half a kilometer from the bridge they turned off on a side road. A sign read "Dalhunden 1 km." Schefler explained: "Two kilometers past Dalhunden there is a bridge over the river Moder, one of the Rhine's tributaries. I'll drop you there. Climb down the bank and wait under the bridge. Someone will be along in a motorboat to pick you up within the hour and bring you across to the German side. We'll meet in Söllingen."

Marais nodded. What else could he do?

"It's quite secure," Schefler said, sensing Marais's reluctance. "In Söllingen there is a man who operates a number of small boats. He works with my employer. It will take him only a few minutes to cross the river." He gave Marais a kindly glance. "Don't worry, my young friend, I won't desert you."

That wasn't what worried him. It was Nicole. What if the border guards decided to ask Schefler about the blonde he'd produced fifteen minutes after chatting them up about the man whose picture they had hanging in their rogues' gallery? Did they tell him the rogue was traveling with a blonde? Had he asked?

"Nicole stays with me," he told the German.

"As you wish," Schefler said without taking his eyes from the road. But he was not pleased.

Beyond Dalhunden the road narrowed again until it became a winding woodland trail. Then they were in the open and within a stone's throw of the Rhine. A laden barge with a white superstructure pressed against the current, moving slowly upstream to Strasbourg. Schefler stopped a few meters from the bridge.

"I'd like my suitcases," Marais said.

"You won't need them."

"Maybe not. But you could have a heart attack between here and Söllingen. It happens."

That caused a fleeting smile. "You are a very cautious man, Monsieur Marais." The voice was tinged with respect. "Very well then, you shall have your luggage."

Rain still fell in a steady light drizzle. More than a mist, less than a shower, it penetrated their outer clothing quickly. Nicole shivered.

Schefler closed the trunk. "The boatman will ask if you'd enjoy a trip to Baden-Baden," he said. "He's a man about my age with a military bearing. Stay under the bridge and out of sight. Sometimes a DST border patrol checks along this road. If they see those suitcases they will become suspicious." For a moment he hesitated as though some further explanation were required, then thought better of it and closed the trunk. "I'll see you in an hour," he promised, and was gone.

When they were settled under the bridge on a section of more or less dry and level ground Marais opened his suitcase and took out a sweater.

"Here, put this on."

She tugged the turtleneck over her head and pulled it down over the damp dress.

"I have a suit jacket."

She took that too. He put an arm about her shoulders and drew her to him. Damp hair brushed his cheek.

"Sorry to put you through this," he said. "But I couldn't leave you alone with that old smoothie."

"I'm glad you didn't," she told him simply.

They sat huddled in silence, staring at the eddies and river mist, waiting for the boat they knew would come. Twenty minutes went by. A trio of water fowl paddled past, making for the inland shallows. Nicole looked at them and smiled. The birds were so intent, so puffed with self-importance as they glided along. Then the sound of a truck punctuated the stillness. Faintly at first, it came from the direction of Dalhunden. Its diesel motor lumbered overhead and continued down the road. But as the noise of its passing faded they heard another engine. This one was constant, like a car parked on the roadside just short of the bridge with its motor running.

Marais placed his finger to his lips. Nicole nodded. A minute passed. Then another. The vehicle remained. A car door slammed. Marais froze, straining to hear footsteps. It was no use. He motioned Nicole to keep down. It might be a fisherman. Did people still fish the Rhine? Wasn't it supposed to be more polluted than the St. Lawrence? No, it wasn't a fisherman, he decided. Not with the car's motor still running. More likely someone had stopped to check. On what? Something they'd dropped at the side of the road maybe.

"I'm going up to investigate." He breathed in her ear. Her eyes were fearful. She touched his cheek as he turned away.

Whoever had got out of the car, he reasoned, would be looking off across the river. There was certainly nothing to see on the land-ward side. By climbing the other embankment he could come up behind unnoticed.

He crawled off, concentrating on his footing. One misstep in the slippery grass and he'd be in the water. Once out from under the bridge he could see the car top. It wore a large blue dome-light on its roof. Police? Border Patrol? Did it matter? Cautiously, he made his way up to the embankment.

The car's uniformed driver stood leaning with both elbows on the hood as he studied the river through a pair of very large binoc-ulars. Static from a mobile radio crackled out the open window. Marais had seen enough. He dropped away. Had they been betrayed? Impossible, or the man would have looked beneath the bridge. A regular patrol, more likely.

But if the car remained much longer their pickup boat would see it and turn back. He couldn't allow that to happen. Why did the man have to stop here? Weren't there any other bridges on his route? Short of getting in and driving the car away himself he didn't see what more he could do.

Within the hour, Schefler had said. He checked his watch. Thirty-five minutes had elapsed since the German's departure. The boat could arrive at any time. That car had to go. He made his way back to Nicole.

"Police patrol," he muttered. "One cop with binoculars watch-ing the river."

"What do we do?"

"Persuade him to move on."

"How?"

"I don't know."

He opened their suitcase arsenal and brought out Daggar Paoli's .44 Magnum with the silencer.

"You're not going to kill him?"

"Not unless he tries to kill me." Marais whispered. He shut the suitcase. "If the car isn't moved the boat won't come in for us."

He could see she didn't approve. Neither did he. But what was the alternative? He eased himself along the bank. A light tap on the head wouldn't hurt the man badly. There would be some rope in the car to tie him up. He could drive back toward Dalhunden until he was out of sight of the bridge. When they reached Germany he'd phone the French police and tell them where to look. Their man would wake up with a bad headache and a tender scalp. No harm done, at least from Marais's point of view. The French police, however, would see things differently.

The man was still leaning on the hood when he got back. Marais flattened himself below the edge of the road. As he lay judging the distance for his running assault, the mobile radio suddenly crackled.

"Central to Patrol Seven. State your position. Over."

Marais tensed. The man straightened. Christ, he was Patrol Seven! He turned, stuffing the binoculars into their case. Marais raised his Magnum. But the man never looked in his direction as he came around the open door and slid into the car.

"Patrol Seven to Central. I'm stopped at position M4. Over."

"Roger, Patrol Seven. Report back to Central immediately. DST Paris has transmitted a photographic ident on two murder suspects, a man and a woman. You'd better have a copy. Over."

"Roger, Central. I'm on my way."

Antwerp, 5:13 P.M.

Normally, Max Kramer closed up shop in his Antwerp office at four o'clock sharp. But today he had decided to stay later. Several matters were troubling him.

First, one of his most trusted couriers had disappeared with a small fortune in cut stones. It had happened somewhere between New York and Rio. The man who had got on the VARIG flight with the attaché case handcuffed to his wrist was not the same man who got off in Rio. Same name; wrong man. And no attaché case. There'd been a number of sensitive documents hidden in the lining of the case. Losing the diamonds was bad enough. Losing the documents could be catastrophic, both to Moscow Center and to himself. If his errant courier had decided to turn the trip into an early retirement, Kramer hoped he had had enough sense to destroy the incriminating papers before absconding with the gems. On the other hand, he could have been kidnapped by a competing agency. They all knew what Traveler was doing in the diamond business.

An operative's career in the field lasts at most ten years before circumstances either at home or abroad force his recall, retirement, defection, or death. Max Kramer had already confounded the odds of longevity. He realized he'd been living on borrowed time. Whether or not his missing courier had defected, absconded, or been spirited away would be difficult to say for a day or two. Whatever the circumstance, Kramer had to be ready.

Next, he faced the Adelaine Mercure business. Stupid woman. He should never have brought her into his warren. If she had talked he was finished already. Even now he could be under surveillance by the thick-headed Belgian police. He had made up his mind this morning as to what to do about Adelaine Mercure and her portrait phobia. If the KGB colonel wasn't back on Monday he'd use her as his conduit to defect. It would be a good move. French stock in NATO would soar. Her colorless husband would probably collect a promotion, or at least a medal, for his negotiating skills, and Max Kramer would be hailed as one more example of Soviet duplicity falling to the triumph of good over evil.

But that was before he'd received word on the missing courier and the strange phone call from Adelaine Mercure less than an hour ago. She wanted a meeting. She said a friend was coming up from Paris who wanted to discuss the portraits with him.

Those damn paintings!

He was afraid to say anything over the telephone. She suggested he meet them in Brussels with his car. They would be on foot waiting at whatever point in the city he preferred. Ten o'clock, if that would be convenient, giving her friend time to reach the city, she explained apologetically. Quickly, he decided that by cooperating he could maintain the present equilibrium until the odds for tipping the balance were completely in his favor.

He suggested the Parc Josaphat in the Schaerbeek District for the pickup. It was central to all roads leading from the city and an ideal location for losing pursuers in traffic should it become necessary.

"The corner of Avenue Louis Bertrand and Boulevard Lambermont. Do you know the place?"

"I'll find it," she promised. "Ten o'clock then?"

This friend of hers added a new dimension to his problem. Had she discussed her espionage activities with the friend? How, he wondered wearily, could he talk about the paintings when he knew less about them than they did?

His phone rang, making him start. It was Boris Titov at the airport.

"Your fears are unfounded." Titov spoke in French.

That was good news as far as it went. "I see," Kramer said cautiously.

"But you're to take no action on the matter until we've talked."

"Agreed." Killing Adelaine Mercure was the furthest thing from his mind at that moment.

"We must meet," Titov said.

"When?"

"As soon as possible."

That was good. He could get whatever information the man had uncovered in Moscow, then continue on to his meeting with the women with a better idea about his own position.

"I'll be at the arrivals door in forty-five minutes. Wait for me," Traveler told Titov. If it hadn't been for the weekend traffic he could easily have made it in thirty.

Paris, 5:22 P.M.

"The place is a few doors down the street from Hermès leather," Comte deBrisay told André over the telephone. He sounded peevish at being interrupted. "I spent two hours with one of your detectives this morning answering silly questions, Monsieur Villeneuve. Why can't you people get together and decide what you want to know all at the same time?"

André apologized for the intrusion and thanked him for his information.

Hermès occupied a trio of adjoining six-storey buildings on the corner of Rue du Faubourg St. Honoré and Rue Boissy d'Anglas. He parked the car in a restricted zone and walked back. The sidewalks were as crowded with people as the fashionable shop windows were with their expensive enticements. He found what he thought was the right entrance and went inside. He was surrounded by silks, perfume, and beautiful women.

"Monsieur?" prompted the receptionist.

She was too lovely to be real. André blushed. His tongue stuck to the roof of his mouth. He produced his ID.

"Goodness!"

She was teasing. He asked for their oldest employee.

"You're not serious?"

"I am." He felt like a eunuch.

She gave him a strange look. "I'll go and find Madame Andanucci. Wait here please."

By the time the coiffured Madame Andanucci arrived he'd managed to adjust to the surrounding feminine pulchritude and could speak without a blush. With a gallant bow he introduced himself again and asked the same question. She regarded him icily as she would an impoverished suitor.

"Do you mean 'old' in terms of physical longevity or years with this establishment, Monsieur?"

He explained. "There was a woman who worked here, Madame. A model. Nineteen forty-six, forty-seven, in that era. Possibly someone employed here during those years would remember her?"

"Possibly." She had a stiff implacability to her posture as though corseted in eternal pain. "What is your interest in this woman, Monsieur?"

"A police matter, Madame," he said. Two could play at the same evasive game.

Her chagrin escaped in a vexatious hiss.

"This model's name, Monsieur?" she snapped.

"Marie Carnot."

Her transformation was immediate. Indigo eyes that had drenched him with contempt were now alert and alive with curiosity. Carefully, she reexamined him. André refused to blink.

"You are investigating the death of Madame Marie deBrisay?" Her voice had changed texture, taffeta to velvet.

He nodded.

"Follow me, please, Monsieur," she said.

Her private office on the second floor had been designed for the financial seduction of the establishment's clientele. The room and furnishings were all done in white and gold: soft sofa, comfortable chairs, a footstool, an enormous full-length mirror in a gilt-encrusted frame and a small discreet writing bureau with floral marquetry on its flap. The atmosphere was intimate. They sat on the sofa. Madame Andanucci rested a braceleted wrist on the back cushions. André declined a cigarette. The gold box went back on the marble-topped coffee table.

"In 1947 I started work with this house," she began. A wisp of a smile melted her lips. "I don't look that old?" She paused to acknowledge his tactful look of astonishment. "I was seventeen. My name was Arsenault then. Marie suggested I change it to Andanucci. She was a little older than I and of course much more beautiful. We worked together at most showings. However, we were never friends. No fights or anything like that. But she moved in a different circle from mine. It came from having no family, I imagine. She lived in the Latin Quarter back then, with her roommate and her little girl, a sweet child of about three with the blondest hair you ever saw."

He brought out the wedding photograph and asked if she recognized anyone. Almost shyly, she took a pair of half-moon spectacles from a leather case hidden within the folds of her dress and adjusted the gold wires over her ears.

"How lovely she looked then," her fingers touched Marie's corsage and moved on. "That's Adelaine, second on the left. She worked here awhile after Marie left. Next to her, Irène Boisson, Marie's roommate. She danced at the Lido a number of years before marrying the manager." A pause while she checked the others' faces. She shook her head. "There's no one else I recognize."

"Can you remember what happened to Adelaine? Who she married, where she went?" He wanted to stay with those who'd had portraits done.

She removed the spectacles. "I'm sorry. You could try Irène. She'd know. She knew all Marie's friends. They were very close."

Irène lived in Reims. She found the address and telephone number in her desk and wrote it down for him. André felt his pulse quicken. He thanked her. She accompanied him downstairs and through.

"Does this help you, Monsieur?"

It certainly did.

For a half hour he drove around aimlessly wondering what to do with the information. In the end he decided to call Commissaire Boule. He'd know what to do.

But when he telephoned Villejuif there was no one home. As he was turning the car toward Reims, an uneasy thought crossed his mind: maybe he was overstepping Boule's mandate by leaving Paris. Should he advise the Reims PJ of his intentions, or Paris? In the end he did nothing, reasoning that silence should always take precedence over discretion in a murder investigation. Though he wasn't so sure Boule would have agreed.

River Rhine, 5:30 P.M.

A small cabin cruiser came spiriting through the mist, its diesel rumbling comfortably, a black, red, and yellow flag hanging wetly from its stern. As it slid slowly under their bridge a lone man appeared on the open aftdeck. He wore a bright yellow slicker and rain hat.

"Would you enjoy a trip to Baden-Baden?" His hands cupped the words.

Marais stood and waved. The boat nosed into shore, grounding on the river bank. He boosted Nicole onto the prow, passed her the luggage and jumped aboard. Gently the cruiser backed away into midstream. They went below. The man in the slicker stood at the wheel. He pointed them to seats. When they were settled he levered the power and the little craft surged out across the wide river. No one spoke until they were closing on the opposite shore, when the man looked over his shoulder and said: "Söllingen!" then turned away before either of them could answer.

Schefler stood waiting dockside at the small marina, his trench coat wrapped around him like a wet winding sheet.

"No problem?" Schefler inquired facetiously.

"Ask him," Marais said. "We were just along for the ride."

They thanked the boatman. Schefler looked pleased. They exchanged a few words in German while the man secured his mooring lines. As they left the dock he gave Schefler a casual salute and called him "major."

"You were in the army?" Marais asked when they reached the car.

He shrugged as though it had been an inconsequential matter. "Nearly everyone of my generation served. I retired as a major," he smiled, "in 1945. An early retirement."

They skirted Söllingen and, keeping to a secondary road, crossed the Rhine plain: Stollhofen, Leiberstung, Weitenung: orderly villages in a sea of intensively cultivated farmland. As they neared the edge of the Black Forest country the flatlands became hills slanted with vineyards. Schefler provided running commentary on points of interest.

"Where are we going?" Nicole asked.

"Varnhaft, near Baden-Baden. We're nearly there."

She shivered.

Marais said: "Can we stop at the first decent-sized town that sells women's clothing? She needs to change into something dry."

They stopped in Steinbach. She bought slacks, walking shoes, some underthings, and a soft gray sweater.

Five minutes later they were in Varnhaft, a dormitory town outside Baden-Baden. A winding road on the other side brought them to a district of expensive homes partially hidden from view by tall trees. They turned into a paved drive that curved through the pines then opened onto a grassy clearing. Beyond lay the house. It looked like a larger version of the place in Haguenau. On the left was a four-car garage with a black Opel parked inside one of the two open bays; on the right, what looked to be a large banquet hall or ballroom with tall adjoining windows that ran nearly the full length of the first floor. Schefler parked next to the Opel. A yellow Passant Estate Wagon and white Bavarian camper filled the other bays.

As they came from the garage a slim white-haired man holding a cane appeared on the front steps of the house. His bearing was erect, though he leaned on the cane.

"Permit me to introduce my superior, Colonel Hugo Hiller." Schefler said as he put down the bags. Hiller bowed and shook hands. His grip was warm and secure. He wore a green whipcord jacket equipped with leather shoulder patches although obviously it had been many years since a rifle butt had rested against either one of the colonel's shoulders.

"Welcome to Germany," Hiller said. "I appreciate your taking time out from your adventures to visit old men." A smile played at the corners of his mouth. "We don't get many young visitors now-adays, do we, Hans?"

Schefler concurred. Hiller spoke French in a quiet precise voice tinged with humor. His eyes were old and gray and flecked with the wisdom of years.

"Well, come in, come in! Let's not stand out here."

He led them inside, walking with a pronounced limp. Yet there was no hesitancy in his movements. In the middle of the hall Hiller stopped.

"I'm forgetting my manners," he apologized. "You must be tired and hungry. A chance to wash up first, yes? We can talk later. Hans will take you to your rooms. Of course you'll spend the night. Yes? Good, then. We dine at eight."

A pleasant-looking uniformed nurse carrying a food tray passed them in the upstairs hall. She nodded silently to Schefler. A door opened suddenly ahead of them and a man stepped out of a room. He held a cut-glass vase with a single wilted red rose.

"Bitte, Nina!" he called after the nurse.

She came back and collected it. The man exchanged a few quick words with Schefler then returned to his room.

"They are medical personnel," the major explained. "They live on the premises."

Marais and Nicole were given adjoining rooms with a shared bathroom. To ensure privacy the access doors from either bedroom had sliding brass bolts on both sides.

"If you need anything just ring." A bedside buzzer connected to the downstairs. "Whenever you're ready, feel free to join us. I hope you'll be comfortable," he added on his way out.

The furnishings in Marais's room were all dark mahogany and brass. Several gloomy scenes of the Black Forest hung from the walls, and had it not been for the wide-windowed view of the back lawns and tennis court the effect might have been claustrophobic. Glass doors led onto a balcony. He stepped out to investigate.

The balcony stretched across the length of the house. He leaned on the rail and considered the view. The tennis court had been abandoned long ago. There was no net and its white boundary lines had faded into obscurity. Through the trees he caught a glimpse of the house and property next door.

Nicole joined him. She had washed her face, fixed her hair, and put on the new clothes.

"How do you feel now?" he asked. She looked wonderful. Her eyes were clear, her whole presence vibrant and exhilarating.

"I suppose I'm relieved more than anything else. I feel safe. And glad we're still together." She linked her arm comfortably through his.

"How are you feeling, Roger?"

"I'm curious," he said after thinking about it a moment. "If I didn't know better I'd swear we'd been kidnapped. And I'm damned if I can figure out why." He sucked thoughtfully at his bottom lip. "Meeting Major Schefler was an accident. But once he knew who we were, why did he bust his butt bringing us here? He doesn't strike me as the Good Samaritan type."

"Colonel Hiller's orders?" she suggested.

"And what's his interest?"

She shrugged. "Maybe we'll find out over dinner."

Reims, 6:47 P.M.

André tried Boule's Villejuif number again in a layby on the outskirts of Reims. Still no answer. He frowned and replaced the receiver. Traffic whizzed past on the autoroute outside the glass kiosk. Maybe he'd taken his wife to the cinema or dinner.

Next he tried the number Madame Andanucci had given him for Irène Boisson. He waited six rings and was about to hang up in frustration when she answered. Lamely, he introduced himself and explained how he came by her number and why he was calling. It was a matter of great urgency. Could he visit her now?

"You mean right now? This minute, Monsieur Villeneuve?" She sounded perplexed.

"If you'd permit me, Madame. I have driven all the way from Paris just to see you."

Reluctantly, she gave him driving instructions for reaching the place. It took a half hour to find the spot after two false attempts along roads that dead-ended at the canal.

Her house turned out to be a renovated lock-keeper's cottage with a red tiled roof. It sat in picturesque obsolescence surrounded by geraniums, roses, and hollyhocks. He parked outside the wood fence and walked to the gate. Marie Carnot's old roommate was on her hands and knees working in the garden. Soft bewitching scents floated on the early evening air.

"Madame Boisson?"

She tilted back on her haunches and examined him suspiciously. "You're the policeman?"

He entered the enclosure and handed her his ID. She shook her head and with effort got to her feet. Her height surprised him as much as her girth. It was difficult to imagine her high-kicking in a Lido chorus line.

"I'd need my glasses, Monsieur. It looks official enough and you look too young to be interested in a woman my age and size." She took off the work gloves and dropped them in a small wicker basket filled with garden tools. "I'll take your word you're who you say you are. So you want to know about Marie?" She wiped her hands on her dress front.

"Whatever you can tell me about her — and the others," Andre said.

They went into the cottage. "A glass of wine?" she suggested. André nodded.

She motioned him to a cane-bottomed chair that had been situated for viewing the drifting canal.

"I read about Marie's death in *France Soir*. A terrible business, if you ask me." She produced a bottle and two glasses from an old oak cupboard and set them on the table. "When I met her back in 1944 she was pregnant. A lonely girl from the Ardennes, pregnant in Paris. Phew! Can you imagine? I felt sorry for her so I took her in, looked after her until the baby came, then got her a job in one of the clubs."

She stopped talking long enough to pull the cork, resuming as she filled their glasses.

"She named the baby after me. Not that it made any difference my being its godmother. As soon as it could travel Marie took the poor little thing back to Charleville and left it with her mother to bring up. Cold-blooded, I thought, but she looked on it as someone else's brat. Not really her own, if you know what I mean. Anyway, here's to her wherever she is!"

She reached across and touched his glass with her own and he wondered if they were toasting the mother or the child. As Madame Boisson drank he asked: "Did she ever see her baby again?"

"But of course. A couple of years later when her mother fell ill she brought the little girl back to Paris for a few weeks." Her flabby features clouded. "By then I had a few problems of my own, you see."

"Oh?" he prompted.

"I was stupid," she shrugged. "I got myself pregnant with an American. His commanding officer wouldn't allow us to marry. The rest of the story you can imagine, Monsieur." Said with a sad embittered smile. "He promised to bring me to America after his discharge. But in the end it was Marie who stuck by me and helped."

"What happened to your baby?"

"She died from a brain fever, poor little thing. Only two and a half years old when she went to God."

She crossed herself, then lapsed into a few moments of thoughtful silence. Outside the window sunset mellowed into evening. Madame Boisson turned on a light.

"You went to Marie's wedding?"

She nodded, sipping her wine. "I was happy for her. We all were. Isn't it every girl's dream to marry a handsome titled millionaire and war hero? I wish the rest of us had done as well. Not that my Henri wasn't a success in his own right, you understand, Monsieur." She crossed herself once more. "But a Comte! I was her maid of honor."

"You knew the other bridemaids?"

"I knew most of them. Some better than others. Why, I even found jobs for three of them when they came to Paris. They were so beautiful. We all were in those days."

He leaned forward. "Do you know what happened to any of them, where they went, who they married?"

She frowned. "We kept in touch until they married or moved away. After that it was a note at Christmas or Easter. You know the sort of thing. A few snapshots taken in the park or on a picnic with the children. Then nothing." She sighed. "Hélène died of cancer back in the fifties. Adelaine married a lieutenant in the army, Rolland Mercure. He was a major the last I heard so he's probably a general by now." She refilled his glass and topped her own.

"Then there was poor Gabrielle," she continued. "Married some young man who'd befriended her when she arrived in Paris. She was by far the brightest of those Ardennes girls, I thought. She had everything: beauty, brains, and determination. She was the sort of person who'd stop at nothing to get what she wanted. Not someone you'd want to cross. I'd have thought she could have done better. Although he adored her, that much was plain to see. But he . . . well, you know what I mean . . . had no money, no family connections, no position. Why, he wasn't even handsome. And he smelled!" Her button nose wrinkled with disdain.

"Do you by any chance remember her husband's name?"

"Boule," she replied. "Bernard Boule. Do you know him?"

Villejuif, 6:45 P.M.

Gabrielle was gone. Boule had found her bloodstained clothing in a shopping basket under the stairs. Of all the hiding places in the house she had picked the one spot where under normal circumstances he would never have looked. He packed everything back in the basket and went into the kitchen, ignoring the ringing telephone. He realized that he was weeping — weeping for Gabrielle, for himself, for the tragedy of their lives together.

The sight of her as a bridesmaid in the 1948 wedding photograph had nearly unhinged him. A bridesmaid three years after their marriage! There was no wedding band on any of the hands holding the bouquets. For years Gabrielle had been lying to him. She had known Marie Carnot, just as she had known the other girls in the picture, the girls in the portraits — the girls of the Ardennes. What was it they had done together?

Somehow he had managed to maintain his composure until André left the office. Then his shoulders had sagged, his mouth had gone dry, and his heart had begun hammering like a caged and frightened animal. An anguished sob had filled his lungs.

He began to weep again. Why couldn't she have trusted him? He had never pressured her to explain the past, who her family were, if they still lived, the names of her brothers or sisters. What terrible dark secret had she been hiding all these years, a secret she believed so deadly that only murder could protect it?

He blamed himself. He had loved her so much that he had placed her on a pedestal like a goddess to be worshipped by lesser creatures like himself. So enraptured had he been that her presence and beauty had blinded him to the fact that she was after all only mortal. Yet he recognized the terrible senseless logic to her actions starting from the day they met.

She had married him not out of love, but out of kindness and self-preservation, secure in the knowledge that with him she would always be in control. Instead of sharing her life she had been living a lie. His love, on the other hand, had been complete and without reservation. Did she not know that he could have forgiven every tragedy in her past, no matter how evil, how frightful, how sordid? Perhaps she had planned on telling him but waited too long, until what had been merely a mound of deceit grew into a mountain of corruption and lies that she would have believed impossible for him to accept.

How little she really understood him! She was a part of his soul, the whole reason for his existence. He could forgive her no matter what she did. Even murder.

He straightened his shoulders and dried his eyes. It was time for decision. His place was with Gabrielle. More than ever before she would need him now. He must go to her at once. Together they would face whatever misfortune might come.

Varnhaft, 7:30 P.M.

The main floor had an elaborate games and trophy room located just off the central hall. Its double doors had been left open. Nicole and Marais could see Major Schefler hunched over a billiard shot as they descended the staircase.

"Do either of you play?" he inquired when they came in.

Nicole shook her head. Marais admitted to a passing knowledge of snooker. Colonel Hiller, seated near the empty fireplace, got to his feet and welcomed them. His face held that same inquisitive interest in Nicole that Major Schefler had expressed back in Haguenau.

There was a third man present. He was shorter than either Schefler or Hiller but appeared to be about their age. His shaven head resembled a cue ball while the skin on his face lay loose and laced with a filigree of tiny lumps and lines as though suffering from internal shrinkage.

"Major Meisser will be joining us for dinner," Hiller said.

"Ulrich Meisser, at your service," he bowed, offering his hand. "Have you ever considered a film career, Monsieur Marais? You have an excellent speaking voice and a handsome expressive face. They're very important in films," he said severely.

"I dare say, Ulrich, but our young visitor has more pressing concerns at the moment than a film career." Colonel Hiller took Nicole by the arm, drawing her away to one of the stuffed armchairs next to the fireplace. Marais followed. "We will eat in twenty-six minutes," the Colonel said, checking his wristwatch. "Meanwhile, I want to hear your story in its entirety. Sit, sit!" and he eased himself into a chair, holding the cane for support while he adjusted his leg so that it stuck straight out in front of him. Majors Meisser and Schefler took flanking seats next to the colonel. Marais moved in beside Nicole.

He listened while Nicole retold their story. The old men sat in silence, nodding occasionally when she made a point. Even Schefler seemed interested in the rerun. When she finished, Hiller gave a disarming smile.

"Do you have anything to add, Monsieur?"

Marais shook his head. She'd covered it all, including the balcony scene when they'd considered the reasons for being brought here.

"Nothing except our gratitude to you for getting us over the Rhine before the roof fell in."

The answer seemed satisfactory. Again Hiller checked the time.

"We will eat now," he announced.

A mantel clock chimed eight as they entered the dining room, another paneled room with an enormous candlelit table that sat thirty-two. There were place settings at one end for five: Hiller at the head, the majors on his left, Nicole on his right, and Marais across from Meisser. The walls were hung with realistic paintings, like Dorfmundt's. A faint odor of stale cigars pervaded the atmosphere.

A waiter in a white jacket with pearl buttons brought in the first course, spinach soup. The colonel picked up his spoon.

"Now it is my turn to tell you a story," he began gravely. "I'm afraid it is not very pleasant." He took a tentative sip of soup, reflected a moment on its quality, then noisily spooned several mouthfuls before continuing. "But it's a story you must hear for two reasons. First, so you can protect yourselves against those who are trying to kill you. And second because . . ." A frown while he considered his wording. " . . . because I am compelled to reveal the existence of a situation and legacy which undoubtedly will alter your life."

His gray eyes fixed thoughtfully on Nicole. The majors likewise stared across the table at her. Marais waited.

"My tale begins in September 1914, when the German Army was stopped at the Marne as the result of a massive miscalculation by General Von Kluck when he marched his forces across the Allies' front, exposing his flank. Within a week our army had been driven back to a line running from the river Oise beyond Compiègne, across Champagne and the Argonne to Verdun. In that week we lost the war. Count Moltke was sacked and Erich von Falkenhayn became Commander in Chief.

"Even the Kaiser's son, Crown Prince Wilhelm, told a reporter from the American Hearst newspapers that we were finished. That sort of defeatism threw his father into a towering rage. But the Prince was quite right." Hiller chuckled. "They never got on, those two. Completely different personalities. The Prince was a gentle man of wit and grace. The Kaiser, on the other hand, was a simpleton and an arrogant fool.

"The Prince had been given titular command of the Fifth Army. And although only thirty-two, he had considerable knowledge about military matters. The Kaiser ordered him to pull his Fifth Army out of the Marne mess and move over to an area around Stenay near Verdun. Plans were afoot to try breaking the French line from a new direction. Prince Wilhelm was not optimistic. But he decided to make the best of it. He took up residence in the villa of Madame Duverdier on the edge of town and then proceeded with his own amusements. His character had one devastating flaw, you see: a sexual appetite of Olympian proportions." He stopped to observe Nicole's reaction. If her equanimity troubled him he managed to conceal it while finishing his soup. As if summoned by telepathy the waiter appeared and removed the empty bowls.

The colonel waited until the fish course had been served before apologizing that the fillets were a day old.

"One of the many disadvantages of living so far away from the sea," he observed regretfully. "Now where did I leave off?"

"The Crown Prince at Stenay," Nicole said. "And his sexual flaws."

Hiller smiled. "Quite right, my dear." He resumed his story. "Naturally the Prince surrounded himself with friends his own age. They were a grand group of young men filled with that wonderful enthusiasm for life that had made Germany great. Fritz von Zobeltitz became the acknowledged court jester. To keep the Prince supplied with interesting females he devised a simple ploy: a tour by staff car throughout the surrounding towns and villages every week spotting comely faces and figures. Formal dinner invitations followed, and the young ladies were brought to the villa with their mothers as chaperones for an evening with the Prince." He cleared his throat and took a sip of wine, then continued, "Those provinces of Alsace and Lorraine had been in German hands since the Franco-Prussian War and much of their citizenry was pro-German. And if they weren't," he shrugged indifferently, "no matter. Prince Wilhelm held a truly royal table at Stenay. The girls came flocking. First with their mothers, later alone once a parental rapport and mutual trust had been established. None of the girls caused any problems over the loss of their virginity. Why would they when it had been taken by a prince of Hohenzollern?

"Naturally the Prince's young officers shared in this bounty. What a way to spend a war, eh? Both sides deadlocked in trench warfare, thousands dying every week, while over in Stenay there's the Prince and his friends living the good life. His father must have been apoplectic.

"Through 1915 and into '16 the war dragged on, the French line still intact, our army probing endlessly for some weakness along the Allied front. The Battle of Verdun, according to the High Command, would change all that. It began on February 21 and continued intermittently until September. When it was over we had traded 350,000 lives for two shattered forts, a few ruined villages, and twelve square miles of the French front. Madness!"

He ate a piece of fish, chewing it thoughtfully.

"In March 1917, Fifth Army Headquarters moved from Stenay to Charleville in the Ardennes. The Prince no longer cared about the war. Many of his friends had died at Verdun. He moved his headquarters into the Château Havetière outside of town. But things were different in the Ardennes. Von Zobeltitz was gone. The people of the district despised the Germans and regarded the Crown Prince as little more than an object of ridicule; a tragi-comic figure in his Death's Head Hussar busby, with his sexual abnormality and eclectic tastes. In Charleville he became known as 'l'homme qui rit' — the laughing man — after a popular play of the time."

The others at the table had finished eating. Hiller nibbled at his fish, washing it down with some wine. He paired the knife and fork neatly on his plate, then sat back.

"So much for background," he said. "Now we reach the crux of this story. Enter Lieutenant Rudi Hoessler, aged twenty and fresh from a photographic intelligence course at Frankfurt. Aerial photoanalysis was in its infancy, and Lieutenant Hoessler could lay claim to all the latest camera techniques.

"He and the Crown Prince met by chance in the studio of Professor Pape, a wartime painter of some distinction. The Prince had come to persuade one of the professor's young French models to accompany him back to the château for the night. Hoessler had come looking for a nude interested in cooperating on a series of photographic studies he contemplated doing during his off-duty hours. They talked, quickly discovering that they shared the same sexual interests. A vista of possibilities opened up for both men. Within the week Hoessler found himself transferred to the head-quarters staff at the château and working directly for Prince Wilhelm. As the son of a wealthy industrialist from the Ruhr, Hoessler fitted easily into the Prince's circle of intimates even though most of them were ten years older than he. Rudi had a quick incisive mind behind a proud handsome face. With his white blond hair and clear blue eyes, he was like a young Siegfried of the *Nibelungs*, even managing to rival his prince's prowess as a sexual athlete."

Their plates were exchanged for the main course: veal, sliced wafer thin and tender, napped with a wine-flavored mushroom sauce. Tiny carrots and pebble-sized boiled potatoes completed the dish.

"Hoessler developed a new approach for attracting females. With the Prince's approval, an official Court painter was installed in a specially constructed atelier in the château."

Although no one had spoken, Hiller sensed that they had guessed the painter's identity.

"That's right," he confirmed. "Karl Dorfmundt became the third man in this sexual confidence game. He'd caught the Prince's eye during an inspection tour near the Somme a week or two before

when the co of the Alsatian Lieb regiment produced several bril-
liantly executed canvases done by a young signals corporal. They
were dark somber paintings showing the horror and futility of war
in a mind-shattering realism. As His Imperial Highness had some
small talent with brush and paint himself, he recognized
Dorfmundt's ability immediately. So when Hoessler suggested that
the plan called for a credible artist, Wilhelm remembered
Dorfmundt.

"The initial approach used on the Ardennes girls was basically
the same von Zobeltitz had used in Alsace-Lorraine, with one
important difference: instead of inviting mother and daughter to
the château for an evening of food and conversation, the invitation
was given as a pretext for discussing arrangements for having the
young lady's portrait done for the Prince's private collection.
Hoessler told a ridiculous story of how His Imperial Highness had
spotted the girl by chance and been so struck by her beauty that
he wanted a portrait done at his expense. If further persuasion was
required, Hoessler threw out some additional bait: a series of photographic studies would be needed before the formal sittings could
begin in order to give the painter time to decide on his style and
approach for the subject. All such photographs would be given to
the girl's parents once the painter began work. A powerful entice-
ment in those days, you must realize. Peasant families who had
been cursed by beautiful daughters understood the value of being
able to advertise their plight with photographs. If someone important happened to see the girl's picture or portrait, and if he happened to be a man of substance, then the family's fortunes were
assured.

"And too, Hoessler's plan had a built-in safeguard once his guests
agreed to allow their daughters to sit for Dorfmundt: none of them
wanted news of their fraternization with the enemy to become
public knowledge. Later, after the parents received the photographs
and their daughters' virginity and morals had been sacrificed on
the Hohenzollern mattress, who would be in a position to complain
— and to whom? Certainly the daughters would never dream of
telling their parents what had happened to them in the château.
Nor would the parents risk complaining to the authorities even if
they discovered their daughters' fall from grace. Oh, it was a very
clever arrangement."

From a side door a man materialized. He wore spectacles with circular steel rims and a dark suit, and looked to be about the same age as Marais. He came directly to Colonel Hiller and whispered in his ear. Everyone stopped eating to watch. The colonel nodded several times as he listened, finally saying "Danke," when the man finished and withdrew.

Schefler and Meisser exchanged glances and regarded Hiller questioningly. Marais sensed their unease. He had the feeling that up until this interruption everything had been following a plan that the old fellows had agreed upon among themselves back in the games room while he and Nicole were upstairs. Had something happened to upset their plan, he wondered?

"Depravity is the most peculiar of human traits, I think," Hiller mused. "When men and women are faced with the inevitability of their own destruction, they can turn into hedonistic animals. Thus it was with Hoessler, Dorfmundt, and the Crown Prince. They knew the war was lost when America threw in her lot with the Allies. Up until then there might have been a chance. But now it was only a matter of time before Germany collapsed.

"At the Château Havetière what had begun as a clever little exercise in seduction to feed the sexual appetites of two men suddenly turned into something grotesque and disgusting."

He took another forkful and squinted at the candelabrum, intent on its wavering yellow light. His sigh was one of sorrow.

"While Dorfmundt painted the girls' portraits, Hoessler and the Crown Prince photographed them. His Imperial Highness became a superb photographer. At first they photographed them in nude studies, later in suggestive pornographic poses, finally persuading them to pose while actually engaged in the sex act with Hoessler or the Prince. Later, other officers were invited to join these orgies. Every photograph and its negative were filed and stored with typical German thoroughness. By the time the war ended the collection held over a thousand pictures.

"The Prince went into exile on the island of Wieringen in the Zuyder Zee. Dorfmundt packed his portraits and shipped them to his parents' home in Haguenau. Major Hoessler — Prince Wilhelm had promoted him for valuable services to the Crown — packed their pornography collection into an airtight empty mustard gas cylinder and buried it in the château garden. By late November

1918, he was back working in his father's business at Oberhausen."

Again he paused to slice a piece of veal.

"I don't understand the point to all this," Nicole said. "It's a fascinating story, Colonel Hiller, but I can't see how it could apply to my grandmother. Why, she wasn't even born until nineteen twenty-seven! It is my grandmother you're trying to connect into all this, isn't it?"

The colonel patted her arm soothingly. "A few minutes ago I received word from an old friend working with the Bundeskriminalamt that a bulletin has been received from Interpol stating both of you are wanted for murder. You for killing your grandmother, and for being an accessory before and after the fact with Monsieur Marais in the Rue du Bac murder on Wednesday and the murders of two prostitutes in the Latin Quarter last night."

"Oh, my God!" she whispered, bringing her knuckles to her mouth.

"The Bundeskriminalamt has been asked to assist the French police should you manage to cross the German border. They want you very badly, it seems. Not for what you did, because you did nothing. Nor for what you knew, because you knew nothing." He ventured a brief sympathetic smile. "But for what they think you know and the power it gives you."

He reached out to take her fingers in his own. She stared numbly at the clusters of liverspots on the back of his hand. Gently he told her: "I'm afraid your grandmother is connected to all this, my dear girl. Karl Dorfmundt painted her portrait at the Château Havetière in 1944 after Major General Rudi Hoessler threatened to expose her mother." His eyes lowered with regret for what he was about to say. "Your great-grandmother was one of the girls Hoessler helped the Crown Prince seduce back in 1918."

The heavy silence was broken only by the guttering candles. Finally, her jaw clenched; two words of invective hissed from between her teeth.

"The bastard!"

"Agreed," the colonel said reasonably. "Yet that bastard became your family's benefactor and made you the inheritor of his considerable estate."

She blinked in bafflement. "Why would he do that?"

"Why not?" Hiller asked. "After all, you're his granddaughter."

Brussels, 10:00 P.M.

Traveler pointed through the window at two middle-aged women standing near the curb in front of the Parc Josaphat.

"There they are! The one on the right is my rabbit," he told Titov.

Both women were dressed in smartly tailored suits and carried shoulder purses. Titov studied the pair as they drove by. It would be a waste to kill them. But then killing anything beautiful was always wasteful.

When they were past, Traveler checked his rear-view mirror. The women had chosen a particularly well-lighted part of the sidewalk on which to wait. He could see nothing suspicious around them. A young man and woman strolled hand in hand toward the corner. A trio of teenage boys were running a zig-zag, laughing as they goosed each other. He'd placed two of his men in the shadows of some trees bordering the park. A tail car, following a discreet distance behind, held three more troubleshooters.

"I'll circle the park again just to be sure," he said. "Then we can pick them up."

"Let me off around the corner. I'll walk back," Titov said.

Traveler protested. "The sidewalk's covered and we have a team on our tail. What more do you want?"

"Do as I say!" Titov snapped.

Traveler stopped. Titov got out. If Adelaine Mercure and her friend were expecting to meet a lone man in a car then that's what had better turn up to meet them, he reasoned, surprised that Traveler hadn't thought of it first. He felt certain the man had something else on his mind besides his nervous rabbit. And that made Titov nervous.

"Don't let them both sit in back!" he cautioned as he closed the door. Traveler drove off without answering.

Titov sauntered back along the sidewalk wondering how much longer he'd have to put up with Traveler. He sensed an imminent explosion from the man. Why couldn't it happen after his tour of duty in Brussels?

He sighted the women and pushed all other thoughts aside. It could be a setup to grab Traveler. There was nothing unusual to be seen on the sidewalk, in the park, or among the night-time traffic swarming past him on the street.

When he spotted Traveler's dark brown Volkswagen pull up to the curb his pace quickened. One of the women stuck her head in the front window. The other stood back and looked up and down the sidewalk. They could easily have been mistaken for two prostitutes negotiating with a customer. After a moment both climbed into the car, one up front, the other in back. He decided to allow thirty seconds for them to discuss his arrival.

He'd counted to twenty-four when suddenly the rear door flew open and one of the women scrambled out. She paused an instant, checking the sidewalk in both directions. He'd nearly reached the car. Their eyes met. It was the other one, he realized, the friend from Paris. But before he could speak, assuring her that she had nothing to fear, she turned on her heel and walked quickly away out into the churning traffic.

He stopped, watching in fascination for the car that was bound to hit her. Tires squealed, horns honked in panic, two Renaults kissed in a crunch of tearing metal and broken glass, then parted careering down the avenue. Yet she made it across to the other side.

Through the windshield he saw Traveler's head lolling against the steering wheel. Something had gone wrong. He leaped toward the car and flung open the front door. Adelaine Mercure's lifeless body fell out onto the curb.

The backup men came running from the park. Their tail car pulled in behind the vw with signal lights flashing. Three more men arrived. They peered inside the vw. Blood oozed from a bullet hole behind Traveler's ear and dripped down on the rubber floormat.

Adelaine Mercure's friend from Paris had suckered them all.

With a series of crisp orders Titov galvanized them into action: bodies into the back seat and out of sight. Get both cars in motion before the police arrive. Back to the Antwerp office, every scrap of paper to be cleaned from the safe, files, and desks. Ditto for Traveler's apartment, everything to be delivered to the Embassy's GRU liaison officer.

"What about the bodies?" someone asked.

"Strip them. Burn the clothes. Weight their ankles with chains and dump them at sea."

"Yes, Comrade Colonel."

They piled back into the cars. Titov waited at the curb.

"You're not coming, Comrade?"

Titov shook his head. "I'm going after that woman."

He watched until they were out of sight, then flagged a taxi. The woman, whoever she was, had to be given credit. Two swift neat kills, then out into traffic where she knew no one would dare follow or shoot. She had style. And he remembered that her face had held no fear when she saw him advancing. What an admirable woman to have as a colleague! How dangerous as an adversary!

"Gare de Schaerbeek," he told the driver. That's how she'd arrived. That'd be the way she'd return.

He paid off his taxi and joined a group of tourists entering the station. The departure board showed a Paris Express leaving track number four at 11:30. She'd be on that one, he decided. He took a seat in the concourse near the doors and waited. At twenty to eleven she came into the station looking like something out of a Eurorail magazine ad. He raised his newspaper, watching her over the top of the page.

She checked the departure board too, then looked at her wristwatch. A trip to the newsstand for some magazines wasted ten minutes. She bought several, then picked a seat at the end of the concourse and settled down. He'd never come across a woman with such extraordinary aplomb. How should he approach her? He decided patience was his best strategy for the time being. Somewhere between Brussels and Paris his moment would come.

In the meantime, how precarious was his own position, he wondered? By Monday morning Traveler's network would begin unraveling across Europe and he would be blamed. Seven experienced agents outwitted by one inexperienced woman — two people dead, and the woman gets away. He winced mentally at what Moscow Center would say when they recalled him.

The only palliative he had would be the woman and the story on François Daumier. Would Moscow be interested? It depended on the woman's identity. But, he reasoned, if it was worth killing two people to protect that secret then the information had to be of some value to someone.

Loudspeakers announced the arrival of the train for Paris. The woman gathered up her magazines and walked over to the platform gate. Titov went to the wickets and bought a first-class ticket for Paris. He boarded close behind, but instead of going to the first-class seating on her right she turned left into a tourist coach packed with noisily exuberant Dutch teenagers.

She picked a seat in the middle of the car and sat down. Two young men dressed in shorts and open-necked shirts immediately offered her a drink from their open wine bottle. Her smile of refusal was dazzling. It would be too risky for him to sit in the same car. He took a seat in first class near the connecting doors. The train started with a small jerk.

At ten-minute intervals he checked in on her through the glass door. The Dutch lads had swarmed around her like honeybees. She appeared to be enjoying their attention.

Near midnight when French customs and immigration officers came on board at Mons he went back to the toilet and taped his pistol to the inside of his thigh. Returning to his seat he saw that the woman had likewise made a trip to the toilet. He averted his gaze quickly when she glanced his way as she sat down.

His diplomatic passport caused a brief stir until a curious customs officer in the next car found a paper bag filled with marijuana in one of the Dutch boys' backpacks. The lad was handcuffed immediately and every piece of luggage coming from Holland searched. By the time they had crossed the border into France three others were under arrest. The train stopped in Maubeuge. The border officials and their shaken prisoners got off, along with those passengers connecting with the Nord-Express to Berlin or one of the local services. A few sleepy-eyed people came aboard. Then, incredibly, just as the train was about to leave, the woman folded her magazines under her arm and got off.

A whistle shrieked. They were moving. She remained on the platform.

He leapt to his feet and rushed to the vestibule. A trainman started closing the door. He pushed him aside and wrenched it open. She was still standing, waiting.

"The door must be closed when the train is in motion; it is the regulation, Monsieur!" The trainman began pushing.

Titov shook him off. "Shut up!" he snarled.

Surprised, the man backed away with his mouth open.

They were gaining speed, moving past the platform onto the dark roadbed. He leaned out and looked back. She had turned away into the terminal. Titov jumped and tumbled down the embankment. Sounds of the train receded. He scrambled up to the tracks, cursing the perfidy of women. His trousers were torn and he'd scraped his knee. Fortunately, the pistol had held secure. After taking a moment to dust himself off he limped toward the platform lights.

She was inside at one of the counters buying a ticket — to where, he wondered. He waited until she'd closed her purse and sauntered off to the adjoining cafeteria before he approached the wicket.

"Monsieur?" the clerk asked.

"That woman who just left. What train is she traveling on?" He gave what he hoped was a lecherous smile and accompanied it with a folded Belgian hundred-franc note that he slipped across the counter. "She looked lonesome," he winked.

"The train from Calais. She's going to Charleville-Mézières." He palmed the bill without changing his expression. "Leaving at 1:15."

SATURDAY, JULY 14

Maubeuge, 12:23 A.M.

Gabrielle sat in the station cafeteria nursing her cup of coffee. A deep and terrible sadness filled her as she thought back to events that were finally catching up with her.

An enormous reception room in the Château Havetière with summer twilight searching through the shadows beyond the tall mullioned windows, a room crowded with uniformed men and beautiful women. The German officers have tight uniform collars that pinch their necks. How do they breathe? There are little silver bowls of nuts and candies in the reception rooms, a string quartet playing softly, everyone bowing and so polite. It's like stepping into a fairyland, everything so crisp and clean. Uniformed waiters holding aloft silver trays of canapés and champagne weave expertly among the throng. Gabrielle is sixteen years and five months old.

She and her mother are guests of General Hoessler. He introduces them to his distinguished visitor, another general, a reedy man with a monocle and big dark circles under his eyes. When they go in to dinner Hoessler seats her mother between himself and the skinny general. She sits on Hoessler's left. The table is huge, with room for over twenty guests. For the first time she sees that many of the women are only girls not much older than herself.

Throughout dinner, Hoessler is charming and attentive, making her feel important and much older than her sixteen years. She has never seen such abundance at a supper table: five courses with two different wines. By the end of the meal she is giddy and more than a little drunk. Her mother is forgotten in a haze of more immediate happiness. Hoessler tells her a very funny story about a miller and his wife who are carrying on separate love affairs in the same village. She laughs boldly at the end of the tale.

He tells other stories about his experiences in France. His French is effortless and correct, his manners impeccable. During coffee he takes her hand and asks for permission to have her portrait painted. Her beauty should be preserved forever, like the Mona Lisa. She is flattered and can feel herself blushing. He is so handsome, his short close-cropped hair so blond it is nearly white. The general's dark blue eyes undress her. She blushes again. Of course she will sit for a portrait.

"Our Divisional artist is very good. Aren't you, Karl?" He introduces her to a melancholy man with sunken cheeks and a shock of nut-brown hair who is seated across from her but farther down the table. The painter shrugs. "What do you think, Karl? Is she worth a portrait?"

The painter agrees. He says that she has excellent facial bone structure. Sittings can start at once. When can she begin?

"Why, tomorrow!" she says without thinking.

"No!" her mother shouts. She is ashen-faced and her hands are trembling. But the general pretends not to notice.

He puts his hand on her thigh. She doesn't jump. It's a game, man and woman. And she is a woman now. The general seems to think so. He leans forward, his face expressionless, fingers exploring delicately. She gasps in surprise, hesitates, then opens her legs to him. Momentarily, his sangfroid is breached. His eyes widen. He massages gently and she feels herself tingling, wetting his fingers with her lubricant. Her face is flushed. The room is very warm. A waiter takes away her dessert plate and the general stops.

"You will come and sit for Dorfmundt?" he asks earnestly as they are getting ready to leave. She smiles and promises. He is a very attractive man, even if he is old enough to be her father.

"You will come back?" he asks again, as though she might change her mind. Of course she'll come back.

Her mother agonizes over the matter. Sadness fills her face, bending her shoulders with its invisible burden. But she does not forbid Gabrielle to attend the sittings. She is silent on their way home in the staff car and does not speak when they go up to bed.

Gabrielle lies awake thinking, remembering the pleasurable sensations from the evening. Her fingers explore where the general's gentle touch aroused her. Closing her eyes she imagines being naked in bed with him making love.

Her fingers move in a steady rhythmn.

She wonders if it will be painful. The first time is always painful, she has been told.

Tonight her climax comes quickly. She shudders in a chill of agonized delight then sinks into a peaceful sleep.

In the middle of the morning a camouflaged DKW *scout car arrives, driven by a young lieutenant. His orders are to deliver her to the château in time for lunch. His name is Oswald Krantz, Ozzie to his friends. He clicks his heels and bows. Her mother is crying as she leaves. Several spears of April sunlight pierce the gray overcast giving a sense of promise to this adventure. They drive through the two checkpoints into the château without being stopped. He pulls up and parks at the bottom of the sweeping stone steps, telling her this is where they'll meet when it's time to return home.*

The front lawns and driveway are crowded with men and vehicles. A motorcycle dispatch rider races in, dismounts, and takes the steps four at a time. She hesitates at the bottom of the stairs.

"Go on!" Krantz yells. "You're expected."

At the top of the steps an armed soldier leads her inside to a trestle table set up beside the front door. Everything is different from the previous evening. Something is happening. Soldiers carrying file folders move quickly between rooms. At the other end of the central hall three officers converse in urgent tones. She feels distinctly out of place. One of the officers at the trestle table demands her name. He has a nasty pinched face.

"Quite right," he says brusquely after she tells him. He points to the curved staircase. "Second floor. The guard on the door will let you in. Off you go now."

On the second floor only one door is posted with an armed guard. Wordlessly he allows her past, stonefaced to her smile of thanks. She is nervous now. There's a coldness to the château in daylight that wasn't there the evening before. The guard shuts the door after her and she is alone in a sumptuous apartment filled with furnishings like those in the Versailles Palace that she has seen pictured in her textbooks.

She wanders through the connecting rooms: a spacious drawing room turned into an office and conference center with ornate desk and two telephones, a bedroom with a high four-poster bed and yellow silk canopy, a bathroom with toilet, bidet, and giant sunken marble tub, and at the end of the interconnecting hall a cosy little library with fireplace and games table set with a luncheon for four.

She hears voices and goes back to investigate. She meets two girls in the drawing room. They see her and wave. Both were at the dinner party. One is dark, the other red-haired. They are beautiful and seem very much at home. Gabrielle is confused.

"I'm Marie," the dark one announces. "This is Hélène." She considers Gabrielle's dress. It is shabby compared to the gorgeous summer prints they are wearing. She smiles and looks beyond to the other rooms. "Is he here?"

"Who?" Gabrielle feels stupid. These two seem so worldly.

"The General. Who else did you expect to meet?"

"No, there's no one here. Just us."

Hélène sighs and sits down while Marie rummages through the desk drawers. She finds a package of cigarettes and lights one. "Do you smoke?" Gabrielle shakes her head. "Neither does La Belle Hélène." She takes a deep drag and expels twin plumes through her nostrils. Gabrielle is impressed with the girl's panache.

"This your first time?" La Belle Hélène inquires.

"Yes," Gabrielle admits.

A somber nod from Hélène. "The first time is the worst. After that you get used to it. He's really quite gentle. Not like some of the others. Ask Marie. She's his favorite."

Gabrielle would rather not. She is confused and a little fearful. Who are these two and why are they here?

"I've come to have my portrait done," she tells them. "By special invitation of General Hoessler."

Hélène makes a face, sucks in more smoke and talks as she exhales. "Of course you have, chérie."

"I don't understand," Gabrielle says. She has a feeling the girl is teasing.

From her chair La Belle Hélène produces an enigmatic smile. "It's all very simple. They feed us, paint us, clothe us, and have sex with us. In return we're expected to stay beautiful and available and provide sexual favors for whoever feels in the mood."

Gabrielle is speechless. Then slowly the implications of her words dawn.

Marie adds, "But only for officers. No NCOs or enlisted men. They use the brothel in town."

"Goodness no!" La Belle Hélène exclaims. "We're the high-priced meat." Her eyes are liquid with tears. She blinks them back and forces a smile. the worldliness and bravado are only an act, Gabrielle realizes, a thin veneer to hide her shattered pride and self-loathing.

*The general arrives brimming with good humor. Murmuring with plea-
sure, he kisses their hands in quick succession, pausing to hold Gabrielle's
fingers against the front of his tunic next to his heart. How has she been
getting on with the other two? Such naughty girls. They all have so much
in common. He doesn't explain what.*

*Hélène smiles sweetly and puts on her shoes. They troop into the library
and take their places at the table, Hoessler talking continuously.*

*"Another red alert. The entire coast under attack from Ostend to Le
Havre. Seventeen divisions in Normandy were ordered to move within
the hour against Allied invasion forces." A good-natured chuckle, the sort
that comes from a tolerant uncle. "You'll all have champagne, of course,
to stimulate the palate."*

*He uncorks the bottle in an explosion of froth and bubbles, filling their
glasses to overflowing. "As it turned out, the exercise was another* okw
*practice given under direct orders from the Führer." He takes his seat and
unfolds his serviette with a practiced flourish, settling it onto his lap,
then tugs open the two top buttons on his gray tunic. "My guess is the
Allies will not attack before next year. In fact I'd wager on it." He pauses
to drink. "What do you think, Gabrielle, my dear?"*

*She doesn't know what to think. Her head is spinning. She doesn't even
know what he's talking about. Instead of replying she sips her champagne
and appears to reflect on the question. Over the rims of their glasses the
other two watch her reactions. She feels like a bug under a microscope. Is
this really a high-class bordello for the general and his officers? He looks
so charming, so at ease. Do men act this way before they rape? Would it
be rape, she wonders to herself?*

*Luncheon is served by two young soldiers with white gloves. The men
keep their gaze studiously averted from the girls. The meal is simple:
lentil soup thick enough to hold a spoon upright, ice-cold chicken salad
and a dark tomato aspic embedded with peas and chopped celery. She
chews thoughtfully.*

*Hoessler carries the conversation with brightly spiced stories about the
local mayor and Council members, their wives and lovers. After an especially amusing anecdote, Gabrielle laughs. The general places his hand
on her knee. She doesn't resist. In fact she doesn't mind at all. The wine
has made her reckless. As if by a prearranged signal Marie and La Belle
Hélène fold their serviettes and depart. She experiences a brief moment of
panic until Hoessler opens another bottle and tops her glass. After filling
his own he toasts her.*

"To the most beautiful woman in the Ardennes. Possibly all of France. Certainly the most beautiful I have ever seen. You make me giddy with desire to possess you, make love to you."

His breath is cool. His lips taste of wine and tobacco as they brush her own. She feels his bristled chin at her neck while he nibbles her ear. Gradually she relaxes, enjoying his loveplay. His fingers tuck beneath the lace edge of her underclothing and he prompts her wetness as before, only this time it is more exciting because they are alone. She responds willingly, adrift in a languid pool of champagne and desire. Slowly he undresses her, caressing her lips, tummy, thighs, cheeks, breasts, so gently, so assuredly. Her breath comes in little gasps. He strips quickly and for the first time she sees him naked and aroused, a muscular old stallion ready for servicing. She shrinks from him, from the thought of what he is going to do. Gently, he reaches out and takes her hand, laying it on his erection. Her fingers curl delicately around its warm unyielding hardness. They go into the bedroom.

They are not alone. Marie and Hélène lie naked and waiting. Hoessler pats Gabrielle's cheek and gives her an encouraging smile; then slowly and with infinite gentleness he lowers himself on to Marie. Gabrielle's eyes widen in horrified fascination. Strangely, she finds herself wanting to participate. Hélène reaches out, showing her what she must do. Later, when the general takes her virginity, her cry is of both pain and pleasure.

But her mother knows what has happened. She is no longer welcome at home. She doesn't care. The general makes arrangements for her to live at the château with the other girls. A life of luxury with pretty clothes, good food, and sex. Lots and lots of sex.

She shares an enormous bedroom with Hélène, Marie, and Monique. The Four Musketeers, they call themselves. Marie is away most evenings, sleeping with the general. She is his favorite. Gabrielle is jealous. Marie is more beautiful. Then, one night as she lies in bed thinking angrily about Marie and the general, the misery of her situation overwhelms her. She wants to run away from the place before it destroys her completely. She doesn't want to end up like the others who have been here longer and grown to accept their situation. But where can she go?

There's a honeycomb of luxurious reception rooms and single-bedroom apartments buried beneath the château. Access is through a heavy steel door and down a flight of concrete steps from the wine cellar. Underground parties are held twice each week for majors and higher-ranking officers. Never does the general attend these gatherings. But all the girls are expected to be on hand.

They begin with polite conversation, schnapps, champagne, and some strange chocolate aphrodisiac that does peculiar things to the libido. Clothes are discarded in orgiastic frenzy. Nakedness allows no distinction between ranks. These are the rules.

Except for Major Meisser.

The major remains in uniform and films the proceedings, though on whose authority is never made clear. Every sexual game, perversion, aberration, and abomination Meisser can imagine is captured. Closeups of sodomy, lesbianism, and mob sex are carefully orchestrated and recorded. Meisser is a hedonistic perfectionist, a cinematographic detail man who demands and gets whole-hearted cooperation from his subjects.

What is the point to an orgasm unless the participant's facial expression can be recorded at the time of climax?

"Bitte, bitte, meine Damen und Herren, let yourselves go!"

What ever had happened to the movies, Gabrielle wondered? Several hours twice a week for how many years? The major must have produced the world's longest continuous pornographic film. And somewhere among the miles of celluloid were sequences in which she and all the other girls had starred; closeups with various German officers embedded in one part or another of their anatomies.

1:04 A.M.

Marie deBrisay's body arrived in Maubeuge shortly after one o'clock in the morning. Irène went to the front of the train and watched the coffin being unloaded onto a baggage cart for transfer to the Charleville-Mézières local from Calais. After the Paris to Amsterdam train had left she went over and sat on the cart, resting her back against the coffin. She felt tired. Yet she was not unhappy with what she'd managed to accomplish in a single day. Her mother's belongings would be shipped to Lyon at police expense once the Comte had confirmed ownership. A requiem mass had been arranged for Sunday in the church of Notre Dame de Grâce de Passy. And if dear old Father Daniel could get the gravediggers to work on a Saturday morning her mother would be buried in the little village cemetery outside Arreux this afternoon. She warned the priest not to say anything to Old Margot, preferring to break the news herself. Irène planned on staying at the house for a few days until Margot adjusted to the fact that Marie would no longer be spending her August holidays at the farm with Nicole.

Where was Nicole, she wondered? No one seemed to know. She hoped she wasn't in some sort of trouble. A headstrong girl, she thought admiringly, not unlike herself at the same age.

The train from Calais arrived. She waited until the coffin was loaded aboard, then joined the few passengers boarding the coaches farther down the platform. Sleeping bodies sprawled in nearly every seat. She found herself a space next to another woman joining the train in Maubeuge. The woman, middle-aged and quite beautiful, had a collection of magazines with her but no hand luggage. She helped lift Irène's suitcase onto the overhead rack, then offered her one of the magazines once they were comfortably seated. Irène accepted.

They began talking.

Varnhaft, 1:18 A.M.

Nicole lay awake tossing and turning long after Marais had gone back to his own room. Her brain wouldn't shut down. Too much had happened too quickly for it to be absorbed all at once. Should she weep over the tragedy of her present circumstance, or whoop with joy at the implications it presented? Her mood fluttered from revulsion and sanctimony to fascination and compassion.

"If you'll excuse us?" Hiller had asked the others after dinner. "I have someone who wants to meet Nicole."

She took his arm and together they climbed the stairs. On the landing he paused, nodding toward the hallway. "Second door on the left. Don't bother to knock. He's expecting you." When she hesitated he added, "There's nothing to fear, I assure you. His mind is crystal clear — and he does love you."

"How do you know that?"

"Because he told me so." Hiller gave her shoulder an encouraging pat and set her in motion. He watched as she hovered over the door handle. She looked back. He nodded twice and smiled. Nicole shrugged and opened the door.

The room lay in shadow except for a single bright tri-light lamp standing to the left of Hoessler's upholstered armchair. The general was working at a small tilted desk of the type used in hospitals. He looked up, then removed his glasses.

"You'll forgive me for not rising. My hips are not quite what they used to be." He spoke slowly, enunciating every word. His French was flawless. He screwed the top onto his fountain pen and set it aside. "Well, come closer. Let's have a look at you."

She moved from the shadows into the light. He studied her carefully, beginning with her shoes. While he studied her, she examined him. He wore a dark gray suit, white shirt, and maroon polka-dot cravat with matching handkerchief in the breast pocket of his jacket — the sort of uniform one might expect to see worn in an expensive private club by the afternoon manager. His eyes were old and veined but incredibly dark blue. The same color as her own, she realized with a start. And her mother's.

Yet in spite of his years he remained an impressive-looking man. The loose facial skin and drooping chin wattles had the texture of finely pebbled leather, but his jaw line, mouth, and posture remained uncompromising. He would, she decided, be a difficult man to refuse or, in the case of his soldiers, disobey.

"Hiller has told you about me?" he inquired when the exchange of stares was complete.

"Yes," she said, more sharply than she had intended.

"You don't approve of having me as your grandfather?"

She thought a moment. "I don't approve or disapprove."

"He told you how it happened?"

"You blackmailed my great-grandmother."

His lips tightened. After a time he waved a liver-spotted hand toward a side chair. "Pull that over here and sit down. I have something to say." Nicole obeyed. When next he spoke his voice was softer. "I was appointed garrison commander for the Ardennes region in July 1940, after France surrendered. It wasn't my choice. General Alexander von Falkenhausen, heading our occupation forces, wanted his garrison commanders to be fluent in the language of the country. It was to be a long-term appointment because the General believed that unless a speedy rapport could be established with the local populace enormous numbers of troops would be needed to hold control of what we had conquered. The policy made sound military sense. Why use ten thousand men in an area if five hundred are sufficient?

"It was not a posting I relished. Not after the excitement of Poland and the campaigns in the west. I had just been promoted, won my spurs, in a manner of speaking, when suddenly it looked as though my combat career was finished for the duration. The same thing had happened in the First War. No sooner had I become a qualified photographic reconnaissance expert than Prince Wilhelm had me transferred to his Headquarters Staff."

"Where you seduced my great-grandmother," Nicole interrupted.

Hoessler shrugged. "I make no apologies for that. I was young and a little bitter at the time. In any case, it was not I, but his Imperial Highness, Prince Wilhelm, who took your great-grandmother's virginity. And many other young women's too, I might add."

"But you participated in the business!" She wasn't going to let him skate away from any responsibility.

He sighed. "Participate? My dear girl, I arranged most of the Prince's liaisons. I was no better than the Royal Procurer. A pimp." He spat out the word. "Do you wonder that I was bitter? I wanted to be a soldier. Do brave deeds. Gain fame and promotion." He shook his head regretfully. "It was not to be. Not then. Nor later when I returned in 1940." His eyes shifted their gaze toward a painting on the opposite wall, a forest scene of nibbling deer and frolicking wood nymphs. "But as a soldier I had to obey orders. Fraternize with the local populace. Gain its trust and, who was to say, perhaps in time its respect. I set up my headquarters in the Château Havetière and invited all local mayors from the surrounding district to dinner. Quite naturally they refused. I was being too idealistic."

"You didn't really expect them to show up?" She couldn't believe he had been that naive.

"At the time I did," he admitted. "When they wouldn't come I tried invitations to prominent local business leaders. They too refused. No one, it seemed, was prepared to have anything to do with Germans. Except the local prostitutes. But then that is a profession which recognizes no distinctions between nationalities or political ideologies. In the end I decided to try those ladies of the Ardennes I had known back in 1917. Finding them wasn't difficult. Their records were on file at the Prefecture in Mézières. I chose carefully; only those who had husbands away and needed help."

"Most had married well. Beauty always has its pick of suitors, doesn't it? You should know that." She hadn't really thought about it in such terms but supposed he was correct. "Several husbands had been killed during the war. Two had run off to work with the underground. Others had made it to England and joined DeGaulle's Free French Army. One had died of natural causes; Charles Carnot, your great-grandmother's husband. He had been an inspector of canals and waterways, leaving her with two sons and two daughters. She had been told that both sons had died near Sedan. The daughters, Soulange and your grandmother, lived with their mother in Charleville. I sent one of my adjutants with an invitation for them to join me for lunch. Déjà vu. That was how it began again."

His gaze returned to her. He leaned forward in his chair, his hands gripping the armrests. "Blackmail was the farthest thing from my mind. I wanted only to prove to myself that it was still possible to establish some sort of amicable relationship between ourselves and the French in that area." His face turned grim. "Unfortunately the Gestapo prevented that from ever happening. The Wehrmacht had no control over policing functions. That responsibility belonged exclusively to Himmler's thugs. So what was the use of my trying to find a common ground with the local populace by extending a velvet glove when S.S. Sturmbannführer Felix Doepner's steel fist was busy behind the scenes smashing my every attempt? In the end I gave up and decided to spend the rest of the war enjoying myself."

"I sent for Dorfmundt. Together we designed his atelier. The underground apartments I had refurbished. Then Major Meisser and his staff of technical people joined us. He had been sent from Berlin by the Ministry of Propaganda to record whatever activities in northern France and the Low Countries might be useful for home consumption. Except for the usual visiting VIPs and photographing footage of damage by English bombers he was as bored as I was. We developed our own forms of amusement."

"With the girls of the Ardennes," Nicole interjected.

"Yes." He paused. "But it was not blackmail," he insisted.

"Did they have an alternative?"

"They could have refused like the mayors and the others."

"But did you offer them that choice?"

Hoessler shook his head. "No, I didn't." So that the revelation of each woman's past hung like a sword of Damocles if she refused his overtures and invitations. He had used them badly. He could admit that to himself now. But not to her. Not yet. "But I loved your grandmother, despite what you may think."

"Your favorite whore. I'd believe that. But love?"

Hoessler winced as though she had struck him. "There is a red leatherbound photo album in that bookcase behind you. Bring it to me." As she went to fetch it he continued: "I first met your grandmother in 1941. She was very young, no more than fourteen. Yet it was obvious she would be more beautiful than her sister. Soulange left home and moved in with me a few months later. Her mother had to get her out of the house. Her constant coming from and going to the château had already brought disgrace on the Carnot name and household.

"She remained for two years, then left for Berlin with one of my junior officers who was being transferred. I went to the Prefecture to see her mother and explain what had happened, but was told that she was at home in bed with the grippe. I drove directly over to the house. Your grandmother met me at the door. I knew at once I had to have her."

He took the album and set it on the narrow desk top. Nicole returned to her chair.

"She never appeared in any of Meisser's photographs or films. You must believe me when I tell you that. I never treated her like the others. She was always special. I loved her."

"She bore your child," Nicole said matter-of-factly.

Her grandfather nodded and opened the album. "My divisional medical officer took care of any unwanted pregnancies, provided the girls reported their condition in time. But I refused to allow him to terminate Marie's pregnancy."

"Why?"

"Because I was vain enough to want a child to carry on the Hoessler line. I had never married. It seemed such a trivial thing to do. But with the Normandy invasion and Europe in the process of being retaken by the Allied Armies it became very important that some part of me survive. Because I didn't think I would. I had no brothers or sisters. My uncles had died in the First War and my father was at home in Oberhausen dying of cancer."

"She was beginning her third month in the pregnancy when orders came for me to pull out. I gave her a few gold sovereigns and told her to look after the baby when it arrived. Then Hiller and I headed east to new defense lines being set up at the Rhine. We never made it. Outside Bouillon a pair of Spitfires caught us on the open road. We should have waited until dark before setting out. The brilliance of hindsight is always such a small comfort, isn't it?"

He tugged idly at an earlobe, remembering the day, the roaring engines and winking cannon fire from the aircraft gun ports as they flashed overhead. A rumble of thunder and they were gone. Hiller's ankle had been shattered. The driver was dead. One of the cannon shells had taken off his head.

"I too had been wounded. A shell had gone between my legs. A bit more to the left or right and I would have lost a leg and bled to death immediately. Instead, the Englishman's cannon had merely taken two large chunks of flesh from my inner thighs and left me alive. When the army doctors finished their repairs my lower quarters looked more like a woman's than a man's."

Nicole's eyes widened in horror. Her grandfather gave a thin smile, the first she had seen from him.

"Over the years I have managed to persuade myself that the wound was a form of poetic justice. It made the situation easier to bear."

"What happened to all Major Meisser's photographs and films?"

"Buried in the garden next to those mustard gas cylinders from the other war. I used waterproof canisters."

"Why didn't you destroy everything?"

"I thought that one day they might be of some use."

"To blackmail the next generation?"

"I prefer regarding them more as bargaining chips."

"Instruments for blackmail is a better description," she countered.

He changed the subject. "I'd like you to examine the photographs in that album." He pushed it toward her and sat back, his fingers pyramided against his lips, both elbows resting on the chair arms as he watched her.

She leafed through several pages. To her astonishment the album was filled with carefully mounted snapshots of her family over the years. There were pictures of her mother as a little girl at the farm in Charleville, as a teenager in Paris at the Sorbonne, with her husband outside the church in Lyon, with Nicole and her brother as children. She stared at each in fascination, wondering who had taken them all, realizing that someone had been spying on her since she was a little girl.

Her first communion, her first boyfriend, walking the bridge between Charleville and Mézières with her grandmama, in each case the photographer had caught her smiling, always oblivious to the silent observer. If she needed proof that her grandfather really cared, the worn, well-thumbed album provided it.

"I have never been far away when you or your mother needed me. Did you know that your father had been working for one of my companies when he was killed in that driving accident? The generous monthly settlement your mother receives for his loss comes from me. I love your mother very much, Nicole. I had hoped that as my daughter she would one day join me in my business. Instead she chose to remain in Lyon raising you and your brother."

Nicole understood. A huge lump rose in her throat at the sadness of it all. Her mother had grown up with Old Margot, a surrogate parent, and had wanted something better for her babies than a hired babysitter and lightning visits by some painted Parisian whore on birthdays and Holy Days. For the first time she understood why her mother so disliked her grandmama. By her mother's steely standards Marie deBrisay was nothing more than a silly irresponsible girl who'd produced a child out of wedlock and then abandoned it.

"Does she know?"

"Your mother? No. She was never told. She would have looked upon it as charity and hated me for it."

"What about my brother?"

"He has your father's amiable disposition and total lack of ambition. He works for one of my companies because no one else will hire him. As a business manager he would be a disaster. That is why I have chosen you as my inheritor."

She closed the album and sat looking at him. Was it compassion she felt, or pity? In his own peculiar way he had tried to make up for what he had done. It didn't cleanse the past or absolve him from responsibility for the misery he had caused. But at least he had tried. And she believed now that he had loved her grandmama. What a tragedy and torture his sexual impotence must have been to him, seeing the woman he loved married to another millionaire industrialist who then refused to embrace his illegitimate daughter. And how much worse for him later when the Comte divorced her and she was free for him at last. Yet what could he have offered that she didn't already have except a love incapable of further consummation? So he had made the wisest choice and left her alone.

"Tell me about this man, Marais."

"I love him." She said it simply, surprised at her boldness.

Her grandfather nodded, satisfied. "From all reports he has great courage. Without courage a man is nothing. Does he love you?"

"I think so."

"If he doesn't then he's a fool. In any case if you intend marrying him let me know." He rubbed his hands thoughtfully. His dry skin gave off a scratching sound. "Your immediate problem is with the French police. They want you and your friend very badly. Fortunately, I am not without some influence in this situation. I believe the matter can be resolved very swiftly by a phone call to Paris. I have given Hiller instructions on how to proceed. It will mean returning to France for both you and the young man. Are you up to that?"

"If I must. I can't speak for Roger."

He smiled again. "I have a feeling that wherever you go he'll follow."

"Would it be safe?"

"Quite safe or I wouldn't have suggested it. You'll leave in the morning. Now, an old man needs his sleep. Would you be good enough to give your grandfather a kiss and shut the door on the way out?"

She set the album back in the bookcase and returned. At his chair she stopped, looking down at him. So frail and yet still so strong. His dark blue eyes regarded her expectantly. Quickly she leaned over and kissed his cheek. His sigh followed her to the door.

"Nicole!" he called. She turned. "I love you too."

"Goodnight, Grandpapa."

Marais was waiting for her. She was too stunned to speak. He understood. He kissed her forehead and told her to go to bed. Colonel Hiller, he said, had a busy day planned for them tomorrow.

After two hours of tossing and twisting she got out of bed and went to stand outside on the verandah. The night breeze was cool. She shivered, clasping her bare arms. Pine needles clicked and scurried along the eavestroughing. In a few hours it would be sunrise, she realized. If they were leaving early in the morning she had better get to bed.

She closed the sliding door into her own room before going next door to Roger. Quietly, so as not to wake him, she slipped in beside him.

"Did you miss me?" he whispered.

Their arms encircled each other. She felt his warmth and comfort flowing into her. "Yes," she admitted. "I missed you."

He loved her slowly, almost languidly. Afterwards she fell into a deep untroubled sleep within his arms.

7:00 A.M.

Breakfast was served at seven sharp on a table flooded with sunlight. The morning room was filled with the smell of fresh-cut flowers and coffee. Major Meisser had left at dawn for some urgent business at his Geneva bank, Colonel Hiller explained.

"I thought he was a movie-maker, not a banker," Marais said.

"A man of many parts," Hiller agreed. "His bank handles most of the general's financial interests. And yours too, my dear," he added, addressing Nicole.

She produced an appropriate smile and spooned a slice of grapefruit. Hiller poured the coffee.

"You are both ready for the journey?" he inquired.

Although the night before Marais had agreed in principle with the colonel's plan of attack, now in the light of day, he wasn't so sure that going back to the Château Havetière with picks, shovels and a chain hoist was all that bright an idea. Politely he voiced certain misgivings. Major Schefler listened attentively, but Hiller broke in before he'd finished.

"You have no alternative, Monsieur Marais!" he admonished. "Tell me, where would the two of you hide? In Germany? No. Switzerland? No. Austria, then, or Italy? I wouldn't recommend either. Perhaps back to Canada with fictitious passports?" He shook his head adamantly. "You can't remain here forever, you know. How can either of you appear in public without being arrested, tell me that?" He buttered a piece of croissant. "Without some dramatic evidence to support your position against these rascals, proving you were innocent bystanders drawn into a murder intrigue devised by others, you will be lost." He wagged a finger. "Make no mistake about it, they will follow you wherever you go. In the end you'll be caught, jailed, and extradited back to France to be held in prison until your trial."

He dabbed blackcurrant jam on top of the butter.

"That is of course assuming they let you live long enough to come to trial." The piece of croissant vanished into his mouth.

"We have the suitcase bomb," Marais reminded him.

"How naive you are, Monsieur Marais. That you could have made yourself," Schefler interjected. "That case is available in any second-hand store in the country and is covered with your finger-prints. Likewise the wires, timer, and explosive."

The pistol and silencer he'd taken from the man on the train had had its numbers obliterated by acid. It would be strictly their word against whoever in France had decided to blow the Interpol whistle. In the end he acquiesced. Nicole remained silent.

Hiller's plan did have merit. The last place the French police would think of looking for them was in a vw camper with West German plates. And Schefler would be following them in the Mercedes with backup, never out of sight, all the way in and out of the country.

"You should be back here late Sunday afternoon," Hiller predicted. "I expect no trouble."

Nor was there when they backtracked across the Rhine later that morning. The day had grown bright and sunny. They crossed in the same cruiser that had brought them into Germany, but with a different man at the wheel. Their helmsman nosed the boat ashore on French soil at exactly the same spot under the bridge where they'd boarded yesterday. As they scrambled up the bank Schefler arrived, followed closely by a second vehicle. He handed Marais his keys to the Bavarian camper.

"It tends to be a shade top-heavy on the turns and sways badly in a high wind. Other than that you shouldn't have any trouble."

Marais promised to be careful. He climbed into the driver's seat while Nicole slid in next to him. The major went around to the side window.

"Follow me to the turnpike. We'll enter it at the Brumath toll gate. Our van will be waiting at the side of the road. Look for it: a green and yellow Benz diesel with two men. Once past the toll you take the lead."

Marais nodded and started the motor.

"Oh, one last thing: the speed limit on the turnpike is 130 kilometers per hour. Today is Bastille Day. A national holiday. Don't exceed the speed limit or the Gendarmes Mobiles will pull you over. They're spotted all along the highway and they're bastards!" he warned.

Marais waited until the Mercedes eased past, then put the camper in gear and followed. He glanced at Nicole.

"You all right?"

"Fine. Did you notice those men who drove the camper?"

He had. Tough-looking lads in their early twenties bulging with muscles and vindictiveness.

"Where did they come from? And two more waiting in the van. Why so many?" she demanded.

"Somebody has to do the digging. I'm not much good on the end of a shovel. We're going to need plenty of strong backs." It was as good an explanation as any. Since last evening's revelations she'd withdrawn into herself, not rejecting him exactly, but nonetheless shutting him out from the turmoil of her emotions. She had come to him last night because she needed him, not to talk, but to love and hold.

Schefler took the ring road, by-passing Haguenau. Ten minutes later they were slowing for the toll gate onto the autoroute. Their van sat parked on the shoulder with its bright yellow caution lights flashing. Two men in shirtsleeves appeared to be working on the engine. One of them sighted the Mercedes. Quickly, they buttoned down the hood and were already climbing into the cab when the camper drove past. Marais slowed to a crawl, watching his mirror until he saw the van was moving.

He collected his toll ticket and sped out ahead of Schefler and his brawny lads, finally settling the camper's speed at a comfortable 120. The other two vehicles spaced themselves well out behind. Heavy traffic rumbled along the autoroute in both directions. Periodically a gendarme motorcycle thundered past, its rider weaving wildly through the traffic lanes. The patrols all carried submachine guns strapped to their bikes.

He thought about the canisters. They lay buried under two meters of garden soil, Hiller had said. The old mustard gas tank from the first war had been made of thick steel plate. It would be very heavy. Major Meisser's film reels were sealed inside a lighter aluminum cylinder of the type used for air drops by the Luftwaffe during World War II. Each of the sixteen-millimeter films was packaged and labeled in its individual can. There were 143 cans of exposed film and another 200 reels of unused stock.

Assuming the canisters' seals had held out ground moisture, and the outer casings hadn't corroded into powder over the intervening years, they would lift them into the van and bring them to Germany. French authorities would then be notified of an impending news conference for all European journalists at which the entire sordid story would be revealed together with supporting facts and live witnesses.

"That ought to flush 'em out, whoever they are!" the colonel had growled after presenting his plan.

Was he really prepared to tarnish the Hohenzollern memory? And what of those others, living and dead, who would be exposed: Meisser, Schefler, the general, even Hiller himself? Surely a simpler way could be found to protect the general's granddaughter against a charge of murder. But offhand he couldn't think of one.

Shortly past noon he turned off the autoroute near Valmy and stopped for gas. They bought fresh sandwiches from a caféteria next door to the service station. Marais handed Nicole a sandwich, paper-thin salami slices wedged between cheese, pickles, and rye bread. They washed it down with an unlabeled bottle of red wine that stung the palate.

"We'll park at the campgrounds when we reach town," Schefler announced. "After dark we'll leave for the château. The van driver has been there before."

"Where?" Marais asked. "The château or the campground?"

Schefler gave one of his enigmatic smiles. "Both," he said. "Just follow the main road into Mézières. You can't miss the campground. It's called Mont Olympe, though it's on level meadowland at the edge of town."

Everyone returned to their vehicles. When Nicole asked to drive the rest of the way, Marais handed her the keys.

"You don't mind?"

"Of course not," he said. "The easy driving is over. You get the hard part."

He remained alert for the first few minutes going through Valmy in case she'd overreached herself. She hadn't. She was a smooth, competent driver. He sat back and relaxed, enjoying the scenery.

It took a shade under two hours to reach Mézières. The town was filled with people. Flags hung from windows and street lamps everywhere. Even the buses and taxis were decked out in colored bunting. Men in uniforms and women in costumes mingled with sidewalk spectators.

A white chalked sign at the entrance into Mont Olympe read "Campground Full." Nicole stopped the camper.

"Now what?"

He swore roundly and walked back to the Mercedes. The van driver approached from the other direction. Schefler rolled down his window. Directly across the road two policemen eyed their curbside conference. They were parked illegally. The major looked uncomfortable.

"There's tourist parking at the château grounds on weekends."

"What about the van?" Marais asked.

"I'll find a place for it in the woods. You go to the château and wait. We'll be there in an hour." He switched to German for the van driver. Marais rejoined Nicole.

"We go to the château and wait. Do you know the way?"

She nodded.

They crossed the bridge into Charleville and took the road for Revin. The château lay in the Bois de la Havetière about four kilometers from town. A line of cars sat parked on the side of the highway waiting to enter the grounds.

"A popular spot for a Saturday afternoon," he said.

They drove past.

"You're not going to join the line?"

"We can come back later. Maybe the crowds will have thinned in an hour. There's no rush, is there?" She knew there wasn't.

He shook his head. "Take your time. We've got the rest of the day to kill."

The highway split to the right, then a kilometer further it split again to the left. A road sign announced "Arreux 3 km." Nicole turned left. After a short distance she swung onto a treed lane which led up to an old farmhouse. Chickens scattered in confusion. They stopped beside a sky-blue Renault sedan parked in the middle of the front yard. She switched off the camper's motor and took a deep breath.

"Can you smell that, Roger? Isn't it lovely?" Her face came alive with pleasure. "It's all right, you can get out. We're not trespassing." She opened the door and jumped down. A chicken fled in a zig-zag of momentary fright before resuming its pecking. Somewhere close by a dog barked. "Remember that farm I told you grandmama had in the Ardennes? Well, this is it!" She took his hand in a pro-prietorial clasp and demanded, "What do you think of the place?"

A two-storey whitewashed stone and plaster farmhouse with pole roof and tiles was light years away from his own concept of nirvana. But then he wasn't a farm boy. Some people liked the smell of chickenshit on a hot summer afternoon.

"Who lives here?"

"Old Margot."

"How old?"

"Well into her eighties, I'd guess. Ancient."

"She drives?" He pointed at the car.

She shook her head. "Probably the hired man from Arreux."

They went to the front door. His skin suddenly began prickling. The place was too quiet, the trees too still. And hired men didn't drive new sky-blue Renault sedans.

The door opened.

"Good afternoon, Monsieur Marais, Mademoiselle Daladier. Do, please, step inside out of that dreadful heat."

The dark gunmetal silencer on the end of the pistol pointed directly at the middle of Marais's guts. The hand holding it was very steady. A question crossed his mind: since he now held all the cards, why was Commissaire Boule sweating?

Paris, 4:00 P.M.

At four o'clock that afternoon Colonel Hugo Hiller phoned François Daumier at his Paris residence. The Minister of the Interior was in his study awaiting the call. Hiller had made the arrangements the night before. He'd asked for a private telephone discussion on "urgent matters of mutual personal interest." Hiller's name meant nothing to Daumier, who insisted that his caller be more specific. But the colonel told him he preferred to wait until the following afternoon in order to give the Minister time to cleanse his telephone lines of eavesdroppers. What he had to discuss was not the sort of thing the Minister would wish recorded. Intrigued, Daumier asked for some hint as to the subject matter. He had, as he explained, a number of public appearances scheduled on Saturday honoring the storming of the Bastille. One of these appearances started at four o'clock.

With some reluctance the colonel identified himself as an employee of the retired General Rudi Hoessler, then went on to say that the matter to be discussed concerned events at a certain château in the Ardennes. That was as far as he got. Daumier interrupted quickly with his promise to be waiting for Hiller's call the next day.

He picked up the phone part way through the first ring.

"Daumier speaking."

His voice betrayed his emotional suffering.

"Colonel Hiller here again, Monsieur le Ministre," Hiller began affably. "Well, it's turned out a lovely day, hasn't it?" Daumier expressed no opinion. The colonel got to the point. "My purpose for calling is to offer you a private exchange of benefits."

Hiller paused, waiting for comment. But the Minister remained silent. Was it possible he'd brought in the Renseignement Général to monitor the call? If other ears were on the line, so much the better. The time for secrets had ended.

"General Hoessler holds a proprietorial interest in a collection of photographs now buried in France. This collection is of considerable magnitude and variety and encompasses a period during our occupation of your country during two wars. Possibly you are familiar with the subject matter?"

There was no reply from Daumier. Hiller decided to push a little. "Are you still there?"

"Yes."

Another pause.

"If you're not acquainted with the subject matter I can outline it for you in greater detail," he offered reasonably.

"That won't be necessary."

"It has come to my general's attention that your police forces are hunting two suspects who are believed to be involved in several murders. A man and a young woman?"

"Yes."

"You know their names?"

"Yes."

"And you know also that they are innocent."

"That will be for the courts to decide, Colonel Hiller."

"Au contraire, Monsieur le Ministre, it is for you to decide, as both of us know. And you must decide now. My general is prepared to offer you — and you alone — his extensive photographic collection in exchange for the freedom of your suspects. It is a fair exchange, no?"

"What is General Hoessler's interest in the suspects?" Daumier inquired cautiously.

"The same as your interest in his photographic collection. It's a personal matter." He gave him a moment to digest that information. "Are you interested in such an arrangement, Monsieur le Ministre?"

"Are you offering an alternative?"

"Unfortunately, no. Except perhaps a great deal of unpleasantness for everyone connected with this affair. My general has no wish to embarrass you."

An audible sigh of resignation and regret escaped into Hiller's ear. "You have a plan as to how we should proceed?"

It was the colonel's turn to sigh.

"Yes, Monsieur le Ministre, I do."

Charleville-Mézières, 4:05 P.M.

Marais's first impression of the front room was that it was almost in total darkness. The curtains were drawn and there were no lights. Gradually, his eyes adjusted from the bright sunshine and his mind gathered in their new surroundings. Boule waved them into the middle of the room and well beyond retaliatory range before he closed the door. Throughout, his pistol remained targeted at Marais's belly.

There were three women at the far end of the room, two sitting across from each other at a polished oak table, the other standing over them with a gun.

"Mama!" Nicole exclaimed.

Marais assumed she meant the one with the white-blond hair in a bun. This must be Hoessler's daughter, an older version of Nicole but without Nicole's unlined facial softness. The older one seated across from her would be Margot, the ancient housekeeper. Where did the well-dressed chick with the gun fit in, he wondered? As his eyes adjusted he saw that she wasn't a chick at all but a cold-eyed woman in her fifties and absolutely beautiful.

"The two of you sit down!" she ordered. "Opposite sides of the table. Keep your hands out front where I can see them." Then to Boule, "Bernard! Get upstairs and see if there's another car out on the road. They may have brought friends."

She regarded them all dispassionately as the Commissaire hurried away. Her voice had a sharp brittle edge like diamonds on glass. Marais took a chair next to Nicole's mother and sat down with the apparent confidence of a man who believes the odds are still heavily weighted in his favor.

What a fool he'd been, arriving in shirtsleeves, with no weapon to defend himself. He deserved to be caught. The female gunslinger he assumed to be a policewoman from Paris. He examined the other two.

Clearly the older one was terrified. She gazed at him imploringly. What did she have to fear? They weren't going to arrest her. He gave her a conspiratorial wink, hoping it would comfort her. It worked; her tired eyes reflected gratitude.

"I don't believe we've met, Monsieur Marais. I'm Nicole's mother, Irène Daladier," the woman beside him said casually. She sounded as if she expected him to shake hands.

"And that humorless-looking creature with the pistol pointing at us all is Gabrielle Boule," Irène continued, "the Commissaire's wife and soulmate. Gabrielle is one of our famous Ardennes whores, aren't you dear?" Her lips tightened with grim humor. But Gabrielle's face remained impassive, her eyes watchful. Marais sat stunned into silence. A sense of raw fear prickled his scalp. Not a policewoman, but Boule's wife? One of the Ardennes whores? She and Boule weren't here to arrest them. They'd come to kill them.

"Not only is she a whore, Monsieur Marais. She's a hypocrite. Aren't you, Gabrielle?"

"Mama, please!" Nicole hissed.

But Irène ignored her plea and in a pleasantly conversational tone described how they had met in the train from Maubeuge, how Gabrielle used her maiden name when introducing herself, even admitted to having known Marie deBrisay when they were girls.

"I was a little surprised when she turned up at the graveyard this afternoon."

"You buried Grandmama today?" Nicole cried out.

Her mother nodded. "Shortly after two."

"Couldn't you have waited?"

"For what? For you to turn up? Don't talk nonsense, child!"

Boule returned. The road outside was clear. He wiped his face with an enormous handkerchief and sat down on a chair drawn from near the fireplace. For a moment he studied Marais with undisguised curiosity.

"Why did you come back, Monsieur?" he asked with the sincere melancholy of an unappreciated man. "Didn't you know I was prepared to let you go? The girl too." He spoke as if there was no one else present at the table.

"You should have mentioned that to Interpol," Marais countered. "They have a Europe-wide warrant out for our arrest. Four counts of murder, including two prostitutes from the Latin Quarter."

Boule blinked with surprise. "Really, Monsieur Marais, your sources of information are extraordinary! You are a man of unusual resourcefulness," he said admiringly. "But that Interpol business is purely a matter of form." He shrugged indifferently. "I would never have requested your extradition, believe me."

"But how were we to know that, Commissaire?"

"True," Boule agreed. "You were working blind. But I'd have thought you might have figured that out for yourself. You seem to have figured out everything else."

"Most of it," Marais agreed blandly, with a confidence he couldn't even begin to feel.

"Ah!" the Commissaire said as he traded glances with his wife. "Suppose you tell me what it is you know, then let me fill in the blanks."

"Well, for starters, Commissaire, I know your wife killed Dimitrios Kouridis on the Rue du Bac last Tuesday and then you decided to frame me."

He held his breath. Very slowly, Boule's face turned the color of wet stone.

Bull's-eye!

"He's guessing!" Gabrielle snapped. "He doesn't know a thing. Nothing!"

Boule removed his handkerchief with his free hand and sopped his face. "No, my dearest, you're wrong. I think he does."

The kaleidoscope of fragmented facts had finally stopped turning. Marais could see their intricate pattern in his mind's eye. Gabrielle had been the missing key to everything.

"Marie deBrisay spotted some portraits in Dimitrios's window. One of them was of your wife, painted at the Château Havetière during the war. There was probably one of poor old Marie there as well." He gave them a sympathetic smile. "When she saw them she panicked. Not because of the portraits themselves but for what they represented. She called your wife for help. Who would be in a better position to get answers quickly than the wife of a policeman?" From their attentive expressions he knew that so far he was bang on. Gabrielle took a step closer to her husband. If he could swing his body around in the chair so he was facing them they'd be almost within reach. He began by taking his hands off the table and using them to emphasize his words.

"Over the years Marie and your wife had kept in touch. I think all the girls from the Ardennes who'd had their portraits done kept in touch." He held out his open hands, acknowledging the logic of their conspiracy. His buttocks shifted slightly on the chair, his body turned a little.

"Between 1941 and 1944 each of them had been seduced by General Hoessler."

From the corner of his eye he saw Irène nodding sternly, as people do when they hear confirmation of their own beliefs from another unexpected source.

"But that wasn't the worst of it, was it, Madame Boule? The fact that you were all deflowered by a Nazi general and then turned over to his officers to be used as their mistresses wouldn't have been quite so terrible if a certain Major Meisser hadn't filmed your sexual gymnastics in the basement bunker apartments, would it?"

Gabrielle took a deep angry breath. Her eyes turned to flint. He eased his legs around from under the table.

"It wasn't altogether your fault, though, Madame. Did you know that?" He reflected a moment. "No, I don't suppose any of you did. The general wouldn't have said anything. But it was because of your mothers you were delivered to the château for seduction. He blackmailed them."

"How?" Boule asked softly. His pistol wavered ever so slightly. My God! They really didn't know why all of it had happened the way it had. Marais felt almost sorry for them.

"Because their mothers had been seduced and photographed by Höessler and the Crown Prince in exactly the same way during the German occupation in the First War."

"Liar!" Boule's wife screamed. "All lies!" A vein pulsated across her forehead and her cheeks flamed in indignation. The Commissaire lifted a hand to restrain her. Angrily, she shook him off. Across the table Old Margot blew her nose and started weeping, her face hidden in her hands. Nicole put an arm around the bent shoulders.

"You're making it up!" Gabrielle shouted.

"No, Madame. You know that I'm not," Marais told her gently. "A number of those portraits in the shop were of your mothers, painted during the First War. And what frightened Marie deBrisay was the possibility that if the portraits were being offered for sale then perhaps the photographs and films were available as well. She had the money to buy them. You offered to have your husband look into the matter. Isn't that the way it happened?"

He sat facing them now, leaning forward with a casual intimacy. Very slowly he began bringing his feet back until his heels were at the edge of the chair and he could transfer his weight onto the balls of his feet. His gaze shifted to Gabrielle.

"But you never mentioned the matter to your husband at all, did you? Instead, some time Tuesday night or early Wednesday morning, you broke into Dimitrios's shop to search for those photographs and films. Dimitrios must have heard you creeping around. Drunk as he was he came downstairs to investigate. That's when you had to kill him, wasn't it?"

"It was unintentional," she muttered.

"So you cut his throat with the kukri. But there were no films or photographs to be found, were there?"

Gabrielle shook her head. "Nothing." Sweat poured from Boule's cheeks into his collar. The silencer now pointed at Marais's knees. If he leaped at them this moment could he catch a wrist in either hand and disarm them? Gabrielle's wrist appeared delicate enough to snap, but the Commissaire's was a different matter. It looked as thick as Marais's forearm. The man was strong. It would be a long shot, but he'd backed long shots before. He took a deep breath preparatory to launching himself out of the chair.

"Then it was you who killed Marie deBrisay!" shouted Old Margot.

Marais froze as both pistols steadied on him again.

"Hands on the table everyone! Madame, sit down or I shall shoot you!" Gabrielle told the old lady. But Margot remained standing, her streaming eyes defiant. She held Nicole's shoulder for support. "I am eighty-three years old," she said in a bitter, cracking voice. "And if you are afraid of me then you'd better shoot because I will not sit until I finish what I have to say."

He had to admire the old woman's gall, but why couldn't she have waited another five seconds before deciding to get up and give a speech? Gabrielle hesitated. Would she shoot an old woman out of spite?

"That young man is correct, Gabrielle, when he says your mother was being blackmailed. I know because your mother and I were friends. And like your mother, when Rudi Hoessler summoned me to bring my daughter to the Château Havetière, I obeyed. You see, Marie deBrisay was my daughter."

Everyone stared at her in astonishment. She seemed to gather strength from their reactions.

"It wasn't her portrait Marie saw in that shop window. Hers had been destroyed years ago after she had been blackmailed into buying it from Karl Dorfmundt." She took a deep breath. "No, the one she saw sitting alongside yours in that window, Gabrielle, was mine." She blew her nose and tucked the small embroidered handkerchief primly back in her sleeve.

"My poor little Marie," she lamented. "What a terrible blow to discover her mother had been one of Hoessler's harlots from another war. She called me that afternoon after she'd spoken to you and begged my forgiveness. Can you imagine that?" Her eyes filled at the wonder of it. "After all the misery my deceit had caused her what did I have to forgive?"

She searched their faces for an answer, her gaze coming to rest finally on Irène. But her granddaughter lowered her eyes with shame. Old Margot nodded in understanding and turned to Boule's wife.

"Oh, Gabrielle! How could you have done it?" she cried. "Marie trusted you. She thought you were her friend. Didn't she give you money to buy your home in Villejuif? Then bought you a car. Even gave you a special key to her house so you could visit without disturbing the staff. And how did you repay her, tell me?"

Silence.

"Didn't you promise to visit Thursday morning after she phoned you about the Rue du Bac murder? She knew that was your doing and she was frightened — not for herself, never for herself, but for you. Marie would never have betrayed a friend. So when she telephoned me and asked what to do, like an old fool I said to talk it over with you. Her friend."

With a shudder she stopped for breath. The physical and emotional effort must have been enormous, Marais realized. But she appeared determined to continue. Nicole looked up at her encouragingly. Margot patted her great-granddaughter on the cheek. Then she nodded and continued.

"You went to Marie, didn't you? And you murdered her because you were afraid she'd go to the police." For a second she wavered, then somehow managed to regain control.

"She promised to call me after you left. When I didn't hear, I knew in my soul that something terrible had happened." She shivered and sank slowly onto the chair. "Later, when I called back, a policeman told me she was dead."

There were no more tears. She stared defiantly at Gabrielle.

"How do I know it was you, you wonder? That's easy. I remember you as a girl. Always the ruthless little manipulator with the sweet smile and no conscience."

Somewhere at the back of the house a window broke.

Everyone froze, listening.

Boule sprang to his feet, stepping back around the chair.

"You fool!" Gabrielle said hoarsely. "They've brought someone with them!"

"Check the rear!" he ordered.

With his gun pointed at Marais he crossed to the nearest curtained window. Gabrielle hesitated. For the first time they had
split their field of fire.

"Go on!" Boule snapped.

Up on the second floor another window shattered. Gabrielle
winced and turned to go. Boule flattened himself against the wall.
He touched the curtain for a cautious peek out at the front yard.
His head turned — only for a second, but it was enough.

Marais charged.

Boule's silencer blew white smoke into his face. He caught
Boule's wrist as he fell, dragging the Commissaire down on top of
him.

The window behind the curtain smashed. One of the women
screamed. Boule struggled free. Marais clung to his wrist, twisting
at the gun. God, but the man had strength.

The curtains parted.

Gabrielle rushed back into the room. Her lips tightened as she
aimed her pistol at the window. She fired, and at the same time
another gun went off above Marais's head, so close it deafened him.
But it wasn't Boule's — Marais still had hold of the Commissaire's
wrist, trying desperately to haul him off balance. With a sudden
surge, Boule kneed him in the groin. Marais collapsed to his knees.
Gabrielle staggered backwards, her mouth open with surprise. Her
gun arm dropped like a puppet's on the end of a broken string.
Boule howled like a wounded animal as Gabrielle slid slowly down
the wall onto the shiny oak floor, a scarlet stain spreading across
her breast. Her eyes were already glazing when she looked down
to see what had gone wrong.

Instantly the Commissaire was at her side, holding her in his
arms, tears and sweat pouring from his face. Marais tried to get
up, but his legs wouldn't obey. The light was fading.

A man stood over Boule.

"Drop it, Commissaire." He held a gun pointed at the side of
Boule's head. "It's over. I've solved our case."

But Boule didn't drop the weapon. Instead he raised it slowly to
his anguished face, put the silencer barrel in his mouth and pulled
the trigger. Marais had just enough time to see Nicole coming
toward him with eyes as wide and blue as a prairie sky before the
lights snapped out.

WEDNESDAY, JULY 18

When the crisis had passed, one of the younger doctors told Nicole that they'd nearly lost Marais during that first night after taking the bullet out of his lung. He began hemorrhaging and they had to open him up again.

She asked if she could move into the infirmary to be near him. It was against the rules. But after Major Schefler and André Villeneuve spoke to the Prefect of the Ardennes and the senior administrator was contacted, all opposition melted away. A cot was wheeled into Marais's room and set up for her at the end of his bed.

For three days she watched and waited and prayed. On the afternoon of the third day his delirium ended and he came back to her.

"Been waiting long?" he inquired. His eyes were very clear but his voice was weak.

She left her chair and sat on the edge of the bed. "How do you feel?" It was a silly question.

He ruefully surveyed the iv needles taped to the back of his hand and forearm, the plastic tubing connecting him to an inverted bottle overhead, the bladder tube dripping into a large glass jar below the bed. He reached out with his good arm.

"Want to fool around?"

"Not until you've shaved," she said, and leaned over to kiss him.

"What the hell happened?"

She told him what the doctors had done.

"And Boule?"

"Dead. Along with his wife. The Russian shot her."

He considered this information. Poor tragic Boule. Caught in a hurricane of events that forced him to sacrifice his integrity, his honor, and in the end his life. All for the woman he loved. Such an incredible sense of loyalty. He found himself admiring instead of hating the poor man. "Who was the Russian?" he asked.

"Outside the window. Don't you remember?"

He nodded uncertainly, trying to fit the pieces together with fuzzy-minded concentration.

"That was Boris Titov," she said, "a colonel in the Russian intelligence from Brussels. He followed Boule's wife here from Belgium."

"Where is he now? I'd like to thank him for turning up in time to save my life."

She shrugged. "Probably hidden away somewhere for formal interrogation. After Major Schefler and the others burned all their movies and photographs at the château on Sunday afternoon, Colonel Titov defected to the French government. Today's papers have the story. Apparently he's quite high up in the KGB."

She saw his eyes close while he tried sorting it out.

"Schefler burned the films and photographs?" he asked.

"The day before yesterday," she nodded, brushing aside her spilling hair.

"But why? I thought we were taking them back to Germany."

It had been hard for her to understand at the time too. But those had been her grandfather's orders to Colonel Hiller. The bargaining chips he had told her might one day be of use. Clever old man.

"We were to bring them back only if the police refused to drop all charges against us. Colonel Hiller made a bargain with the Minister of the Interior, François Daumier. Even managed to get it in writing through the German Embassy in Paris. It wasn't necessary, as things turned out, because André Villeneuve had already reported that Madame Boule and the Commissaire were the ones responsible for everything that happened."

He closed his eyes again. She waited, wondering if he was thinking or dozing. After a few minutes they opened and she told him the rest.

"Colonel Hiller kept his word anyway. Mama and Margot went to watch. André took them in his car. The Minister of the Interior flew in by helicopter. The entire château grounds were cordoned off. After the canisters were opened they used gasoline. Nothing remained afterwards except the metal movie reels. Then Mama and Margot went home. Major Schefler left yesterday once he knew you would be all right. "That just leaves you and me."

His eyelids were beginning to droop once more.

"Your mother has come to terms with everything?"

"I think so. She's talking about moving back here to live with Margot. It's funny, isn't it? I mean how things have a way of working out. If I hadn't lost my grandmother she might never have found hers."

She nodded approvingly at this thought. It was high time her mother found some happiness.

"She's no longer the same, Roger."

"None of us are," he murmured thoughtfully. There was still something more to be explained. He fought off the lethargy that kept trying to engulf his mind. Some little part still missing. What? Then he remembered. "The Minister of the Interior. How did Hiller manage to get him to agree?"

"Charles Carnot was grandmama's eldest brother. He didn't die during the war. He traded identities with a dead comrade and became François Daumier, hero of the Resistance. He came back after the war to find his mother accused of collaboration, his sisters gone. Worse, he discovered the secret of what had been going on at the château.

"He confronted his mother — Margot — demanding an explanation of why she had allowed it to happen. So she told him. And then she told him something else: that the man she had married in 1919 was not his father. Charles Carnot senior had been her benefactor. He'd agreed to marry her and give his name to the child she was carrying. The baby's real father was Wilhelm, Prince of Hohenzollern, heir to the German throne.

"Margot had told my grandfather this when he came to see her in 1941. She showed him a photograph of Daumier as a young man going off to war. Ten years later he saw the same face in a French magazine. Daumier had been photographed at a banquet honoring leaders of the Resistance. Through his agents he had Daumier's fingerprints checked with those of Charles Carnot, deceased, on file with French Army records. They were identical. François Daumier was an army deserter and a bastard Prince of Hohenzollern, a man married to one of the château whores from the Ardennes. Think of what the Opposition and newspapers would make of that story!"

Marais nodded. For a long time they shared the silence of the antiseptic room. Then finally he roused himself.

"Do me a favor, will you?"

"Name it."

"Marry me?"

Very tenderly she took his stubbled cheeks in both hands and kissed him.

"Only if you promise me you'll get better."

He promised.

REUTERS. PARIS. JULY 21 . . . IN A SURPRISE ANNOUNCE-MENT FROM THE ÉLYSÉE PALACE THE PRESIDENT STATED THAT HE HAS ACCEPTED WITH RELUCTANCE THE RESIGNATION OF FRANCOIS DAUMIER, MINISTER OF THE INTERIOR, FOR REASONS OF ILL HEALTH. NO REPLACEMENT WILL BE DECIDED UPON UNTIL AFTER NEXT WEEK'S CABINET MEETING. . . . END.